LINES THAT BIND

PART ONE

CIRCLE OF TRUST

BY ANNA LAZARIDIS

LINES THAT BIND

PART ONE

CIRCLE OF TRUST

ISBN 978-0615871660

Cover design by George D.K.
Cover Illustration by ©quayside/Fotolia.com
Interior Illustrations by Vasiliki Mitakou

www.linesthatbind.com

DEDICATION

For my beautiful daughter and loving husband whose
unwavering love and patience have made all this
possible.

And to my parents for always being my rock, and the
little voice inside my head.
I love you all.

"Sometimes even to live is an act of courage."
— Lucius Annaeus Seneca

PROLOGUE

ITTING THERE alone on the cold, tiled floor, phone in hand, brought back the sharpest and most painful memories. The second I heard the sound of my name rolling off her tongue my back stiffened and my throat went desert dry, knowing that my life was about to take yet another sudden turn.

By the tone of my aunt's voice I knew I had no choice but to listen. I hadn't spoken to her in approximately five years and fiercely unexpectedly, she called inquiring about my well-being. I could feel myself infuriatingly clench and unclench my fist as I held onto the receiver – tempted to hang up and allow her to think what she liked.

Affixed to the rhythm of her voice, I continued to listen, nonetheless. It was one of those conversations that didn't really lead to anything. She asked about the weather, my friends, school – deliberately avoiding the main reason she had called.

Heard it in her voice, sensed it in the long pauses she took between questions that there was something bothering her, something truly important.

"Will you be visiting us anytime soon?" she finally asked, after a long awkward break.

A whole kaleidoscope of thoughts and emotions flooded through my head as I rummaged for my next words, yet none came out. Instead, I fell completely silent – the same dead, ominous silence that prevailed as they led me quietly to the car some years ago. That day my Aunt Leslie's eyes mirrored a longing for something better than the situation at hand, but the true pain was etched on her face as they drove me away – a clear indication that the whole ordeal was something beyond her control.

In a sinister merciless manner, my dreams, home and family had materialized into a five-year confinement at an all-girls boarding school. I had sensed the tears building up, but my aunt had never been one to express emotion, not when the decision was final. At some point I tried to rationalize my predicament, even accept it for what it was – not that I ever knew what it was all about, but still, I made up excuses for them all. They were my family, after all.

Even so, how could she? I was only thirteen. My aunt had about five years to explain, almost five years to make things right. I didn't make a fuss – didn't say much that night.

In spite of the fact that I had been carefully admonished to respect the laws of our kind, and refrain from asking questions, my burning curiosity often overcame my scruples, but not that night – that night I left quietly. In truth, I was a rather dutiful thirteen-year-old – compliant in every way.

"Well Caitlin, I was hoping you would come out this weekend."

Her persistence drew my thoughts to the present. "This weekend?" I swallowed back the shock. "You can't possibly be serious! What are you saying?"

My response to her request had met a strange long, ill pause. She had wanted me to drop everything and return to Oaks.

"Yes Caitlin, this weekend." She added with an even more rigid tone, stubbornly unyielding.

My stomach in knots, I didn't know what to say. Even though I was deeply hurt and betrayed I still felt ludicrously indebted to her. She did raise me after the untimely death of both my parents.

"It's November, mid-semester, senior year, I can't miss my classes." I said pleadingly, not finding anything smarter to say to convince here that what she was asking of me was inconceivable.

"For the weekend, Caitlin – you don't have school on the weekend."

I pursed my lips, restraining the urge to scream – to snap that I would rather stick red-hot needles in my eyes than return to Oaks, but my response was on autopilot.

"I'll see what I can do." I answered, unsure of why I couldn't simply say no. There was no refusing her.

Even though my answer was completely against my better judgment my curiosity had got the best of me.

ACKNOWLEDGEMENTS

First and foremost, I would like to extend my warmest thanks to Traianos Panagiotidis, Evgenia Patsoni, Olympia Tzima, Sissi Vavoura, Sofia Georgiadou, Vaso Iliadi, Maria Politi and the twins; Stavroula and Illiana Ntitoura, for such support and inspiration.

And a great big thank you to my creative team, especially George DK and Despina Terzopoulou – could not do all this without their knowhow and invaluable input.

The Call

Illustrated For Lines That Bind - Circle of Turst

ONE

THE RETURN

MY DAY SEEMED TO BE GOING surprisingly well, so far. Come to think of it, nothing wildly exciting had ever come about, or even mildly arousing come to that, but that was perfectly fine, because nor had anything gone terribly wrong during the thirty-six hour drive back home to Oaks.

Even so, it was still only mid-afternoon allowing ample time for something disastrously wrong to happen.

I had, I thought, considered every possibility and had formulated plans to deal with any eventuality, no matter how catastrophic. But I was only just reaching my final destination, and had no way of foreseeing the dreadful choices that would be forced upon me by the day's end.

For the moment, however, there was only silence – unnerving in itself, inciting a sequence of short quick breaths, slowly easing the panicky feeling of having reached my past, the place I once called home – The Cathcart Estate.

With my forehead up against the white-knuckle grip I had on the steering wheel, I reluctantly turned off the engine. My thoughts raced back and forth over the years, swinging into focus and then out again. I shook my head utterly frustrated, feeling as though something had come unhinged in my head allowing my terrors to come spilling out into reality.

"I can't believe I'm actually doing this," I seethed uneasily. "Why? Why the hell couldn't I simply say no?" My mind was darting about frantically, reaching for answers I clearly didn't have.

For several seconds I kept my eyes closed, trying to void my mind of everything beyond the sound of my choppy breathing. I was not ready to face everyone after all those years.

There had been a time, not many years before, when there had still been a glint of nostalgia, when I would have given anything to be back in Oaks. But that was then, things were radically different now.

Those times, wild and warm and exciting, I had loved best of all, but there were other things to think about in the long dark years of my absence.

"Just breathe, damn it. Just breathe." I kept repeating, hoping it would be enough.

Since kicking myself didn't even come close to what I wanted to do for allowing myself to get into this mess, I did the next best thing – I clasped my fingers tightly around the worn leather, violently shaking the steering wheel, coming up with the most brilliant array of profane utterances, using it as an outlet for my pent-up frustration.

Thankfully, good Old Betty was used to my bursts of rage, the tears, and the multitudes of unanswered whys. I found that talking to Old Betty was a great release. The best part was that she never complained or ever talked back.

Eventually, as the storm inside me began to abate I leaned

back. Motionless, I sat there staring into space for at least an hour, parked right outside the towering wrought iron gate unsure of so many things.

At some point, during the butt-numbing drive to Oaks, I convinced myself that everything would be fine. It was most helpful to think of pleasant, happy things, things that might distract my mind and help me cope with what was to unfold the second I reached the front door.

"Enough," I muttered, shaking my head to expel all the rotten memories. There was no point in getting angry and berating myself, it was too late now, too late to turn back.

I pushed against the rusted car door to let myself out. "Oh, c'mon, Betty," I grunted, pushing with all my might. "Damn it! Not now, girl!"

The colder the weather, the harder it was for the rusted hinges to unlock. Finally, with one last push the screeching metal gave way, practically landing me on the asphalt-paved road.

Cursing profusely, I awkwardly pulled myself out of the driver's seat.

Upright and intact, I allowed the crisp evening air to help soothe my anxiety and after several attempts at slamming it, the car door finally shut behind me with a loud screeching bang. Standing there, under the evening sky on the side of the road, I allowed my eyes to roam the area, savoring the scenery I had once taken for granted.

I can't believe I'm actually doing this, I thought.

I was on my feet, turning slowly in a circle, scanning the strange beauty of the rolling hills and vast areas of woodland which sprawled further than the eye could see.

This secluded community had once been my home, but now it

only reminded me of the dreaded presence of everything and everyone I detested.

Without any warning, a cold gust of wind threw me violently against the car door and suddenly a pang of fear thudded against my ribs as I felt a warm brush across my face – as if someone or something were breathing against my winter kissed cheek.

Terrified, I lifted my cold hand to my left cheek and looked around but saw nothing. I would have been immersed in the anxiety that gripped me had my attention not been quickly drawn to the glare of oncoming headlights, which blindingly obscured my vision.

Another cold gust whipped by me as I straightened myself out. It was then that I realized that depriving my mind and body of sleep those past few days was not such a great idea after all. It seemed to skew my senses, making them far more sensitive than was necessary.

The oncoming car neared. I had always thought that coming back would be a mistake and just then I saw the reason why. A sleek red BMW unexpectedly pulled up in front of my beat-up old Ford; the comparison was yet another reminder of why I didn't belong in Oaks.

I strained my eyes to see who was behind the wheel, but the lights were simply too bright for that time of day, preventing me from making anything out. The eerie slam of the door and the sound of footsteps approaching only heightened my natural response to flee.

"Oh great, that's all I need." I mumbled the second I realized who it was.

I tried to relax and compose myself not expecting to see anyone apart from the family on my short visit, but it was rather foolish to believe such nonsense – nothing in Oaks went undetected. I had remained silently staring; transfixed with wonder, until the most obnoxious voice I had ever come across in my existence spoke to me. "Caitlin...," she said hesitantly, making sure she was not mistaken, "didn't know you were back in town." She continued to say with her signature snooty tone, checking me up and down in utter contempt. "You look different."

Deep inside where anger once had pulsed like spouting lava at the mere sight of her, there now seemed to be nothing left but vacant echoes of past memories. Megan's deep-set eyes, however, fixed and fiery with inner turmoil, revealed the extent of her true feelings for me, feelings that apparently hadn't waned over the years.

With subtle movements of unparalleled grace, Megan took a few steps closer and stood there, displaying a smug expression. Her silhouette suddenly came in line with the glaring headlights catching the bright beams as she stood there staring, causing an angelic effect around her long blond hair. There was nothing angelic about her; she was far from anything good.

Even now, she couldn't hide the fact that she disliked me, finding me very plain and too ordinary for her taste in friends, not that I ever hoped to be one. She was cruel and ruthless to those she despised.

Unfortunately, I was at the receiving end of her sadistic comments all through my formidable school years. However, now it was different, now she would be dying to know what I was doing back, otherwise she would not have wasted her precious time on me.

Relax! I kept repeating in my head. *Just breathe, how bad could it be?*

Surprisingly, even after all those years, the feelings of inadequacy had once again resurfaced the moment I heard her slithering voice.

Dressed from head to toe in nothing less than the last word in fashion – next to her I looked worn and disheveled. My faded jeans were no match for her sleek trousers and tight fitting blouse which, coincidentally, was buttoned just enough to make any man crazy, revealing all her attributes.

Please go away! I thought, hoping that somehow she would vanish into thin air taking her pink Prada tote bag with her.

Paralyzed from the shock of seeing her, I scrambled to think of something to do. I realized that I couldn't just stand there without saying something; it would have only confirmed her mistaken opinion of me. "Megan," I smiled warmly, "wow, you look great. It's been quite a while, hasn't it? It's nice to see you," I finally said, swallowing back the blatant lie. "I'm only here for a short visit."

Her perfectly shaped eyebrow arched up slightly, clearly unconvinced of my confidence. Her gaze bore deep into my eyes. "Will you be enrolling in Oaks High to finish senior year?" she asked, hypnotically.

I hadn't felt it for some time, but the peculiar feeling of having someone rummage through my mind was quite acute, severe even. Evidently Megan was, without a doubt, searching my thoughts to see if I were lying or planning something. Unlike me, she was gifted, like everyone in town.

The sensation of having someone in my head was indubitably like no other, easily compared to the onset of a major migraine – hundreds of pins poking successively in my brain. The longer she stared the deeper she probed.

I didn't flinch, didn't want to give her the satisfaction, though my eyes were treacherously defying my wishes. "I'm only here for a short visit," I quickly repeated, reaching for the car door with a polite, but awkward smile, masterfully turning my back to her, blocking her piercing gaze. The sharp pain suddenly subsided and instinctively, with the back of my hand, I quickly rubbed my eyes dry.

"Got something in your eye, Caitlin?"

I shifted my gaze to her momentarily. "No," I told her emphatically, "I'm perfectly fine – must be my allergies. It's spineless, cold-blooded swamp dwellers that I'm most pervious to." I smiled wickedly, "I must be close to one."

She snickered distastefully, visibly annoyed at my comment.

Ignoring her, I turned my attention back to getting the car door open. I growled in hopeless frustration, pulling on the damn thing with all my might. *Betty, not now! Please, don't be stuck now!* I prayed, not wanting to make a fool of myself – not in front of Megan of all people.

The screeching of the corroded metal was deafening, amplified by the sheer silence of my surroundings. Megan's all too familiar snickers of displeasure and contempt at my poor excuse of a car made my blood boil. All the same, I was not going to get cross with her. I was not going to be there for more than two days, so there was no need to get into any sort of confrontation.

My dilapidated 55' Ford T-bird fell short of any comparison, in her present state that is. Betty was a barn find. What did I expect? Even the owner himself tried talking me out of buying her. I thought vintage, he said scrap metal, insisting that I look for something that needed less work, something that didn't require duct-taping the fiberglass top to keep the elements out. But it was love at first sight – a 'steal', I thought at the time.

"Caitlin," Megan said breezily, running her fingers through her long, blond hair in an unnecessary tidying movement, "the door isn't going to fall off, is it?"

I was not really sure, so I kept quiet and continued fiddling with my stuff.

"I'd help and all, but – well – you know…."

"That won't be necessary," I answered, discretely looking over my shoulder towards her. "I'm fine Megan, thanks anyway." I turned my attention back to my belongings.

Collecting a few things from the passenger's seat, I muttered a few select adjectives under my breath, those few I had over the years reserved for Megan's sake. I turned, hoping that she got the point and moved on, but I quickly paused, and in the pause, I noticed her leaning up against my car. *She's really asking for it*, I thought.

I felt one corner of my mouth tip upward in a wicked little smile, determined to get her to leave. Taking a step forward, I locked at her – I mean, really looked at her straight in the eyes, giving her full access to the vile images I conjured up in my mind – images of what I would do to her if she didn't leave me alone. "I dare you to see what I'm thinking about now," I said grinning widely.

Her eyes widened as she quickly got the message and straightened up, knowing my resolve. "You don't need to be rude about it, Caity," she crowd, making me cringe with the shortening of my name. She dismissively wiped herself off, clearly disgusted by my car. Megan looked down at her hands appallingly. "Saved it from the compactor, did you?"

"Why do you care? And the name is Caitlin," I corrected her with clenched teeth, trying desperately to control my temper. I never really cared what people called me, but this was Megan

Gordon, and I was not going to let her belittle me. "Seriously Megan, aren't we a bit too old for these games?" I asked. She rolled her eyes and looked away. "Look," I exclaimed, drawing her attention. "For what it's worth I'm not happy to be here either."

"So, why are you back?"

Good question, I thought. "Just here to see the family."

Her eyebrow arched even higher. "Really? After all these years you want me to believe that you simply came back?"

"What's it to you, anyway?"

"Just saying, Caitlin – it's weird, that's all."

I had enough, I took a step forward, she, instinctively took a step back.

"Megan, please just go." I said, clenching my teeth. "We're way too old for this, and I'm way too tired. I had a long day, trust me."

I wasn't lying. I drove straight through, without thinking of stopping anywhere for fear of changing my mind and cutting my trip short by turning back. The few pit stops to fill up the tank were enough to have me rethink my decision.

The reason that I made it that far was thanks to my school's Head Mistress, Ms. Leedey, who surprisingly exhibited a great understanding with my having to miss a few days of school which was completely out of character, helping further my curiosity. She had hugged me tightly and reassured me that everything would be okay.

I swallowed back the tears because I didn't want her to see me cry, but then I cried anyway and she looked at me in astonishment as she wiped my eyes with the back of her hand. "What's the matter, Caitlin?" she asked.

"I don't know. I – I just don't know. Why – why now of all times?"

"Come now, sweetie. No worries," she said stroking my hair. "They're your family. It'll be fine. I promise you."

I was convinced that my aunt had spoken to her because in all my years at Stone Hurst, Ms. Leedey had been rather protective of me, hardly ever leaving me out of her sight.

Switching my thoughts to the present, I noticed Megan's confused expression. "God, Caity! You're not tired, you're just weird," she said, concentrating on my face, trying to read my blank expression. "I was wrong about you, you haven't changed one bit. You're still as strange as ever."

I lowered my gaze, acknowledging the fact that there was some truth to what she said.

"Pathetic," she snorted, turning on her high heels and with the graceful click-clack back to her car. She lazily circled her head as she opened her car door. "Well, I guess I'll be seeing you in class." Without even the slightest glance back, she slid into the driver's seat and took off, leaving a cloud of dust behind. I didn't have the chance to correct her on her wrong assumption. *Did she really think I was back for good?*

In a hopeless despairing panic, I realized, looking at Megan disappearing around the bend that it would not take long for the news of my arrival to catch on. Not that I was anybody important, but my presence would certainly stir up some old memories – memories, for some, best left forgotten.

As the sun slipped beneath the horizon and the air grew even colder, I wrapped my arms around myself as the cold slowly seeped its chill into my bones sending shivers down my spine. I shrugged off the negative feelings, and with a few bags in hand, I anxiously pushed the heavy, intricately designed gates open. The wrought iron was meticulously forged to create an array of roses and thorns. It was a work of art, crafted somewhere in Europe hundreds and hundreds of years ago.

Halfway up the cobbled driveway I stopped to get control of my erratic breathing, and then I walked on, and with each step I could feel myself turning hotter and pricklier with fear.

Quickly, I froze at the sight of the incredibly charming, European cottage style mansion looming up ahead with its high pitched roofline and decorative arches. The formidable estate indulged one's senses. If ever a home made a statement, an eloquent, understated but clear statement, of good taste, it was the Cathcart Estate.

The driveway was as I remembered, laced with small lights to guide the visitor to the entrance. On both sides an array of towering trees sprawled across the grounds, casting shadows in the mid-evening light, enhancing the enchanting surroundings.

By design, I left Old Betty by the side of the road allowing myself ample time to walk up the long path and calm my nerves. It did little good. With every step, I could feel my body tensing all the more.

"You can do this," I whispered, trying to talk myself into the daunting prospect of seeing everyone. Suddenly, I couldn't breathe. "You're not doing this. Get a grip!" I ordered, trying to verbally trounce myself into submission.

On reaching the main entrance, I tilted my head up to see the brilliantly hand carved arch which depicted the same design as the gate – the signature Cathcart roses lacing their way around the whole curve of the arch.

"Here goes nothing," I exhaled, ready to knock on the door.

Before my hand could even reach the brass knocker, out of nowhere, I felt a feather like touch across my left cheek, again. I turned around roused by a sense of danger and quite frightened as I sensed that I was not alone.

"Who's there?" I asked, but no one answered. A burst of cold air flailed some loose strands of hair in my face as I continued to look around.

Seeing nothing out of the ordinary I remained silently still for a couple of minutes until I decided that it was probably my exhausted mind, again, playing tricks on me. Shrugging it off, I stretched out my free hand, and finally got up the nerve and knocked on the door, knowing that the echo would be heard throughout the house.

I waited nervously, not knowing which family member would answer. *What would I say once the door opens?* I wondered, biting my bottom lip in anticipation.

Just then, I heard the lock click open. "Dear lord," I whispered, holding in my breath anxious beyond belief. My blood was coursing through my body with such force I could feel it draining from my brain. I knew I stopped breathing because I could feel my chest constricting.

The second the door opened something inside me shifted and then a deathly calm washed over me, extinguishing the agitation.

There was a pause during which things became all too quiet. Now, as I stood there still as a statue, a tranquil silence replaced my bursting anxiety. Powers were being used out in the open, first by Megan and now this. It was like somebody had hollowed out my emotions – used a tranquilizer to still my nerves.

Feeling nothing was foreign to me, but surprisingly welcoming.

"Caitlin?" I heard my aunt's unmistakable voice say. Tall and commanding and yet delicately poised in every line and movement, my aunt stood framed in the arch of the doorway, her beauty glowing, warm and seemingly glad I was there. She stared for a few seconds looking at me with those translucent grey-blue eyes.

Too sedated to react the way I would have liked, I simply stared for a few seconds and finally said, "Aunt Leslie...."

Even saying her name was difficult in my otherwise ransacked brain. My throat was bone dry. I couldn't look up. Desperately needing to do something with my hands, I fondled half-wittedly with my stuff, giving me the time to think of what to say next. I thought I had practiced this in the car on my way there, but now nothing, a blank. Where had all the anger gone? I felt naked, stripped of my defenses – completely numb and dead inside.

"Oh, honey, come in you'll freeze," she said, helping me with my things, shutting the door carefully behind me.

Instantly, the familiar scents from my past rushed right through me. The foyer was one of the most architecturally detailed parts of the house. It was steeped in fine detailing. The visual impact of the splendor of the magnificent house always took my breath away; now more than ever before.

Aunt Leslie gracefully held out her hand, waiting for me to hand her my coat. I nervously shrugged out of it, handing it to her, but I kept my long scarf around my neck, needing my hands to keep busy and the length of the finely knit accessory was most effective. I twisted and twirled the fringed ends between my fingers till there was nothing but knots.

"Let me look at you," she said, lifting my hands to the side, as if I were five again, "you've grown, Caitlin." Her voice was tinged with a hint of sadness as she returned my hands to my side.

Perhaps she felt guilty for missing out on so many years of my life. Whatever the reason for her saddened expression, it disappeared just as fast at the sound of footsteps.

"Abbot," she exclaimed, "Look who has come for a visit."

How was it even possible that my uncle was not aware of my arrival? Aunt Leslie made it sound as though I was simply in the neighborhood and decided to pop in for coffee. I thought that they would all be aware of my arrival. They must have all known that I would never return, not like this, not without some warning.

Why would my aunt keep this from him? Why did she call me in the first place?

"Caitlin," Uncle Abbot pronounced, beaming a great big smile, looking rather pleased to see me, "didn't know we were expecting visitors."

"She's not a visitor," Aunt Leslie snapped. "This is her home!"

The two of them stared at each other for a moment while the air between them crackled. Never having heard her speak to my uncle in that tone, I was taken aback by her curt response. There was anger underlining her every word.

Abbot Cathcart just stood there in a confused state of mind. "Of course it is dear," he said with a soft soothing tone, "I'm just happy to see her after so many years. I didn't mean to suggest that she wasn't welcomed." Finishing his words he turned to me, "How about a hug?" he asked.

I obliged, squeezing my uncle hard, and then gazed quizzically up into his eyes as he cupped my face in his hands and in that split second I realized why I had felt numb – void of all feelings; it was my uncle's doing. Of course he would use his gift to diffuse the charged atmosphere; he hated conflict.

A quick memory of how close we used to be flashed through

my mind. Uncle Abbot was forever planting big kisses on my forehead, and glow with pride at my little accomplishments. Quickly, I recoiled, reminding myself of the pain these people had caused me, and I took a small step back.

"Welcome home child," he finally said with deep affection. "You must forgive your aunt's outburst. She's been all wound up for some time now."

I shifted my gaze to my aunt to see her reaction, but there was none. Her features remained stern and unyielding. A musty cigar smell lingered as my uncle took a step back. His choice of words was meant as a warning, meant to prepare me for the worst in my aunt.

He was the only person in my life that had ever made sense, the only one who was selfless to the core. Uncle Abbot was always very careful with his words, never getting cross with anyone. His deep and authoritative voice could surely silence a room, but he knew how to handle situations without ever raising an octave.

"Uncle Abbot," I sighed. It was then that a slight but appreciable amount of emotion surfaced through the deep deathly calm. Tears stung my eyes at the sound of his name on my lips.

His brow quickly lifted at the sound of emotion in my words and said, "You have grown quite strong, young lady, resilient to persuasion. Quite – quite interesting."

I turned to my aunt for clarity, but nothing. She continued to stand there motionless. "Come now child, there's no need for tears," said my uncle in an afterthought, putting his arm around my shoulders, leading me to the den. "You have grown into a beautiful young lady."

I didn't respond.

"So, tell me Caitlin," he added, dropping his gaze on me, smiling that all too boyish smile, "how has life been treating you these past few years?"

Puzzled, I looked at him. Was he kidding me? I was not sure what he wanted me to say. Where would I start? Was he simply making small talk – wanting to get my mind off the weirdness of the situation? I didn't know what to do.

On entering the den, my uncle gestured for me to sit near the open fire, on one of the two mahogany framed spoon-back armchairs.

Large and heavily furnished with formidable leather sofas on either side of an imposing double-height French Louis XIV stone fireplace, the room was as I remembered, with the finest Persian rugs gracing most of the dark oak floor. Now my aunt and uncle were seated side by side, on one of the elegant sofas that blended so perfectly with the carefully chosen antique furnishings. Aunt Leslie smiled warmly and quietly directed me to sit.

Uncomfortably perched on the edge of the armchair, I sat there in stunned silence, waiting for them to speak first. My uncle reached for the antique box filled with cigars.

He took one out, trimmed the tip and then lit it, allowing his head to rest back, continuing to eye me while inhaling the smoke; letting out puffs now and then.

"Are you warm enough?" Aunt Leslie asked, looking overly concerned.

Chit-chat aside, I knew she was trying to warm up to a much deeper conversation, but for some reason she couldn't. I looked across the room directly at her. "I'm fine, thanks, just a bit tired from the trip." They both looked at each other, sharing a private thought. "Emily? Kyle?" I asked, wondering where my cousins were.

"The kids went to the movies. They should be back soon."

The way she said the word 'kids', was, to say the least, amusing since my cousin Kyle was twenty-two and Emily, the closest thing I had to a big sister, had turned twenty a few months ago.

For many minutes we sat in awkward silence. The sound of crackling wood in the fireplace rose and fell in hypnotic rhythms, and I listened in entranced silence.

"Aunt Leslie?" I finally said, weak and shaky from the long drive. "I know I just came and all, but I'd like to freshen up before we sit down and talk." I didn't want to sound too forward, but the only thing I wanted at that point was some time alone.

All grown up now, with a mind and a life of my own, I was not afraid anymore. Thankfully, I didn't have to answer to anyone. I quickly wondered if Kyle and Emily even knew I was there. *Maybe they used the movies as an excuse to get out of this....*

Instantly, even before my mind had the opportunity to completely formulate and process the content of my passing thought, I sensed lightness, as impalpable as air across the side of my face. "They don't know," she whispered, shockingly standing right next to me, "I haven't told them."

My anxiety, which had begun to subside, flared anew. How she managed to traverse the length of the room within a blink of an eye made the hairs on the back of my neck stand on end.

I quickly stood and picked up my belonging, realizing that she was using her powers in the open, reading me like an open book. Of course she knew what I was thinking, that's what always amazed me about the Cathcarts, and many others there in Oaks. They never talked about special abilities – they didn't have to.

Searching my pockets for the car keys, I turned to my aunt momentarily. "I parked the car on the side of the road. I'll need to move it," I said, looking for an excuse to get some much needed fresh air.

"Kyle can put it in the garage once he gets home. You needn't worry," she said, putting her hand on my arm, "Now, let's get you settled in."

She led me up the circular staircase to the second floor. The mahogany handrail felt smooth to the touch and the wooden floor all too familiar under my feet. *Four, five, and Six*, I counted each step to myself and there it was – the sinister sound of the sixth step creaking.

As far back as my first memory of the house, the sixth step always made a sound under anybody's weight. When we were really young, Kyle, Emily and I would sneak out of bed at night only to raid the kitchen – especially on nights when we knew the fridge was well stocked with my aunt's homemade sweet treats. We always made sure to skip over that one step because Aunt Leslie was known to sleep with one eye open.

Lined with oil paintings and large ancient artifacts, the upstairs hall was more or less a small museum, with every last item belonging to my aunt's extensive private collection.

The moment we crossed the corridor, I felt a cold stream of ice freezing up my spine, stopping me dead on the spot, staring at the double doors that led to my parents' old bedroom.

I stood there agaze in fear and wonder, not really sure what to do with the feelings that quietly surfaced from the cold iron hold that my uncle's powers had on my emotions.

Immersed in dark and mazy thoughts, I couldn't move. I didn't for some time notice the sound of my aunt's voice. The quiet interruption stopped my boggled memories, cold.

Stunned, I turned to her.

Her face was white and set. "It's only a room," she said, trying to guide me further down the corridor towards my old bedroom. Never before did the existence of that room bother me. I knew my parents had passed away. I came to terms with not having a mother or father around long ago. My aunt and uncle raised me – the Cathcarts were my family. Being my mother's sister, Aunt Leslie seemed to love me as much as she loved her own children – that's how she acted anyway.

But why would this bother me now? Why would the thought of my parents cause me to act this way? I wondered.

"You're tired sweetie. Your exhaustion has heightened your senses," she said, answering my thoughts again. "You'll see, tomorrow everything will be back to normal."

I had forgotten how ordinary it was for her to read people's thoughts. Unlike Megan, Aunt Leslie was a master of her craft, an Ellri of the Inner Sanctum. I felt absolutely nothing when she used her gift; no pain accompanied her mind reading.

"Yeah, guess you're right. I am rather tired." I replied, completely exhausted. I could feel my limbs ready to collapse. I wanted to ask her why she wanted me there, but I knew it could wait. Aunt Leslie slightly tightened her grip around my arm. "I guess our waltz down memory lane will have to be postponed till further notice," she added with a smile. "Don't worry though; we have all the time in the world."

I didn't know what she meant. She knew that my visit was just that – a visit.

Too tired to think, I let the conversation die, knowing all too well that she could clearly read my thoughts if she wanted to. In the posture of total exhaustion, I was led to my old room in silence. It was the farthest down the hall. "You ha`en't slept at all, have you?"

I raised my gaze to her. "No, not since I left Stone Hurst."

She shook her head in utter disbelief. "Why do you continue to do that? Your body needs its rest. You have to sleep. You're not a child anymore, Caitlin. You cannot continue to deny your body rest; especially now."

Not up to getting into any sort of argument over the fact that I only slept three to four hours a day, on average, I nodded in agreement.

On entering the room I paid little attention to the details, aware of only one thing, the bed and how soon I could get some sleep.

"We'll talk in the morning, Caitlin. You need your rest," she said preparing to leave. "Before I go, I just wanted to say…," She paused briefly, "thank you for coming home. I – I have missed you so, so much."

She waited momentarily for some sort of reply. I had nothing to say. I surely didn't share in the sentiment.

Not wishing to lie, but not caring to share my true thoughts on the matter either, I stood there motionless. Dropping her gaze to the floor she quickly closed the door behind her.

I gave myself a mental shake and mechanically plopped my things in one of the armchairs and stretched on the bed to rest for a few minutes. Part of my mind railed at me, *Coward! You're pathetic! You should have said something – tell them how you truly feel about being back.* But the emotional numbness was stealthily suppressing my true feelings, suffocating any need to vent my inner most thoughts – so I closed my eyes and ears to it all.

TWO

REUNIFICATION

HOSE MOMENTS between sleep and my awaken state I became aware of a strange exaltation of infinite space and vertigo, and then a confusion of sensations that seemed unrelated to anything real. I tossed and turned half the night unable to dispel the unusual rush of being carried away by indefinable emotion. The sensations only sharpened as day approached, and I seemed to become a part of them. *Justin!* I thought and exhaled, burying my face in my hands, flushed with the sheer impurity of my inner thoughts.

Agitated by my inability to control my emotions anymore, I pulled the covers over my head and blocked out the morning light that suffused every corner of the room. It temporarily remedied the situation, but didn't help in erasing the mix of feelings.

Nestled comfortably under the warm comforters, I drew the conclusion that those abstract, whirlwind of emotions were clearly due to Justin's proximity. It had to be him. He was way too close for it to be anything or anyone else. I could sense him miles away, have done so my entire life, felt the distance between us my every waking hour. I was drawn to him like a bright beacon in the midst of a storm.

It was not until much later that I was finally ready to face the morning. Poking my head out from under the covers, I took the liberty and looked lazily around my old room. I was happy to see all my dolls and stuffed animals as I left them; my desk, my books, everything just as if time had stopped. I didn't want to get up, the bed felt so right, so comfortable, contouring perfectly to my body, unlike the beds at Stone Hurst which were hard, military like.

Just then, I sensed that I was not alone. A figure stirred slightly at the foot of my bed. I sprang up, only to be blown away by a radiant smile and luminous eyes, sparkling with mischief as she regarded me.

"Emily," I squealed, surprised to see her.

Though the anxiety behind her smile was well hidden, my cousin beamed with delight. "Hey, you're really here," Emily cried, bouncing up from the foot of my bed to give me a hug. "I can't believe you're actually here," she said softly, caressing my cheek, studying my face. She seemed to be finding it hard to believe that it was really me. Her voice began to falter under the strain of emotion. "You've changed. You're all grown up, Caitlin and there's something else, something different in your eyes."

I couldn't help but stare back. I knew she was always beautiful, but now she was simply stunning. Her silky blond hair was pinned slightly back into one of those perfectly styled knots, exposing her long, elegant neck, enhancing her porcelain features. Her eyes, slightly lighter than Aunt Leslie's, a pale greyish-blue which quickly drew you into its hypnotic glance. She was only fifteen the last time I saw her, but even back then she was very attractive, popular in school and most talked about in Oaks. Like all others in town, she too dressed stylishly, in very expensive clothes. Emily could wear anything and still look ethereal.

My eyes remained, uncouthly, fixed on her face.

"Hellooo...?" she said, with her corky laugh, attempting to make me stop staring. "I'm happy you decided to come home," she added, jumping off the bed. "I can't imagine how awful it was in that boarding school. Ah, and those uniforms. How did you cope?"

I was on the verge of telling Emily that it was her mother's telephone call that led me there, when I forgot betrayal and anger alike in a sudden rush of joy as Kyle barged in, heaving me off the bed, twirling me in circles.

"Stop! Please stop! C'mon, just stop," I pleaded, cutting him off in mid twirl.

"Sorry, did I hurt you?" he asked concerned.

"No – no, I'm fine," I shook my head taking a small step back. "You – you simply took me off guard."

"Can't believe you're back, little sis."

It took me a few seconds, but I finally raised my gaze to his whimsical smile. He was all grown up, ruggedly handsome with perfectly aligned features – more handsome than I remembered. Kyle was quite simply drop-dead gorgeous and as modest about his looks as Emily was proud of hers. The girls at school used to follow him to his classes just to get one last look before the bell rang.

"Kyle," I exhaled and turned my gaze to Emily and back to him. I must have gone back and forth a couple of times because I noticed their heads moving as mine was. Without any warning I felt drained – my knees were just about to buckle under my own weight when I took a step back to get a hold of the bed. Anticipating my distress, Kyle had his arm around my waist in no time at all, supporting my weight. "Now, don't you go fainting on us, little sis," he said, sitting me carefully on the bed. "If I remember correctly you were never one of those damsels in distress types."

"I'm fine," I reassured him. "I didn't sleep well last night and the drive here was rather endless," I explained, in a faint breathy voice which slowly faded into a long silence. "Well, it's simply all too much," I muttered, turning my gaze to both of them. "I – I can't believe how much you've changed. You both look great!"

Kyle winked at me and smiled. "You're not half bad yourself, sis. Looks seem to run in the family."

I giggled – first time in God knows how long.

Emily came and perched herself next to me and held my hand in hers. Then with one of her critical glances she scanned me from head to toe. "This won't do," she exclaimed, shaking her head in disapproval, fiddling with my hair, trying to do something with it. Seeing that there was absolutely no hope of salvaging it, she dragged me to the bathroom. "Go wash up and please, please do something with that hair," she ordered.

Kyle chuckled. "Leave her alone Em, she's perfect just the way I remember – dirty and scruffy."

Emily shook her head in utter annoyance.

"What now?" he complained. "Why the heck are you always rolling your eyes at me, Em? Not everyone wants to be your clone?"

Emily made a face and turned her back to him.

Unwilling to get into an argument with her, Kyle made his way to the door and just as he was about to exit the room, he abruptly turned around and smiled devilishly at me, saying "See you downstairs, Scruffy. Make sure you clean behind the ears."

I giggled – *second time today*, I thought.

"You're such a buffoon," Emily screamed and without a second of hesitation picked up the first thing in reach and hurled it at him in the hopes of hitting him. Lucky for Kyle, the projectile was a soft, silk-lined pillow.

He was deliberately using me to bait her, and she fell right into his trap.

"You missed!" he said amusingly, irritating Emily even more.

I couldn't help but smile at the comical ordeal. Only Kyle's quirkiness could awaken such dormant feelings of happiness within me.

"You're such an ass!" she yelled, stumping her foot in frustration. "Go away, will ya!"

"Whatever, Em," he childishly answered and turned to leave, leaving behind him a faint wisp of hope.

"What a jerk," Emily muttered, "What an idiot! He has no right," she said, shifting her gaze back to me. "Now go, get ready and come downstairs for breakfast."

Before I even had a chance to respond, she exited the room, closing the door behind her. I had, at first, been terribly surprised and excited, but soon after both my cousins left, reality hit home once more.

"What am I doing?" I scolded myself, "I shouldn't even be here." These were, after all, the people that had kicked me out – the people who stood there while my world came crashing around me.

How can I be this happy to see them?

Annoyed at myself for proving Megan right – I was pathetic after all – unable to stay mad at any of them. I kicked the end table only to shudder from the pain.

Even with strangled emotions, I hadn't felt that alive for quite some time. My dreams for the last five years were of their faces. The faces I had grown to love. They were the only family I had known. There was a small, hidden part in me that knew or at least hoped that I would understand the reason they all felt I had to be sent away.

Long, rejuvenating moments later, I drew a towel around me and combed out the knots in my waist-long hair, making a mental list of what clothes I had shoved in my bag. Turning around to get another look at my room, I noticed something sprawled on the bed. It was a pair of designer jeans and a light skinny fit cardigan waiting to be worn. *Must be Emily's*, I thought.

I contemplated wearing my own clothes, but I knew they needed ironing. Not being up to that just yet, I pulled on the low-waist jeans and put on the top. They were surprisingly fitting and right. Emily had always been much slimmer and taller than I growing up, but now we seemed to be the same size.

Giving no further thought to my attire, I quickly collected my hair loosely pinning it back with my favorite butterfly hairpin; giving it time to dry naturally.

Heading downstairs, I instinctively stopped on the sixth step and bounced up and down making squeaky sounds.

The distinctive noise must have carried to the kitchen because Kyle's laughter shook the whole house. "Get your ass in here," he yelled.

Having caught the mouth-watering drift of crisp fried bacon from the kitchen, I picked up my pace. Even though the kitchen was at the far end near the den I seemed to have reached it in record breaking time. I must've been hungrier than I thought.

I could hear their voices clearly now, talking about Kyle's graduation ceremony. *He must be finishing his studies*, I thought as I entered the kitchen where a long, convent-style, pine dining table dominated the spacious room.

"In my last semester at Yale," he said, as soon as I stepped foot in the kitchen, obviously answering my thoughts, "I have a few weeks left and then I'm all done."

I stood there for an uncomfortable minute wondering what to do. Now, trying to cover my unease, I widened my smile as I struggled for my next words. "Wow! Congrats Kyle. Wow, didn't know you had Yale in you."

"I didn't...," he looked right at me and pulled out a chair for me to sit, "mom and dad pulled a few strings and made things happen. All the same, I'm graduating now so I guess I did have some latent abilities after all."

I took the seat he offered and said, "So, what are you majoring in?"

Kyle took a quick sip of his freshly brewed coffee and said, "Economics, of course – what else is there?"

"That makes sense," I exclaimed, recalling his childish fascination with the stock market.

Aunt Leslie couldn't keep her eyes off me. She was clearly pondering something, not knowing how to put it into words.

"Look at you," Kyle enthused, drawing my gaze back to him. "You're beautiful."

His comment took me by surprise. It was not like him to compliment me, not this early in the morning, not any time of day for that matter. Apprehensively, I looked down assessing my clothes, straightening out my top. He was surely comparing the before and after images he had of me in his mind.

"Emily is to thank for the overhaul," I said looking down at my hands.

"I doubt that." Kyle took a quick sip of coffee. "It's all you, beautiful. Emily had nothing to do with it and don't let her tell you otherwise."

I reddened, feeling awkward.

"I'm attending Yale as well," Emily said, changing the subject.

"So what did you do Uncle Abbot, build them a new wing?" I didn't mean it to sound sarcastic, but I could tell from Emily's foul expression that she didn't find my words amusing.

"I got accepted the old fashioned way," she continued, looking at me angrily, sounding spiteful. She had clearly taken offence to what I said. "Mom and dad didn't need to pull any strings for me to get in," she added, turning her gaze back to her breakfast, deliberately ignoring me. Emily didn't appreciate the fact that I thought she didn't deserve to go to such a prestigious school.

I realized, at that precise moment that I unintentionally had hurt her feelings.

Just as I was about to apologize she looked directly at me with those piercing eyes and said, "Caitlin, after you left things changed...." She stopped momentarily and took her frustration out on her breakfast, poking the heck out of her ham and cheese omelet. "Things got much better. It was hard at first, but then everything was much easier."

I knew the eruption was long overdue, and her words were cutting into me cruelly, making me feel even more desperate than I had been before.

If they were so much better off without me then what the hell was I doing back?

Each syllable continued to ring in my ears long after she had verbalized her spite. It came out so naturally. I was not sure if she knew how potent her words were to me. My heart started beating a mile a minute, triggered by her venomous response. I was infuriated with thoughts of how wonderful their life must have seemed the minute they had sent me away.

How could she just sit their eating her breakfast after saying something like that?

I felt draped in anger. I stood and turned my back to them, holding onto the kitchen counter, sensing the earth shake under my feet. A crystal-like sound clinking in the distance rang in my ears. I was so frustrated that I couldn't make any sense of what I felt or heard. *How dare she?*

Those years away were the hardest thing I had to endure. I didn't expect her, of all people, to throw it in my face. Not quite equipped with the appropriate skills to handle such a situation, taking deep breaths to control my rage seemed to be, at the time, the only way to get a grip of what was about to boil to the surface. I had a lot of practice over the past few years to channel my pain and anger. At one time it used to get the best of me, but now I was old enough to control it. It still, however, took all of my self-control not to leap at Goldilocks and pull out her hair – strand by golden strand.

Uncle Abbot approached me apprehensively; I sensed it in his stride. "Now you know she meant her grades improved for the better and not her life without you," he said, trying to defuse the situation.

I turned and glared at him over my shoulder not knowing how to react to his words.

"My God Caitlin, you didn't think I was talking about you leaving, did you?" Emily was on her feet now trying to explain herself. "Everyone here, especially me, was torn to bits on your decision to leave."

I half turned to face her. I kept my hands clutched onto the counter, a safe distance from scratching out her eyes. "Did you just say it was 'my' decision to leave?" I spat out, angrier than ever. "What the hell are you talking about? I was only thirteen years old. Since when do thirteen-year-olds know what's best for them?"

My head started throbbing. The memories of that night all flushed over me like a tidal wave of emotion.

"Breathe! Breathe in deep!" Aunt Leslie ordered. Standing right next to me, her eyes bore into mine. "Try not to lose control, Caitlin." Her persuasive whisper slithered into the fast whirling center of my thoughts. "Control your temper, otherwise you'll hurt someone."

Uncle Abbot even closer, placed his hands on my shoulder and within seconds, in my persuaded brain, everything mellowed. The whirling stopped, and my thoughts came slowly, but very sharply into focus. Astonishingly, all was calm again. I could feel my body relaxing, my mind clearing up.

"That's my girl," he said smiling. I quickly felt as I did last night – numb inside and out.

Aunt Leslie's piercing gaze still focused on me. "Are you okay?" she asked knowing the answer long before I did.

"Yes, I'm fine," I responded, taking another deep breath in the process. The rage I felt had completely vanished. "Thank you, Uncle Abbot," I said, knowing his gifted touch saved me from an awkward situation.

Turning to face Emily, I noticed Kyle's position. He looked the way I felt. His whole body shifted in front of Emily shielding her from imminent danger. *Why the defensive stance?* He knew I would never hurt her – no matter how harsh I thought her words were. He stepped away more relaxed now, having assessed the situation and returned to his breakfast.

"I'm so sorry," said Emily, taking hold of my hand, "I didn't mean it to sound like...." She instantly squeezed my hand tight. Her apology was cut short by the knock on the door.

The loud echo bounced off the walls enhancing the sound of the thud. Emily let go of my hand and returned to her seat without finishing her unnecessary apology. Kyle, preparing to head for the door turned to me and said, "You need to behave yourself and be nice." He patted me on the head playfully. "Behave!"

It was a good thing I was freakishly calm, because his comment would have angered me even more. Was I the only one making sense in that house? How could they all believe that it was my choice to leave, five years ago? Why was Aunt Leslie not saying anything?

And then, my face suddenly turned stone cold. My legs felt dangerously wobbly. The torturous feeling that I have known all too well growing up had once again resurfaced. This time the intense burning sensation in my veins was even more potent than ever before. I could feel him getting closer. The pain escalated to his every step.

"Not him – not now," I muttered through clenched teeth. I squeezed down so hard that any more pressure and my teeth would have surely shattered. "I shouldn't have come back,"

I circled my head desperately looking for a safe escape. The back door seemed to be my only hope for avoiding what was to come. The pain was immediate now that he was so close, intense and unrelenting.

Turning to exist, Aunt Leslie unexpectedly caught my arm pulling me to a full stop. "You're not one to run," she said, "besides; he's sensed your presence as you did his." She smiled and let go of my arm. "It will be ok, you can handle this."

It was not him that I was afraid of, it was me. I had absolutely no control of myself when he was around. From childhood the mere sight of Justin Bradford would trigger a chaotic spiral of emotions. It was like a reaction to some chemical in my blood. When he was only a few feet away the physical pain of needing to be near him subsided only to be replaced with a feeling of immense elation, but distance – distance made the pain unbearable – a burning so deep that it made me sick on many occasions. I thought I got control of this while away, but being there now only ignited the suffering.

I cleared my throat and braced myself not knowing how I was going to react on seeing him. *Why is he even here?*

The agonizing burn rushed through my body once again. I felt sick. The pain of it became unbearable, and for a moment I shut my eyes trying to shut it out, but it was useless. The turmoil came through with every breath of air, spreading like wildfire in my blood stream. The second Justin entered the kitchen I clutched the counter as the horrible sensations faded, leaving me nauseated and shaken.

The pain finally abated as if smothered by a sheet of calm, and a heightened awareness of his presence surfaced. A new sensation, however, quickly reared its ugly head. I felt like I was being pulled – pulled towards him by an invisible rope.

"Abbot, Leslie," he said, entering the room ignoring my being there.

His voice! There was nothing as magnificently alluring as his velvety, smooth voice. That instant my uncle beamed an amazingly warm smile and said, "Good morning, Justin. How's the family this morning, son?"

"Great," Justin replied, just as happy to see my uncle. "Dad told me to tell you that he's expecting you at eleven to finish off your debate."

Abbot's chuckle filled the air.

William Bradford and my Uncle Abbot were both quite scholarly. They would spend countless hours discussing trivial matters, each holding a cigar in one hand. It was masterful to watch two equal opponents arguing their points. When I was very young I used to sit on the floor in front of my uncle listening to them talk. Their voices passionate – never losing control of their emotions. They could debate for hours on end. It was entertaining for me to see who would back out – neither ever did. They would simply postpone the discussion for the following day.

What would today's topic be about? I wondered, trying to redirect my mind to a much safer topic.

"Hi Em," Justin said, turning his gaze to my cousin.

Emily smiled at him momentarily and then circled her head to face me, visibly confused about why he was purposely ignoring me. I was only standing a couple of yards away.

The next few minutes seemed to pass like a dream – a grim, unreal sequence unfolding in slow motion. His back suddenly became stiff taking him a second to turn to face me. Noticeably uncomfortable, his eyes locked onto mine for what seemed an eternity. I stopped breathing, or at least that was how it felt. There was a long, dreadful silence – a silence that pulsed with confusion and tension.

It was Justin who spoke first. "Caitlin…." His voice was a raspy, uneven tone, a clear contradiction to his stone-cold expression. He seemed to be fighting his own inner battle, apparently finding it hard to accept the fact that I was there. Evidently, he was as insanely uncomfortable as I was.

I ground my teeth behind my soft smile. "Hi Justin," I said, responding rather hastily, hating myself for sounding so eager. I swallowed hard, unwilling for him, of all people to realize what an effect he had on me. My body's reaction to the few feet that separated us was ruining the calm façade I was trying to display. I wanted to seem composed and mature, but it was Justin who was serenely self-possessed.

With the utmost composure he looked around the room to all the other faces clearly confused about something. "Is there a good reason why she's here?" he finally asked, completely ignoring eye contact; refusing to even repeat my name for the second time.

Surprisingly, I was deeply hurt by his response, though I shouldn't have been considering all those deliberate hurtful things he had said to me that fateful night.

"She's where she belongs," answered Kyle in a bewildered tone. "This is her home, Justin."

I decided, then and there, that I was not going to stand and listen to this. I had already gone one round with the family, I was not about to go another with Justin. I knew my limits; besides, I would not be able to concentrate with him around.

As I was about to walk past him to head outside for some fresh air, Justin grabbed my arm with force meaning to stop me. I wanted to scream, but not because of the pain of his grip, but because having him so close tormented me. His warm breath against my skin momentarily diminished any ill feelings I had for him.

"Where do you think you're going?" Justin asked, turning me in his direction – snapping me out of my little daze.

"Anywhere I damn well please," I swore, pulling my arm free from his vice with all my might. His touch left a burn much deeper than the surface of my skin.

Justin's piercing gaze locked onto mine once again. It took all of my concentration to stay upright and not fall down. I was not about to make an idiot of myself – not now – not with him there. "I need some fresh air, if that's all right with you." I finally heard myself say.

I was proud. I sounded strong and determined. Looking around I noticed that everybody else had returned to their breakfast except for Aunt Leslie, who was monitoring me, waiting for some kind of reaction.

"Why are you here?" Justin asked, in a commanding tone, taking one step back to put some distance between us.

"That's none of your...," I was about to push past him when my butterfly hairpin suddenly fell to the floor, breaking the silence with a piercing crash, causing my hair to cascade to the side. I bent down to pick up the elegant heirloom which was handed down to me by my mother, hoping that it didn't break in any way. "Idiot," I whispered, hating myself for being so clumsy.

A butterfly covered in beautiful stones with its wings spread, decorated the top section. To ensure that the full beauty of the butterfly was visible, the ornate design was hinged to sit over the hair while the prongs were secured in the hairstyle. It was my favorite thing to wear – something my mother actually wore herself. Now in my hand, I examined the delicate butterfly to see that it was intact. Seeing that it was, I tossed my head to the side to direct the loose hair away from my eyes. Justin's fingers were about to wipe some loose strands from my face when, hesitant at first, he pulled back, realizing it was not his place. His hands were quickly bunched in fists at his sides, and his face was contorting with impotence and fury, groaning under his breath, clenching his teeth – obviously detesting everything about me.

Hating him, I pushed him to the side and advanced towards

the door collecting my hair, pinning it back once again. Disregarding his foul mood, I grabbed my coat and headed outside. I needed fresh air – needed to clear my head.

My emotions were completely out of control. Nothing was going according to my own little plan. Surely, Justin was not part of any scenario I had concocted.

The back of the house was my only escape, for now, and I had to place some distance between me and him because the mere thought of Justin caused my stomach to flutter. I couldn't handle his eyes on me as they caused sheer havoc to my sanity. I needed time – time to figure out my next step, to talk to my aunt and get everything straightened out, to apologize to Emily for thinking she could be so callous. "What a mess I've made", I muttered, kicking some dirt to the side, "Great! Just freaking great! And it's only morning."

Totally disappointed at the way things were panning out, I looked up at the trees wrapping my coat tighter around me. I had forgotten how beautiful everything was.

The outside of the house was as refined and impressive as the inside. The branches swayed ever so lightly, casting shadows on the ground. It was brilliant in places where the sun filtered through. Walking around the grounds aimlessly, I recalled the endless hours of playing hide and seek with my cousins. The immense trees were perfect for hiding. The grounds that the estate covered were breath-taking in every way. In spring, from the running stream to the wild flowers that outlined the horizon, the sight and smells were second to none. Aunt Leslie's flower gardens would fill the air with their scent.

Now however, on the onset of winter everything was bleak, dead and grey; the flowers were gone and most of the trees stood bare, awaiting their chance to be revived by nature.

A feeling of calm began to finally spread through me. Closing my eyes, I took a rather deep breath and shook my head vehemently in the hopes that my mind could somehow erase the memory of his touch. It was then, in the middle of my tranquility that my back quickly stiffened. *Oh, great,* I thought. *Just what I need!*

I knew it was him – didn't need to turn to confirm what my heart already knew. Justin was standing right behind me. His sweet voice awash with curiosity shattered my defenses to a million pieces. "Not a trace of you in five years…," Justin paused, apparently struggling to get the words out, "and suddenly you're back?"

In all the years I have known him, Justin had never spent more than a few minutes talking to me. He always seemed uncomfortable around me, finding some asinine excuses to leave. We never actually talked – I mean really talk. It would explain why his questioning tone threw me off completely.

He remained rooted to the spot without the slightest notion of wanting to come any closer. There was a stiffness about him that made him seem so vulnerable and fragile that I thought he might break if I as much as touched him. The distance between us was merely a few feet. I purposely avoided eye contact trying to figure out why he seemed as lost as I was.

Moments later when our eyes finally met, my mind immediately scrambled for coherency. The pools of cobalt-blue looked at me, causing my racing heart to bounce hard and fierce against my ribs, responding to his splendor. "What is it with all of you?" I wailed, allowing my anger to surface. It was my only remaining defense against his brilliance.

I hadn't realized it inside, but he looked different, older. His looks were much more defined. Justin Bradford was the only man in Oaks who made Kyle look ordinary. His dark hair set off his perfectly sculptured features and flawless, white complexion. It had been five years, but my memory of him was unquestionably astute. Time hadn't altered his teenage good looks; instead, it accentuated them.

Justin took a deep breath as if ready to speak, but before he got in a word, I motioned for him to stop. "Do you really think," I started to say even louder, "that I would ever come back here if Leslie hadn't asked me to?" I was satisfied that I had finally told somebody my true reason for being there. "I'm not crazy, Justin. I don't just get up one morning and decide to ruin everyone's life by returning. I'm not cruel like some people."

The words were meant to hurt and I was sure they had some effect because his whole posture seemed to shift uncomfortably. His wounded gaze fell to the ground refusing to look at me. I knew those memories would have flooded back as soon as I spoke – that was my intention after all.

Seconds later, Justin gazed over to me and simply stared. For a moment he seemed to hesitate, and when at last he stepped forward, his movements were trembling and unsure. Then he abruptly stopped and said, "You said Leslie called you?" He sounded surprised. "Why would she want you to come back now?"

I shrugged my shoulders. "I don't know. She called me the day before yesterday and wanted to know if I could come for a visit. She sounded determined to get me here. Sorry if it's an inconvenience," I added, intentionally sounding spiteful.

Smiling devilishly, Justin took a few steps closer, lessening the distance between us. "Not at all an inconvenience," he muttered, looking content – happy even. As if drawn by an irresistible force, our eyes met and lingered, unable to break away. He continued to stare, demolishing any sort of wall I tried to build over those five years. *What's wrong with me?* I thought. *What the hell am I doing?*

He was simply standing there, but his presence alone made me question my own sanity – no other way to explain the intoxicating effect he had on me. Justin's grin widened in satisfaction, enjoying what his closeness was doing to me.

His breathing suddenly deepened. But although my body was ready to give itself up with immense gratitude, my mind refused to surrender itself to his charm. I was not sure how I was supposed to react to the attraction I felt.

From the time we were children I was aware of some strange connection between us, but Justin never let on that he felt anything of the sort. Even if he had, I was way too young. Being almost four years older, he was in no position to allow anything to evolve between us. Now, however, we were no longer children – those rules didn't apply.

Justin simply stood there studying my face. I wondered how I looked to him. I was only thirteen the last time he saw me. His expression was difficult to read. I couldn't tell if he approved of the changes the years had on me.

He smiled again.

Apart from the pounding of my heart, it was disturbingly quiet. The awkward silence loomed for a few more minutes. "You're actually here," he said taking yet another step closer, dangerously lessening the distance between us, which triggered a rabid breathing-frenzy on my part. It was then that he unexpectedly slid his left hand around my waist and pulled me towards him – merged with him until I could feel the breath from his lips and the toned muscles in his arm against my back.

This can't possibly be happening, I thought, finding it even harder to breathe now that he was actually touching me.

The hardness of his body came crashing on my chest as he tightened his hold. I couldn't believe he was doing this. My heart was pulsating under the force of his grip. Justin's free hand smoothed my hair to the side and looked at me now with even more intent, trailing his fingers down the contours of my face, brushing them against my dry, chapped lips.

"You're really here," he whispered, barely audible.

At that point, I was like a deer caught in headlights. Having absolutely no control of my brain or body, I remained there, putty in his arms.

I tried to clear my mind, to take control of my senses, but it was useless. I couldn't break away from him – heck, I couldn't even find the will to try. I simply stared back, confused at how I felt. In seconds, Justin hesitantly loosened his grip and carefully let me go.

Taking a few steps away from him was disturbingly agonizing – like forcing two titanic magnets apart. Everything around me seemed to draw me to him, fighting off the pull made me faint, my legs were once again wobbly, everything was moving in circles. I was about to fall when Justin swiftly caught me in an embrace saving me from embarrassment.

"Sorry, I didn't mean to...," he grinned, not letting me go. "Seeing you here today, well....," he couldn't find the words to explain what he felt. He simply sat me down on the ground. "Are you okay?" he asked tenderly.

I continued to stare in disbelief.

"Take a deep breath," advised Justin, beaming with

satisfaction at having such a strong effect on me.

I grimaced, wanting to scream, to let him know that all I have been doing since my return to Oaks was take deep breaths, but I kept my mouth shut, kept the thought to myself.

His eyes quickly turned to granite, but I could tell that there was pain in their depths, glimmering flecks of confusion and utter frustration.

With his fingers through his tussled hair he turned and said, "I've forgotten how strong the bond is, Caitlin. I figured through the years it would've faded, but I guess I was wrong."

My heart caught in my throat. I collected myself and finally stood up. "Bond?" I scuffed angrily. "That's ridiculous," I said under my breath. Anger seemed to be the only shield I had against what I felt for him.

There was talk among the Ellri that some of the gifted were born with a life-bond to another that they were bound in life as well as in death. The thought that this could be a description of Justin and I always jarred images of us walking on a stretch of beach holding hands like we see in movies.

I was so young, so stupid back then to think that we had any sort of future together. Bonds only had been known to occur between members of the pure blood lines. Unlike me, Justin was a direct descendant of his lineage, more powerful than most. I on the other hand had absolutely no gifts – a freak as far as our kind was concerned.

"I know what you're thinking, Caitlin," he said, with a wide grin.

In that split second he made me realize the reason behind his devilish smiles. I bit my bottom lip feeling stupid for having forgotten how easy it was for him to read my thoughts.

"Damn it!" I screamed, annoyed at giving him the satisfaction of knowing how I felt. "Damn you! Don't waste your gift on me, Justin." I suddenly felt him searching, probing my deeper thoughts – defying my wishes. "Damn it, stop that! You're impossible!" I yelled, looking at him now angrier than before. "There is no bond between us, and if there ever were you sure broke it years ago," I snapped, sensing his discomfort. "You are as bound to me as any other. I'm not like you Justin and I'll never be like any of you!"

I wanted to sound unforgiving – wanted it to be as painful as his last words to me five years ago.

Shouting at Justin made me feel marginally better. A dull calm descended. A relief from the stinging pain of earlier. My head felt oddly clear, but I still wanted to run – run far, far away.

"Caitlin, we're not through," he said grabbing my arm again. "There are some things we need to clear up."

"Clear up?" I looked at him questionably, "What in the world do we have to clear up? You made yourself perfectly clear a long time ago, remember? I'm not here to stay, if that's what you're worried about."

I yanked my arm free feeling the pull his closeness was exerting on me. Looking into his eyes made me even dizzier. Angry at my lack of self-control, I took a step back agitated by my own weakness.

"I can't think when you're around," I finally confessed, shaking my head in confusion.

My revelation seemed to agree with him. Justin's stone look broke into one of those smiles filled with satisfaction. I didn't realize, till then, how much my statement was stroking his ego.

"Monday morning I'll be on my way," I said, trying to erase the cocky smile from his beautiful face. "You can all go back to your normal lives once I'm gone."

The second I finished my statement, Justin swiftly grabbed both of my arms pulling me closer, his eyes spitting sparks, clearly angry. I didn't expect him to react the way he did to my simple remark.

"There's absolutely nothing normal here without you," he said angrily, shaking me ever so lightly. He let go just as fast, dropping my hands to my side with such force that it almost knocked me down. I knew I got the best of him, but for some reason it didn't give me the satisfaction I was hoping for.

Justin stormed off without looking back, mumbling foul words to himself. I was content for the time being. It was nice for once to have the upper hand.

In a fleeting moment the sensation of needles probing my mind emerged. *"Don't think we're through, Caitlin,"* said Justin, using his powers to project his thoughts. I could hear him crisp and clear as if he were right next to me. To the non-gifted hearing voices would have sent anyone running to the nearest shrink. I, on the other hand, being raised in Oaks was used to these mind games.

"Go to hell," I screamed to the invisible intruder. "Damn it, leave me the hell alone!"

I could hear his laughter ringing in my ears. Only then did I realize how strong Justin's powers were.

Now, at twenty-one, he must have already ascended like all his ancestors before him. I shivered at the thought of him holding me so tight. In the middle of all that chaos, I smiled in the realization that it was the first time Justin and I ever shared an intimate moment.

How strange, I thought, smiling even wider, relishing in the fact that he obviously felt something for me.

The Return
Illustrated For Lines That Bind - Circle of Turst

THREE

FURY WITHIN

MILY WAS HEADING UP the stairs as I entered the house and as soon as she saw me she came running towards me, beaming with happiness. "Did you enjoy your little reunion with Justin?" she asked adoringly. "You know, he's still here," she added, "went upstairs with Kyle."

"He's still here?" I asked surprised that he hadn't left.

"Caitlin, he's so hot, isn't he?" I rolled my eyes not knowing what she expected me to say. "Come upstairs, we have five years to catch up on and a birthday party to plan," she added, fussing with my hairpin. "What is it with this hair?" she complained, pushing some loose strands behind my ear.

I was still shaken by Justin's response, not sure if I had heard her correctly.

"Wait! Party – what party?" I asked, in complete ignorance. As soon as I structured the question I knew she was talking about my birthday. "No! No way! You can't possibly mean that. Em, I'm not staying," I blurted out.

"Oh, come on Caitlin. I'm dying to throw a party and your

birthday would give me a great excuse to invite Marc...," She paused at the thought of him and added smiling deviously, "and everybody else we know of course."

Marc was the son of Dominick and Adrianna Falcone, one of the oldest families of our kind. I always knew that Emily had a thing for him, but I had thought that after so many years something would have eventually unfolded.

"Nothing," she said, out of the blue, answering my own thoughts. "Marc has never made a move."

"Emily? You didn't tell me your powers surfaced?" I was accusing her of holding back a major piece of information, knowing that she could read my thoughts as clear as if I had spoken them.

"Two years, and five months," she boasted. "One day I woke up and felt a bit dizzy, different sounds which made absolutely no sense rang endlessly in my head. It was like putting my ear up against a blender and turning it on. I was disoriented for a few days, but mom walked me through it and here I am," she said, lifting her arms in the air to show her excitement.

"Wow, I didn't know it was that simple."

"Simple? I assure you that there was nothing simple about it. I was in agony. My head throbbed, and I was literally in physical pain." She continued to explain, shivering at the thought of her ordeal with her gift. "Anyway, enough about my stupid powers – now – about the party?"

"I don't think that's possible I'm...,"

I was going to tell her about my leaving on Monday, but just then my aunt walked in and cut me off, by saying, "Emily, you can talk to Caitlin later and make arrangements. I need to speak to her myself, if that's ok with you?"

Emily didn't look too thrilled to be interrupted, especially when a party was at stake. "Yeah, fine mom," she said, rolling her eyes. "We'll talk later, Caitlin," she added, heading up the stairs.

Seeing Emily walk away triggered my need to apologize – to clear the air from my earlier outburst. "Em, before you go," I said, turning towards her, needing to get some things off my chest, "I'm really sorry about earlier – about the misunderstanding. I should've known better than to think – well, you know."

In no time at all she skipped down the stairs and gave me a big hug. "What's a few words between sisters," she said smiling gloriously, displaying her perfectly white teeth. "Love ya, Caitlin," she added with her voice an octave higher – visibly touched by the whole incident.

"Love you, too, Em, and I really am sorry."

Emily kissed me on the cheek and disappeared up the stairs leaving me to fend for myself.

We stood there my aunt and I, looking at each other, both lost for words. There were so many things to clear up and so many explanations to be given.

"All in good time, Caitlin," she said. "You must be patient and trust me to know what's good for you."

This was the second time she spoke those words to me – once now and once five years ago. For some reason I trusted her, even then, hoping that I was right about her loving me as much as she did her own children, but why all the secrecy now? She knew I was old enough to handle anything.

"We need to talk somewhere quiet," she said, pointing to the main study.

Without even the slightest touch to the door handle my aunt effortlessly opened it with a quick flick of the hand. Feigning comfort, and attempting to hide my apprehension about her using powers out in the open, I entered the room first, focusing all my attention on the oil paintings hung on the far wall, and on the treasures that lay within.

Never before had I seen her exhibit the slightest ability and now she was clearly trying to make a point. In seconds, the smell of old books inundated my lungs.

I had always loved this particular room. Growing up in this old house I came to consider the study my sanctuary. All four walls were lined in bookshelves from top to bottom, crafted in the sixteenth century by local craftsman. Most of the books were first editions of great literary writers – masters of their craft. It was overwhelming to anyone who entered the main study for the very first time.

Spacious and quite conventional, it retained its original oak beams, and wooden floor. The most indispensable feature of all was the fireplace – embellished with silver picture frames of the family and some priceless antiques. My grandparent's frame stood out from the rest – biggest in size and most impressive in style. Grandfather Cecil and grandma Cordilia were, after all, my mother and Aunt Leslie's parents. It was only natural for my aunt to have the McDevitts front in center on the mantel.

The windows dressed in velvet curtains were hidden behind the massive oak desk I loved most of all. It was usually laden with all kinds of books; new and old – mostly very old.

The Cathcarts had the largest collection of all the families. Uncle Abbot took extra care to furnish it with the latest pieces as he saw fit. He would make such a fuss when he brought home a new addition. "Guess what I have," he would say, waving the leather bound book in the air. He knew to look for my face among the family members because I seemed to be the only one who shared his love for reading. I spent endless hours sitting in front of the fireplace absorbed in a book. It was my personal escape.

Aunt Leslie knew that this was the only place in the house I felt most comfortable in; otherwise she would not have led me there. Unexpectedly, she pushed a pile of text books across the desk – Biology, Calculus, English Lit…

"What's this?" I asked, looking down at the pile.

"You cannot expect to go to school without books now can you?" she said casually. "I enrolled you in the Advanced Placement program here in Oaks High." Her expression was hard – ruthless.

"I don't follow. What school are you talking about? I have a school, and books back in Stone Hurst."

"Caitlin, don't walk away!" My aunt shouted the words as I pushed the text-books back to her side of the desk and started for the door. "You must understand!"

"Oh, I understand loud and clear," I said, turning to face her. "How dare you! How dare you tell me what to do! Is this why you called me back after all these years? Don't tell me you're concerned about my education. You don't get to tell me what to do any more, Aunt Leslie. I'm leaving first thing Monday morning."

"Ok, look," she said, pressing her hands together, "I've talked to Mr. Patterson and arranged everything. You're starting Monday morning at Oaks High, and finishing your senior year here, with us."

"You're not listening to me," I pronounced. "I'm leaving on Monday!"

Her composer was unnerving. "I've also made arrangements with your old school," she continued to say. "Your things should be here by Monday, Tuesday the latest."

So infuriating was her resolve that it caused me to take a step back. She was not asking me if I wanted to stay, she was ordering me, deciding once again on my future. My anger ignited a rampage of other, far more suppressed emotions.

"Are you out of your freaking mind?" I screamed, raising my voice at her for the very first time in my life. "Are you crazy? How can you do this to me, again? I have friends at Stone Hurst. I have a life to get back to."

What life? I thought. *Who was I kidding?*

I kept to myself most of the time being the new kid and all. Boarding schools were not the best experience a young child could have, especially for a thirteen year old starting in the middle of the school year. My days were filled with homework and extracurricular reading. Only on rare occasions did we take field trips. For the most part, the students at Stone Hurst were all from affluent families who would travel abroad the first chance they got, leaving me and a few other children behind in the quiet halls of residents. I was content with my arrangements, never asking for more.

This year was the most bearable of all. I decided to make something of my life. Tired of crying myself to sleep at night, I got a part-time job cleaning up a local café in the evenings before closing. It was nothing special, but the fact that I was actually somewhere other than my room was invigorating.

It took me a few years to control the physical pain I was experiencing because of the distance that separated Justin and I, but I found ways in dealing with it. Stone Hurst was finally feeling like home.

I made some friends, but only in passing. It didn't amount to much since all the students at Stone Hurst had such busy schedules. I was the only one who remained in the resident's hall

all through summer. Alone with my thoughts for three months out of the year was, to say the least, the worst of all. Had it not been for the well-stocked Library in the main building and the trivial chores Ms. Leedey had me do, I would have surely gone crazy.

Good old Ms. Leedey came to check on me from time to time to see if I needed anything. She even took me on excursions to local museums and restaurants, introducing me to new things and experiences. It was not her job to care for me, but soon I depended on her, considered her family. As far as I knew she never had any children of her own, so she felt protective of me, connected in some way. I enjoyed our conversations, they were all very enlightening. She had experienced so much in life – seen so much of the world and I her polar opposite, absorbing in all the information – like a sponge always wanting more.

"It's for the best," said Aunt Leslie once again, drawing me back to the present. "Your life is here."

"No!" I yelled even louder, "I'm going back. No one wants me here."

"Don't be ridiculous! Everyone wants you here."

"If that's true, then why, why did you send me away?" She dropped her gaze to the floor as she did every time she had no answer to give. "Caitlin, you suffered enough alone, it's time you were with your family."

Her words caused anger to surge up in me in a hot dark wave. "My family?" I wailed, lifting my tear-wet face, all choked up, barely able to speak the word. "Where was my family when I needed them night after night? Where were they when I prayed for someone to come and get me? I was only thirteen, Aunt Leslie, and all alone. How dare you speak to me about family?"

"Caitlin, please control your anger," she said in complete

disregard of my words. "You must stop and get control."

Angered even more, my voice became louder, "You betrayed my trust, promised never to leave me. How dare you stand there and pretend to care. I needed you Aunt Leslie." My voice suddenly choked with sobs. "Tell me, where the hell were you when I needed you?"

I quieted at the sound of books crashing to the floor.

Confused, I looked around and noticed that the floor was covered with fallen picture frames, papers, books even the wall paintings were all tilted and some even ready to fall off.

Too upset to care, I stood still, my breath coming in slow, shuddering sighs. "I can't be here. I shouldn't be here," I yelled again, intent on making her understand, "There's no reason for me to be here," I kept repeating, if by some miracle it would start to make sense to her.

The tightening in my chest got worse. I could feel myself losing complete control of my emotions. Five years of bottled up, suppressed anger, all surfacing now in torrents. I could feel my body shaking now, more than ever in physical pain – the burning in my veins, ignited; intensifying my agony.

At that moment there was a rap at the door. Ignoring the sound I walked towards the fireplace turning my back to the intruder. I was in no mood to confront anyone else.

I racked my brains to think of why. Why now? Why did she want me to stay now? I hoped against hope all those years ago that someone would come, but no one did.

The pain in my chest was now a pounding thud. Aunt Leslie was in two minds about opening the door, but did so anyway.

"Did you feel that?" he said in awe.

Not now. Not him too!

"Yes, don't worry, she's fine," my aunt answered.

"Caitlin," Justin, sounding exceptionally concerned, "are you okay?"

His voice was deeper, calmer nothing like earlier. I felt him getting closer with every step – gradually soothing the burn in my veins. With a feather like motion he placed his hand on my shoulder and turned me round to face him.

My face now flushed from the warmth of the fireplace – my tears completely out of control. Maddened by his audacity, I shoved his hand off and pushed him to the side, wiping away my treacherous tears. "Don't you dare touch me!" I screamed "Don't you ever touch me!"

Justin stared at me bewildered and then looked angrily towards my aunt. "You can't be serious," he shouted, sounding even angrier than I was.

He must have read my thoughts of what had just transpired. His shock was unmistakably carved on his face. I sensed the volatility in his words.

Though Justin seemed calm on the surface, I was alarmingly aware of his anger rising. He was usually even-tempered and had the ability to seem cool in the hardest circumstances – now for some reason he was completely beside himself.

"Leslie, what are you thinking? She can't stay here," he said, looking at me knowing his words would hurt. "She must leave. She doesn't belong here."

I was not sure if I had heard correctly. I knew that he was not happy to see me that morning, but still, this was too much. I was stunned. *What have I ever done to them?*

I wanted to run, wanted everything to go quiet. The room was spinning so fast that I couldn't think straight. *He didn't want me there.* It was the second time I heard him verbalize those words. Just like five years ago – Aunt Leslie on one side and Justin on the other. But back then they were, at least, both playing for the same team.

I stared at both of them fully aware that I had absolutely no say in the matter. Then, the realization of my true circumstance set in. I had absolutely nowhere to go, without any means to survive on my own. I was stuck.

Mentally confused and unable to think with clarity my mind made no sense of what my aunt and Justin were arguing about. I wrapped my hands around my waist, barely hanging on. "Stop it! Both of you! Just stop," I heard myself say through the tears. "I can't win, can I?"

Silence

"You want to break me, is that it?" There was pain in my words, and resentment. But what hurt most was the betrayal.

I shifted my gaze to both of them. Then a stiff silence hung over us for many long, awkward moments. I flung my hands in the air in defeat. "You're both too strong for me. Decide what you wish and I'll obey," I finally said, completely beaten.

Their expression was ghostly – motionless. They didn't expect an outcry. Justin looked like somebody had punched him in the gut. I couldn't stand there any longer, not with both of them staring at me. It was clear that they were keeping something from me, unwilling to let me in on the secret. Utterly lost and hurt, I stormed off, leaving them behind in the study and headed for my room. I could still hear Justin's voice continue to talk to my aunt in an aggravated tone. Already up the stairs, I couldn't make out what he was saying as I headed to my room with tears feverishly streaming down my face.

Once I reached my parent's old room I stopped and with one quick push I opened the double doors to their chamber and walked in tired and confused. Desperate for someone's understanding, I fell on the bed taking hold of the pillow under the satin covers. My whole body ached. I didn't know what to do. I lay there motionless for quite some time, even my tears had run their course.

Wiping my face with my sleeve I sat up and held my legs to my chest, trying to control the rush of emotions. My mind chased itself in circles, and my thoughts twisted in all sort of directions. Looking around, I noticed that the room seemed much smaller. It was in impeccable order, just where my parent's had left everything so many, many years ago. Seeing my mother's possessions, for the most part, was rather comforting. When I had wanted to be left alone, this was the place I would run to.

Nobody ever bothered me in this room.

I used to crawl under the bed with my parent's picture in hand, hugging it so tightly that it literally hurt my little arms. I would fall asleep on the floor under the bed only to have Uncle Abbot collect me each and every time, returning me to my own bed further down the hall. The years after my parent's passing were very difficult. I refused to eat or even speak. I missed them so much, asked for them, cried till I couldn't cry anymore; my aunt and uncle surely had their hands full.

Sitting there, lost in my memories, I pulled the butterfly hairpin out of my hair and traced its wings with my fingers, missing my mom even more. Moving it around in my hands, the stones, unexpectedly, caught the beams of light that came through the window and created prisms on the wall, opposite the four poster bed.

I followed the dancing lights to the painting that hung across the room. It was a family portrait of my father in his brilliant three piece suit looking as handsome as ever while mother sat in an elegant chair, wearing a long cream colored lace gown with me in her lap. I must have been only a few months old when the painting was commissioned.

Sadness suddenly overtook me, causing my tears to resurface. I needed them so much, needed them to reassure me that everything was going to be okay. "Mom...," I wailed calling out to her, hugging my legs even tighter, "Mom," I kept repeating over and over between the sobs with my face in my knees. The gasps turned to moans that were of my mom's name, then the moans to silence.

I suddenly heard Justin say, "Caitlin, you shouldn't be in here." He approached the bed and in one swift move picked me up and carried me away.

Purely for selfish reasons, I didn't fight him off. The chemical reaction my body had to his was warm and soothing; putting an end to the burning in my blood the instant he touched me. How something so sweet sprang from something so lethal was baffling. I didn't care what it was at that moment. Justin's embrace was making me feel better.

His hold got even tighter, reacting to my thoughts. "Relax, everything will be all right," he said, trying to console me as he entered my room, propping me on my bed carefully, taking care to pull the covers first.

"I must go home," I whispered, looking up at him, exhausted from the tears.

Justin sat on the edge of my bed, without a trace of discomfort. I took a deep breath and closed my eyes in an attempt to regain my composure. I didn't want to say anything that would cause tears to well up again. I kept my eyes shut for a while trying to choke back the incessant emotions that kept sprouting up.

"You are home, Caitlin," Justin finally said, pushing my stray hair to the side, allowing his hand to linger.

I looked down at my hands and pulled on my sleeve feeling quite awkward, and then slowly lifted my eyes to his, to see what he was thinking.

Only inches away, Justin's eyes looked dark, full of thought and contemplation. We were never this close before, apart from earlier. My mind couldn't figure out why my body reacted to him so intensely. I was going crazy with the sensation of his lips being so close to mine.

Justin didn't move, lost as I was in the moment. He leaned forward lessening the distance between us. I didn't care about hating him anymore, everything about him was welcoming.

He smoothed my hair to the side again, this time sliding his hand to the back of my neck, pulling me even closer. There was no distance left between us. I could taste his breath on my lips. He unexpectedly leaned away, searching for something in my expression. "You're really here," he whispered softly.

His words felt like a knife through my heart. My eyes still sore from the tears, filled once again in pools of pain. I felt beaten in more ways than one. Then, as I sat there, staring into his eyes, I wondered what it would truly cost to open up to him. My body surprisingly froze at the thought. I felt sick to my soul as the memory of his harsh words the night I was sent away played over and over in my head like a song gone awry. Justin's expression suddenly changed as well, hardened in a matter of seconds. He pulled back ever so slowly never losing eye contact.

"I'm sorry," he said.

I was not sure what he was sorry about.

"I just can't seem to control this thing I feel when you're this close. It's...," he couldn't find the words to explain what he was feeling. Instead he pushed back his hair with both hands and turned away.

It was comforting to know that he felt the pull as much as I did. But even so, allowing things to get that far really annoyed me. He, however, didn't seem at all bothered. Within seconds he was in my mind again searching for explanations.

"Justin, please. You have to stop," I said, in a low soft voice. I didn't have the energy to yell. "Why does everybody presume to have the right to go through my thoughts?"

"I can't speak for the others, but as far as I'm concerned, I can't help it. I want to understand what you're feeling and thinking."

"If you want to know what I'm thinking, all you need to do is ask. That's what ordinary people do."

Justin cracked a smile. "Caitlin, if you haven't noticed, there's nothing ordinary about us."

"I don't know about you," I answered, "but I'm as ordinary as they come."

He circled his whole body to face me. I sat further up, pulling my hair to the side combing it with my fingers. He looked at me again with one of those irresistible glances. I could feel my cheeks ablaze with uncontrollable excitement. To my surprise he stroked my cheek and let his gaze scan over me from head to toe. "Caitlin, I wouldn't go as far as to call you ordinary," he finally said, moments later, lifting his eyes to mine. He was about to take my hand, when I quickly pulled it away. I needed it to think. If he touched me again I wouldn't have been able to form a sentence.

"So, have you and Leslie decided on my future once again?" I said, wanting to sound unforgiving. "Justin, I need to leave. I can't stay here. You both need to be reasonable."

"You have school on Monday," he said, in a superior tone, sounding like my uncle. "I talked to Leslie and she's right. This is the best for you."

"Justin, please! Why are you all putting me through this

again?" I was begging, "I don't belong here. I should go back to Stone Hurst."

It was the second time in my life that I was pleading for his help.

His eyes darkened once again and looked at me. "I need you here," he said. "The last five years have been murder. Having you so far away was insufferable and the nights not being able to read your thoughts were pure anguish." He sighed, shaking off the memories.

I looked at him in disbelief.

Justin's declaration rang so true to my ears. His words were a mirror image of my own torment. I knew exactly what he meant. When we were young the feelings I had for him were unbearable at times. Justin's absence hurt me physically as well as emotionally. I thought it was an ordinary crush teenagers had, but I knew better. When he came round to visit Kyle, it was the only time the pain subsided. He didn't need to be in the same room just in the vicinity. I felt his presence in my bones, in my blood, in my heart.

Over dinner one night, so long ago, giggling Kyle suggested that Justin had difficulty staying away from our house. "He's your best friend," Uncle Abbot had told him, unsure of why Kyle was acting so stupid at the dinner table.

Emily looked at Kyle and started laughing as well. The duo had been keeping a secret from me. I could tell by their reaction.

"What is it?" I had asked.

Kyle collected himself and tried to explain his theory through the giggles. "Justin doesn't come round here for me, Caitlin, but for you," he said, with a wicked smile.

Aunt Leslie looked at him appallingly. "What do you mean?" she asked, quickly absorbed in the conversation.

"I think there is a bond between them," Kyle responded, looking at his mother's expressionless face, "How else would you explain the poor guy's suffering? She's too young for it to be anything else."

She turned and looked at Uncle Abbot. Her face had marbleized, she didn't flinch. Uncle Abbot picked up his plate and took it to the sink, trying to break the tension. "Nonsense," he said, brushing aside the whole conversation. "Did you guys finish your homework?" he asked ending the ordeal.

That's when I knew that the feelings I had for Justin were beyond anything normal – way beyond my control. The harrowing years without him at Stone Hurst incited bouts of depression and endless hours of agonizing pain. It had nothing to do with missing my family it was clearly the reaction of being so far apart.

The Ellri had once explained that bonds were the strongest connection our kind could have with another person. Normal people called them soul mates, but in our world it was much more, much stronger.

There was a physical need to be around that person, a magnetic pull – no force on earth greater. This at times did describe Justin and me. It did explain my attraction to him at such a young age, but it simply couldn't be the bond because life bonds were rare and only known to occur between family members of the pure blood lines.

We were not in the same hierarchy in the blood lines. Justin was the first born in the Bradford family, making him quite unique as far as powers were concerned and the purest of blood. I, on the other hand, had absolutely no idea where I ranked. My father, who was only a distant cousin of Uncle Abbot's, was not even from the immediate Cathcart blood line. It was the reasoning behind my lack in gifts.

"Caitlin, look at me," Justin said, putting an abrupt halt to my whirling. "You'll be fine. No more talk about leaving, you need your family and I'm not letting you go again."

I looked at him, truly looked at him.

"I need to talk to my aunt," I said, pushing myself out of bed, "I'll be eighteen in a week. I don't need anybody's permission to leave."

"Don't be stupid, you're better off here. Where would you go? You can't go back to Stone Hurst," he exclaimed, running his fingers through his hair, clearly annoyed at my refusal to understand.

Visibly frustrated at my persistence, he got to his feet. "Damn it Caitlin, you're much stronger than I am. If you want to leave, go ahead and leave. I won't stop you, but how can you stand the pain of being apart? Doesn't it tear at your soul?"

He stood there waiting for an answer. It was only the faintest and most uncertain of feelings, but I recognized the answering tremor in my own mind as one of fear, fear of leaving him again – fear of never seeing him.

Justin was about to say something else, but instead he irritably pushed his hair back again, looking even more frustrated. "Fine! Leave! Leave if that's what will make you happy."

Without a second to spare he headed for the door and slammed it shut; leaving me stunned and with tear-filled eyes. My gaze remained transfixed on the door. I brushed away the tears with the back of my hand and closed my eyes tightly. I tried to close my ears, and mind also, to the things that became all the more confusing. Nothing ever made sense.

Refusing to let his words get the best of me, I headed to the bathroom to splash some water on my face, to help me snap out of this depression. I needed some time to think, some time to figure out what I was doing back, to decide what my next step was going to be.

Justin was not in the house anymore. I could feel the void growing within; the overwhelming need to be with him, once again, crept its way to the surface, the pain caused by the distance rekindled into an agonizing burn – much stronger than ever before.

I concentrated hard, closing my eyes as tight as humanly possible, willing the pain to subside. It used to take hours, but now, after years of practice I was able to reduce the acidity to a faint discomfort.

For long moments I continued to look at my own reflection, wondering how I got myself into such a mess.

"Let's just go," I told my own reflection. "Why put ourselves through all this?"

Go where? I thought. *Where could I possibly go?*

I shook my head knowing that there was absolutely no way out of this situation. Any way I looked at it, I was trapped by my own inability to express what I truly felt for them all – to let them really know what they had put me through.

Pathetic is what I was – Megan was so, so right. I was truly weak and utterly pathetic.

FOUR

UNFORESEEN

S I AWOKE FROM A DREAM, tears slid down my cheeks and I sat up in bed brushing the tears aside. What a sad, sad dream that was – full of grief and despair. Yet I couldn't remember what it had been about, just a voice carrying all the sorrow in the world had somehow threaded a path through my mind.

Deciding that walking it off was the best remedy, I wandered down the long corridor outside my room, as I did thousands of times when I was a child. Never having taken a nap before, the inertia and sluggishness due to sleep hampered my attempt at brushing aside the traces left behind by my dream.

Taking the time to admire the art that lined the endless walls of the upper quarters would have surely, at other times, eased my mind. It was there that I found the much needed silence to think, to straighten out every little detail that lingered in my head.

The sight of the beautiful tapestries which hung on the far walls depicting scenes of another world – a world full of magic and mystery surely helped in finding my center.

Once, when I was eight I had asked Aunt Leslie if what the people of Oaks had was Magic. "No," she had answered, "nothing unnatural with all our gifts. You see," she continued to explain holding me in her lap, "from the beginning of time some people were born with gifts, endowed by our creator. Some of these abilities were much more evident in some than in others."

"What do you mean?" I had asked looking up confused, with thousands of questions whirling in my little mind.

"Well," she said, giving me a tender kiss on the nose, "every person on this planet is talented in some way or another. Some people are able to tell stories in such a way that they seem more than real to the listener. Others might have a better perception of what is going on around them. With the passing of time these heightened abilities evolved as did mankind. So there is absolutely nothing unnatural about the town folk."

"Then why doesn't the rest of the world know we exist? Why can't the people here use their gifts openly? Why all the secrecy?"

"Umm – all good questions," she said, smiling. "In ancient times things were quite different. People with gifts were considered godly, not freaks as they are in our days. In ancient Greece for example, Pythia was considered to be a priestess in the slopes of Mount Parnassus around the eighth century. She was the most prestigious and authoritative oracle in the ancient world. She was a human like the rest, only with a heightened ability to foresee events. Though now, most would consider the possibility of her ever having existed, a myth. There have been many throughout time. Our history books are filled with these gifted individuals, mostly stories passed down from one generation to the next. There have always been people with gifts; as far back as we know – some in science and others in politics.

With the course of history some gifts became more powerful."
She tried to simplify the details as best she could.

"At one time…," she continued to say, "The world was reborn with new ideas and religions. For fear of heresy, these exceptional people were cast out from society, believed to be witches or demons. Many were stoned, hung, burnt at the stake others even killed at birth, simply because they bore a mark. The only way to survive those dark times was for the gifted to look for others like themselves. So, hundreds of years later secret societies were created, families of wealth and power came to be."

Mesmerized I continued to stare at her – hung by her every word. "Why is there an imbalance of power among the gifted?"

"It's not an exact science, Caitlin. We've noticed that the older the family line and the purer their blood line, the stronger the powers became." I turned to look at her – now more baffled than before. She must have anticipated my next question, because as she spoke she smiled, a perfect gleaming smile that illuminated her inner beauty. "Yes, blood line," she said, ignoring my disgusted expression at the word 'blood'. "What I mean Caitlin, is that we're human after all, so it is understandable that many of our kind got involved with others less gifted. So, with time the blood lines weakened and with each generation some gifts diminished even disappeared."

"Oh," I said, fascinated.

"Only five pure bloodlines exist to date, "she explained further. "My bloodline, the McDevitt, then there is the Korbs, the Falcone, Abbot's bloodline the Cathcart and Justin's, the Bradford. They each have pure ancestral trees dating as far back as the pyramids and even older. Three of these lineages decided a few centuries ago that the New World would be the most appropriate place to raise their children. In order to secure the purity of the blood lines and protect everyone from prying eyes, they decided to create our community here in Oaks."

"What happened to the other two bloodlines, the Korbs and the McDevitt? Where are they? Why didn't they come live here in Oaks?"

She seemed hesitant to answer my question. "They, being the oldest of our kind, remained in Europe." Her posture suddenly shifted, stiffened in a way.

There was a moment, only a very brief moment, in which I needed to construct my next thought "Aunt Leslie?" I looked at her skeptically, "Oaks has more than just the three bloodlines."

"Yes, of course there are others," she said, smiling once more. "Just because people don't belong to one of the great families doesn't mean that there aren't others out there, blessed with gifts. They're not as potent as ours, but they're exceptional, nonetheless."

"Fat-head, Megan Gordon doesn't belong to one of the bloodlines, does she?"

My aunt tightened her embrace. "No, no she doesn't."

"Then why does she live in town?"

"Well, that's because, years ago the Ellri had decided to protect any gifted person by giving them residence in Oaks. So people who were banished by their society were given a home here, given a place where they could finally fit in. Keeping our society and abilities a secret was an unwritten rule that they each had to abide by." My eyes dropped in disappointment. "What is it sweetie? What's wrong?"

"Why don't I have any gifts?" I finally asked, raising my gaze to her brilliant grey-blue eyes. "I'm part of the bloodline, aren't I? I'm a member of the family, a Cathcart. There are kids in school much younger than me that have had powers from birth. They're abilities aren't anything special, not like the powers the Ellri have, but still they have something."

"Of course you are a member of the great families. You shouldn't worry about not exhibiting any gifts."

I huffed, infuriated. "Sure, easy for you to say. You don't have to go to school every day and be teased about being different."

"Caitlin, being different is what makes you so special, makes us all special. Don't be shy about not fitting in."

She loved me way too much to understand my school's social politics. I got to my feet and leaned in closer, taking her face in my small hands. "Aunt Leslie, you are clueless as to how awful being different is. I go to school with Megan, did you forget? She is evil, I tell you. EVIL!"

My aunt was visibly amused by my adult-like nature. Tenderly, she took my little hands in hers and squeezed them tight. "No child is evil, Caitlin. Megan is as different as you are. She just doesn't want to face up to it. Don't be fooled by her confidence. It's a ploy to make you feel unimportant. You are special. For some unexplained reason your gifts haven't surfaced yet."

"When – when will they surface?"

She shrugged her shoulders. "Sometimes they skip a generation or just one person in particular."

"That's not fair! Of all the people in Oaks, I had to be the one it skipped?"

She put her hand under my chin guiding it upward, so that she had full view of my disappointment. "You are gifted Caitlin, just not in the way you think," she answered, trying to sooth my smothered hopes.

The memories were so many. She tried explaining things as best she could. I knew now that there was something more, something deeper to the whole story. Some of the Ellri were known to control the elements while others could manipulate people's actions and dreams. These were more than simple parlor tricks. They were all very careful with their powers – rarely using them out in the open.

"Self-control is power," they would tell us.

Combined, the eighteen members of the Ellri, in Oaks, were not a force to be reckoned with. They were all amazing people, educated and worldly. They didn't stay rooted in Oaks, but instead traveled, seeing the world around them. However, they did leave their children behind. Aunt Leslie and uncle Abbot had never left my side while growing up. They felt more comfortable here in town so, when the other Ellri decided to travel, they were left caring for a brood of uncontrollable children. Our house was full of mischief and mayhem.

Those were the days, I thought.

A house full of rowdy, gifted individuals – what could go wrong, usually did go wrong. Some kids, like Justin and his best friend, Marc Falcone were born with gifts that outmatched the rest. They were, among other things, able to manipulate people's thoughts as well as their actions.

Let's just say, my aunt and uncle had their hands full, keeping those two under control.

Once, I was told that when Kyle was only ten years old, he had invited Marc and Justin for a sleep over. To my uncle's surprise, he found Kyle pounding his hands against his chest believing he was a monkey, dangerously close to falling off the banister, in an attempt to reach an imaginary banana. Justin and Marc's manipulation of Kyle's mind was a constant game among the best friends.

The three of them together, were completely out of control

most of the time. The memories were many, but it was best, I knew, to stay focused on the present.

It was late in the afternoon and I was helping Kyle with the dishes – agreeing to wash if he did the drying. He was in a rush to go out, so he agreed to anything that would make the chore bearable.

It was a quaint dinner, with different topics thrown around the table. We talked endlessly about everything and anything, but eventually every conversation returned to the topic of my return to Oaks High.

Aunt Leslie didn't look my way not even once – probably not wanting to chance a reenactment of that morning. She knew I had enough for one day. She ate quietly, only answering direct questions and later left the table with a simple order for us 'kids' to clean up.

After we finished the chores I went to my room and sprawled on my bed. I was happy the day was slowly coming to an end. Too many things had transpired. Honestly, it was one of the longest days of my life.

"Caitlin," Emily said, swinging my door open, "come downstairs, there's someone here to see you."

Draped in apprehension, I headed downstairs only to be stopped dead in my tracks at the sight of Tyler Falcone gazing up at me. There was something grown up in the rigid contours of his Italian good looks and in the dark intensity of his deep brown stare that made me beam with pleasure at the sight of my childhood friend. We knew each other practically from birth. He was only a few months older so we were classmates and best friends from pre-school and up until that godforsaken night.

Pausing only long enough to allow my surprised expression to fade, I noticed, from the corner of my eye, Emily smiling, trying to hint at how handsome Tyler was. She instantly threw me one of those winks, full of underlining meaning.

I rolled my eyes at her, turning my full attention back to my long lost friend. "Tyler," I squealed, "I can't believe – I just didn't expect...." I was way too emotional to structure a sentence. I really didn't expect to run into him and there he was.

Grinning sinfully, he stared back. "Caitlin, I heard you're in town and I had to see for myself," he said, looking me up and down. "It's been a while and you look real good." He sounded a bit over the top.

I reached over and gave him a big hug. "You don't look half bad yourself." Tyler was clearly just as happy to see me – his embrace tightened just a little too much. "Um, Tyler?" I said, barely able to breathe. "You're sort of hurting me."

He quickly loosened his embrace and stepped back, scanning me with those expressive almond shaped eyes. "I'm sorry. I just can't believe you're back. It's been way too long, Caity."

"I missed you too, Tyler." I hugged him one last time before taking an awkward step back.

Emily seemed uncomfortable standing there having nothing to say. "Well, I don't want to be the third wheel," she said, and scurried off.

"Are you up for a walk?" Tyler offered, paying little attention to Emily, "It's nice out for this time of year. Come on, don't make me beg. It'll give us time to catch up."

"Sure, I'd love to," I answered, all too happy to get out of the house and clear my head. "It's been a long day. A walk would do me good."

I eagerly grabbed my coat and followed Tyler outside. It was not until much later, after a long trek down the twisting woods, that we came to a stop. "Have you been crying?" he asked, turning his gaze to me. "Your eyes look a bit strained."

"Being back has made me a bit too sensitive," I said smiling. I didn't exactly lie, but I didn't want to give him a glimpse into my sordid morning.

Tyler kicked a pine cone to the side and circled his head to me and said, "Emily tells me you're starting school on Monday. Is that true? Are you back – back for good?"

I paused for a silent moment, not sure how to answer. "Yeah, it would seem so." I kicked the dirt with the tip of my shoe, hating having no control of my life, yet again. Tyler continued to look at me through the corner of his eye. "I don't know what to tell you, Tyler. I honestly don't know. I guess I am back."

"It's going to be fun having you here. We can finally do all those things we said we'll do in our senior year. It was so boring without you, even Megan missed you."

I raised a brow of discernment, smiling, knowing all too well that it was a conspicuously loud lie. We started laughing knowing that Megan and her friends didn't care either way.

The walk was truly invigorating. I felt absolutely comfortable. Tyler was like an old worn sweater – warm and just what the weather required. We sat on the wall on the farthest side of the field, like we did on innumerable occasions in the past. It was centuries old – ruins really. It had served as a boundary separating the Bradford estate with the Cathcarts. Useless now, the relationship that Justin's parents, Shannon and William Bradford, had with my aunt and uncle was far greater than any wall could separate. Now it barely stood at all. There, Tyler and I would spend most of our time after school, close enough to home, but yet far enough to feel free.

"I can't believe I'm here," I whispered, taking it all in. I didn't mean to say it out loud it just slipped.

"You don't look too happy. Didn't you miss me?" he asked boyishly.

I leaned into him, nudging him in the ribs. "Of course, I missed you, but I have a life back there now."

"Caitlin, you belong here, with us. You're one of us and that will never change, no matter how far you are."

"I know Tyler, but it's been too long. Everything is different, but yet the same. Look at you. You're so grown up. You've changed so much."

"That's just on the outside, Caitlin. I'm still the same old annoying friend." His sweet smile widened. "I just want you to know that I didn't believe any of the things people were saying about you when you left." Tyler turned his gaze to the ground avoiding eye contact – feeling awkward about opening up that can of worms.

"What were they saying exactly?" I asked, interested in knowing what the town folk thought about my sudden departure.

"Oh, you know how small towns work Caitlin. There were rumors that you were tired of being caged up here. Having no powers allowed you the freedom to live normally. You could easily live with the non-gifted, outside Oaks. Why in the world would you choose to stay here, within these limits?"

"Is that what they thought? They thought that at thirteen I suddenly decided to pack up my things and go, leaving behind my family and friends? That's – that's ridiculous."

"What else could they have thought? You kept to yourself, doing your best to keep everyone at a distance. They just assumed you couldn't take it anymore and split."

Infuriated, not at him but at what people thought about me, I jumped off the wall and stood right in front of him – fuming with contempt. "How absurd," I said, louder than I had intended. "I tried blending in with everyone, but they made it nearly impossible. They mucked me about my lack in powers on a daily bases. You saw how Megan and the rest of them goaded me. I chose to take the high road, refusing to play into her trap. How could they think I wanted this?"

"Caitlin, I know. I was there, remember?"

I rubbed my forehead as to rub out the lingering effects of all those bad memories.

Tyler stroked my arm to comfort me. "So, are you going to tell me why you left in the first place?"

I exhaled and sat back down. My hands twisted tightly in my lap as I kept my gaze lowered. "There's really not much to tell, Tyler." I glanced over to him. "I wish I knew. I really do. I have no idea why they felt it was necessary for me to leave. I'm as much in the dark as you."

He looked at me confused – clearly unaware of all the details of that dark night. "How can you not know? I mean, how is that even possible?"

We lingered in deathly silence for a few awkward moments. Then I asked. "Do you remember the night I left? I was over your house."

"Yeah, of course I remember. It was a momentous occasion. The first time I kicked your butt in trivial pursuit."

I couldn't help but smile at his personal recollection of the worst night of my life.

"When I got home that night my aunt had already packed my things. I had no choice in the matter. A car was even waiting for me, to drive me away."

Expressionless and unable to speak from the shock, Tyler took my hand and stared at me in horror. "I didn't know, Caitlin," he finally spoke after a few minutes of stony silence, "nobody told me. They let me believe that it was your choice and that you wanted to leave. How naïve was I?"

"You weren't naïve Tyler, you were thirteen."

"I should've known you wouldn't have left without saying something to me." He shook his head in disbelief. "So, why return now, after five years and not sooner?"

"I told you, I'm not sure. I'll get to the bottom of it, don't worry," I reassured him, sounding optimistic and carefree – shrugging it off as a mere trivial matter.

I didn't think that Tyler should be dragged into my problems, but my unanswered questions were like a silent scream in my mind.

"Anyway," he said smiling, "that's the past. I'm glad that your back and have put the past behind you."

I nodded in agreement, not wanting to lie any more than was absolutely necessary. "Thanks for coming by, Tyler. You can't imagine what it means to have you around."

The topic of my unexplained departure aside, it was nice to sit there and talk to Tyler. It took my mind off the fact that once again my life had taken a turn. My questions were so many, but none that Tyler could answer. For some reason, from the moment I stepped foot in Oaks I couldn't come to grips with the waves of sadness that washed over me. In Stone Hurst I found a way to block everything out, but here, now, everything was too raw for me to handle.

"Monica is going out with Toni," Tyler continued to say, giving me a play by play to catch me up on the school gossip.

"Monica and Toni," I repeated, wanting to sound interested in the conversation, but I wasn't. I simply didn't care to know who's dating who. I just wanted to hide under a rock and disappear.

I could hear Tyler talking on and on about all the students at school. I was not paying much attention to him – too depressed to care.

He must have realized that I tuned him out because there, in the middle of his sentence, he unexpectedly stopped and stood up. "I'm boring you with the details. C'mon, let's grab something to eat," he said, grabbing my hand. "We can go to this new place that just opened."

"I can't. I'm sorry," I responded pulling my hand free, "I have to find Leslie and talk to her about school; besides, we just had dinner, how about a rain check?"

"Your call," he said satisfied, "you know I'm going to hold you to it."

"I wouldn't have it any other way," I said, pleased with his understanding.

We walked back to the house talking about this and that, nothing concrete or remotely interesting – not to me anyway.

Poor Tyler I thought.

He's making such an effort to make me feel at home and I'm in such a foul mood.

He suddenly stopped in front of my aunt's rose bushes and was searching for something.

"What are you looking for?"

"I want to give you a flower," he said.

"Its winter," I reminded him and looked down at the half dead rose bushes. "What flower?"

"Dorothy, you're not in Kansas anymore. You're in Oaks, remember? Have faith."

He squatted in fronted of the rose bush and took hold of one of the dormant stems. I couldn't figure out what he was doing and then, suddenly, it simply came to life. From black to dark brown, the rose bush was being revived from the root up. Small leaves and thorns popping up everywhere – it was truly amazing.

The rose bud little by little unfolded its velvety petals as if it were mid-spring. I just stood there in awe. It was miraculous how different it looked against the dead of winter. I was genuinely smiling. Tyler snapped off the stem and handed it to me. I held it up to my nose breathing in its rich scent.

"You like?" he asked, already knowing my answer by my elated expression.

"You know my aunt is going to kill you for using your powers, but for what it's worth I love it, thank you," I said, enjoying the moment once again. "Your gift is getting stronger Tyler."

"Yes it is," he boasted "You haven't seen half of it."

"Wow, it's amazing. Can you bring anything back to life?"

"I don't bring things to life, Caitlin. I simply bring out their full potential. The rose bush wasn't dead just asleep for the winter. It's happy now – looking beautiful again."

"It's beautiful, but not in its element. The Ellri are right, Tyler, we shouldn't mess with nature."

"I'm not messing with anything. This is who I am," he said, sounding wounded at my criticism. "I wanted to give you a flower, that's all. I don't understand why we have to hide who we are. I mean, what good are these gifts if we can't use them?"

"I'm the wrong person to debate the issue with," I said smiling. I reached over and kissed him on the cheek. I looked back at the rose bush, now in full bloom against the lifeless backdrop. It was so out of place. "I'm sorry, Tyler. I'm really out of it today. You know that I didn't mean to sound so critical," I heard myself say, trying to rectify the situation. "Your gift is awesome – as are you."

Tyler didn't speak. We reached the house in complete and utter silence. Hurting his feelings was not my intention, though that's all I seemed to be doing since my return – first Emily and now Tyler.

What kind of person am I?

Emily was there to meet us, at the foot of the stairs, beaming her award winning smile. "I've got an idea," she said, as soon as we closed the door.

There was an unmistakable, wicked little twinkle in her eyes.

"Tyler?"

"What is it Em?"

"Well, you see, I was thinking…,"

He chuckled. "That can't be good."

She grimaced at his poor attempt at poking fun at her. "Ha, ha – very funny! Are you trying out for class clown this year, too?"

The soft smile was quickly erased from Tyler's lips. "What is it this time, Em? What has that gorgeous mind of yours thought of this time?" Emily's eyes were filled with satisfaction. "Well, it's Saturday night and all, and I was just thinking that it'd be great to take Caitlin out."

I glared at her. "You really don't need to do that, Tyler. It's been a really, really, really long day. I don't see how going out will make it any better."

"Nonsense, we need to celebrate your return, Caitlin," she said, ignoring my protest. "You can rest tomorrow." Turning to Tyler she continued with her plan, "Why don't you get your cousin Marc to pick us up in about an hour and take us all out? We can go to 'The Raven'."

I continued to shake my head in disapproval, but there was no winning once she had made up her mind – stubborn as always. I could tell Tyler liked the idea; his eyes had lit up like a match on fire.

"Sure, of course if that's what Caitlin wants, that's what Caitlin gets," he said, furtively ignoring my contradiction.

"I wasn't aware anybody had asked me what I wanted or didn't want since I got here. You all seem to know better."

Emily pulled a face, and turned her full attention back to Tyler. "Ignore her. Of course, she wants to go out. You don't expect us to be locked up in here all night, do you?"

"I'll get right on it," he answered.

Quickly, before I had the chance to express any sort of argument, he turned on his heel and scrambled to the door, but before he exited he circled back and, unexpectedly, planting a kiss on my cheek. "Welcome back, Rose," he winked, making sure I caught the pun, and then left.

Frustrated at my knack for getting myself into thorny

situations, I turned to Emily irate at her tenacity. "What the hell do you think you're doing?"

"I don't know about you," she answered amused, "but I'm going upstairs to see what I'm going to wear tonight. Haven't you heard? I have a date with Marc Falcone."

"You sneak," I accused, following her upstairs, "You're using me to get together with Marc?"

"A girl's gotta do, what a girl's gotta do," she laughed. "C'mon, stop complaining. Let's see if we can find you something to wear. I doubt if that bag of yours has anything to salvage."

"I'm not up to going out tonight. I'm still exhausted from the trip," I tried to convince her that it was a bad idea, tried to change her mind and call the whole thing off.

"Don't be a sour puss, we're going to have fun, you'll see. Besides, Tyler would be heartbroken if you bail out now, seeing how you owe him for being so rude earlier. The guy was aiming to please you with a flower. You shot him down cold."

"Why do you do that?"

"Do what?"

"Stop reading my thoughts. It's irritating. Can no one have secrets in this town?"

She stopped in mid-stride and turned to look at me. "You should know the answer to that, Caitlin. Now stop the whining and let's get ready."

Reflection

Illustrated For Lines That Bind - Circle of Trust

FIVE

TRIED AND TESTED

EMILY MUST HAVE TRIED ON TWENTY outfits, looking just as beautiful in the next one as she did the one before. I was surprised to find her so self-conscious about her appearance. She must have realized how stunningly attractive she was.

"What are you girls doing?" Aunt Leslie asked walking in the room, looking at all the clothes Emily threw on the bed. "Are you going somewhere?"

"Caitlin and I are going out with some friends," Emily answered, assessing her appearance in the full length mirror.

"Oh, that's nice."

The conversation sounded versed, strangely weird how mother and daughter were verbalizing their thoughts, as if it were something common for them to do. I was sure that Aunt Leslie knew exactly what Emily was thinking and vice versa. They did this for my sake, so I would feel normal.

"What are you wearing, Caitlin?" Aunt Leslie asked.

"I'm not sure if I'm going," I answered, trying to put some

order to the array of garments sprawled on the bed.

Emily turned on her heel, infuriated and stared at me from across the room, "You are going and you are going to have fun," she ordered. "Here, try this on."

She flung a top and trousers at me – purposely aiming for my head.

"Emily!" Aunt Leslie exclaimed, shaking her head disappointedly at her daughter's impudent deed. Nonetheless, she smiled and left the room visibly happy at seeing Em and I together again.

I decided to be compliant – not wanting to dishearten Emily after she tried so hard to make me feel at home. I tried the top on first. It was a long sleeve cashmere wrap around in a pale rose pink. I could see it outlined my every curve, making me feel extremely conscious about my body.

Emily sensed my dilemma and casually came up next to me. "You've filled it out quite well," she said smiling, tugging on my sleeves to smooth out the fabric. "Now, that's how you wear it," she said, reviewing the overall effect. "You look beautiful. Poor Tyler won't know what hit him tonight."

My back suddenly stiffened. I grabbed onto the edge of the wardrobe, feeling somewhat dizzy.

"Justin's approaching," I exhaled, under my breath. I sensed him on the move, approaching the house at toxic speed. The closer he got the more intense the feeling became.

"He's picking up Kyle," Emily answered hesitantly, unsure about divulging the information. "They're going out tonight with the girls. Caity, are you going to be okay?"

I was not sure which felt worse – the physical pain of having him approach or her words which hit me like bucket of ice. "What girls?" I asked, trying to veil the distress in my voice.

"Nothing serious – you know them. Girls fall at their feet all the time. You can't expect him to sit around waiting for...," she cut the sentence short, not wanting to wound me any more than I already was.

"Who's Kyle dating?" I asked, ignoring her remark, trying to warm up to my next question.

"Sandy Stevens," she said, casually looking at herself in the mirror, straightening out her outfit. I could feel her looking at me through the reflection.

"I've never heard of her."

"She's new in town, moved here with her family two years ago. The Stevens are very nice. They seem to like Kyle which, unfortunately, doesn't say much about their taste."

I knew Emily loved her brother dearly. Being his sister gave her the divine right to poke fun at him whenever she pleased.

"And Justin – who's he seeing?"

The thought of him touching another girl, the way he touched me earlier was unbearable.

"Well, I'm not sure who the flavor of the week is," she said, looking at me. "You shouldn't worry. They mean absolutely nothing to him. You must know that."

"Why should I care who he dates?" My words weren't at all convincing, betraying my true feelings on the subject. I took a few steps towards the oval gilt mirror and scrutinized over my reflection. "I don't think I can carry this off, Em," I said, shifting my gaze from the mirror to face her – trying desperately to change the subject away from Justin's love life. His closeness was bad enough without having to think of him with another girl. "This top is just not me."

"Oh, please! Put on the trousers," she ordered.

The smoky-grey, low-riding trousers flattered my hips, waist and thighs with tailored flare. I had to hand it to her, she knew fashion. They hugged my body in all the right places; accentuating curves I didn't even know I had.

"Perfect," she commented, surveying her creation, "here, try these on, they should fit. You wear a size nine, don't you?" Emily handed me a pair of designer pumps.

"Yeah, nine – nine and a half depending on the shoe." I responded, happy to see that the leather Jimmy Choo pumps fit just fine?" I looked down at my happy feet and said, "Should I ask how much this outfit costs?"

"You'll feel much more comfortable not knowing."

"That much, huh?"

She nodded. "Now about your hair and makeup," she grimaced, pushing me towards the vanity.

Emily sat me down – back facing the mirror, removing the hairpin that held up my long hair, allowing it to cascade freely down my back.

Ignoring all the little moans and groans that escaped my mouth, she brushed through it and then started twisting and pinning it back with all sorts of things. Once finished she took out her makeup bag and scattered its contents on the vanity. She started with my eyes, then my cheeks and last she put a coat of lip gloss on my lips.

"All done," she said, looking down at her work. "I must say sis, you are to die for."

I got up and headed for the full length mirror.

The second I saw my own reflection, I took a step back, happily surprised with the end result.

Only Emily could make a ponytail look that elegant and my makeup – flawless and natural looking – nothing over the top.

"Well? Do you like what you see?"

"Are you kidding me? I've never worn makeup. The only thing I wear is Chap Stick."

She smiled warmly. "That's what big sisters are for, silly," she said standing, staring at our reflection, "You know that Chap Stick is not considered makeup, right?"

I nodded, leaning, playfully into her. "I'm clueless, I know."

Emily finally decided on wearing a cream hued sheath dress which featured a black waist belt – very feminine and alluring.

"We're going to drive the Falcones crazy," she said smiling devilishly.

I didn't know about driving them crazy, what I did know was that all eyes were going to be on me tonight so I was happy Emily was going to be there. Her presence always drew more attention than anyone else in Oaks. That instant, I felt a sharp jab up my spine. The intensity was overwhelming – folding me over in agony. Justin was somewhere in the house. He was close, but not close enough to rid me of the burn.

"Are you Okay?" Emily looked concerned. "You're both going to kill each other if this continues. You need to talk to the Ellri. This is ridiculous."

"It's nothing I can't control," I said, trying to reassure her, not wanting her to worry. I didn't want to duck out now. She seemed so happy – excited about this evening. I wanted her to have this date with Marc. "Em, I need a second – a second to control this."

She nodded in understanding.

I sat down on the edge of her bed and shut my eyes – shut them real tight. It took longer than last time, but I was able to get control, not complete control, but enough to continue with the evening.

"Are you sure about this?" Emily asked, concerned. "If you're in pain we can stay in."

"Pain?" I scuffed.

It was strange to hear her define what I felt with such simplicity. There were no words or phrases to define what I felt. Everything seemed pale in comparison. "Don't worry, I'm used to it. I'll be fine, really."

"Only if you're sure about this," she said, holding out a waist-length fitted cashmere Peacoat with luxurious satin lining.

I took it from her hands. "I'm not sure about anything," I said, being brutally honest. "Let's get going."

She stood there motionless.

"C'mon Em, you didn't get me all dolled up for nothing, did you?"

She giggled and wrapped her arm around mine. "You're beautiful, you know that don't you?" she said, as we headed down the corridor.

"The only thing I do know is that you'd say anything to get me to go out tonight."

She laughed knowing there was some truth to what I said. Her laugh was contagious.

Descending the stairs, I saw Kyle at the entrance talking to Tyler. Emily quickly pulled on my sleeve and whispered, "That's Marc standing next to Tyler."

"Yeah, I figured as much," I said, taking her trembling hand into mine. "Relax will you?"

She nodded obediently.

From the corner of my eye, I caught a glimpse of Justin. He looked at me with a lost expression. For a second I thought he wanted to say something. I smiled, but quickly my smile vanished the second I shifted my gaze to his right. I realized that he was not alone.

His companion was striking – tall and slender with long,

brown curly hair and legs that would shame any model.

They look good together; a perfect match, I thought.

I swallowed hard, cringing with distaste. I didn't know why I hated the girl, I didn't even know her, but yet, the sight of her alone, filled my mind with volatile thoughts. Venomous images of the two of them together, swirled in my head, causing a spiral of ill emotions. *Will this day never end?* I took a deep breath and made my way straight to Kyle, simply smiling at Justin and his breath-taking date.

Marc Falcone exhibited the warmest of smiles. He was a year older than Kyle, about twenty-three. His mother Adrianna and my aunt were really close. I was pretty sure that the two families would be looking forward to Emily and Marc dating. Years ago I had overheard both women talking about how nice it would be for the 'kids' to get together.

Feeling Emily's anxiety I grabbed her hand once again to calm her, not realizing till then how much she liked Marc. "Hi, guys," I said, knowing Emily was in no shape to speak.

"It's nice to see you again, Caitlin." Marc spoke first, with genial intentions. "It's been a while."

I felt awkward. "Yeah, it has," I finally said, rather shyly.

Kyle put his hand over his heart. "Daaaamn, Caitlin! You sure do clean up good. You're beautiful," he exclaimed amusingly, "And you sis. Well, you know what you are."

I saw Emily make a face at him which only instigated Kyle's laughter. She playfully whacked him across the arm, cutting his amusement short.

It was long moments later, after the uncomfortable formalities ended, that the guys continued on talking about whatever it was they were previously talking about.

Emily had joined in the conversation, as well. Justin, on the other hand, remained a few feet away, engrossed in whatever his alluring companion was saying.

Indifferent to the conversation, I looked over my shoulder toward the couple, and saw that Justin was looking directly at me. Quickly, and totally embraced at being caught peeking, I circled my head forward. I fought the need to look at him again, fought against my natural need to be around him.

I had to concentrate – concentrate hard. On other occasions, the sting in my veins would have abated the moment he was close, but now it was different, much stronger than this morning, making me sick knowing what he was doing to me.

I took a deep breath, determined not to ruin the night for Emily.

Marc did up his coat. "We should be heading off," he said, looking in Emily's direction. "It'll be a waste to stand around here and chit-chat on such a beautiful night."

We all agreed.

Kyle, being in his playful mood, placed himself between Marc and Tyler, wrapping his arms around their shoulders. "Hope you guys can handle them," he said, motioning to me and Emily. "Let me warn you both," he continued, to poke fun, "they're a handful."

Shrugging Kyle off, Tyler came and stood next to me, taking my hand and raising it to his mouth. He kissed the back of my hand tenderly. "You're insane Kyle," he started to say, "Caity is not a handful, she's perfect, just like a rose in winter – beautiful and one of a kind."

He winking at me and kissed me on the cheek, making it perfectly clear to everybody around that we had shared something intimate – an inside joke of sorts. I didn't fuss about him holding my hand, or the fact that he kissed it.

At that moment, we all turned our heads to the sound of Justin storming off. He headed into the study, slamming the door shut, swearing under his breath – leaving his date unattended. Kyle and Marc flicked a glance at each other, visibly worried about their best friend. Justin was pissed for some reason and there was nothing either of them could do to remedy the situation.

"Tyler," Kyle said only moments later, "buddy, if I were you, I'd take out life insurance right about now."

Marc instantly chuckled, as did Emily. Though, there amused expressions didn't last long; they were abruptly wiped away as soon as Justin's date approached our group and said with her deep and sultry voice, "Kyle won't you introduce us?"

"Of course, where are my manners?" Kyle said, taking her hand in his. "Caitlin, this is my girlfriend, Sandy," he finally said, letting the bomb drop.

I didn't know what to say – blinded by my own mixed emotions, I had misinterpreted her role. "It's nice to meet you," I replied, not being able to come up with anything more original. My mind was otherwise disposed.

Sandy unexpectedly gave me a quick hug and a peck on both cheeks. "I've heard so much about you, Caitlin," she said, excitedly. "I've been dying to meet you. Kyle has several great stories about you guys growing up."

"I'm sure he does," I said, turning to Kyle, wondering how much about me she knew. "Well, it's a good thing we're all going out, then. We can all get to know each other better tonight."

Kyle stepped in and wrapped his arms around Sandy's waist, tenderly giving her a kiss on the shoulder. "Not tonight, Caitlin. Thanks for the offer, but we have other plans." He winked at me and smiled deviously.

You didn't need to have much imagination to know what he

was planning for that night. Realizing what his words were implying, Sandy turned and smacked him on the arm. "I can't believe you," she yelled, angrily.

"Oh, come on sweetie. I was just playing."

Hearing him pleading for forgiveness made us all laugh.

"Don't give in to his charm, Sandy. He's a pig," Emily said, getting back at him for his previous remark.

Sandy was not going to stand for Kyle's impropriety. She walked off fuming – Kyle was at her heel groveling, begging for forgiveness.

"Poor Kyle," Marc said, shaking his head.

"He deserves it," Emily responded, looking intently into his eyes. Marc smiled warmly.

In the midst of all the drama, somewhere in the depths of my subconscious, a ringing sound drilled deep and hard. Then, Justin's voice was back in my head. *"I want to talk to you,"* I suddenly heard him say, clear as day, just as it was this morning. *"Now!"* he commanded.

I was agitated at first by his insistence, but I excused myself nonetheless, and went to find him.

"Don't do that! Stay out of my freaking head," I told him the instant I entered the study, closing the door behind me.

Justin was pacing back and forth noticeably preoccupied with his thoughts. We were close again and it was getting harder to breathe.

"What do you want now?" I asked, sounding more annoyed then I actually was.

He finally stopped pacing and leaned one hand against the window frame, looking out into the night. "You feel it, don't you?" he finally asked, in a hushed voice. I wanted to say yes, say something, but instead I just stood there. After long silent moments Justin turned and glared at me, "This pain, this is what I've felt for the last five years while you were away."

My heart instantly shrank back at the sound of his words. His eyes were darker than I remembered, hard and unyielding.

Justin reached out and grabbed my arm and pulled me closer. My mind and stomach alike were trapped in a whirl of emotions. "Tell me Caitlin, do you take some comfort in knowing that you torment me with your existence? Do you?"

Infuriated and bitter, Justin let go of my arm just as fast, and traversed the room, pushing back his hair with both hands. "Damn you, Caitlin," he growled.

A wild howl of grief clawed its way in my gut. I wanted to scream, cry even laugh. I didn't know what to feel; all my emotions were compressed violently into one great knot that caught in my throat. What I did know was that I was going to be sick.

With my arm, tight around my waist, I leaned against the edge of the desk, crouching over. With two long strides, Justin was quickly by my side, his features were strained. "Caitlin, are you alright?" he asked, coaxing my chin up to face him. "What's the matter?"

"You're making me sick," I responded, wincing with discomfort.

"Freaking hell," he cursed, and to my surprise took the liberty of lifting me up into his arms, holding me tight, knowing that the contact would sooth the discomfort.

I kept my eyes tightly shut; praying that the vertigo would fade. My face was up against his neck taking in his scent; feeling better by the second.

Justin sat down on the leather sofa and cradled me in his lap. "It's never been this strong." His voice broke the deafening silence, "It's getting worse with every hour. I could feel you miles away today," he confessed. "We need to tell the Ellri. It's nothing like when we were young. I don't have the strength to…." Justin broke off the sentence and brushed his magnificent lips up against my forehead.

I burrowed deeper in his embrace, indulging my senses; finally quenching the burn. Like an addict on a binge for gratification, I basked in the way his closeness was making me feel. The scent from his cologne, alone, was enough to rouse a shudder. I simply couldn't get enough of him.

"How do you feel?" he asked minutes later, gazing at me with his beautiful deep blue eyes.

"Now that you're calm, much better," I pronounced, keeping my head against the curve of his neck. "Every time you get angry the feeling intensifies."

For a short moment he was deep in thought. "Caitlin, I think you're right, that's what it must be."

"Right? Right about what?"

"I must be projecting my feelings onto you without even knowing it. The bond we share seems to be evolving, changing – growing somehow." I shook my head, refusing to accept the reality of our special connection. "There's no bond between us, Justin," I finally said, straightening myself out, preparing to stand, pushing myself free from his hold, feeling much better and more confident. With stealth reflexes, Justin pulled me back into his embrace. "Where do you think you're going?" he said, smiling his all too perfect smile.

"My date is waiting."

"Date?" he grunted. "Aren't you worried about being in pain again if you leave me behind, here, all alone?"

He was antagonizing me by design.

"I've left you behind years ago, what makes you think I can't handle it now?" The words just blurted out, I didn't mean them, but I was not about to fess up to my true feelings – not now – not with him looking so smug. "You simply need to control your anger next time and I'll be fine."

His eye brow curved up, skeptically. My words were meant to wipe the stupid look off his face, but he was obviously aware of my true thoughts.

Annoyed at allowing him to get so close, I finally pushed his hands aside and lifted myself to my feet; standing there right in front of him fixing myself up, smoothing the creases from his hold – intentionally tantalizing him as much as womanly possible.

Justin groaned under his breath and stood up towering over me – only inches away. I could feel his warm breath on my brow.

"Caitlin," he said, cupping my chin with his hand, turning my head up to face him. "If you tell your date to keep his hands to himself, I'm sure we won't have an anger issue."

I pushed his hand away with force.

"What I do with Tyler is of no concern to you."

I looked intently at him wanting to sound unwavering, "You and my aunt wanted me to go to Oaks High and I'm going; bright and early on Monday, but as far as who I am or am not seeing, is none of your damn business!"

He took a step back, looking distracted by his thoughts, and then said, "You're right. It's not my place to intervene." Justin's voice sounded more brazen than ever before. "If you want to be with Falcone, I understand. I'll keep my distance."

I went cold. "Justin I didn't mean...."

He motioned for me to stop. "Enjoy your date, Caitlin," he said, and marched out of the room.

Carried Away

Illustrated for Lines that Bind - Circle of Trust

SIX

ALARMED

HE CENTURY OLD, traditional Irish pub with wooden trimmings, was the oldest bar in town. I had never been inside The Raven before, but I used to hear the craziest tales from Kyle.

Mr O'Malley, the owner, was a real character. I saw him on many occasions pacing up and down the street, scratching his head absentmindedly and muttering to himself in Gaelic, as he tried to find a solution to his problem.

Apart from his brawny appearance and striking red hair he was a loving man who assured the parents of Oaks that there was going to be no drinking for youngsters in his pub.

He was gifted like the others, with the innate ability of spreading merriment in the worst situations – able to incite feelings of elation and harmony. Young, gifted individuals could be a handful for any one person, but no one could resist Mr O'Malley's gift.

He would climb on top of the counter, to get a panoramic view of the rowdy crowd, and break out into one of those old Irish songs. The instant his breath left his lungs, the atmosphere would be infused with tranquillity and peace. The singing was his own personal touch, a way of entertaining everybody, since he didn't need to sing in order for his gift to work.

I guess it's going to be soda for me and Tyler tonight, I thought.

Marc and Tyler were real gentlemen. They led us inside, showing us to our seats.

Mr. O'Malley waved and yelled out over the voices, "Welcome back, Caity girl. Gooda see ya, lass." His deep Irish accent clearly cut through all the noise and music.

I waved back, smiling as best I could and said, "Good to see you too."

He winked and motioned that we'll talk at a later time. As quick as a thought he returned to serving his customers, pouring foaming glasses of stout and lager.

Related somehow to uncle Abbot – I was not clear on the details – he'd come over quite often and sit with my uncle, sharing the latest jokes. The whole house would tremor with their laughter.

"It's your first time in here, isn't it?" asked Marc, unzipping his bomber jacket, revealing the sleek striped, five button vest that pulled together his outfit with a little edge.

I let my gaze scan over the décor, saying. "It actually is."

It seemed much more than a place for drinking; it was part bar and part living room. With its timber floors and displays of Irish bric-a-brac that represented Irish music, literature, sport and history, it surely made one feel warm and welcomed.

The pub was not very crowded for Saturday night – nine o'clock was not exactly peak hour, though, there were a few familiar faces; mostly younger members of our tight knit community. Nevertheless, I could feel everybody's eyes on us. It was not every day they saw the Falcones and the Cathcarts together. But on this occasion I was pretty sure the stares were my doing. I felt them probing – searching my mind. It was a bit uncomfortable, nauseating even. I felt an acute seasickness, but nothing I couldn't handle.

Marc sat across from me and suddenly said, "You should feel better in a second, Caitlin. I've blocked them out. They're too young, inexperienced."

"You can do that?"

He nodded and quite suddenly I felt balanced once again, I had found my equilibrium; the nausea faded.

I smiled at Marc, only then did I realize how handsome he was. I could see, now, why Emily liked him.

Like all the Falcones, Tyler included, he was also blessed with rugged Mediterranean good looks. His dark brown hair emphasized the brown in his almond shaped eyes.

This was the first time I had ever sat with him. Being four years my senior, never gave us the opportunity to hang out.

Marc and Emily seemed to have mutual feelings for each other. I could read it in their eyes. He looked at her lovingly and with her every word you could tell that he was one step closer to heaven.

Their eye contact rarely broke. He was so into Emily that he gave no notice to the waitress who had been patiently waiting by his side to take our order, incidentally wearing insanely short, black shorts.

"What can I get you," the girl said, smiling at Marc's surprised expression.

"Oh, sorry about that," he said awkwardly, "Yes, well, we'll have two beers and two cokes." The girl paused, waiting for him to continue. Like a lost puppy, she gazed into his eyes. "That'll be all, thank you," he said, cueing her to leave.

I studied Marc as the bar maid took the order. His manner was a mix of being pleased and distracted, for although he smiled, now and again a tiny frown creased his brow as though something nagged him.

"Sure, okay, two beers and two cokes, coming right up," she said. Lacking skill in manner and movement, the waitress sashayed to the bar, causing a few customers to turn their heads.

"What was that all about?" asked Emily.

Marc simply shrugged his shoulders. "Don't really care to know."

Emily smiled content in knowing that Marc paid little attention to the girl who seemed enamored by him.

Tyler, however, seemed completely preoccupied, drawing Marc's attention. "You can't be serious."

"It's done, just drop it."

Apparently, I missed something.

"C'mon Marc, I'm eighteen for heaven's sake. Give me a break – a coke?"

"I don't know what your complaining about, you said it yourself, only eighteen. But if you still feel strongly about drinking, why don't you take it up with Mr. O'Malley? I'm sure he'd love to hear your reasoning."

Tyler knew when to back down. There was no argument to be had with good old Mr. O'Malley, he would not have it. He strongly believed that people could enjoy themselves so much more without the influence of alcohol. It was strange that a man with such convictions would consider opening a pub.

Marc patted Tyler on the arm. "I didn't think so."

It was not until much later – after Tyler came to terms with the fact that he'd be drinking a coke for the night, that our conversation totally absorbed me. Marc talked about his visit to Italy the year before. He went to Tuscany and Palermo to see some of his distant cousins. Emily was lost in his words. It helped that Marc was a talented orator. His depictions were so vivid and colorful that we were all consumed by his story. He got to meet some of the other families as well.

"I met some of the Korbs," he said, turning in my direction, like it was meant to mean something more to me. "They're an amazing bunch, especially the twins; Clancy and Albion. Their telekinetic abilities are quite advanced. They can move objects in perfect coordination. I saw them play tennis once, without the application of physical force. They sat on the sidelines while Clancy controlled one racket with his mind and Albion the other."

Marc shook his head, lost in his recollection of the amazing feat. "You had to be there."

"That's amazing," I exclaimed, completely at awe "how old are they?"

"Only twelve and they can do so much more. They can even share their power by passing it to the other. They are under strict supervision by Caradon, their father and Ellri."

"So young...." Was all Emily could say, visibly as amazed as I was.

We all knew that the Korbs were the strongest of all the bloodlines, dating back thousands of years and keeping their blood line completely sterile. It was no wonder their powers were so great at such a young age. As our conversation continued, the pub continued to get all the more crowded with the passing hours. I pretended not to notice the stares, but the pounding in my head kept getting stronger and stronger. There were too many trying to read my thoughts.

Soon, the intense pressure triggered an onset of tears. I noticed, by his concerned expression, that Marc was fully aware of what was happening.

He reached across the table and took hold of both my hands.

Visibly disturbed with what was happening; Emily simply stared, and said, "I'm so sorry Caity, this must be killing you."

"We shouldn't have come here," said Marc, shifting his gaze to her. "There's simply too many."

He shut his eyes tightly and lowered his head, mumbling some unintelligible phrases. I closed my eyes as well, allowing his words to flow into the vortex of my mind, soothing the escalating pressure with each syllable.

Some minutes later, in the whirlwind of my scrambled brain, I felt calm. The acute, stabbing pain had miraculously lessened, but unfortunately for me, it was replaced by a wave of hushed sounds, sounds that became all the more deafening.

"We shouldn't be here with all these people. We should have gone somewhere, less crowded." Marc's voice was full of remorse. "I didn't think it was going to be this bad."

I looked up through my wet eyelashes and feigned a smile. "It's ok, I'm fine." I lied unsuccessfully. I didn't want to ruin Emily's chances with Marc, but the reality of the situation was something my eyes couldn't hide.

"You're not fine, Caitlin," Marc said deeply concerned. "They won't stop probing and some are quite strong. I can force them to stop, but it would mean hurting some of them and I can't chance it."

Having full control of his gift he needn't lift a finger if he wanted to harm or even kill anyone or even everyone in that room.

My head was viciously pounding from the voices which

swirled in my mind. I couldn't believe how intense the piercing was. I wanted to excuse myself and head for the ladies room, but I knew standing up would make me feel even worse. I needed some time to deal with this on my own. I knew I could, somehow, but I needed time – something I simply didn't seem to have.

Tyler instructed me to breathe. He asked the waitress for the check and collected my stuff. "We need to go. It's dangerous in here," he said, looking around the room.

Again, I felt nauseous from the unquantifiable pounding in my head, ignoring the jarring pain down my arm, my teeth clenched against the howls of frustration that tore at my throat while hot tears spilled down my cheeks. But there again in the middle of my unbearable suffering, I felt a familiar knot in my stomach. *Justin*, I thought. *He must be here somewhere.* Weak and disoriented, I attempted to look for his face in the crowd, but I couldn't find him.

To help me to my feet, Tyler put his arm around my waist. At first I stumbled and landed back in the seat. It took all my strength to keep from falling – keep from blacking out from the sheer agony of it all. Tyler tightened his hold, allowing me to lean into him. "I got ya," he said, "Just relax."

Drained from the ordeal, my body simply gave in and everything darkened.

"Caitlin? Caitlin?" I heard Tyler's angst voice say, shaking me.

I opened my eyes lazily. "I'm fine," I repeated in a breathy voice.

"We have to go, now!" Marc said, in a commanding voice. "To the side," he ordered.

I was not sure who he was talking to, but then I saw what three little words from his mouth could do. A path from our table to the door simply opened. He parted the crowded room like Moses did the sea. I had never seen anyone use their power out in the open before – not someone who had ascended. They knew better than that. None of the customers were remotely aware of his manipulation. They just moved out of the way instinctively, not knowing it was Marc's doing.

"Sorry Caitlin, but we need to get you out of here," he said, leading me outside, but his quick stride was suddenly cut short by Justin.

"Caitlin," Justin said, coaxing my chin up. "What the hell...?" The moment his gaze fell on mine, his whole manner had changed. Justin stiffened as soon as he caught sight of my anguish stricken face.

At that precise moment and to my horrid surprise, he shifted a menacing glare towards everyone in the bar and in seconds they all bowed their heads in complete submission, frozen, waiting for some sort of order. I was not even sure if what I was witnessing was even real.

"Justin, knock it off," Marc bellowed, pulling him by the arm, "you're going to kill them. They're just curious. You need to control your anger."

Turning his gaze away from the customers, Justin turned and glared at Marc. "This is your fault," he said, shoving Marc's hand to the side. "What the hell were you thinking bringing her in here? If anything happens to her," Justin paused, and looked at me momentarily and then turned his gaze back to Marc, "It's your head. You of all people should've known better."

His words were dripping venom.

"Justin, please!" Marc grabbed his arm again. "You can't blame them for being curious. You need to stop. Some of them are too young. You'll kill them."

"Who says they deserve to live?"

Lost in a false calmness born of exhaustion both emotional and physical, I wiped my cheeks with my sleeve and studied Justin's face.

"Stop the nonsense, Justin," Mr. O'Malley ordered from behind the bar. "Now lad – don't make me force ya."

Justin shifted his gaze back to me and our eyes locked momentarily, and just then, everybody in the pub continued on with what they were doing as if nothing had happened. They were not aware of how close they all came to meeting their maker.

Marc tugged Justin by the arm, "We need to get her outside, now," he said, raising his voice. "I didn't consider the danger. I'm sorry. I should've taken better care, but this simply isn't the time and place to discuss this; Caitlin needs to go."

His apology was heartfelt. Even in my state of mind I could sense his sincerity. *Poor Emily,* I thought. This night was not turning out exactly as she had planned. I didn't want to ruin her evening any more than I already had. I could tell that she was really worried about me; her face was too calm even for her. It was then that I reached out and gripped onto Justin's wrist, raising my head to eye level.

He quickly read into what I was thinking and at once turned to Marc. He told him to stay with Emily and that he and Tyler would take me home.

Emily was hesitant about staying behind, but Justin reassured her again. She kissed me on the cheek one last time and asked, "Are you sure you don't want me to come along?"

"Stay," I told her, swallowing back the bile in my throat. "Justin and Tyler will take me home, enjoy your evening. I'll be fine." I lied, third time in one night.

Tyler was still holding me tight, unwilling to let Justin help. Not the slightest bit amused by Tyler's gallant gesture, Justin motioned for him to let go. "Falcone," he hissed through clenched teeth. Cursing under his breath, Tyler reluctantly passed me over to Justin as a young child would a borrowed toy.

With his strong arm wrapped around my waist, Justin held me up, leading me outside. "Do you have a death wish or something?" he barked, the second we were out in the parking lot. "They could've killed you if Marc wasn't there to block most of them."

"I know. I shouldn't have come. I have no business being here," I said, hoping he caught the double meaning.

Irritated by my last comment, Justin helped me in the back seat of his Audi S5, recommending that I lay down. Without any hesitation, Tyler jumped right in, helping me stretch out as much as humanly possible in such a cramped space. The car was obviously designed to be sporty, not a makeshift hospital.

Justin drove while I sat in the back seat with my head on Tyler's shoulder, allowing him to massage my neck in the hopes of alleviating some of the pressure.

"Caity, I'm so sorry," Tyler kept repeating, softly in my ear, caressing my back. The more affectionate Tyler became the more tense Justin's posture was – accelerating the car even more. Tyler's ease seemed to infuriate him. *Too bad*, I thought. He'd just have to bear it tonight because I wanted Tyler there – his soothing massage was actually helping.

The, otherwise, fifteen minute ride seemed endless in the condition I was in. I wanted nothing more than to crawl into bed and die. Once at the house, Justin instantly threw his car keys to Tyler and barked out the orders for him to go home. Turning his full attention to me, he carefully helped me out of the car and supported most of my weight, knowing that I was in absolutely no condition to walk.

Before heading up to the entrance, Justin shifted his gaze back to Tyler. "Don't worry, she'll be fine. The Ellri will be here soon," I heard him say in my lightheadedness. "Thanks for being there for her."

Tyler simply nodded his head, and drove away in Justin's car. I rested my head against Justin's shoulder unable to speak, keeping my eyes tightly shut, trying desperately to suppress the overwhelming need to vomit.

Through half closed eyes I saw that my aunt and uncle were there at the entrance waiting.

"The leeches – they could've killed her," said Justin angrily.

Aunt Leslie simply patted him on the shoulder leading him up the stairs. "Now, now don't worry," I heard her say, "She's stronger than you give her credit."

My head was on fire. I kept my eyes shut to block out any hint of light. Caringly, Justin placed me on the bed wiping my tears away with his elegant fingers. He had dimmed the lights in my bedroom, figuring I'd feel much better.

"How bad is it?" he asked, perched on the edge of my nightstand.

"Bad," I answered through the pain, "really, really bad."

I knew I couldn't lie to him, the distress was written all over my face.

"I'm going to kill Marc. He should've known better," he mumbled under his breath.

"I wanted to go out tonight," I lied, swallowing back the nausea that crept up my throat. "Look, I even got dressed up." I motioned up and down my body to point out my attire. "I even wore makeup. It's not Marc's fault. I suggested going to The

Raven." I hated that he blamed his best friend. It was my fault for agreeing to go. I should have put my foot down and refused Emily's invitation.

Justin scanned me up and down again. "You look beautiful," he finally said, smiling at my poor attempt to redeem Marc, "It's too bad you can't lie to save your life."

I involuntarily smiled at his innate ability to see right through me. "What happened tonight?" I asked, squirming in pain, wanting to wane off the subject of who is to blame.

"You've been gone for the past five years. It's only natural for people to be curious. Everybody just wanted to know the truth. So, instead of just waiting to learn the reason for your return, they were simply trying to dig for information in your head." With a soothing touch, he stroked the tension from my brow. "Under normal circumstances one or two people probing wouldn't have been a problem. Tonight however, the bar was full of Readers. You're lucky Marc was with you, otherwise they would've turned your brain to mush."

"Mush huh? That doesn't sound too bad," I mumbled, mustering up the energy through the excruciating pain. "Remind me to thank him later."

Long quiet moments later, Aunt Leslie came in, followed by Uncle Abbot and two other Ellri; Shannon and William, Justin's parents.

Justin quickly kissed me on the forehead and got to his feet, crossing the room to sit in the armchair in the far corner.

"Thought you were going to keep your distance?" I said smiling, responding to his previous declaration of how he was to stay away from me. Justin simply winked at me, and turned to our visitors.

His mother approached the bed and stood over me. Shannon's

shoulder length, black hair was pushed behind her ears on both sides to reveal her high cheekbones and rosy complexion. There was absolutely nothing plain about this woman, her beauty, radiated from within; tender-hearted and good-natured she would never refuse to help anyone.

William who stood to her left was quite handsome for his age as well. The dimples on his face added to his allure. Tall and slender he exuded confidence. It was quite easy to see where Justin got his good looks.

"Caitlin, you've grown into a beautiful young woman," Shannon said, looking to Justin from the corner of her eye.

"Thanks," I mouthed, squirming from the pain.

Her features suddenly darkened.

Without saying a word, Shannon placed her palm on my forehead, assessing the damage. She turned to the others and just looked at them. I could tell they were communicating by the way they concentrated on each other's gaze.

My aunt came to the other side of the bed and sat herself down. She took hold of my left arm with one hand and placed her other hand on my forehead on top of Shannon's.

Shannon unexpectedly gripped my free hand, and without any warning I felt the purest form of pain. It felt like a surge of burning lava coursing through my veins, causing my body to convulse completely out of control.

"Please, let go," I begged, through clenched teeth, "it's killing me. Make it stop," I screamed.

Both Shannon and Aunt Leslie kept their gaze locked on each other. From the corner of my eye I noticed William and Uncle Abbot holding Justin firm in his seat; keeping him from approaching.

My head was going to burst, I was sure of that.

"Caitlin," Aunt Leslie yelled. "Will you please concentrate?"

Was she kidding? Couldn't she see what was happening?

"Close your eyes and breathe deep. You'll be alright," she insisted.

Stray thoughts ran through my numbed mind, but being tired of the day's events, I decided to call it quits. I closed my eyes and let my mind drift off to the bottomless pit I knew all too well; the place I called my solace.

How long the frenzy lasted, I didn't know. What I did know was that once in my solace, everything went calm and quiet.

I did this often in Stone Hurst, keeping me sane through the difficult times. I felt peace and tranquility in this particular place in my mind. Even Justin's absence didn't bother me. I loved it there – knew that nobody could reach me.

The darkness that enveloped me was welcoming. There was nothing like it in the world.

My erratic breathing slowly returned to normal and the pain finally subsided.

SEVEN

SOLACE

IS PLEADING VOICE cut right through my serene surroundings, "Caitlin, Caitlin, please, please open your eyes." I suddenly heard. "Come on Caitlin, open your eyes." Justin's strained voice was laced with concern.

Disoriented at first, I finally opened my eyes little by little so that they could slowly adjust to the light. My head felt lighter – much better. Quite deficient in energy, I looked around the room lethargically, only to see Shannon's worry-stricken face looking at my aunt, holding her hand as though she needed comforting. Uncle Abbot looked much the same, but he was standing on the far corner of the room, completely lost in thought. Then, I focused my eyes on the most beautiful thing in nature – Justin's face, only inches away from mine.

I wanted to speak, but my throat was on fire – dry and coarse like sandpaper. After swallowing back the raw taste, I shifted my gaze and scanned all their faces. "Is everyone okay?" I finally asked, grimacing from the putrid taste in my mouth.

Suddenly there was a commotion. Aunt Leslie and Shannon

rushed to my bedside while Uncle Abbot and William stood at each post.

"You're back, are you feeling better?" It was Justin's silky voice that sliced through the silence.

"Of course I am," I answered trying to swallow. "Thanks Aunt Leslie. Thank you Shannon, I feel much better."

They looked at each other, visibly confused. "We didn't do anything," Shannon said, in wonder. "Whatever you did, you did alone. I've never seen anything like it. You were gone for over an hour," she continued to say, "without breathing, not even a heartbeat."

Now I was the one confused. *What did she mean over an hour – it didn't feel more than a few minutes. And what was that about my heartbeat?*

"Physically, you were here but otherwise gone," Uncle Abbot broke in – his face much softer now. "Have you done this before?"

"Almost every night at Stone Hurst," I admitted – not sure why they looked so shocked.

"Where do you go, dear?" It was William's turn to ask.

"I don't know what you mean," I swallowed hard, preparing to explain. "In my first week away I felt this agonizing pain. I knew it was from missing all of you. It kept me awake. It was unbearable. Ten days without a nights rest would drive anyone insane," I said, turning my gaze to Justin, aware that he would be the only one who could clearly understand the effects our separation had on me. "It hurt so much being away. It was torture."

I closed my eyes and shook my head, trying to erase the rotten memories. It was hard for me to recall those first few weeks in exile. "Then one night," I continued to say swallowing back the tang in my mouth, "I closed my eyes, trying to forget that the pain existed. I felt myself slip away into sheer darkness. It was like nothing I'd ever felt before. For the first time in many nights I felt content and relaxed.

The head mistress, Ms. Leedey, even allowed me to sleep-in for the duration of the day, realizing I needed my rest. From that night on, I did the same thing over and over again slipping into my personal solace. Each day the transition became easier, effortless. It was the only way to escape the pain."

Shannon turned adoringly toward her son and stroked his cheek. "That's why you couldn't sense her at night," she said, lovingly.

Confused, I turned to Justin. "What's your mom talking about?" I asked.

"The feeling we share, no matter how unbearable the pain, is the only thing that keeps us in tune with one another," Justin said, smiling tenderly. "A few years ago it unexpectedly stopped one night. I couldn't feel anything but a deep hollow feeling, like a part of me had died. It scared me at first, but by morning the intensity of the burn returned."

Terror-stricken, I just stared at him, "I wasn't aware you'd be affected. I'm truly sorry."

Justin smiled, trying to sooth my guilt. "No need to be sorry. After the Ellri assured me that you were alright and in one piece, I actually enjoyed sleeping without the intensity of our bond. I worried at first, but then relished in a calm and relaxing sleep."

"Your ability to transcend...," William said, allowing his voice to trail off, completely oblivious to the core of our conversation. Apparently, he was preoccupied with matters of more significance. Minutes later, he continued to talk as we all stared at his perplexed expression, "It's amazing, Caitlin. Only Ellri of the higher order are known to possess such a gift. For a girl this young – it's – it's simply unheard of. You haven't even ascended yet." He looked around for clarity. "How is this possible?"

"What's the big deal?" I said, looking at each and every one of them. "I simply close my eyes and breathe deep, an idiot can do it."

"It's much more than that," Uncle Abbot added, now sitting on the foot of my bed with one hand on my leg. "You see Caitlin, transcending is a gift like no other. It allows you to go beyond any natural boundary."

I shrugged my shoulders unaware of the significance. "What good it did me tonight?"

"Your ability will grow with time. The control you have shown here was far greater than I have ever seen in someone so young, especially for someone who hasn't ascended yet. If it weren't for your gift, you'd be dead now, child – that, we are all sure of. Your gift is what saved you last night. It's the reason you are alive now."

My eyes widened in response to his words – even Justin was visibly shaken by uncle Abbot's alternative version of tonight's events.

"But, Marc was there. He's the one who helped. I didn't do anything."

Uncle Abbot patted my leg. "Marc knows his limits and so do Tyler and Emily. The things inside your head today would have killed any of them. Your gift protected you, more than you give it credit."

I looked at my aunt. "But you said I didn't have any gifts."

"I never said that, Caitlin. What I did say was you needed to be patient. This morning when you were angry with Emily, didn't you feel how strong you were? Didn't you feel the whole house tremor in reaction to your mood?"

"Is that what that was?" I asked surprised, recalling the incident in the kitchen and in the study.

Uncle Abbot got to his feet and headed to the door. "Your gift will only get stronger. You must learn how to rein it in," he said looking around the room. "They're coming," he motioned to the others. "Bring Caitlin downstairs, Justin."

My uncle was deeply absorbed in thought by something far more of import and headed out the door, followed by Justin's father. Shannon, however, turned to Justin and gave him a loving smile.

They didn't have to verbalize their thoughts. They just stared at each other for a moment. Sharing from what I could tell a personal conversation. "I will, don't worry," Justin answered. Shannon satisfied with her son's answer, turned to me and caressed my cheek before she headed downstairs. Aunt Leslie, however, lingered behind, holding my hand, smiling a weak smile. "You did great tonight, I'm really proud of you," she said. "I knew you could handle it."

"Was it all some sort of test?" I asked, looking at her confused. "You could've at least warned me?"

She must have known the dangers of my going out. She knew people would be curious to know about my whereabouts for the past five years.

"Caitlin, you shouldn't fret over insignificant details," she said, heading for the door. Justin looked rather upset. His stern voice stopped my aunt in mid-stride, "Leslie, what were you thinking? Caitlin could've been killed!"

"But she wasn't, was she?"

She exited the room, short after.

"What a day this has been," I spoke, trying to break the

silence. I quickly lifted myself off the bed and sat on the edge. "I assume all the Ellri are here? We should go downstairs."

Justin continued to stare at the closed door, lost in his thoughts. "Yes, they're here," he finally said, turning his beautiful face towards me, "but you don't have to do anything but rest. You must be exhausted. You should try to get some sleep." He motioned for me to lie down. "I'll explain things to the Ellri."

Still baffled by what had just transpired, I looked at Justin questionably. "Does this mean that I'm gifted like you guys?"

Justin looked at me beaming a great big smile. "Whether you want to believe it or not, you were always one of us."

He reached out to caress my face, but I pulled back just enough to make him drop his hand to his side. Clearly hurt, Justin walked across the room and leaned his hand against my desk half turned. "Do you need help getting ready for bed?" he asked, turning to face me.

I must have turned three shades of red at the thought of his hands on my skin. Reading my mind, his lips formed a cunning little smile. His cobalt-blue eyes lit up at the idea of undressing me. "I'll be fine. I can manage on my own," I answered. "Are you sure the Ellri won't mind?" I asked, wanting to change the subject.

"They haven't come here for you, Caitlin. They had arranged this meeting a week ago."

"Oh, I wasn't aware that they met regularly."

"Lately they have," Justin offered, sitting in the armchair across the room. "They need to reach an agreement on something. I'm not sure about what, but it must be important. This is the third meeting this month."

"Do you think it has anything to do with my arrival?"

"No, I don't think so. Why would that be a problem?" He

didn't sound too convinced with his own words. "Caitlin, aren't you just a little bit happy to be here?"

"I am. It's just that there are so many unanswered questions. I feel just as lost as I did five years ago," I admitted for the first time.

"I'm happy you're here, if that counts for something. Now, get some rest," he ordered.

I put my head back on the pillow. I could feel my eyes getting heavier. Justin was right, I was tired. His presence subdued the burning sensation I usually felt by his absence. It felt good to have him so close. Finally, I closed my eyes, drained by the day's events.

"Sweet dreams, sweet Caitlin," I heard him say softly – not meant to be heard. I turned to the side and let sleep take me – happy that he felt as I did.

The sound of Kyle and Emily arguing woke me from the soundest sleep I had in years. I felt surprisingly good for a person who was almost killed the night before.

"Did they wake you?"

I opened my eyes lazily, taking in the sound of his voice. *Did he stay here the whole night?* I reddened at the thought. It did explain, however, the calm I felt – no burning like all the other sleepless nights.

"Caitlin, to answer your question, I did stay all night," he said smiling.

Odd how, straight from sleep, clad in last night's clothes, he still managed to look devastatingly handsome.

I shifted my body into a sitting position, leaned my back against the headboard. "But I didn't ask a...," I grinned. "Oh yeah, I forgot. My thoughts are public domain. I get it."

"Did you sleep well?" he asked approaching the bed.

"Like a baby, thanks to you, but you really didn't need to hang around all night. The armchair couldn't have been comfortable?"

"As long as you're rested it was worth the sacrifice."

"Does my uncle know you're here? He'll kill you if he doesn't," I warned.

Justin chuckled. "Don't worry he's the one who suggested that I stay the night. As long as I was on my best behavior," he said, displaying a mischievous smile. "Abbot figured that you'd be more relaxed if I were around; besides, did you really think I'd be up here without his knowing? I mean, your uncle is an Ellri for heaven's sake."

"Guess you're right. I haven't thought about all this in quite some time. The supernatural wasn't exactly a common topic in Stone Hurst."

For a space of time I sat silent, and let my mind empty again. I brought my hair to one side and combed through it with my fingers. "Abbot really suggested you stay the night?" I raised my confused gaze to his. "It's hard to believe that he would allow such a thing. Why would he do that?"

"It would seem the Ellri are aware of our connection. Seeing how we both react when we are apart and with last night's events, Abbot felt you needed a break from the burn."

"Oh! That was thoughtful of him."

I made a mental note to thank my uncle for his deep understanding. It was not easy for people like my uncle to forgo their deep rooted morals and beliefs – no matter the circumstances. Allowing a boy in my room went against everything he stood for.

His decision to let Justin stay, only magnified last night's pending danger. It was then that I became aware of how close to death I truly was.

"Good morning Caitlin!" Emily said barging into the room. "I hope I'm not disturbing." Her grin was wide and lined with mischief. "So Justin, did you sleep well?"

"Veeerrry well," he answered purposely playing into her trap – smiling that wicked little smile.

I could see that Emily couldn't get enough – enjoying Justin's mood for games. "Will this be a permanent arrangement then?" she asked even more amused.

No sooner did she speak when Kyle walked in, pushing her to the side, "Mind your own business, Em," he said, turning to me and Justin with one of his whimsical smiles. "Good morning guys, sleep well? Leslie's made pancakes and we don't want to keep her waiting."

Justin got to his feet and followed Kyle to the kitchen. They were laughing and pushing each other like two, four-year-olds. Emily stayed behind, fuming at her brother's childish behavior. "Juveniles!" she screamed behind them.

"Why were the two of you arguing this morning?" I asked, heading for the bathroom, purposely leaving the door wide open. I threw some cold water on my face hoping it would wash away all memory of last night, brushed my teeth and pinned my hair back with my mother's lovely butterfly hairpin.

"Arguing? Oh that, Kyle was just being himself," she answered shrugging it off. "Come on, get dressed everyone is waiting."

Looking down I saw that I was in my favorite flannel pajamas. "Who put these on me?" I asked mortified at the thought of Justin seeing me naked.

"Don't worry, he was a perfect gentleman," Emily said reassuringly. "He waited till I got home and asked if I could help."

"Thank God!" I exclaimed.

"Caitlin," her voice only a whimper, "sorry about last night, had I known I was putting you in danger I'd never have suggested going out."

"Besides the near death experience," I said trying to lighten the conversation, smiling at her to ease her guilt, "I had fun. It was a nice change for me."

"I'm truly, truly sorry."

"Don't worry about it. Really Em, I'm fine." I gave her a quick hug. "So, what did you and Marc do after we left?"

People like me should never try doing two things at once. Especially, trying to get dressed and hold a conversation simultaneously. I almost fell over putting on my jeans, using the bed post for support. I finally caught my balance. I could tell that Emily was holding back the giggles.

"You and Marc...?" I asked wanting to know the juicy details.

"It was unbelievable! It did, however, take me a good hour to calm him down. He blames himself you know?"

"He shouldn't. He did all he could."

"That's the problem Caitlin, he didn't. I mean – he couldn't. It was difficult for him to contain his instincts. Marc's powers are growing day by day and making it harder for him to control. Let's just say that last night he felt the full force of what he could have done and it scared him."

"I can't believe I ruined everybody's evening. He must hate me!"

"Hate you? Why in the world would anybody hate you? He found you undeniably cute and strong. He was more amazed at your ability to keep calm under the circumstances."

I shook my head to banish the memory. "Em, enough about last night's ordeal. Tell me about you and Marc." I was dying to know if they hit it off. It was so obvious that he was into her.

"I'm totally in love with him," she declared, twirling on her heel, blissfully content of how last night went. "He is the epitome of gorgeousness and perfection."

"Wow!" I exclaimed. There was not much more I could say after such a heartfelt declaration. She deserved to be happy and from what I could tell from last night, Marc was just the man for the job.

As we descended the stairs, Emily was still lost in her love cloud. I wondered if I would ever feel love; the kind she felt for Marc. I knew my attraction to Justin was much stronger than anything in this world, but I knew it couldn't be love. It was too instinctive – chemical, something beyond feelings. If the undeniable pull we felt suddenly ceased, would we still feel the same about each other?

The smell of breakfast interrupted my thoughts. I hadn't noticed how hungry I was till then.

Once in the kitchen I noticed sitting at the head of the table was Uncle Abbot with his newspaper in hand reading the latest trends in the stock market. Kyle was next to him pouring maple syrup on his stack of pancakes; making sure not to miss a spot. Aunt Leslie was, as always, sitting there eating quietly. I was making a mental note of their faces, never wanting to forget this picture for when I would have to leave and then, there he was. Justin's back was facing me, but I sensed his awareness of my presence. He was not going to turn, not with my uncle there.

"Good morning girls," Aunt Leslie said getting up to serve us breakfast, "sleep well, Caitlin?"

"Perfect!" I purred.

Justin was clearly satisfied with my reply. Continuing to look down at his plate he cracked a smile just enough to catch Uncle Abbots attention. My uncle's eyes were on fire. He didn't like the underlying meaning of Justin's content smile.

"Sorry for not coming down last night to see the Ellri," I quickly said, defusing the situation.

"Don't worry about it child. You rested, that's what matters." Uncle Abbot quickly returned to his paper ignoring Justin – for now.

After breakfast the four of us cleaned up while uncle Abbot and Aunt Leslie retreated to the den. "What do you girls have planned for this glorious Sunday morning?" Kyle asked helping with the dishes.

"I don't know about Caitlin, but I have a date with destiny," said Emily, beaming.

Kyle seemed to be taken off guard by her bubbly manner. He was, from what I could tell, amused, "Poor Marc! Somebody ought to warn the poor bastard – needs to tell him what he's getting himself into." Kyle was doing his best to infuriate her. Luckily for him, Emily was oblivious to his snaring comments; probably day dreaming about her outing with Marc Falcone.

Thank God! I thought. Otherwise they would have started arguing again.

Realizing he wasn't getting anywhere with his sister Kyle turned to me. "What about you, sis? Do you have anything planned?"

"Actually, I need to talk to Leslie about school. If I have to go tomorrow I'd like to get started on studying so I can catch up. I'm sure the students here are way ahead of me."

"It's sunny outside Caitlin – rare for this time of year. Don't spend it inside with your nose in a book." Kyle was so sweet when he tried to act the older, caring brother. "Justin, why don't you take her somewhere?"

"He doesn't need to do that!" I snapped, averting Justin's gaze. "I need to get ready for school."

Justin, ignoring my comment, simply turned and faced his best friend. "Kyle, I need to go home anyway. I have a few things to do before lunch, before I have to leave for Cambridge."

My chest constricted at the thought of him leaving. *What's so important in Cambridge?* I thought.

"Harvard," he answered, facing me for the very first time since breakfast. He was reading my thoughts again. "You're not the only one with school tomorrow you know?"

"Harvard! Huh!" I heard Kyle say from a distance in disgust. "You could've gone to a real school brother, but you chose Harvard." A Yale and Harvard rivalry was in our midst. Kyle was making such a fuss.

"Down, dog," Justin commented, referring to Yale's mascot of Handsome Dan, the bulldog. "You Yalies just wait for this year's Regatta. You'll be licking our shoes like the good dogs you are."

"We're going to cremate you Crimson," Kyle said, raising his voice.

"You might've snapped a seven-year Harvard hold on the varsity-eight trophy, but be prepared to lose this year."

They continued for some time going back and forth talking about their teams – calling each other by their school's nicknames. For some reason the Ellri believed that it was good for the young people of Oaks to attend University, even though they had an upper hand when it came to academics as well as athletics.

Grades were not a factor. The Ellri knew that people like Justin and Kyle could anticipate the questions on Exams. Schools outside of Oaks were not protected by the Shield of Knowledge as were the ones in town. The gifted could do what they wanted. The reason behind attending University was to get a well-rounded education by interacting with ordinary individuals. To see the world as it is outside the parameters of our close-knit community.

The thought of Justin leaving was hard to swallow. I was quickly saddened by the mere thought of having him so far away, but I knew that I had to somehow sever these feelings, stop whatever this was from getting any bigger.

"It's almost the end of term, and finals are in a few weeks," he said. "The campus isn't that far from Oaks. I can be there and back in no time. I wouldn't need to stay on campus if you'd rather I stay here, in Oaks," he added, looking concerned. "Staying here will ease the pain."

My mind came to a screeching halt. *Time to end this*, I thought. "You needn't bother." I said with resolve. Justin held my gaze. "Don't get me wrong, I'm really thankful for your help last night, but,"

I scrambled for the right words to cut the tie, "trust me – I'll be fine without you. I have been for some time now. I didn't need you then, and I certainly don't need you now."

Kyle and Emily's expression of disbelief was testament to how harsh I sounded. I was purposely being hurtful, wanting him to hate me – wanting him to stay away. My physical need to be around him would not stand in the way of my better judgment. The pain of being apart I could deal with, but the deep wound left by his betrayal was still open and unwilling to heal.

"Well then," he said calmly, his face a mask, his eyes intense and unreadable, "there's nothing left to say now, is there?"

I lowered my gaze, while inside I felt so wretched it was all I could do to stop myself from crying.

"Kyle, Em, see you guys later," he said and stalked off without a second thought, determined to put distance between us.

I stood motionless with my eyes fixed on his back. *It's best he hate me.* I assured myself. I knew in my heart that he would not be bothering me anytime soon. With his every step I could feel him distancing. I knew he felt the same discomfort, it was in his walk. The unusual sensation started with a gradual warming, then stinging and as soon as he slammed the door shut, the torment of the full force of the burn rekindled. I breathed deep to push the discomfort aside and regain my balance.

"That was a bit harsh, Caitlin," I heard Kyle say bitterly, defending his best friend. "He means well. It wasn't easy for him these past five years either. You can't imagine how he felt when you left. It took all the Ellri to keep him from coming to get you."

I shook my head in denial. "You're lying. You're all lying," I accused.

"Caitlin, you're wrong! Justin….."

"Kyle, that's enough!" My aunt said standing in the doorway. "Both of you leave, Caitlin and I need to talk."

"But mom, she needs to know the truth. It's not fair to Justin. Caitlin needs to know!"

"Kyle, I said that's enough. Now go!"

He was not at all ready to drop the subject, but he knew better than to go against her wishes. With a few foul utterances under his breath, Kyle left the room agitated at not being able to clear the air. His devotion to Justin was commendable, but why did he feel he had to lie to justify the unjustifiable? Emily left short after, leaving me to stand facing my aunt all alone.

"Why am I here?" I yelled, enraged with all the secrecy.

She just stared.

"Why now – why after so long?"

"Caitlin," she broke in, gently reaching for my arm, "listen, please."

"No! Don't you dare touch me! You forfeited that right long ago."

Taking a silent step back, her face turned pale and tired. "Your questions are all valid, and I'm aware of how confusing and frustrating this is, but you have to believe me when I say that you have to trust me."

"Trust you? Are you kidding me? How can I? You are being so vague and holding out on things I need to know. It's my damn life you're playing with, Aunt Leslie. I won't have you controlling it anymore! I need to know what this is all about, and I need to know now!"

"It won't be long, sweetie. You'll have all your answers soon enough. You need to be patient."

"Patient? I think I've been more than patient with all of you. Hell, I've been simmering in patience for the last five years. It's time I knew what the hell is going on."

Her eyelids lifted to pierce me with a gaze that would have had more impact on me were I not so angry.

"The Ellri will decide when the time is right, Caitlin, not you! There are rules to our way of life created to protect us all. No short cuts will be taken – not even for you." Her authoritarian voice fluctuated with each syllable expecting unquestioning obedience. As I drew a sharp breath, I caught the troubled look in her eyes, and quickly decided to put an end to my appeal. I moaned and buried my face in my hands. "Just forget it! I can see there's no point in arguing with you."

"Please understand, sweetie, there are things in motion here much greater than the both of us." I remained silent and immobile. "The only thing I can tell you is that Kyle was accurate in describing Justin's response to your leaving. It did take all of us to make him see that it was the best thing for you. His powers of persuasion have grown tremendously with his ascension. We had our hands full fighting him off, swaying him to our way of thinking."

"He acted in his own interest, I can assure you," I replied under my breath. "It's the burn he wanted to extinguish. He didn't do it for my sake." My feeble attempt to explain Justin's actions was lost on my aunt. "Caitlin, I don't understand why you're fighting something so natural. You and Justin were born to be together. Even the Council of Nobe is aware of your bond, and they're never wrong, child. This type of connection doesn't happen very often – once, maybe even twice in a millennium."

"The Nobe? What does this have to do with them?"

"In time, Caitlin, I've said too much as it is. Now, about school tomorrow."

"No – it's not fair," I raged furiously, tears starting down my cheeks as my frustration hit breaking point. "You can't make me do this. You just can't. I'm not thirteen anymore. I let you turn my world upside down once before, but never again! I'll do as you wish only when I get my answers. Do you understand? I really need to know what the hell is going on."

Her gaze softened. "I'm sorry, but you'll have to wait for your answers. Until then, your only responsibility is to finish your senior year. Hard as all this might seem, you must realize that we're all here for you. We'd never do anything that wasn't in your best interest."

"So wait. What you're telling me is that you want me to pretend that five years of my life didn't happen? To act as if everything is normal? Is that what you expect me to do?"

She didn't answer right away, just stood there staring at me. "School is all you need to worry about for now. Leave the rest to the Ellri. We only want what's best for you."

I put my hands over my ears, tormented by her resolve. She remained silent, giving me the time needed to set right the muddle inside my head. It was not until much later that she began to speak, "You will be fine in Oaks High."

I simply raised my gaze to her as I rubbed my eyes with the back of my hand.

"Caitlin, the building itself, as you remember renders student's powers useless upon entering the great hall. The Shield of Knowledge will keep those who want to pry out of your head. However, you will need to be escorted to and from for a couple of days so we won't have a repeat of last night. Soon, your own powers will block everybody out allowing you to drive yourself to school. You should be fine before winter break."

EIGHT

NEW BEGINNING

OST OF WHAT I KNEW concerning the Nobe, I had learned from my uncle. When I was really young, I came across a book on the Nobe while hanging out in my uncle's private study.

Curious to see what it was all about I leafed through a few pages before my uncle pried the ancient, leather bound relic from my small hands – not allowing me anywhere near it from that point on.

What I remember best of all, is that the volume brandished with the crests of the five different bloodlines. The symbol bore the lineage sign of each family and a date was forged in the middle. The oldest was the Korbs' family crest which was rather simple compared to the other more decorative ones – a triangular shape with the Latin words 'LUX ET VERITAS' adorning each side of the three-sided polygon.

Having spent hours being tutored in the dead languages, I knew that the word meant 'light and truth'. In the middle of the triangle roman numerals depicting the year 2000 BC were interwoven with symbols of the vine of life. It bewildered me. It was the oldest, biggest family to date, and still going strong somewhere in Europe.

That night over a cup of hot chocolate, my uncle had explained that the truly gifted members of the bloodlines ascended in stages. They ascend as teenagers when their powers start to strengthen, and then if they are lucky they ascend again, sometime later in life, as did my aunt and uncle and become Ellri. Only the strongest of the bloodlines, the ones whose gifts are no match for nature and mankind can ascend to the next stage and become immortal – can become Nobe.

He told me that the Nobe were the balance that kept us human, that one Nobe alone was stronger than all the Ellri combined. They see to it that none of the gifted interferes with nature or mankind's natural evolution and due to their enhanced gifts they simply choose to blend in with society. Only when you become a Nobe can you learn who your counterparts are.

Their powers are vast and mighty and intervene only when the Ellri are unable to help. Even though the Nobe are known to live among us, they never make their presence known to any one of us. These immortals of such immense power could easily take the shape and form of anyone they wanted, but they rarely did since they didn't need to be physically present to make their needs known. The Ellri kept in tune with them through their thoughts.

Uncle Abbot made it perfectly clear that the Nobe are the most supreme beings second to the Creator. "They are human like you and I, born to protect this world." he had said. "To keep to true balance the Nobe created the Council of Nobe by electing seven members of their kind to represent the bloodlines. Each line had one representative, but the Korbs being the largest and oldest of all five families had three Nobe in the Council. Every few hundred years the existing council steps down and leaves room for new Nobe to rule."

It had been the first and only time in my life that the existence of the Council of Nobe had been discussed. It was blasphemous to even bring them up in mere conversation. Thinking back now to that night only heightened my awareness of the seriousness of my present situation.

It simply doesn't add up. I thought. *The Ellri are meeting more than ever. Aunt Leslie referred to the Council of Nobe in casual conversation as if it meant nothing. Something is, most definitely, up.* Now more than ever before, I had to figure out why I was summoned back and what role I play in it all.

For the very first time in years, my mind was clearer than ever. Aunt Leslie's words about Justin suddenly rang true. I let my head fall back against the leather sofa as I ventured a throaty whisper, "What am I going to do now?"

Confused, I closed my eyes momentarily to think. There were no specific thoughts in my head, only faint traces of what needed to be said and done. My brain simply couldn't work around the idea that he had wanted me there, that Justin actually had fought for my return.

In that fleeting moment, I clutched my chest wondering if it were humanly possible for my heart to ache any more. *Why didn't he say something, say that I was stupid to treat him so vile, say something – anything?* I bit my lip hard to stop myself from crying. *Did the Ellri have anything to do with his actions five years ago?* I had to find him and explain, at least apologize. *Would he ever forgive me?* I wondered. I had made such a mess of everything.

Without a moment to spare, I ran upstairs looking for Kyle,

hoping he would know where to find Justin. Without knocking, I barged into his room. Kyle looked as if he were expecting me. "Haven't they taught you manners in Stone Hurst," he said facing me, sitting at his desk fiddling around with CDs.

"Kyle, I need to know where Justin is."

"You're driving the poor guy crazy, Caitlin. I just talked to him. He's on his way to Cambridge."

"Did he say when he's coming back?"

Summoning a wavering smile, Kyle threw aside the CDs and led me to the bed. I sat on the edge, wringing my hands nervously.

"Caitlin," he said touching his hand to mine, "Justin will come back, don't worry. He just has a few things to straighten out first."

My heart contracted as a deluge of tears surged to my eyes. "Kyle, I was horrible! How could I say those things to him?"

"Yeah, well, you'll just have to apologize as soon as he returns, won't you?"

I nodded as I wiped the stray tears from my face. "When do you expect him back? How long will he be? He's coming back, isn't he? "

"I'm not sure, sis. I've never heard him sound so despondent. Don't worry, it's a guy thing. He'll snap out of it eventually. You'll see!"

"Eventually...?" I inhaled a large volume of air. "How long is that? How long is 'eventually'?" My eyes darkened with remorse. "Kyle, I really need to speak to him. You were right, I was harsh. I didn't mean any of it. What am I going to do?"

Smiling, Kyle stroked my back. "You really need to relax. These things have a way of working out."

He turned his head up towards the ceiling and closed his eyes.

I was not sure what he was doing. Motionless and quiet, he remained in that position for a few minutes and then he spoke, "Justin's confused and driving like a maniac. It's a good thing you can't hear him, Caitlin. He's cursing up a storm."

"You can actually see him? You can hear him?" I asked, absolutely dumbfounded.

"Of course I can – as clear as I can see you. Let's leave him cool off a little. He'll come round." Kyle rested his arm on my shoulder. "You know Caitlin, loving someone doesn't need to be so difficult."

I turned and gaped. "Where did that come from? Love – what love? I'm not in love with Justin." I exclaimed. "It's this stupid bond we share. Whatever it is that we feel, we can't help feel it."

Kyle shook his head. "If you saw what I and everybody else sees when you two are around each other, you'd know that if that's not love, than nothing is. I've seen how you both react around each other. I must admit it was annoying at times when we were young, but you must realize that the bond is only physical. You and Justin are so much more than that."

I dropped my head into my hands in utter disbelief. "It can't be," I muttered. The room was suddenly spinning. My veins burning even more responding to Justin's escalating anger.

"It can't be what you said, can it? No, impossible! Kyle you don't know how we feel – how our body makes us react. It's all jumbled together. It has to be the bond – it just has to!"

Kyle pointed to my head and said, "Don't over think this. Don't analyze things so much. You feel it – he feels it – what's there to think about?"

"Is he in as much pain as I am?"

"I can't tell. He's blocked me out. He's strong. I don't want to push him, not when he's like this. He knows you want to speak to him – at least I got that much." I was breathing heavily, allowing Kyle to stroke my back. "You need to relax, Caitlin; otherwise you're going to make yourself sick."

"To late for that," I admitted putting my face in my hands.

"Everything is going to be fine, sis, you'll see."

I sat there for a few minutes, gathering my wits about me and then slowly stood up and gave him a quick peck on the cheek. "Thanks for the pep talk," I told him, smiling through the discomfort.

"Anytime! Now go – get some rest and take your mind off all this. Let time remedy the situation."

"I will," I answered with a horrible dryness in my throat. "Kyle, you're the best. I've really missed our talks these past few years."

His face brightened up as he said, "The feeling is mutual, Caitlin. It was hard for me not to have somebody to pick on. You're much more fun than Emily. She takes everything so seriously."

Pushing the thought from my mind, I smiled and made my way back to my room, mentally sifting through everything Kyle had told me. I crawled into bed needing to stop the intensity of the flame that consumed my blood. I closed my eyes and transcended to find my solace. *Finally peace*, I thought. Now I could finally rest, without the pain of missing him.

A few hours alone with my thoughts were enough to revitalize me. I had arranged for Tyler to come over later on that night to talk me through the classes. I didn't want to go to school any more than I wanted to be there, but school seemed to be my only salvation as it would keep my mind busy until I figured things out. Lessons aside, ignoring the agonizing pain was futile.

As soon as I slipped back to a conscious state the feelings drenched me like a bucket of ice water. I knew Justin was quite far, but for some reason the pain kept escalating, venomously circulating in my blood stream.

Not knowing what to do to alleviate it, I achingly made my way downstairs hoping to find help from my aunt, but instead I came across Uncle Abbot along with Justin's father, William Bradford and Tyler's dad, Marcellus Falcone at the foot of the stairs.

"Good, you're awake," Uncle Abbot said, cracking a weak smile.

I swallowed back the discomfort and answered, "Yes, I needed a nap, badly." Then I turned to our visitors, "It's nice to see you again William and you Marcellus."

"Caitlin, are you feeling alright child?" asked William "You look exhausted."

"Actually, I'm not alright," I confessed, biting my bottom lip. "The pain – the pain is much worse. It's never been this strong. I can't seem to get it under control – it's – it's wearing me down."

Justin's father placed his hand on my shoulder and said, "Is there something we can do?"

"I'm not sure if anyone can do anything. It's my cross to bear." I knew I sounded melodramatic, but that's how I felt. I was not going to censor my feelings for anyone any more.

Marcellus took a step forward. "Caitlin, it doesn't have to be this way. We can't extinguish the burn, but we can minimize the potency if you let us?" I looked at them puzzled and turned to my uncle for confirmation. "Is that even possible? Can you really make this go away?"

"There is only one way to find out," he said, taking me by the arm and in a shrouded deathly silence, I was led down the hall like those condemned to death. Past the kitchen and to the farthest right was my uncle's personal study. I felt tendrils of uncertainty wrap themselves around me as we made our way down the hall. As soon as we entered the room there was an underlining hint of lavender meant to mask the potent smell of my uncle's habit of smoking cigars indoors.

"Here, have a seat, Caitlin," Uncle Abbot said casually, motioning me to sit.

I was not sure which seat to take, so I took the closest to me. The heavy leather armchairs in the middle of the formidable room formed a perfect circle. Like the main study, the walls here were engrossed in hand carved bookshelves filled with written works encased behind glass doors. These books were much different than the others in the main study – all ancient documents and relics from former ages. No one was allowed to touch them without my uncle indicating his consent.

"What we'd like you to do is concentrate really hard on my voice, sweetheart and do as I say," Uncle Abbot instructed. "If the pain intensifies we will stop. You control how far we go, not us." I nodded in understanding. "Don't be scared to speak your mind, okay? We are all equals here now."

"Okay, just make it go away, please."

How much more could this hurt? They didn't seem to understand the intensity of the burning in my blood. I was not about to miss the opportunity to rid myself of this torment. Just then William stood in front of me and said, "Close your eyes child and don't open them until I say. Do you understand?" I nodded. "It is really important for you to trust us." I instantly closed my eyes obediently. "Concentrate on one thing and one thing only. It can be anything."

My mind drifted to my all too familiar abyss, but I was surprisingly able to clearly hear them as they directed me – guiding me through the process. The pain quickly disappeared as it always did when I fell into my black hole. But I knew that as soon as I re-entered consciousness the fire would still burn in my blood.

Without any warning, I felt a warm glow on my face, radiating from within, spreading to every muscle and every cell of my body.

The intoxicating effect lasted only seconds and then there was a hum-drum of voices in my head, but there was no way of deciphering what they were saying or whose they were. Unexpectedly, the sounds stopped and an eerie silence followed. I was conscious of my need to open my eyes, but I was abruptly ordered not to.

In the long seconds that followed a whirlwind of emotions swept over me and then came pain. The purest and grossest in form, free of any extraneous elements.

A sudden jarring impact came down on me, concentrating primarily on my right wrist. I fought to keep from screaming by biting down hard, but even that didn't seem to lessen the acute burning sensation. It felt like a stream of pulsating lava flowing through my veins, moving down my arm, burning its way to the surface – first through the tissue and then as the pain culminated it broke through the skin.

I knew no natural ailment could bring the avalanche of blood rushing to the area. I felt faint, but still in excruciating physical pain.

Tears ran down my face, but again I was ordered to keep my eyes shut. I squirmed and winced from the acute discomfort trying desperately to do as they wished. In that instant I felt a hand as cold as ice over my burning wrist diminishing the burn, leaving a detectable amount of soreness on my right wrist where the fire had been before.

I continued to keep my eyes shut, not that I had a choice in the matter, but at least the worst was over.

Sitting in stunned silence, I felt someone wrapping something around my wrist. It felt oddly comfortable. As I sat there I was strangely aware of everything around me – aware of even the slightest dust particle that brushed past me – able to pick up the slightest movement and sound.

The lack of sight seemed to heighten my other senses. The next few minutes passed in tranquil silence enabling me to home in on a peculiar sound – a melodic rhythm of pounding human heart beats.

Concentrating even more, I was surprisingly able to distinguish four different rhythms, which meant that now there were four people in the room – not three as before. I could tell where each person stood in the room by the sharpness of their heartbeat. Now, someone was moving closer because the sound of their heart was becoming all the more clear, crisper in a way.

"Good girl, Caitlin," I suddenly heard a soft whisper say.

What was that? I wondered, moving my head from side to side. It was not like anything I had ever heard before. It couldn't be classified as a human voice, it was ethereal – a sound within a sound. Not only was it audible in my solace, but also in the room where I was sitting. It was as though something or someone was both next to me in the study but also in the darkness of my solace. The whisper was completely foreign to me, but comforting. A veil of calm fell over me, my mind was completely aware of this being's radiance. No words to describe the euphoria that swept over me.

"Caitlin," I heard my uncle summoning me, "you can open your eyes now if you want. Join us sweetie."

At first I was unwilling to leave my solace for fear of losing the majestic being. But my uncle called out to me, ordering me to open my eyes.

Hesitantly, I did as he asked and opened my eyes to see only three familiar faces looking back at me. At that moment I realized that the agonizing pain of Justin's absence was not as intense as before, but it was still there, a faint reminder of what it was before – bearable.

I guess the experiment worked after all. I thought looking down at my freshly bandaged right wrist.

"What happened? I asked, searching their faces.

"Caitlin, how are you feeling? Are you okay?" William asked, with a low soft voice. "You slipped away again – your solace, is it?"

I nodded. "I'm fine, but my wrist...."

"Your pain threshold is remarkable. It's unprecedented, young lady. What you just underwent only few would have come out alive."

"It was intense," I admitted, continuing to look at my bandaged wrist. "Did I do something wrong? Did I do this?" I asked holding up my bandaged wrist.

"No, you were amazing," Justin's father said. "You couldn't have done any better. We're very, very proud of you, young lady."

"What happened to my wrist?" I asked, holding it tight. "Did you guys burn me?"

"Us – no Caitlin, we didn't burn you. You did this to yourself – in a way. It's been known to happen, but we've never seen it in action. You branded yourself, Caitlin." Marcellus explained.

"Branded myself? But why – why the heck would I do that – how?"

"Branding is a way for the mind to remind the body of the full force of the physical pain. Having minimized your ache, your body reacted by imprinting a memory of it on your wrist."

"That's insane!" I stared down at my bandaged wrist. "I guess it worked, huh? I mean, I can still feel the distance between me and Justin, but it's nothing like before. It's only a fraction of what it was – a tingle in comparison to the high voltage of before. It's nothing I can't handle."

I looked up at them only to see them staring back at me. "Okay, so where's the fourth person?" I finally asked.

There was a sudden complicit silence between them.

"For crying out loud, Uncle Abbot, I felt this being beside me – heard its heart beat. Don't look at me like I'm crazy!" My voice was trembling trying to make sense of what it was that I sensed.

"What are you saying, child?" asked Marcellus.

All three men simply stared.

"There was someone else here. I felt them. Whatever it was or whoever it was stood here – not here per say, but right beside me in the darkness of my solace," I said, lifting my bandaged wrist to show them. "He – she – whatever it was – was right here with me."

"You're under a lot of strain, Caitlin. The thing you think you felt and heard was your own heartbeat. You did this child," William said, trying his hardest to convince me. "The ancients believed that branding happened only to the truly gifted. You should be proud of yourself. It was quite a thing to watch."

"No," I pronounced, "I know what I sensed. It was...."

Marcellus didn't let me finish my sentence, instead he began to say, "As you said Caitlin, you will still feel the distance between you and Justin, but it won't be as intense. Your bond to one another is rare and very strong. We shouldn't mess with something so extraordinary."

Marcellus quickly looked up closing his eyes like Kyle did earlier. "Justin is fully aware of what transpired. Your pain is as much his as it is yours.

"You mean he felt what I just felt? All of it?" "Well, not exactly the full force, but enough for it to be uncomfortable. So you see, Caitlin, it is not a cross you bear alone, after all."

I lowered my head, nodding in sombre understanding. "Aunt Leslie tried to tell me the same thing earlier." I tightened my grip on my bandaged wrist. "When can I take the bandage off?" I asked, not wanting to think of Justin just yet.

"Keep it on for a few days. You'll know when and what it means." There was a sudden knock on the door. Shannon came in looking quite proud of me. It would seem that all the Ellri had gathered. "We're ready for you," Shannon said, addressing the men. She gracefully moved next to me and caressed my cheek motherly-like and said, "You were brilliant!"

"Was I?"

"Of course you were," she reassured me. "Now, don't rush yourself and be patient. Justin, can help you sort everything out." She lifted my bandaged wrist looking impressed. "You both need each other, Caitlin," she added, giving me a wink and a smile. Shannon quickly turned and left just as fast to join the others.

Tyler came a few hours later, lugging along his school bag. We sat on the floor of my room with our text books spread in front of us. I felt much lighter as the pain was just a fraction of what it used to be and the funny thing was that I didn't even feel it when lost in conversation.

The first few hours it felt really strange not being able to feel

Justin's absence so intense, but Tyler's persistence in wanting to see what's under the bandage was a welcoming distraction.

"Let it heal first," I reprimanded him by punching him on the arm.

"It's so cool, Caitlin. I can't wait to see what it is."

"Same here," I said, picking up a random text book and motioned to Tyler, "let's get started, shall we?"

"Leslie arranged for you to be in all my classes. She thought it would be easier for you. You won't have a problem with first period Calculus because we're only on unit five and Mr Travis is awesome. He has a unique way of explaining things. Even I understand it. You should know that Megan and the rest of her friends are in our class. So, you'll be in for a treat"

" You're kidding, right? Please tell me you're kidding!"

He shook his head no.

"Oh, great!" It was the only thing I could say to his revelation. "My first day back in school and I have to endure the Brat Pack in the first hour? Someone must really hate me!"

We started laughing. It was a nice change to be there with Tyler. We always used to work on class projects together. It was customary for all our teachers to appoint us partners on any assignment. Having him there was going to make school bearable.

Tyler was the studious and meticulous type and I the one who would always neglect to iron out the details. I rushed through things being bored of school. Unfair as life was, I used to get far better grades than him, and it used to drive him crazy.

He helped me with Monday's homework. Calculus was murder and so was Chemistry, my least favourite subjects. Not that I found them difficult. I just didn't have the patience. English Literature, now that was my calling. I loved the classics. I never did understand why this course was called English Lit. It didn't only include writers from England. The greats; like Robert Burn was Scottish; James Joyce was Irish and my all-time favourite Edgar Allan Poe was American, nevertheless, I was spellbound by their techniques.

More than two hours later we were called down for dinner. Aunt Leslie had prepared a lavish feast full of little delights. We headed towards the main dining room where Aurelia and Marcellus Falcone and their younger children were standing waiting to be seated. Aunt Leslie had invited them to return the favour. Their son Tyler was, after all, helping me in school.

We all took our seats. My aunt and uncle sat at opposite ends of the table. I sat between Tyler's younger siblings Natalie and Michelle. Kyle, Tyler and Emily sat across from us making faces every chance they got. To onlookers it would have seemed a formal occasion, but to us it was not. The great families of Oaks were all very close. They were an extension of each other. By any standard, they were a seamless correlation of understanding and mutual respect.

We coursed through the meal with light conversation. Serious matters were never discussed over dinner.

"How are you adjusting?" Aurelia turned to me and asked with her deep Italian accent. "Being back I mean?"

Her hair was cropped and raven black. She had a sophisticated aura about her, always dressed in the latest Italian fashion. She was the youngest of the Ellri more in tune with youth culture. Naturally slim and well-built you would never have guessed she was a mother of three teenagers; Tyler the oldest at eighteen, Natalie fifteen and Michelle only thirteen.

"I'm surviving by the looks of it," I said, not meaning it to sound funny, though they all laughed.

Recounting the extraordinary events of the previous two days, I came to the realization that my life had gone from extreme desolation to the polar opposite. Looking around to all the faces I have dreamt about seeing on those lonely nights in my exile, I couldn't help but feel a deep sadness.

Ignoring the chatter that was going on around me, I feigned interest on what was on my plate. Overwhelmed by the strangeness of all that was happening to me, I looked quizzically down at my bandaged wrist. Not feeling the intensity of Justin's absence needed some getting used to. For so many years I had stayed awake hoping that the pain would subside and now that it had, I felt nostalgic of its power over me.

Would he be feeling the same? I suddenly wondered. *He might not be feeling anything at all – he's much stronger than me.* The thought sent shivers down my spine. *He wouldn't want me anymore.* The sudden realization consumed me. I could feel my chest constricting as the thought took form. I looked up to take a deep breath when I noticed Marcellus eyeing me.

"Have you?" Marcellus asked pointing to my wrist.

"Felt anything of Justin?"

Marcellus nodded

"No," I answered grimly and let my mind empty to see if I could feel the intensity again. "No – nothing."

"Everything's going to be just fine Caitlin, give it time." Marcellus spoke to me without having to utter a syllable. His voice, however, was clear and sharp in my mind. He was in my thoughts the way Justin was on several occasions. Just as fast he casually turned to Uncle Abbot and continued their conversation on their own theories of world economics.

Dinner dragged on for quite a while. It was getting real late and it was a school night. In no time at all, the Falcones gathered their children and finally headed home. I helped my cousins clean up. It didn't take long. We simply stuffed everything in the dishwasher this time.

It was just too much to do by hand. Aunt Leslie and Uncle Abbot retired to the den leaving us to clean up.

"I can't believe I have school tomorrow."

Kyle patted me on the back, "You'll be fine."

"Easy for you to say – a new school in the middle of semester is murder, I should know."

"Kyle and I will drive you to school tomorrow if that'll make you feel better?" Emily said, collecting the linen tablecloth.

"I'd love that, but isn't it going to be a bit too early for you?"

"No, we'll be up before you. I need to go attend classes and Kyle needs to see about graduation. My semester isn't done yet and I have tons of things to do."

"How long will you guys be gone?" I asked.

"Only for a few days, I have to be back by Friday to organize a birthday party, did you forget?"

"You really don't need to do that," I insisted.

"I know I don't need to do it, but I want to do it."

"It's not necessary, Em."

"Nonsense – I want to. You deserve to have a little fun, Caitlin. You have been so depressed from the moment you stepped foot in Oaks and I'll be damned if I sit by and let this continue for much longer. I can't stand to see you like that anymore. A party is what you need to get your mind off of everything that is going on around you."

"You really think that a party is going to help, this?" I exclaimed, raising my bandaged arm in the air.

"Yes it will, Caitlin. I know you have fended for yourself for the last five years and I'm not going to lie and say I understand why, because I don't. But you're here now and you need to move forward. I want to see my little sis smile like she used to. Like it or not, I won't let you hide behind all this nonsense – it's your birthday, for heaven's sake!"

I tried to reason with her but she was not going to let me have my way. "Okay, Okay! I'll agree to the party only if you promise it to be a small family affair."

"A family affair…?"

I nodded. "Yes – only the family."

Reluctant to agree at first, she paced back and forth pondering something. "Okay, only the family."

"Great, so we agree, Em – nothing over the top."

"Sure – yeah! But in all honesty, I can't promise you anything," she said smiling, walking away having the last word. I didn't know what she had up her sleeve.

Oaks High
Illustrated for Lenah That Bind · Circle of Trust

NINE

MOONLIT

HE HOUSE WAS unrecognizably quite with everyone doing their own thing. It was nice to finally have some time to myself. I grabbed my coat and headed down the corridor and out the back door. The lights from inside the house were just enough for me to make my way safely down the few steps that led to the back yard. The moon did the rest, pouring through the branches like a spotlight, showing me the way to favourite place – the bench under the old Willow. I propped up my feet and hugged my knees. It was the stillness that I needed. I looked down at my wrist, replaying the day's events in my mind, wondering what it was all about.

"The longest two days of my life," I exhaled, smoothing the dressing around my wrist.

Unexpectedly, soft lights flooded the darkness, lining the winding paths that spanned the estate. It looked enchanting – surreal in so many ways. Blanketed by the tranquil surroundings, my wayward thoughts finally eased up allowing room for peace and quiet.

Sitting there for an unknown length of time with my head resting on my knees, a new sensation coursed within me. It was not painful in any way, but it was there all the same.

With terrifying suddenness, an indignant, high-pitched screech shattered the silence into a thousand fragments. The back door swung open and there was Justin, standing frozen, visibly not knowing what to do. His regal blue eyes all the more vibrant under the shadowy surrounding. The smooth brilliant planes of his face were now pale and tired.

"Leslie told me you'd be out here," his voice was soft and tender, "it's a bit cold don't you think?"

"No – no, it's perfect," I swallowed, trying to sound as calm as possible – rather hard with him standing right there, looking the way he did. "I needed some alone time to clear my thoughts."

He uneasily turned to the door. "I see," he said raising his brow. "If you want me to leave, I will."

"No. Stay. I want you – to stay." My mind was in a daze from Justin's presence. I couldn't get enough of him. "I thought you were heading to Cambridge?" I added coolly, trying to seem comfortable with him in such close proximity.

"I couldn't concentrate on anything all day. I've been driving around for hours trying to decide what to do," he admitted uncomfortably.

"Did it work?"

He brushed back his dark brown hair with his left hand looking rather anxious. "It clearly didn't. You were everywhere - in everything," he finally said smiling. "You're going to drive me crazy, I hope you know."

I breathed in deep, "For all its worth," I said looking at him, hoping against hope he knew how bad I felt about earlier, "I'm glad you're back. I was having a hard time without you too."

Soothed by this pleasant vision I didn't want to play cat and mouse anymore, not with Justin. His smile widened, "You must be freezing," he said, awkwardly sitting himself next to me.

"I'm fine and happy that you're here," I confessed looking up at his expressive eyes. "I owe you an apology for earlier. I didn't mean any of that this morning. It was stupid. You didn't deserve it, especially after you did so much for me last night. I had too many things on my mind and well – I was hurtful."

Justin was clearly surprised at my admission of guilt. Shaking his head, he suppressed a shudder – his discomfort now more visible. "You never have to apologize to me, Caitlin, ever!"

Our eyes locked.

To sever the tension, Justin motioned to see my bandaged hand. Without any hesitation I stretched out my arm offering my wrist. The second he took my hand, his touch triggered a wave of unparalleled emotion. To keep myself in check I refused to look at him – kept my gaze anywhere but his eyes.

"I can't leave you for two seconds and you go hurting yourself," he said, looking down at my injured wrist. "You certainly seem to have had a busy day. What's this?"

It took me a few seconds to structure my thought – it was not easy with him holding my hand. "I seem to have branded myself." I finally said. "But you already know that, don't you? The Ellri told me that you experienced the pain along with me."

"Did they?" he asked, giving me a sideway look.

"Justin…," I had to stop and breathe before I spoke again. "When you left this morning the pain was unbearable. I was writhing from it, trying to get control. There was nothing I could do to minimize the burn."

Explaining the day's events in one short sentence was rather humbling. His hold got instantly tighter in response to my words.

"Uncle Abbot believed that they could help reduce its potency. They did in a way, but our connection is too strong for them to break."

He lifted his gaze to mine "Did you really need the Ellri to tell you that we're inseparable?" he asked, softly caressing my cheek with his hand. "Don't you feel it every second of your waking day?"

I looked at him wondering how I was able to survive without him all those years. "Justin, I'm…," I stopped and looked down to the ground, "I'm just so confused and tired of everybody hiding things from me. I don't know who to trust. I've been here for two days and I've already got into a fight with Emily, almost got my brain turned to mush, I hear voices in my head, I brand myself on the wrist and if that's not enough for any one person – I have first period Calculus with Megan Gordon bright and early tomorrow. How much can a girl take?"

Justin's husky laugh filled the air – visibly amused with my rendition of the events. "Well you seem to have made it out alright, considering." he chuckled. His mood was noticeably uplifted – hypnotic even. "Let's see what you're hiding under the bandage, shall we? It doesn't hurt, does it?"

I shook my head feeling a slight sting, but no real pain. I watched him slowly unwrap the gauze. He was very careful; taking his time. "Am I hurting you?"

"No more than usual," I answered jokingly.

"Is that supposed to be funny?"

I giggled.

"Hey, be nice!" he said smiling, continuing to attend to my wrist. "Did they explain why you were chosen to bear a mark?"

"They said it had to do with my body's reaction to the pain. They were vague on the details, but the experience itself was enlightening. I felt something strange. I know I didn't imagine it." I wanted him to know everything that transpired in Uncle Abbot's study, but Justin quickly finished the last round of gauze; ignoring my last statement. I was not sure if he even heard me.

"Don't you want to see?" he asked, gazing back at me.

Too enthralled at his perfection, I hadn't noticed that my wrist was completely exposed. We both looked down simultaneously. The coarse skin was still raw from that morning, but the shape was that of a small triangle – barely noticeable.

"What's the matter?" he asked.

"I thought it'd be more elaborate," I sighed, sounding a bit disappointed at the simplicity of the design. "What does it mean?"

"I'm not sure. You need to ask the Ellri for answers."

He started reapplying the gauze. His whole mood had changed – more thoughtful for some reason. He knew more than he let on.

"Justin, you need to stop doing that," I said, looking right at him, "stop keeping things from me like all the others. You need to help me understand. I can't figure this out on my own." My eyes betrayed me once again flooding with tears. "I need to know, please Justin."

I wanted answers now more than ever. I felt drained and running on empty. It felt that anywhere I turned I came up against a brick wall. My voice was shaky and my pulse was thudding in my ears.

Uncontrolled tears kept rolling down my face. "Do you all like tormenting me? See how far you can push me?"

"Look at me Caitlin," he commanded, coaxing my face up – taking my scarred wrist in hand. "Get those thoughts out of your head. I hate to see you like this, I wish I had your answers, but I don't. You must believe me. I'd do anything to make you happy again."

"Then tell me why? Why did you want me to leave five years ago?" I asked, standing up, pulling my hand free from his grip. "What did I ever do to you – for – for you to hate me so much?"

I looked at him pleadingly – my voice shaky from the tears.

He stood up as well – only inches away. "Hate you?" his voice weak with emotion. "Caitlin, how could you ever believe I hated you?" He brushed away my tears with the palm of his hand. "You have no idea what it was like for me to be away from you – not to see you," he confessed, looking hurt that I would ever think such a thing about him. He lifted my chin so I could look at him. "My life meant absolutely nothing without you in it."

My heart skipped a beat because his words were echoes of my own desolation. He felt as I did – was the only one who could understand my pain – my solitude,

"Come here," he said, slowly wrapping his arms around me – bringing me up against his body.

The warmth felt good against the cold, night air. We stayed locked in an embrace lost in each other's touch. I buried my head in the curve of his neck feeling like I belong for the very first time in years.

The feel of his skin aroused feelings I didn't know I had. I looked up only to see his gaze on me. The world around me disappeared. Justin was all that mattered.

He smiled ever so softly – caressing my cheek with one hand. "Caitlin," he whispered, "thought I'd lost you forever."

He leaned his forehead against mine for a few seconds and then simply touched his brilliant lips to mine – soft at first. The lingering sensation was overwhelming. His mouth was savoury and perfect. I leaned up against his body bringing him harder against my lips. Justin's hold tightened to my eagerness.

I could taste my tears on his mouth. I wanted him more than I ever wanted anything in my life. Justin pulled back ever so slightly just enough to see if I would resist. I whimpered to the treachery of his lips. He kissed me again, this time passionately.

"Caitlin," he was having a hard time saying my name, "We can't do this – not with all these things hanging over our heads." He pulled back again, this time straightening out his body to regain control of himself.

Embarrassed, I dropped my gaze to the ground and said, "I'm sorry. I didn't mean to...."

Justin took my hands in his. "Why are you apologising?"

I shrugged my shoulders. "I seem to be doing everything wrong."

"Why would you think that? I'm just saying that you're going through so many changes all at once. Maybe this isn't the time for...."

I turned my face up to meet his gaze, "Two completely different things, Justin." I reached out to smooth the intensity from his brow and gave him another kiss. Like an addict I was pulled even harder towards him, unable to resist.

"I'm serious, Caitlin! I won't be able to stop if you keep doing that."

"Who wants you to stop?" I smiled at him wickedly.

Justin lifted me up in the air like a disobedient little kid and sat me back down on the bench.

"What's wrong about wanting this?" I asked hurt.

"Are you sure this is what you want? Can you honestly sit there and pretend not to wonder if this is all because of this bond we share and not your true feelings for me? This morning you hated me and now this. You need to be sure, Caitlin," he was determined to make me understand his reasoning. "I can't decide for the both of us."

Frustrated, I looked up at him shaking my head, "Stop rationalising everything, that's my job. I want this. I want you." I couldn't have made my feelings any clearer. We had just shared our first kiss – eighteen years in the making and he was ruining my high. I put my face in my hands and felt embarrassed for being so forward. "Maybe it's you that doesn't want me, Justin." I said hurt.

"You don't believe that, do you?" He sat on his heels in front of me, trying to work out how he was going to explain things. "Five years ago I was sixteen, but you – you were only what – twelve or so – twelve Caitlin. It made me sick to be so attracted to you. It was maddening trying to stay away. I couldn't sleep, couldn't eat. I was a walking time bomb. I came over as much as possible to ease the damn pain, but then I kept seeing you with Tyler and it drove me crazy. I know it shouldn't have, but it did. He was able to be with you, touch you, laugh with you, and play with you. It killed me to see you so comfortable around him and then...," He suddenly stopped and stood up – his face all serious and expressionless.

"And then – what, Justin?" I asked wondering why he stopped so abruptly. He looked at me not wanting to continue. "And then – what?" I insisted sounding angrier than before – wanting to know the reason.

"And then you left. You left me, Caitlin."

His words felt like a cold slap across the face. I stood up unable to bear sitting down and listening to what he had to say. I couldn't believe what I was hearing. How could he be blaming me? My heart was thudding in my ears.

"I – left you!" I yelled, beside myself. "I came to you that night

Justin. After my aunt told me that I had to leave because I didn't belong here. That it was best that I stay away from the family and above all, you. My world was crumbling down around me. I didn't believe her. I needed to hear it from your lips. I knew I was young, but I couldn't have been that wrong about what I felt. Of all people, I expected you to fight for me."

I started trembling from the recollection of that night. "I came to you, asking for your help to talk some sense into her, to tell her she was mistaken. Instead, you pushed me, shoved me away; stood there detesting me. You wanted me to leave more than she did. I wasn't even given the chance to see Emily and Kyle. I didn't leave you, Justin! You both discarded me from your lives – threw me away as though I was worthless."

"Caitlin," he reached for me, but I pushed his hand to the side.

"Caitlin, be reasonable. You have to believe me when I say that I was the last person who wanted to see you go. Nobody would listen to me. The Ellri insisted that you had to leave. They didn't explain why. They knew you'd come to me that night. They had foreseen everything, every detail. I agreed to say all those things to you that day, believing that you would see right through them. I told them you wouldn't believe me. You should've known I would never want you to leave."

He sat down with his head lowered. "You came over begging for me to help you; crying hysterically. Do you even know how hard it was for me to see you in so much pain? I had no choice. I told you that you were immature to be acting like that. That you needed to do what your aunt asked of you, that there was nothing between us and that what you felt was merely a crush. God Caitlin, the way you looked at me that instant is engraved in my memory, haunts me ever since. How could you believe that I wanted nothing to do with you? That it was best you left. You were supposed to know. You were supposed to know I didn't mean it. Instead you just stared at me and walked away in silence and the next day you were gone."

My heart stopped. I couldn't feel a thing. His words tore right through me. I played and replayed that scene in my mind over

and over again for the past five years only now, for the first time, did I see the whole picture. Justin was as much a victim as I was. The longing I had for him every day of my life was just as strong for him – just as painful. He couldn't have wanted me to leave.

"I didn't know. How was I supposed to know?" I heard myself say. "I was thirteen for heaven's sake, Justin. The two people I cared most about in my life had wanted me to disappear, saying they'd be happier without me." I sat next to him, burying my face in my hands. "How was I supposed to know?"

"Caitlin, we have to stop doing this. We keep hurting each other to what purpose? This is not how it's supposed to be." He lifted my hand to his lips and kissed the inside of my palm. "I should've fought harder, I shouldn't have agreed to anything. Could you ever forgive me?"

Justin couldn't even look at me. He clearly felt remorse for what he did – ashamed to have hurt me so deeply. I could handle my own pain, but I didn't have the strength to see him like that.

"Justin, we were both too young to know any better. We did as we were told."

I tried justifying the last torturous years of my life.

"You don't need my forgiveness because you did nothing wrong. You thought you were acting in my best interest."

He shook his head. "You left because of me. It's entirely my fault. I made you believe all those lies."

"No – we are both victims here. They all underestimated our bond."

His brow lifted. "So, does this mean that you finally accept the notion that there is a bond between us?" he said smiling.

"I always knew there was something between us. I was simply too mad to accept it for what it was." I finally confessed, smiling.

He cracked a smile and caressed my face. My heart started racing.

"Caitlin, I don't deserve this. I should be punished for the way I treated you. Every day I was tormented thinking of you all alone and the damn pain kept intensifying reminding me of my betrayal. You're too easy on me."

"Am I?" I said, winding my hands around his neck kissing his sweet lips.

His mouth responded instantly.

"This type of torture I can handle," he said, still trying to get over his deep regret. "I'm truly sorry."

"Don't be. I've never been clearer about anything in my life. I've been fighting this thing we have for so long – hating it for existing, but this is where I want to be. It's not you who owes me an apology it's those who tore us apart that need to explain the reason for our hefty sentence. Why did the Ellri want me to leave, Justin? What did I do that forced them to come to such a harsh decision? "

Justin's beautiful eyes looked at me with profound understanding – caressing my face with his strong hands.

"I know you have many questions you want answered. So do I, but it's late, Caitlin. You need to go inside and get some rest for school tomorrow."

I looked at him confused.

"Where did that come from?" I asked at how fast he changed the subject.

"Your uncle insists we drop the subject and that you need to get some rest."

Justin pointed to his head.

"He's in my head, Caitlin. He wants you inside and in bed."

"Really, don't tell me he's been listening in all this time?"

"No, don't worry. We can block people out, but being an Ellri, he can break my barrier when the need arises."

"Do I really have to go to school?"

Justin nodded. "I'll pick you up after and we'll see what we can do."

"Can't I ditch?" I started kissing him again using any means of persuasion.

Justin's face was as happy as it was handsome, glowing with

pleasure. Slowly, he removed his lips from mine. I saw his eyes had narrowed slightly.

"You little vixen," he laughed. "You're a temptress and a schemer. You're trying to seduce me to help you skip school."

"Is it working?" I continued to kiss him breathing in short, excited bursts.

His hands slipped around my waist and started tickling me. I was doing everything I could to hold back the laughter.

"Stop, Stop! You win I'll go to school. But whatever happens to Megan Gordon is on your hands," I said, fighting back the giggles.

"Poor Megan, she doesn't know what she's in for! I know you'll play nice. Now off to bed," he said, pushing me to my feet.

"Aren't you coming?"

I was intentionally taunting him – reminding him of our sleeping arrangements of the previous night.

"As much as I'd love to, I think your uncle's invitation for a sleep-over has expired. I'll see you tomorrow," he said, reluctantly letting go of my hand.

I turned and paused momentarily, looking into his beautiful blue eyes. "I'm really home, aren't I?"

He nodded, caressing my cheek. "You are where you belong."

I pushed myself up on tiptoe to kiss him good night before going back in the house.

Justin swiftly pulled me up and passionately kissed me one last time. I was once again in heaven.

"Sweet dreams," he said, holding my face in his hands, "Now go inside before I change my mind."

"Promises, promises," I said laughing as I walked away.

First Kiss

Illustrated for Lines That Bind - Circle of Trust

TEN

AWAKENING

USUALLY, MONDAY MORNINGS were the worst. Today, however, superseded any other. First day of school in the middle of term; how worse can things get? The only reason I hadn't put up a fight over going was because I felt that Aunt Leslie was looking out for me. Something deep down told me that she had as much to do with my leaving as did Justin. I had to get to the bottom of whatever all this was, but first I had to survive my first day at Oaks High. Thankfully, the memory of Justin's lips on mine was the only thing that made that morning remotely bearable. Our first kiss was magical – better than I had imagined it would be.

"Are you ready, Caitlin?" Emily was dressed and ready to go. "Hurry up already! Get dressed and meet us downstairs for breakfast."

Still in my pyjamas – frantically stuffing books in my school bag, I was unable to get Justin's touch out of my head. Every little detail of his mouth and face saturated my thoughts.

"I'm almost done," I lied. "I'll be down in a minute!"

"Good morning sleepy head," said Kyle, poking his head in the door. He was dressed real sharp, looking handsomer than ever. His gaze scanned me over, causing him to smile. "Are you planning on getting dressed or are you trying to make a fashion statement on your first day back?"

"I'll be right down," I repeated, through clenched teeth. "We can't all look good when we wake up."

My compliment visibly lifted his spirits.

"You're going to school no matter how much you flatter me. Save your mesmerizing charm for my best friend. Your cutesiness won't work on me."

"I'd thought I'd give it one last try," I said giggling.

"It's nice to see you laugh, Caitlin. Is it due to my irresistible personality or because Justin came over last night?"

I could feel my face turning red from the memory of Justin's kisses. Kyle shook his head – reading my inappropriate thoughts. "Never mind, I don't want to know." he said, turning to leave. "Get dressed already!"

I freshened up and threw something on. I didn't even take the time to look in the mirror. I simply brushed through my hair and pulled it back, fastening it with by butterfly hairpin. School bag in hand I headed for the kitchen.

"Where are Leslie and Abbot?" I asked, seeing that their seats at the breakfast table were empty.

"They left earlier this morning, probably another meeting with the Ellri," answered Emily while pouring herself some juice.

"They've been meeting quite a lot. Is there something wrong?"

"Don't think so, Caitlin. Mom would've said something if it were serious. She can't keep much from us now that our powers are heightened."

"She's an Ellri; she can keep anything from anyone!"

Emily was suddenly pondering the thought. "I haven't thought of it like that before. You're right." She turned to Kyle and looked at him, "Do you know anything about these meetings?"

He was halfway finished his toast when he got up and placed the dish in the sink. "Its seven thirty in the morning, don't you two have better things to discuss? Boyfriend issues to solve or whatever girly things you two usually talk about?"

He blatantly ignored her question leaving the room.

"He's right, Caitlin. Let's just drop it. The Ellri know what they're doing. We shouldn't waste our time worrying."

She looked at her watch stuffing what was left of her breakfast in her mouth. "We're already late, c'mon."

"I'm going to be late on my first day back?"

"Don't worry. Mom has arranged everything with Mr Patterson. For the first few weeks you'll be going in later than everyone so there won't be a problem with those lame jerks who wish to poke around in that little head of yours. You don't want a repeat of Saturday night, do you?"

"No, I guess I don't."

I gulped down my orange juice and grabbed a nice juicy apple on my way out. *What the heck am I getting myself into?* I thought shaking my head.

It was a long – loud ten minute drive to school as Kyle and Emily fought over which radio station to listen to. They exchanged an array of adjectives – an amusing display of spiteful camaraderie at that. Up ahead in the distance I could see Oaks High. It was a three story brick Georgian Colonial; once a grand mansion. It was bequeathed to the town of Oaks by one of the families and later became a school at the turn of the eighteenth century, allowing the gifted to have a formal education. Once there Emily got out of the car and walked me to the front office. Ms Morris at the front desk handed me my class schedule and locker number. She welcomed me back to Oaks and wished me good luck in my senior year.

"First floor right," she said, pointing to the carved oak staircase which connected the first and second floor.

I was really nervous. Emily took my hand and squeezed it tight. "What are you worried about, Caitlin? It's only high school."

Was she kidding me? Most horror films were based on high school experiences.

"Yeah, guess you're right," I said as I took a deep breath and waved to her goodbye. Climbing up the wooden stairs was easy; knowing that I'd have to eventually enter a classroom was what was terrifying.

Room one-fourteen – there I was outside of Calculus. I could hear Mr Travis talking to the class. *Now or never,* I thought. I opened the door and apologised for being late. Suddenly, all eyes were on me.

Mr Travis' baritone voice broke the silence. "Welcome Miss Cathcart, take a seat and let's begin."

It's been a while since somebody called me by my surname. At Stone Hurst the teachers would only use our last names if we did something wrong. I saw Tyler sitting close to the front of the class, pointing to the seat he had saved next to him. I made my way, head down, trying not to make eye contact with any of my new classmates. Quietly, I sat down and took out my book. Mr Travis was rambling on about computing the derivative of some function, writing different equations on the board. It was not hard to tell that nobody was paying much attention to the lesson. Most of my classmates were whispering amongst themselves –

my name being repeated over and over again. They kept turning and staring.

"That's enough!" Mr Travis slammed his book on the desk, "Stop talking and concentrate! You'll be tested on this. Miss Gordon," he said, turning to Megan. He handed her the chalk. "Why don't you show everybody how well you understood Continuity and Differentiability? Why don't you come up to the board?"

As if struck dumb with astonishment, Megan looked around the class only to see that everybody was desperately holding back a laugh. "That's not fair, Mr Travis," she whined, in her ridiculously high pitched voice. "I wasn't the only one talking."

Holding the chalk like a cigarette between his stubby fingers, Mr Travis dismissively motioned for her to sit. Showing total indifference to her plea, he turned to the rest of the class, clearly disappointed. "Would anybody else like to take a crack at it?"

Tyler raised his hand. "I'll do it," he said and quickly went to the board.

It took him less than a minute to write the functions. Impressed, Mr Travis looked over Tyler's work and seeing that it was perfect continued on with the lesson. Afraid of being called up to the board everybody finally paid attention. I still got some side stares, but nothing out of the ordinary. As soon as Tyler sat back down I called him a nerd. He made a face and turned his attention to the lesson. I took some notes trying to concentrate – trying to ignore the fact that Megan and her evil friend Loraine kept looking my way passing notes back and forth.

The first-period bell finally rang.

"You did it, Caitlin. You survived first period, only six more to go," Tyler said, teasing me.

He knew how much I hated being there. We collected our

things and headed to English Lit. The halls were teeming with students rushing to their next class.

"Caitlin," she said. I couldn't believe my luck. Megan along with Loraine and Kim stopped me in the hall, "so you're going to finish senior High in Oaks after all?" Megan stated obnoxiously.

"It would seem that way," I answered, looking to Tyler for help, but he was engaged in another conversation with another student.

"We saw you at The Raven on Saturday night. But you left early. Were you okay?"

I tossed a stray bit of hair back, over my shoulder nervously. "I was a bit tired. I did only get in the night before." I said, trying to sound as placid as possible.

She must have known what happened. It was there in her voice. She was trying to point out the fact that I didn't belong with her kind, believing that I was not gifted like her.

"You were there with Tyler, right?"

I didn't answer

"So does that mean that you guys are – like going out?"

From the corner of my eye I saw Tyler turn in our direction. He obviously heard her comment and wanted to save me from the awkward scene.

"Caitlin, let's go," he said grabbing me by the arm. "We're going to be late. See you girls."

"Bye, Meg," I said waving to her, "loved our little chat. We'll talk later, okay? Bye, bye now." The distaste was etched on her ridiculously flawless complexion.

"Stop provoking her," Tyler said, tugging on my arm.

"Why? It's so much fun. That little bitch deserves a good smack across the face."

"Don't talk like that and don't say that word."

"I can't say 'bitch' – why?"

"I don't know. You're better than that."

"Bitch, bitch, bitch, bitch…." I turned and saw him rolling his eyes. "Okay! I'm sorry she just brings out the worst in me."

"Well then, don't stoop to her level."

He was making a good point. "According to Megan," I started to say, holding back the need to use the 'b' word again, "it would seem that we're an item, Tyler."

"I don't care what she thinks as long as she leaves you alone."

"I'm fine with it, don't worry."

Tyler's face lit up. "So you don't care if the whole school thinks that we're going out?"

"Why in the world would they care about who I date?" I looked at him baffled that anyone would take the time to mention me in casual conversation let alone talk about my love life.

"Caitlin, you're the hottest topic of the year. Everyone here wants to know everything about you."

"What's there to know?"

"You don't get it, do you?"

"Get what?"

"Caitlin, nobody in this school or better yet in this town has ever been outside Oaks for more than a couple of weeks. You on the other hand have lived among the non- gifted for five whole years."

"I haven't thought of it like that," I said in a state of mental numbness.

I was so absorbed in my misery these past five years that I didn't even consider what an extreme gesture it was for the Ellri to send me away. But then I had no gifts, they must have known that I was in no danger of being found out or able to hurt anyone.

Would they have done the same if I were someone as strong as Marc or Justin? I wondered.

"You'll just have to get used to the stares for the time being, until something more interesting occurs and everyone's attention is diverted elsewhere," Tyler said, trying to comfort me. "Now come on, we're going to be late for English Lit."

The day dragged on as all school days do, apart from the persistent stares and comments, it was not as bad as I thought it would be, but exhausting all the same. The sound of the last period bell rang like music to my ears.

"It's over," I muttered collecting my belongings.

Dying to get as far from school as possible; I jumped out of my seat and headed for my locker.

"Hold on, Caitlin, where do you think you're going?" Tyler was trying to catch up.

"I need to get out of here. I can't take another minute."

"I feel the same way, but I can't let you go just yet."

"Why? What do you mean?" I said, turning to him looking worried. "Is there something wrong?"

"No, nothing's wrong. I just have instructions to keep you here until most of the students are gone."

"You can't be serious." I looked at him in desperation. "How long will that take? I want to leave."

"Caitlin, don't look like that. It'll only take a few minutes. Do you really think that you're the only one who hates being here? Look around you, silly, we all feel exactly the same. Don't let the smiles fool you."

Tyler was always able to see the brighter side of things. He was always so positive it was good to have him in my corner. We sat on the stairs in the great entrance waiting for the school to empty. I could feel Justin waiting for me outside. My heart started beating faster by each agonizing minute we were apart.

"I don't think I need to ask why you're smiling," Tyler said, looking a bit glum.

I wasn't aware that I was smiling. "I'm just happy this day is over." I lied, knowing how uncomfortable he always was with my feelings for Justin.

"Spare me, Caitlin. Only one thing makes you smile like that, actually one person."

"I'm sorry Tyler it's just," I tried to explain it to him, but he cut me off by standing up and headed for the door. I followed, hating myself for making him feel bad.

Only a couple students remained hanging around outside, it was finally safe for me to exit the protective Shield of Knowledge. The fresh air in my lungs along with my astute awareness of Justin in the distance was rather welcoming.

"Don't," Tyler said turning to face me, "don't excuse your feelings to me. What kind of a friend would I be if I didn't want to see you happy? I'm not saying that I like the idea of you and him, I never did. But if he makes you smile than be it."

I simply stared at Tyler – was not sure how to react to such heartfelt words.

On impulse, I reached up and hugged him with all my strength causing Tyler to, unexpectedly, lose his balance and topple over with me right on top of him, laughing hysterically.

"I'm so sorry," I tried to say through the laughter. "I didn't mean to – did I hurt you?"

We helped each other straighten up. "I don't think it's me you hurt," Tyler said, looking toward the parking lot at Justin.

I could tell he was angry. The look Justin gave Tyler was menacing. "Don't worry, he's not mad, Caitlin. He simply wants to make sure you're not hurt," Tyler explained, excusing Justin's foul expression.

"I hate that you can all read each other's thoughts. I feel like an invalid."

"Trust me," Tyler said leading me in Justin's direction. "It's not as great as it seems."

Acting all mature and proper, we finally reached Justin. He was leaning against his car looking like a runway model preparing for a shoot. My blood was racing. I wanted nothing else but to run into his arms and melt in his kisses, but I contained my instinctual needs.

"Sweet car, can I take her for another ride sometime?" Tyler was admiring Justin's sleek black Audi S5, ignoring his foul mood. "Caitlin's not hurt, if that's what you're worried about," he continued to say avoiding eye contact. "She just knocked me off my feet as she always does." Tyler turned in my direction and winked.

"Falcone, make sure you're more careful next time or it'll be me doing the knocking," said Justin, not finding Tyler's pun at all amusing.

Tyler took a threatening step forward. "Yeah, well I'd like to see you try!"

Justin didn't budge, he simply stared at Tyler – sharing some thoughts of his own, I was certain.

"Grow up, both of you," I said, walking away, agitated by their incapability of being civil towards one another. In two long strides Justin blocked my path. "Where do you think you're going?"

"You're being ridiculous. I understand Tyler acting like an

infant. No offence Tyler," I said turning to look at him, making sure he was not offended by my remark.

Tyler simply waved me away turning his attention back to the sports car. "But I expect you to act your age."

Justin put his arms around my waist and pulled me to him with force. "So, what exactly does that entail, sweet, sweet Caitlin?" his voice low and full of promise.

"Stop patronizing me, Justin." I shoved him to the side to escape his alluring gaze. "You know I can't think when you're doing that."

"Fine, I see you're in no mood for fun." Justin said, shifting his gaze back to Tyler. "Do you need a lift home?" he asked my best friend.

"I parked in the back, thanks anyway. See you later, Caity," Tyler said, winking at me whimsically.

Tyler walked away and left me standing in front of the Audi stunned at how easily they both brushed aside their differences.

"How do you do that?"

"Do what?" Justin asked walking to the passenger's side of his car.

"A second ago you were both ready to rip each other's heads off and now you're all goody-goody with each other."

Justin held the door open. "C'mon Caity."

"You're incorrigible!"

"Don't you want me and Tyler to get along?"

"Of course I do, but...," I was about to sit when Justin pulled me into his arms and leaned me against the car.

"But nothing – I wanted to do this all day," he said, slowly leaning in to kiss me.

I couldn't feel anything except for his warm lips on mine. My body was on fire and my mind completely taken by storm. He stopped abruptly, smiling at my surprised expression.

"Now get in," he said with a wide, satisfied grin on his handsome face. "I want to show you something."

It took me a minute to collect my thoughts. "Where're we heading?" I asked, still spellbound by his kiss.

I could tell he was reading my thoughts because he had a smile on his face full of content and satisfaction.

"I wanted to show you this years ago, but I knew it was not my place to intervene. Leslie would have never allowed it.

"What is it?" I asked, being more curious now than ever. "Isn't she going to get mad?"

"So what if she does, Caitlin? What if they all do? They can't hurt me anymore than they already have. They used me to get to you. They manipulated what I felt to hurt you. I won't stand for it anymore."

ELEVEN

THE ESTATE

HE CEASELESS UNEASE that had been prodding at me since my return to Oaks veined through my mind like a nest of snakes. "Justin," I said shakily, "you're scarring me. The Ellri will find out about whatever you're planning on showing me. I want to get my answers – get to the bottom of this, but I won't risk you in the process. Nothing's worth that."

He took my hand and kissed it.

"Don't worry, they already know. They would've intervened by now if they didn't want me to show you. I thought about this place a lot as we were growing up, but with time I completely erased it from memory."

"Why now? Why would they want me to see it now?"

He gave me a sideway glance. "Last night out of nowhere I see it clear as day right in front of me. I knew it was not a dream. Somebody was guiding my mind. Only all the Ellri combined have that much power over me."

"Why would they do that?"

My stomach was churning. It seemed as though we had passed the town limits – we were too far from Oaks. It was the first time I ever headed in that particular direction. I didn't recognize anything. The forest was much denser now.

"Don't worry, we're still in Oaks – we'll be fine."

Justin took a left on a secluded road. I could just make out an opening up ahead and then there in front of us was a towering wrought iron gate not much different from Uncle Abbot's, but this one was more intricately designed. On both sides of the gate towering walls were erected to keep any intruder out. Justin turned off the engine and stared ahead in complete silence. I could tell he was worried and uncertain about taking me there.

"Where are we?" I asked "Who lives here?"

"Nobody lives here anymore," he said, turning to me, interlacing his fingers to mine and kissing the back of my hand.

It was a gesture of comfort not like the other kisses he had given me. I was profusely aware of how dire the situation was. I couldn't get this harrowing feeling to subside.

"There's nothing to fear," he said, responding to my anxiety. "Do you want to see what's behind the wall?"

I must have looked confused. The gate was locked with a formidable chain, approximately as thick as my arm.

He didn't expect us to climb over, did he?

"If you don't feel comfortable, we can go home." A smile finally appeared on his brilliant face.

"No," I answered, "I'm curious to see what the mystery is all about"

No sooner did I answer him than he turned to the gate and simply motioned it to open with his free hand. Instantly, the rusted chain dropped with a loud thud to the ground and the forlorn iron effortlessly opened on command, letting out a piercing sound of metal grinding against the rusted hinges.

Words had failed me.

"I told you, Caitlin my powers have grown since I ascended and are getting stronger day by day. You look spooked," he said squeezing my hand, "didn't mean to frighten you."

"I'm not afraid, Justin – not of you. I just didn't know you can do things like that."

"You'll be amazed what the mind can do once you harness its full potential," he said, sounding proud of his accomplishment.

"Apparently you have."

"Not at all, for the time being I'm limited to trivial things like what you just saw. But I haven't reached the stage of transcendence."

I looked at him questionably, "The Ellri said I transcend, but how can that be? I don't have any real gift."

"Caitlin, your ability to withstand dire circumstances is unfathomable. Your mind disappears and your heart almost stops completely. I don't know where you go, but it is amazing."

I simply looked at him. I didn't understand why he would consider my insignificant ability superior to his awesome power.

"The place I slip to – my solace is nothing compared to what you can do."

"You still don't get it," he said, lifting his hand to caress my cheek. "In order for me to reach your level of concentration and oneness with myself I would have to live two life times. You on the other hand haven't even ascended and can slip in and out any time you choose – controlling your every thought and emotion."

"I wouldn't say that. I have no control of my emotions."

I was still not sure why they all thought my gift was so special. Maybe they had misunderstood what I did exactly. Justin started the ignition and headed down the driveway.

"With time your gift will reveal itself as mine did, but first you need to accept it for what it is and let it evolve to its full capacity. You might not see it now as it is in its infant stage, but the power is growing inside of you and with each day it saturates your every cell until you have full control of it."

"I don't want to sound impatient, but how long might that take?" I know he heard the doubt in my voice.

"You'll see soon enough." He brought my hand up to his soft curvy lips and kissed it again. "You'll be exceptional."

Engrossed in our conversation, I hadn't noticed how picturesque the lush grounds were. There we were, greeted by a turnabout drive and a large sculptured fountain, smack dab in the middle. But years of neglect had veiled its once pristine magnificence.

Justin slowly pulled up to the pillared entrance. The luxurious manor was imaginatively conceived after Old World charm. Greco-Roman details abounded – Renaissance in proportion. The massiveness of the structure was overwhelming. He turned off the engine and got out of the car. I couldn't move. I was at a loss for words – at awe from the sheer splendour and beauty of the structure.

Justin came round and held the passenger door open.

"Would you like a look around?"

He took my hand and helped me out of the car.

"It's breath-taking isn't it?" he asked responding to my amazement.

"Aren't we going to see inside?" I said, finally able to structure a sentence.

"Not yet. Come on! I want to look around. I haven't been here for so long."

"Justin, what is this place to you? It must be really important.

But why now – why do the Ellri want you to see it now?" He stared at me not knowing how to word it. "To me it's absolutely nothing, but to you Caitlin, to you it's everything," he said warily.

I felt my face harden. "To me..?" I was stunned. I sat down not taking notice where. I just looked up at him dumfounded. "Why did you bring me here? Whose is this place?" My voice faltered at the end.

I sensed that what I was about to hear was not exactly good news. Justin stood in front of me unable to sit. He looked distraught – unable to find the appropriate words to say what he brought me there to say.

"Justin, the suspense is killing me. Out with it! Remember, I'm quite gifted when it comes to stressful situations. I can handle it," I said, trying to lighten up the mood.

I was actually petrified by his inability to say what he wanted. I knew it was serious. He took a deep breath as if he was going to jump off a cliff. "Caitlin, this belongs to members of the Korbs family."

"The Korbs? Wait – I thought that they had remained in Europe. What do the Korbs want in Oaks?"

"They are in Europe, but this estate belongs to a member of their family. It belongs to Winston and Carolyn Korbs," he said, looking at me to see if what he said registered.

"Okay, so, what does that have to do with me?" I asked confused. I didn't know what to do with the information he gave me.

Justin sat next to me, taking my hand in his. "Caitlin, I'm talking about Winston and Carolyn – your parents."

The minute the words left his mouth my blood froze. My world started spinning. "My parents – Korbs – Justin you must be mistaken. My parents are Winston and Carolyn Cathcart. What do they have to do with the Korbs?"

"I'm not sure. I don't know all the details. What I do know is that when your father and mother moved here from Europe your father took the Cathcart name in order to cut himself off from his lineage. I can't tell you much more than that because I simply don't know anything else, but the Ellri surely know more."

I shook my head trying to make sense of what he said. "Why would it bother my father what his last name was?"

"I think he did it to protect you in a way. Perhaps he did it to deter you from asking questions about the Korbs family. Honestly Caitlin, I'm not sure why they would keep your ancestry a lie."

My mind couldn't wrap itself around the idea of why somebody would keep this from me. "I'm a Korbs?" I asked, baffled by the uncertainty.

"Yes, your birth name is Caitlin Eileen Korbs," he said, barely audible.

He was trying his hardest not to shock me. But everything he revealed was quite distressing.

I looked at him wide-eyed "How do you know all this and I don't?"

"Let's just say I did a little mind searching of my own growing up. The Ellri are not the only ones who can dig around, soul searching for information," he said, kissing my hand. "Your first and middle name are derived from old Celtic names meaning 'pure light'. It always made sense to me," he said smiling magnificently. "Every time I looked at you, I lit up like a light bulb."

I giggled. Justin was trying to add humour to an otherwise

difficult situation. His attempt at being funny in the most awkward circumstances was noteworthy.

"This is all too much," I said, cradling my head in my hands, unable to believe what I was hearing. I had a thousand questions to ask, but I didn't know where to start. "Why didn't Aunt Leslie tell me all this after my parents passed away?"

"I don't know. Your parents moved out of this house and in with your Uncle Abbot a few months before you were born. Everybody in town believed that your mother wanted to be with her sister during her pregnancy, closer to the town center. I know I'm not making much sense, but I'm telling you everything I know."

"I'm a Korbs? How can that be?" I felt absolutely nothing – sat there in utter shock, questioning my entire existence. "So, let me get this straight. Basically," I started to say looking up at him, "what you're telling me is that my life has been a complete fabrication. I'm not a Cathcart as I once thought but a Korbs and my whole name is Caitlin Eileen – Korbs? Stop me anytime you feel I've missed something." I said, trying to sound sarcastic.

"I know this must be hard, but you needed to know the truth. I couldn't keep something this important from you."

"They should've said something, Justin."

"Don't beat yourself up over it. It's just a name. I'm sure when you ask Leslie and Abbot they'll give you all your answers."

I stood up and breathed in deep. "I have a feeling that it's much, much bigger than a mere name."

For some reason there was a part of me that was not at all surprised to find out that my world was not what I thought it was. I had many questions growing up about my parents especially my father and Abbot's kinship. Both man bearing the same surname, but having absolutely no hint of resemblance. It was strange really. I always believed that they must have been distant relatives of sorts.

"I didn't want to be the one to tell you because I don't have the answers you need, but last night the visions were all too clear, Caitlin. I knew they wanted me to bring you here."

There was not much Justin could do to help make things smoother. I knew deep down that he felt helpless – wanting to rid me of all this rubbish.

"I was summoned back to Oaks for a reason. Crying about it isn't going to get me my answers." My head was spinning faster. So few questions had been answered in comparison to how many had been raised.

"Don't worry," he reassured me. "You're not alone in this. Not anymore. We'll figure all this out."

"Five years, Justin. Five years of wondering what I did wrong. It couldn't have been them, I thought. No, not them – they were all perfect, raising me with so much love. I must've done something wrong. It must've been me, right?"

I was simply thinking out loud. Justin listened quietly.

"Five years of beating myself up, and all for what, for a name?"

I looked at him with tears in my eyes.

"Why would they need to keep my last name from me?" I shook my head finding it impossible to comprehend. "The thing that frightens me most, Justin is this ominous feeling that is eating me up inside. It's much more, it has to be. It's much bigger than my name – than what we share."

He reached out and took me in his arms and kissed me on the forehead. "There's nothing in this world more powerful than what we have. You need to remember that."

I stretched my hands around Justin's neck and pulled myself up to kiss him. His lips melted into mine. The sweet sensation ran through my body flooding me with his every touch. No bond could be this strong – cause such unbridled feelings.

His every muscle tightened around me, holding me even closer. "We'll get through this I promise," he said, kissing me again this time more tender and loving. "Caitlin," he said loosening his hold. "Do you want to see the inside of your house?"

Justin let go and strolled towards the entrance.

I suddenly felt completely drained and pale with the thought of entering my parent's home. I couldn't think. I was suddenly rooted to the spot. I was not fully ready to face the truth not now, not this soon.

My mind needed more time to work through all the emotions. My chest suddenly constricted and I could feel myself losing the ground under me. I felt Justin's hands catching me just as I was about to fall. He carried me to the car and helped me in.

"Simply breathe, Caitlin," his voice sounded strained. "I'm so sorry. This was too much for any one person to handle. We'll come back another time."

He buckled me in, and went round to the driver's side and started the engine. I was completely still. I didn't know what to feel. We were already on the dirt road leaving behind my past.

A loud clank broke the silence. I turned to the side-view mirror and saw the colossal wrought iron gate close behind us on Justin's command.

The drive back was rather quiet. I looked out the side window wondering what everything meant. It was the onset of November, and the sky was a high, pale blue. A brilliant, low winter sun irradiated the surrounding area.

Opening the window to get a better view, a flood of air as clear, sharp and cold as a bucket of ice hit my face. I smiled a weak smile, my eyes streaming with the chill and sudden awareness that I didn't know who I was anymore.

Justin didn't say a word, looking straight ahead not knowing how to console me. He took an unexpected right hand turn instead of going straight. "Where are we heading?" I asked. "My house," he answered. "The Ellri are at Abbot's having another meeting. It's best you confront them at a later time. You're not up to it now."

He parked the car and came to help me out. "I'm fine," I told him. "Don't worry. It's just that everything came at me all at once. I'll be fine," I repeated wanting to reassure him.

Justin took my hand and walked me up the steps to the grand entrance. The house was a pivotal point in my life. It was those steps I kneeled on pleading with Justin to help me five years ago.

I loved everything about the French inspired home. The stone building with its hipped roofs and flared eaves was elegantly proportioned. It was testament to Shannon's class and style. The French doors across the front were welcoming with one lantern flanking on either side of the entrance. The landscaping was also done to emphasise her love for symmetry.

Once inside, Justin led me to the kitchen. "We need to get something in that stomach of yours. I don't want you fainting on me again," he said, rummaging the fridge.

"There must me something wrong with me. I never fainted before I came to Oaks. Now it seems that's all I've been doing."

He chuckled. "You'll be fine."

In no time at all he whipped out a whole array of different dishes – leaving me wide eyed in surprise. "Don't look so impressed. My mother prepared all this for later on tonight. Now, stop staring at me."

"I can't believe I'm not a Cathcart." I heard myself say out loud.

"Justin, what am I going to do? How am I supposed to be angry at Aunt Leslie and Uncle Abbot?"

He didn't speak – allowed me to get everything off my chest.

"I'm not really mad about them sending me away. I'm indebted to them for raising me after my parents'...,"

I breathed deeply.

"But how can I forgive them for keeping my identity from me?"

"You don't have to be angry at anyone," he said, reaching for my hand "This is the way life is sometimes. We have to work with the hand we're dealt. Leslie has done, I'm sure, everything she can to protect you from whatever this is. You'll need to find the strength to face them. It's time you knew the whole truth."

"It won't be good."

"There is nothing bigger or more painful than the truth, Caitlin. But that doesn't mean we turn away from it because it suits us better to be in denial."

I have never taken the time to think about how articulate Justin was – wise and eloquent beyond his years. I knew it was because his parents were much older when they had him. I figured the formal upbringing had something to do with it.

Justin held my bandaged hand playing with my fingers.

"We'll get to the bottom of this soon enough" he said, sounding distant, thoughtful of how things might turn out. He reached over and kissed me on the lips. It was short and sweet, but enough to get my heart beating a mile a minute.

Before The Storm

Illustrated for Lines That Bind - Circle Of Trust

TWELVE

BROKEN IN TWO

 ELPING JUSTIN CLEAN UP, I leaned over the kitchen counter to reach the cupboard in order to put away the last cup when, unexpectedly, he took the glass from my hand and effortlessly placed the item in its rightful place. I was trapped between the counter and his well-defined body – alarmingly aware of his closeness.

A few minutes passed with neither of us moving. My back to him, I could feel his breath on my hair. Justin pushed a handful of strands to the side, exposing the back of my neck. Leaning in, he traced soft kisses up and down, causing my heart to flutter.

I turned to face him and ran my fingers through his hair, pulling him in for a kiss. Justin's mouth was warm and wanting. I could feel his heart beat against my chest as he pulled me taut against his body. I didn't want the feeling to ever stop.

"I can't seem to get enough of you," I heard him say, trying to catch his breath. I pushed myself even closer wanting to satisfy his need. Justin hesitantly broke away – pulling himself back.

I just stood there. "What is it?" I asked, longing for his touch.

"My parents are on their way," he said, reluctantly, taking another step back. "The meeting must've finished for the night," he added, pulling me back into his embrace. "Its best they don't find you here."

"They probably already know I'm here. I should talk to them," I answered, refusing to give into his request – kissing his chin and then his lips.

"Of course they know you're here, but you don't need to go into this right now. You need to have a clear head if you want to get all your answers."

This time it was me that broke from his hold – irritated at his persistence. "I'm not going to hide from any of them Justin. I haven't done anything wrong. They're the ones who owe us explanations not the other way round."

"Look," he said persuasively, "I know you want this all out in the open, but today has been a bit much, don't you think? First school, and now this – you need to learn your limits, Caitlin. Tomorrow everything will be clearer and you won't be ruled by your emotions."

I knew he was right. I was acting impulsively not looking at the bigger picture. I needed to get my answers, but one more day was not going to change anything. I lived eighteen years without knowing the truth; I surely could survive one more night.

I circled my head to the sound of Shannon and William entering the house. The overwhelming respect I had for Justin's parents was what kept me from sneaking out the back door. "I'm going, but only the same way I came in," I said, planting a quick kiss on his sweet lips.

His displeasure was marked on his disapproving expression. "It doesn't need to be like this. It can wait."

"I'm not going to say a thing. I promise."

He raised a brow of apprehension.

"I swear, not a word."

"This I have to see," he said smiling, taking my hand.

He led me to the foyer where his parents stood, taking off their coats. "What were you kids up to today?" Shannon asked, knowing all too well the answer.

I held my breath and tightened my grip around Justin's hand. He sensed my anguish and walked me closer to the door, making for an easier escape – completely ignoring his parents. Within a fraction of a second he suddenly stopped inches from the exit, releasing his tight hold. He stood there in eerie silence, invoking an onslaught of fear on my part.

"What is it?" I whispered.

He didn't answer. Instead, he snapped his head round to face his parents.

"Save it mother," he grunted, staring right at her, "she's had enough for one day."

I knew there was more to his words. I couldn't hear a word they were saying, but Shannon's furious expression was a clear indication of how volatile Justin's thoughts were.

"You had no right, Justin," she finally spoke, "It's not your place to intervene.

"Like hell it isn't," he barked, "I have every right to help Caitlin figure this out."

In that fleeting moment, Shannon glanced over to William and then back to Justin, exhibiting the most severe of looks. "Don't think for a moment that you know what's best for her. You have no idea what this is."

Justin's anger was escalating, as was the indefinable feeling of terror that infiltrated my thoughts, and then came excruciating pain. Suddenly, my breath was caught in my throat as I was about to scream from sheer agony. Justin snapped his head round to face me, startled, attentive and, it was easy to tell, very much afraid.

"Caitlin? What the hell is going on?"

I had no voice to answer. Something was shifting deep within, something so fierce that it altered my state of mind. My scar was tearing right through me with malice, triggering uncontrollable tears to stream down my face.

"Caitlin!" Justin yelled, displaying a strained expression. His parent's didn't move, not one inch.

There was absolutely nothing I could do to diminish the pain. I tried to concentrate as I did on numerous occasions, but this was new, different. I was overpowered, thrown to my knees; experiencing a rapid onset of something deadly, sharp and acute. My wrist felt like it was on fire, burning me to the core.

"Make it stop," I begged, looking at both Ellri.

Justin tried to approach, but there was some kind of barrier between us. Something or someone was holding him back.

"Justin, it hurts, please make it stop," I wailed, unable to restrain the blood-curdling pain.

He attempted to take a step forward, but William pulled him to a stop. "Don't Justin," he said, in an authoritative voice. "It must take its course."

I didn't know what he meant – I didn't care. In the hopes of extinguishing the burn, I fervidly unwrapped the gauze from my wrist. It didn't make the slightest difference. Whatever it was, I was meant to bear the full brunt; no mercy would be spared. There was a long, painful silence as I looked pleadingly toward Justin, a silence that pulsed with fear and tension. In that moment, only a very brief moment, Justin broke from his father's hold and quickly came to my side.

"Everything will be alright, Caitlin," he said, only inches away.

I reached out my scarred hand wanting to hold his for comfort.

"No Justin! Don't." I heard Shannon's worry laden voice echo through the hall. Don't!" she screamed.

Before she could even finish her warning, Justin took hold of my hand. The second our skin came into contact my spine jolted back; felt as if I was snapped in two. My screams were muted by the consuming rush of adrenalin that coursed through my blood stream. A surge of energy so fierce and pure accumulated in my wrist that to my horror, an inexplicable force passed through my hand and into Justin, propelling us apart, catapulting him yards away; landing him on the floor with a back-breaking thud.

"Justin!" I screamed, fearing that I hurt him. "Justin," I wailed again waiting for a response.

"What the hell was that?" I heard him say, more annoyed than in pain. "Caitlin? Caitlin? Are you alright?"

Crouching and writhing in pain, I couldn't answer through the tears. I had my head in my knees as my body shook violently. The fear came, not so much from the events themselves as from the way that they occurred, unexpectedly and for the most part, uncontrollably. Just then, I felt a cool breeze rush in through the front door. I raised my head slightly, only to see the Ellri filing in, one by one. To see all eighteen of them together, was rather disturbing. My fear suddenly culminated, outweighing the tremors and pain.

My uncle and aunt stood motionless at the entrance, looking surprisingly calm, too calm considering what I was going through. None of them spoke. Standing shoulder to shoulder, they formed a tight circle, encompassing both Justin and I.

"Please, Aunt Leslie, it's killing me," I implored. "What's happening to me? Please, do something. It's killing me,"

She stood there like a statue in deafening silence.

Didn't she care?

"Aunt Leslie, PLEASE!"

Justin sat on his heels a few feet away. His beautiful face seemed as strained as mine was. Was I doing this to him? Was I dragging him down with me?

"Justin? What's happening?" I asked in agony.

"Caitlin, you need to concentrate," Uncle Abbot said, not waiting for Justin to respond.

My wrist was on fire and my heart thudded vigorously, pressing against my chest, constricting my supply of air. "Justin?" I wheezed, needing to know that he'd be alright.

"Concentrate, Caitlin," Shannon said in distress. "You're going to kill each other if this continues much longer. Please child."

I couldn't believe my ears – she was pleading for her son's life. I looked away from Justin's intense stare, it was crippling me. The possibility of any harm coming to him quickened my heart beat, everything suddenly came into focus. I folded my hands around my knees, hugging myself tight – closing my eyes in the process. I dropped my head so I couldn't see the hurt in Justin's eyes. At that split second I felt the earth open. Everyone disappeared and everything went black. At first I had thought that I must have fainted, but then why was I conscious? *My solace,* I thought – *must've slipped into my abyss unintentionally.*

On other occasions I was more comfortable there, but unlike

other times, the pain didn't cease, it had followed me to the depths of my inner world. I took in deep breaths and tried to erase the uncomfortable feeling, but nothing seemed to work.

My thoughts were of Justin. If anything were to happen to him my life would be over. I shuddered at the thought of the agony imprinted on his face. My pain intensified all the more at the mere thought of endangering him.

"Concentrate child and regain control of yourself," I heard a faint whisper within a whisper say.

I was in the presence of brilliance. *The fourth heartbeat*, I thought. Its energy radiated in my darkness. Even though I couldn't see it, I felt it in every pore of my soul. The whisper was neither female nor male. It was like a melody carried in the wind. Breathy and slow, it slid sweetly between notes, but with skilfulness that suggested the seeming lack in tone was intentional.

"I can't, it's too much for me to handle," I cried.

"If he is your life than he is worth fighting for." The whisper was now clearer even closer.

"It's the burn. I can't seem to extinguish it. It's too much. I don't even know what I'm doing or even how I'm doing it."

"You need to decide if his life is worth the burden of your bond."

Was the voice giving me an ultimatum?

"What are you saying?"

"It's your choice, child."

I was now in pain and confused. "I don't understand. What choice?"

Then came silence, and then, even more, brain-numbing silence.

"You need to focus. Focus and choose whether Justin is worth the anguish your bond is putting you through. He might feel the intensity, but you carry the burden. It is your choice and your choice alone." For a space in time I remained silent, unable to speak from the shock.

"You can choose to cut this line that binds you to him ones and for all. The choice is yours, young mortal."

"You're having me choose between feeling this pain and Justin's life? His life is my life," I said, swallowing back the intense emotion. "I refuse to live in a world without him. I'd sooner suffer than cut this thing that binds me to him."

I felt its radiance on my face "Then learn to curb your gift, tame it before it breaks both of you."

I felt weak and beaten. "Justin – all I care about is Justin. He needs to be okay, he needs to be well."

A soft, breathless caress brushed across my cheek and then nothing – absolute silence.

Long moments later, in the midst of my agony, I felt the same soft touch on my wrist. In seconds, the pain disappeared, replaced by a serene euphoria.

"Your gift is in transition and learning to control your power is paramount. If you continue to spiral out of control, you will hurt the one thing you cherish most. Next time we will not be there to hold your hand. You will have to suffer the consequences."

"Who are you?" I asked.

"You have a lifetime ahead of you, don't fret about trivial matters. Your balance and peace of mind should be your only concern. Get your answers and act wisely, Caitlin Eileen," said the whisper within the whisper as it faded into my darkness.

Sinking to my knees, I waited until the whirling shadows that had seemed to be closing in around me began to lighten. I could see them clearly now, standing around the bed, looking down on my motionless body.

They must have moved me, I thought.

My aunt's face was taut and severe, holding back her true emotions – her hand in Uncle Abbot's. I looked around the room, and there, lying next to me was my life – my purpose for being.

The color from Justin's face had faded, leaving his skin as thin and transparent as air. Justin's face was cold and expressionless; his body stiff. He looked fragile and distant. The revelation of his appearance shook me to the core.

"Justin!" I screamed, feeling as if surfacing from the depths of the darkest sea. Catching air in my lungs was painful and my mouth was on fire. "I can't breathe," I said through gasps of air.

The commotion was deafening. The Ellri hovered over me, looking perplexed at my features.

"Caitlin, try to relax. Breathe short deep breaths. That's my girl. Now, are you in any pain?" Aunt Leslie said, holding my hand "You scared us, sweetie."

"Justin, what's the matter with Justin?" I asked, trying to inhale at each syllable.

"He'll be fine. It was a bit much for the both of you."

"Shannon? Is he really going to be alright?" I asked, knowing she would give me an honest answer.

"His perfectly fine – stubborn – but fine."

I leaned over and kissed him on the lips – ignoring everybody around us. His skin was nothing like I remembered. The warmth was replaced with cold hardness.

I turned to Shannon in wrenching remorse. "Did I do this to him?"

"No Caitlin. You were out for so long that he exhausted his power reading you – trying to find you."

"What do you mean long? I was out for only a few minutes. Why would you say I was out for 'so long' when I wasn't? "

My uncle came and sat next to me on the bed. "I don't want to frighten you child, but you should know that it's Wednesday afternoon. You've been out for almost two whole days."

"That can't be. How can that be?"

William circled his arm around Shannon's shoulders. "The Nobe know no time, child. Each second you spend with them can be a life time for us."

"The Nobe?" I asked completely stunned. "William, the whisper was a Nobe?"

Aunt Leslie motioned to the Ellri. "She needs her rest. Let's all leave them be for now." She perched on the side of the bed and planted a sweet peck me on the cheek "You can stay till he wakes, it shouldn't take long. We'll be downstairs with Shannon and William. If you need anything just call."

"Aunt Leslie, about my name…,"

"You need your rest now Caitlin, all in due time," she said, kissing me again this time on the forehead. "I'll be downstairs."

THIRTEEN

INTO DARKNESS

I WAS PROPPED UP with a pillow, revelling in Justin's perfection – he was flawless in every way. With each passing minute the color slowly returned to his cheeks. Tucking myself under the covers, I nestled my body next to his, needing his touch to calm my nerves. I let my fingers trace the contours of his sculptured face savouring everything about him.

"Come back Justin," I whispered, burying myself in his chest, taking in his intoxicating scent. I closed my eyes and cuddled up next to him – waiting for him to surface from his deep trans. "Come back," I kept repeating, hoping that he could hear.

Less than an hour later, I heard Justin's weak voice say my name. "Caitlin?"

"I'm right here."

His sweet voice was shredded and frail – barely audible but harmonious to my ears. I pulled slightly back to get a good look at his face. His complexion was warmer now, more alive than before.

Justin pulled me against him – crushing me against his hard body.

"Don't ever leave me again," he said through the exhaustion.

"Are you okay? You scared me to death, Justin."

"You were the one without a heartbeat for the last two days and you're asking me if I'm okay?" His voice was strained, but he conjured up a sweet smile.

"I don't care about my heart; it's yours I'm concerned about. Don't you dare do a stupid thing like that, ever again," I said, chocking up. "If anything had happened to you I don't know what I would have done." Tired as he was; he lazily swept my hair from my face and caressed me. "Get some rest," I said, trying to keep my breathing steady from his touch.

He coaxed my head up to face him. Even more tired now he kissed me softly on the lips and whispered, "I love you, Caitlin."

I leaned in and kissed him, holding back the tears in the realization that he was able to put into words what I was willing to lose my life over.

His body gave into the enervation and carried him off to sleep. Quietly, I slipped out of bed taking care not to wake him.

My legs were lethargic from the day's events. Unable to move from the numbness, I stood motionless till the feeling subsided. My eye caught sight of the small bandage on my right wrist that hid the rawness of my scar.

Light-headed as I was, I slowly made my way downstairs to meet the others. Uncle Abbot was waiting for me at the foot of the stairs anticipating my arrival and said, "Come Caitlin, it's time we got you home."

The drive home was only minutes away, but the quiescent silence was full of tension. I had so many questions to ask, but no will to ask them. I pressed my forehead up against the window and let the cold soothe the flame under my skin. I stared out into the darkness wondering where I go from there. Being eighteen in a few days, I had hoped that I would at least have some things figured out. Such days, I felt all alone – nestled in my own little cocoon, unaware of the dangers that surrounded me.

How could I be expected to look forward to something when there is no forward to go? Yet looking back would seem wiser. But back to what? The misery of not knowing who I was anymore submerged me to unfathomable depths. The eerie feeling of something horrific looming ahead was imbedded in my subconscious. I needed to get to the bottom of what this gloom was veiling.

With her arm around me, my aunt led me to my room and helped me change for bed. My limp body shifted under the covers trying to find a cosy position for the night. Just then I noticed the black circles under her pain-stricken eyes. I seized the opportunity offered by her closeness and reached for her hand.

"Sorry if I scared all of you," I said.

She looked at me lovingly, as she did when I was little. "Nonsense Caitlin, you did what you had to do. Your gift is rearing its head rather quickly, affecting both you and Justin. No apologies are warranted for saving both your lives. I just wish," she stopped in mid-sentence, not wanting to continue, not at this time anyway. "Get some sleep sweetie. You've been through enough."

She tucked me in and brushed her lips on my forehead.

"Do I have to go to school tomorrow?" I asked changing the subject to lighten the mood.

She smiled knowing all too well how much I loathed going. "I've arranged for you to return on Monday. Tyler can tutor you on the things you'll miss this week. Now get some sleep."

Opening the door I glanced up and down the street. Seeing that the coast was clear, I slipped out into the night traversing a cobbled path and entered a winding labyrinth- type structure. The walls were high and the smell in the air was pungent. There was decay all around me – death and despair hung in the putrid surroundings.

Immediately, the darkness enveloped me as I moved through the paths unheard and unseen. Just then, I heard footsteps behind me. That moment, I turned round hoping against hope that I was mistaken, but knowing I wasn't.

Through the darkness, I could barely make out the villainess silhouettes of two faceless beings. I realized that they were there to do me harm. I quickened my pace. To my horror, the footsteps quickened too, they seemed to be gaining on me.

With my heart in my mouth unable to breathe I felt the cold sweat trickle down my face. My pace was fast, but theirs was faster. It was then that I lost my balance and fell to the muddy ground. I tried to get up but couldn't find my footing. They were getting closer and fast.

Finally, on my feet once more I ran and turned in all directions trying to lose them in the maze of walls that towered over me on both sides, but I felt them on my back – could feel their closeness against the hairs on the back of my neck and then a touch....

I opened my eyes startled. "It was only a dream. Just a dream," I kept repeating breathing in hard. I shook my head trying to erase the images from memory. I never had a nightmare before. Its effect on me radiated through my whole torso cringing at the mere thought of those beings. The silhouettes in my dream were so real so sinister.

I was sure it was the result of all the anxiety and stress of those couple of days. My mind and body were surely responding to the chaos, that is what I believed at the time, anyway.

Still dark outside, I turned to the side for sleep to take me. It was useless. Restless all night I tossed and turned, opening my eyes every few hours. My mind refused to give in completely.

The morning light finally, peered in my window feeling warm and comfy against my drowsy face. The sun was finally out, but I didn't have the strength or will to get out of bed. The knock on the door was welcoming. I didn't want to be stuck there all alone.

Aunt Leslie came in holding a tray with breakfast. "Good morning? Did you get any rest?"

I tried circling my head to look at her, but my neck was dreadfully rigid as was the rest of my body.

"Aunt Leslie I can hardly feel my arms and legs, why is that?" I asked, trying to push myself in an upright position.

Instinctively, she placed the tray on my nightstand and propped up the pillow, supporting my back and helped me get comfortable. "Having experienced so much strain with your transcendence, you'll feel weak for a day or two."

"Great!"

"What did you expect? For two whole days your body was motionless; in a comatose state. It's only natural you feel drained."

"Why does my body respond so violently? Why does my heart have to stop?" I asked needing at least this explanation for now.

"When you transcend it requires endless supply of energy. Your body compensates by draining just enough of your life-force to bear its undertaking. As your power grows the transition will become effortless. Your heart doesn't actually stop completely it slows to a deathly pace. This permits your body to relax and reach the place of awareness you call your *solace*. It's truly a fascinating gift." she explained looking ridiculously proud of my ability. So many questions were churning in my mind making it impossible to file them in order of importance.

"Why was my pain so forceful and severe compared to other times? It wasn't merely my reaction to Justin's anger that triggered all this, was it?"

She perched herself on the bed, realizing I had many questions needed answering. "Justin had a minor role to play. Your bond allows you to share the deepest emotions, but it does not define either of you. The immense pain you felt that day was not Justin's doing. You are slowly ascending and your powers are escalating at an unusual rate," she said wiping my hair to the side. "Your capacity to endure that much power that particular moment was minimal so involuntarily your body took over your mind and slipped you into transcendence, allowing you time to deal with the occurrence. You simply had, what the non-gifted call, a fainting spell. But multiply it by infinity and you'll get a rough idea of what you experienced"

Unintentionally, I stared at Aunt Leslie looking absolutely terrified. She lifted her hand and cupped my face in reassurance. "It's nothing to fear sweetie, your natural abilities are growing and evolving. There's nothing greater than reaching your full potential as a human. The gifted and the non-gifted alike all strive in life to reach a stage where they know that they have done all they could to achieve greatness. It comes in different stages in our life. With each human experience, difficult or not, we develop – enhancing our endurance to pain and learning our personal limits. There is nothing greater than our natural instinct to persevere in the direst situations. That's what makes us all human."

I was suddenly feeling better about my predicament. It was nice to know that I was not the only one faced with personal demons. The thought that everyone in the world could tackle their problems somehow reinforced my willingness to tackle mine.

"Aunt Leslie, when Justin reached out and touched me why was the force so violent that it threw him back?'

She fumbled with the sheets – creasing them just right. "He should've known better than to approach you. You could've both been permanently hurt." Her eyes were shadowed by her dark thoughts. "Fainting," she finally said smiling, "is not your only gift, Caitlin. You are capable of titanic feats. Your body and mind simply responded with great control, knowing that if he came any closer you could've easily killed him."

I gasped.

She smiled. "So, you see Caitlin, being tossed a few feet was actually circumventing imminent doom."

Shivers ran down my spine at the thought of ever causing harm to Justin.

"Slowly you will be able to manipulate your gifts. The Ellri are all very proud of your self-control. Even in your critical state, two nights ago, you were able to defuse the potency of your power. You shouldn't take your gift lightly Caitlin, if not contained you can cause harm to those around you."

I looked at her in horror. Her words amplified my insecurity. "How am I supposed to control this? I don't even know what this is."

She took my hand and placed it over my heart. "This will guide you," she said. "Never doubt yourself, Caitlin. The Ellri will assist you in learning how to channel your power. But it is your heart that will pilot the control needed in each situation.

Don't ever question it – let it guide you."

She picked up the glass of orange juice from the tray and held it up to my mouth – I took a sip. The liquid burned its way down my throat causing me to cringe from discomfort.

"You have to eat to regain your strength. Stop acting like a baby and drink," she said, forcing me to consume the content of the glass. She was back to being Aunt Leslie again. There was no arguing with her when it came to our wellbeing. As soon as I took a bite of the toast, she had another something waiting to stuff in my mouth. I was full and content. "That's my girl," she said. "I'll be downstairs if you need me."

She dusted off the covers, carefully collecting any crumb that might have fallen. Tray in hand, she was about to leave when my question stopped her dead. "Aunt Leslie – about my parents?"

"Your health is what is important now and everything else can wait. You'll get your answers soon enough. But you and Justin must allow us to do what we think is right. Each decision is crucial for all of us, Caitlin. Justin had no right taking you there."

"But he thought…."

She didn't allow me to finish. She simply headed for the door. "All in good time, Caitlin, now get some rest."

I pushed my body under the covers again and closed my eyes trying to sleep. "Caitlin Eileen," I heard myself say, still not believing my ears. I closed my eyes and drifted off to sleep.

A little while later the sound of someone being in my room forced my eyes open "Wake up, Caitlin," she said, arousing me from sleep. Emily's voice had woken me. I looked around – stretching my arms not knowing where I was.

"How long have I been sleeping, Em?" I asked, confused and disoriented.

"Well, let's just say long enough. It's Friday morning and you need to get out of bed to get your blood circulating."

"Not again!" I was at a loss for words, "Friday? That can't be, can it? Was I asleep that long?"

"It would appear so, now get up!"

She pulled the covers off and pushed my legs to the floor. They felt perfectly normal – the numbness I felt the previous morning was gone. Emily helped me up, but I was fine – quite able to fend for myself.

"I got it!" I said, turning to her gratefully.

"Do you need any help getting ready? A nice bath would do you good."

"I'm not up for a bath, but I'll take a quick shower to freshen up. Now stop hovering and let me be. Didn't you have classes or something this week?"

She let go of my hand and sat in the armchair at the far end of my room. "I told you I'd be back on Thursday. I came late last night with Kyle." She looked at me more serious than before. "Caitlin, you gave me a scare last night, you know."

"Me? How? What do you mean? Wasn't I asleep?"

"You were talking in your sleep, unintelligible to me, but you seemed to be in some sort of distress. Mom came and eased your restlessness, but it was still a bit scary."

"Really – I'm sorry if I frightened you. I – I don't remember anything from last night."

She was up on her feet again going through my dresser, pulling clothes out for me to wear. "We definitely need to do some shopping. This is appalling." She was referring to my collection of casual jeans and sweats.

"I like my clothes!" I exclaimed defending my personal style.

"Fine, wear what you like, but I'm going shopping this

weekend and you're getting a new wardrobe."

"You don't need to do that Emily, seriously"

Next to her, stashed in the corner, was a large cardboard box. "What's that?" I asked, pointing to the object hidden well in the corner of my room.

"It's your stuff form Stone Hurst. It arrived on Tuesday while you were completely out of it."

"It figures! My whole life fits in one box. Sad, isn't it Em?"

"Your life is here with the people who love you. This box is only some of your material belongings. Don't get the two confused, Caitlin. You can do without the one, but not without the other."

"I know. You're right."

"I'm always right," she said smiling. "Anyway, hurry up and get ready. I don't know how long Kyle can keep Justin from coming up here."

"Justin's downstairs? Wait, why didn't I sense him?"

She shrugged her shoulders.

"Don't worry! I'm sure you'll be back to normal in no time."

I lit up just thinking of him. My heart started beating quicker at the thought that I'll be seeing him again.

"He wants to come up, but dad's dead set against it. He said that too many house rules have already been broken."

"He didn't actually say that, did he?"

"Well, he didn't verbalize it if that's what you mean. His thoughts were loud and clear, nevertheless. Poor Justin is sitting on pins and needles."

I rushed to the bathroom to take a quick shower. I could hear Emily laughing at my eagerness. The water was invigorating. I let it soak me a little longer than usual. With my hair pulled back I wore my jeans and sweater and rushed downstairs. There were familiar voices coming from the den so I slowed my pace and controlled my breathing so as not to seem so excited at seeing Justin.

"Come in child," Uncle Abbot said.

I was about to take my seat when Kyle picked me up and started hugging me. "Caitlin, welcome back from the dead," he said with a chuckle. "I was so worried."

I could see Uncle Abbot didn't find it funny, "Enough Kyle, let her go," he said with a demanding voice.

"Yeah Kyle, let her go!" I heard Justin's threatening tone

Kyle kissed me on the cheek and grimaced. "I was just having fun."

"I know," I said, giving him a bear hug. "I'm glad you and Emily are back."

"Of course we're back you didn't think we were going to miss the party, did you?"

Then it dawned on me. *The party is tomorrow, I'm finally turning eighteen.* "It's going to be a small family affair, right Kyle?" I asked fishing for details.

"You need to ask Em. I have no idea."

Visibly tired of our childish conversation, Uncle Abbot got up, shaking his head in annoyance at today's youth. "I'll be in my study," he said, picking up his cigar and headed to the door.

In no time at all Justin picked himself off the leather sofa and took me in his arms twirling me around kissing me on the nose amusingly. It was so nice to see his smile again, but even though I was exhilarated about being there with him, I was not able to fully allow myself to enjoy the moment; something was dragging my mood through the mud. Without releasing his hold, Justin turned to his best friend and pointed to the door.

"I know when I'm not wanted," Kyle said showing off his pearly whites in one of his devious smiles.

"Don't let the door hit you in the ass," Justin answered laughingly.

With everyone gone bit by bit Justin leaned in to give me one of the most precious gifts he could ever give me – himself. His lips were soft and sultry. I held his face with my hands pulling him down harder on my mouth.

Wrapping his arms around me he pulled me up against his chest and continued to kiss me gently. His breathing was much heavier now and more passionate.

"Don't you dare leave again," he said under his breath continuing to kiss me.

I pulled back just a little wanting to gaze into his beautiful deep blue eyes when out of nowhere deep seeded emotions of great sadness and sorrow deluged my thoughts. There was no controlling the sudden realization that nothing came without a price. *What would be the cost for loving him so much?* I suddenly thought, having everything else in my life turned upside down. A tear rolled down my face betraying my deepest emotions.

Justin's expression suddenly altered sensing the shift in my mood. "Why are you doing this to yourself?" he asked, looking troubled. "Whatever is making you feel this way, Caitlin needs to go. Get it out of your mind."

I dropped my gaze to Persian rug as darkness enveloped my every cell. It was beyond my control. One minute I was happy to be in his arms and the next I feared losing him.

"Look at me, Caitlin," he said forcing my eyes to his. "I'm not going anywhere. Do you understand? Not unless you want me to. We will be the ones deciding our fate."

I nodded knowing that with each passing day, I was one step

closer to finding out the truth. I felt it in my bones. The choices I would have to make would be detrimental to my life. I feigned a smile knowing full well that he read every last thought and doubt.

"Is what we have Caitlin not enough? Do you really believe that I would allow someone or something to come between us?" His eyes filled with rivers of sadness.

Why can't I be happy for today, for having him here – now?

"Justin, I'm so sorry for ruining this," I tried explaining through the tears and the melancholy. "It's just these past events have made me question everything I've ever known," I said, sniffling back the tears. "I don't know who I am anymore. I feel like I'm being pulled further and further down into a bottomless pit."

"We'll get through this, you'll see."

I nodded in agreement, but my tears continued to flow freely down my face.

"God, Caitlin. I can't stand seeing you tear yourself apart like this. We'll get through this, I promise."

I folded my arms around his waist and hugged him even tighter – never wanting to let go. My body trembled from the intense emotions that were engorging my mind – not knowing how to stop my grief.

"My life is a lie," I cried into his shirt, depressed beyond repair, unable to shake off the dark sinister thoughts that kept creeping up, dragging me even further down into the slums of my soul. It was as though something or someone was pulling me deeper and deeper into the furthest and darkest part of my mind. The control I had managed to cling to since my arrival back in Oaks had shattered. I simply sank to the floor in a spasm of sobs and shudders.

"What have we done to you?" Justin exclaimed, taking my face in his hands, looking down at my grief-stricken expression. He gathered me against him. "Caitlin, you need more rest. This is too much for you."

We stayed there, on the floor for a few more minutes. I wept in harsh, aching gasps wondering if my bones would shatter from the sheer power of it. Justin helped me up and led me to the stairs. I rested my head, crying on his shoulder, allowing my tears to run their course. As we approached the stairs, I noticed Uncle Abbot standing there not saying a word, sympathising with my misery. He moved out of the way allowing us to pass. Justin stopped and looked back at my uncle. Aunt Leslie had just reached the banister and was about to draw near, but Justin wouldn't let her.

"We did this," he said through clenched teeth, causing my aunt to freeze in place. "I hope your secrets are worth this." He looked down at my pale face. "Does she mean absolutely nothing to you?" His voice was much louder, full of rage. "Can you see any logical reason for her torment? It's time you all end this now or God help me!"

Not waiting for any sort of recourse, Justin quickly turned his back to them and continued walking me back to my room. "I'm so sorry Caitlin," he said, drying my tears as he helped me to the bed.

He sat next to me stroking my hair trying to comfort me. I wanted to emerge from the dark pit that engulfed me, but I was being dragged even deeper down with each passing moment. Justin didn't speak, not that there was anything he could say to help me out of this death hold. A flood of tears now streamed freely, I needed to let go. Apparently, I was not as strong as everybody had thought. My past had just caught up with me, and was suffocating me with all its lies.

Later, when things to me seemed to offer absolutely no hope – when everything seemed barren and black, I heard Emily come in. She didn't say a word, just sat on my side of the bed leaning her forehead against mine. I could hear the distress in her breathing.

"Everything will be alright Caitlin," she said teary eyed. "We all love you. We do. You must know that. Everything will be okay."

I was impervious to her words. The void grew deeper and wider pulling everything and everyone down alongside with me. Even the air seemed to be impregnated with misery and grief. I closed my eyes in defeat unable to conquer my own demons, unable to snap out of whatever I was struggling against.

Nobody spoke. Motionless we lay there under the dark cloud that covered us. Just then, I heard somebody enter my room – was not sure who it was. I was too far gone to care.

"What is this?" I heard Kyle yell at the sight of all three of us. "Caitlin, you get your butt out of that bed before I kick it out. Do you hear me?" His voice was nothing like the Kyle I knew – now more serious and stern. I could feel Justin's body tense ready to leap at his friend for speaking to me in that tone. "I mean it Caitlin," Kyle said determined to be heard. "Get your ass out of bed, now!"

Unexpectedly he pulled Emily off the bed and dragged me violently by the hand to the full length mirror adorning the corner of my room. "Is this who you are?" he asked angrily at my reflection. "Is this who you want to be? This is not acceptable, Caitlin." His voice was a whole pitch louder yelling at me, forcing me to see my real self. Becoming impatient Kyle had, at last, begun to shake me, "Stop it, Caitlin," he said.

Suddenly Kyle snapped his head round and stretched out his hand to stop Justin from advancing. In seconds, a transparent film of iridescent light instantly wrapped around Justin blocking his advancement, keeping him pinned in place. The harder he tried to break free the stronger the shield became, twisting even tighter around him. "You don't want to do that, Justin. Don't fight me on this. It's for your own good," Kyle warned. "Her powers are pulling all of you down. You're lost in her misery as much as she is. Caitlin needs to snap out of this and get control of her emotions before it consumes all of you."

Kyle's last words were the push I needed to surface from the depth of my dark thoughts. I turned and looked at Justin and Emily realizing how tired and sad they looked. I was literally destroying their spirit. The smiles I remembered were replaced with tormented stares.

Wrenching my shoulder out of Kyle's grasp, I broke free and ran out of my room – destination unknown.

I simply wanted to distance myself, as far away as humanly possible. The need for fresh air was what drove me even further down the hall. I staggered teary eyed down the steps – close to falling over on numerous occasions. I ran down the corridor and headed for the back door.

To my amazement it flung open as soon as I reached for it. I shrugged it off as yet another unexplained phenomena in this strange town.

The only thing I cared about was being outside.

I ran – ran as far as my legs could take me – until I could run no more. With my hands on my knees I crouched over and took real deep breaths, trying really hard to dispel those disturbing thoughts that kept whirling in my head.

After a few minutes of heavy breathing and several

profanities, I might add, I stood upright and took one last deep breath. The crisp cold air filled my lungs with an awareness I never had before. I finally surfaced from the gloom – soothing my foul mood.

Kyle was right; I was not that person in the mirror. I was not that weak girl that stared back at me. Five years ago, maybe, but not now, not if I could help it.

What the hell was that all about? I wondered. *What got into me?*

Five years ago I allowed myself to be pulled down, depressed for so long; preferring to die than bear the pain. I left that person behind and promised myself never again.

I yelled, "No!" – screamed my thoughts out loud to the sky, "You will not break me! I didn't allow this to consume me at thirteen; I sure as hell won't let it get me now."

Taking another deep breath to relax my muscles, I was pleasantly distracted by the sound of the gurgling water in the distance beckoned me.

I strolled down to the stream spellbound by the way the sunset burnished the rippling water. I held my breath, ripe and hopeful in the soft evening air until something brushed across my cheek.

"Caitlin Eileen," I heard the sound of my name carried in the air. "Don't fight it, mortal. Let the emotions take you. You'll feel much, much better."

I turned in circles, but saw nothing and my fear was like a silent scream in my mind as I was seized and carried by the sinister sound of the voice.

"Who are you?" I asked.

"Little Caitlin," I heard the sound again.

I was sure it was my mind playing tricks on me, because there was no one around. Within that moment of questioning my own sanity, I felt Justin standing a few feet behind me. "Was that you?" I asked horrified.

He looked confused.

"Did you hear that?" I asked again.

"Hear what?"

Justin looked confused. I quickly shook the whole sordid ordeal off and said, "Nothing, don't worry about it. I guess I'm just tired."

"You're going to catch your death out here," he said, taking a few steps towards me; wrapping my coat snug around my shoulders. He hugged me without saying another word.

I leaned back against his chest. "It's not the cold that I fear."

He didn't respond but simply tightened his embrace.

"I'm fine," I reassured him, in a weak attempt at sounding convincing.

"I know you are." He kissed the top of my head.

After a long silent pause I spoke again. "I simply need to learn to restrain my emotions before I hurt any of you; just wish I knew how. I don't even know that I'm doing it," I stopped, swallowing back the tears.

More silence

"These feelings just washed over me and took over. Guess I needed to get all that out of my system. You can push your emotions only so far down before you eventually blow a fuse."

"You've got a lot on your plate these days. Anyone of us would've buckled under the pressure having to endure what you've been through this week."

"Yeah, well I could've harmed both of you. What kind of person does that?" I turned myself round in his hold to face him. "Are you and Em okay? I'd never forgive myself if something happened to you. I'm an emotional wreck."

Justin simply looked at me, stroking my cheek, "We're both fine. Don't beat yourself up. It's part of the ascension process. Marc, Kyle and I all had to go through it during our ascension. It takes time to run its course and deal with the different emotions."

"You mean you guys had felt what I just did?"

"Sort of, the difference with you is that your gift is transitioning all at once. We were aware of our powers from birth and learned to deal with the changes in stages. You'll need to exert much self-control. The Ellri will guide you all in good time." His eyes met mine. "Your powers are growing – imbedding themselves in your system. They need time to contour to your specific needs. Getting control of your emotions and realizing that it is your gift that is causing this shift is imperative."

"I hate this, hate that I can't control any of this," I said, looking at my bandaged arm "I keep hurting you without meaning to."

He laughed finding my words funny somehow, "It seems that our bond causes us to project our feelings to each other. As long as I have you Caitlin, you can hurt me all you want."

"I love you," I finally said, gazing up into his mesmerizing eyes.

The words simply came out. It was something stronger than the physical bond we shared; it was carved much deeper into my soul. Justin's delight was mirrored on the smooth surface of his flawless complexion.

"I didn't hear you, what did you say?" he asked, smiling knowing full well he heard me just fine.

"I love you!" I repeated, emphasising each and every word. "Did you hear me now or would you like me to repeat it?"

"As often as possible, I would hope," he said, kissing me softly under the evening sky.

First Dance

Illustrated for Lines that Bind - Circle of Trust

FOURTEEN

BLISSFULLY

USTIN'S EYES DANCED in delight, "Caitlin, I just realized that I've never taken you out on a real date."

I was surprised that after everything that had just transpired he would mention something so ordinary and simple.

My eyes came uncertainly to his "I think we're way past first date standards." I said, kissing his scrumptious lips.

"Okay, you need to stop that – no more of this," he said, taking a step back. "I'm going to pick you up tonight and we're going to do what normal people do on a first date."

I beamed in delight. "And what would that be, Justin?"

"You'll just have to wait and see."

He gave me a quick peck on the forehead and released his hold.

"This is ridiculous," I protested, missing his touch.

"Caitlin, I'm serious. I want to do this the right way. It's enough that so many things in our life have happened against our wishes. It doesn't have to be that way between us."

"Justin, you don't have to do this, everything is perfect."

"Just because we were born into this doesn't mean you get to miss having a first date," he said, raising an eyebrow questionably, "unless you've been on one before." He gazed at me wondering if he had missed anything from my past.

I smacked him lightly on the arm, embarrassed to have yet again gotten myself in an awkward conversation. "Who would I possibly date in an all girls' boarding school?"

His bright smile widened even more – satisfied by my response. "You see? My point exactly – you need to have a proper boyfriend, one who will pick you up at – let's say nine tonight and take you somewhere magical and if all goes well, sweep you off your feet."

"He's already swept me off my feet on numerous occasions." I said smiling.

"Not like tonight he hasn't."

"You really want to do this, don't you?"

"I've wanted to do this from the moment I saw you in the kitchen on your first day back."

"Really?" I squealed, not expecting him to say anything of the sort. "I thought you wanted nothing to do with me that day, seeing how you reacted and all."

"I knew you were there, Caitlin. I felt you as soon as you returned to Oaks. I was unsure how to react. My body wanted to take you in my arms, but my mind wanted to hurt you for leaving. How was I supposed to behave? Anyway, that's all in the past, insignificant details. Tonight then, be ready by nine."

Without giving me the opportunity to object to his plans, Justin quickly took my hand and led me to the den, ignoring my nagging complaints.

As soon as we entered the room my aunt and uncle, otherwise absorbed in conversation, stopped abruptly and turned to face us knowing Justin's intentions before I even did.

"Leslie, Abbot," Justin said, addressing them in a cordial and formal manner. Aunt Leslie was already beaming a bright smile – evidently excited with what Justin was about to say. "I would like to have your permission to date your niece, if that would be alright with both of you."

I stupidly stared in amazement. I had seen it happen in movies – even read it in books, but never in my wildest dreams did I think I would be witnessing it first-hand. Aunt Leslie approached giving him a motherly hug and turned in my direction and kissed me on my cheek. She just stared with admiration at the both of us.

"Abbot," she commanded, motioning to my uncle who was as lost for words as I was.

"Yes of course dear," he answered snapping out of the shock of it all. He sat up resting his cigar on the elegant crystal ashtray contemplating how to respond to Justin's request.

He stood and stared for a long while before he said, "As long as you take care of my little girl young man and see to it that she's happy." My uncle caressed my cheek. "Justin, I have no objection to you da – da – dating, Caitlin. Not that I haven't been dreading this day for the past eighteen years." He turned to my aunt as she patted him on the arm. Seconds later, and much more serious, he added, "This certainly doesn't mean you have free reign of the house, young man. Rules are rules."

"Yes sir, of course." Justin took his hand in agreement. "Then it's settled," Justin said, turning to look at me. "I'll pick you up at nine."

In no time at all, after thanking my aunt and uncle for their time Justin turned and simply walked out of the door, leaving me standing there speechless. My aunt was, by the looks of it, enjoying my awkwardness.

"It would seem you have a big night ahead of you, Caitlin and an even longer day tomorrow, being your birthday and all. I suggest you get going if you want to be on time for your date."

Uncle Abbot was in no way sharing in her enthusiasm. He groaned under his breath. He might have agreed to Justin's proposal, but that didn't mean he had to like it.

"Your aunt is right, you go have fun Caitlin, but don't forget that with your powers being in transition you are much stronger than he is. If he tries anything funny don't hesitate to use your gift. Throw him across the room if you have to."

Aunt Leslie's appalled expression quickly disappeared when my uncle burst into laughter at his own over dramatization of tonight's events.

"Sweetie, you best get going if you want to be ready by nine. You have lots to do. Oh, and if I were you, I'd go formal, real formal – old Hollywood formal."

"Really?"

She nodded.

I was half-way turned to go – to stay. "I got it, formal – old Hollywood. Okay, formal." I didn't know what to do. "Formal – really? It's only a first date?"

"Trust me, sweetie. Justin is going all out tonight."

Stupefied I stood there staring.

Uncle Abbot chuckled. "Go already!"

"Oh – yeah – okay, I'm going."

The sudden realization that I had an actual date with Justin Bradford had finally seeped in.

Then it struck me – what the heck do I wear? I'd have to

borrow something from Emily again. I was surely not ready for anything like this – not a hint of elegance in that duffle bag of mine.

As soon as I passed my parents room something caused me to stop and turn around. I paused in front of their door and simply stared at the intricately designed brass handle. I reached to open it several times only to pull back, reluctant of going through that horrid cycle of emotions again.

This has to stop, I thought.

In the aim of getting past this overkill of scarcely suppressed feelings, I decided there and then to go through my mother's belongings to see if she would have something suiting for the occasion. Though I had a very vague memory of her, all her pictures proved her elegance in style and refined taste for detail.

Hopefully Aunt Leslie didn't give everything away, I thought. *She wouldn't, would she?*

I walked to my parent's walk-in closet opposite their king size bed, hesitant about opening the double cherry-wood doors in fear that all their belongings would be gone – given away. As I pushed against the antique handle the light scents of vanilla suddenly wafted in the air as soon as the double doors opened. The faint scent filled my lungs with the aroma I knew all too well – triggering a wave of memories that deluged my otherwise happy mood. Refusing to let anything bring me down, I continued on my quest to find the perfect dress for my first date with Justin.

"Get a grip!" I told myself hating how emotional I got over trivial matters.

The rich cherry-wood added to the luxurious feel – shelves filled with their personal touches. *How I missed them both.* Up ahead was the rack that held her beautiful couture dresses. I took my time mesmerized by her style and grace. She must have looked amazing in everything. There, last but not least, was my favourite dress, the one she wore in the family portrait.

I took it carefully out of the garment bag and held it up – marvelling at its smooth texture and flare. The subtle champagne color lace only added to its elegance. Excited about my find, I quickly unzipped my jeans and took off my sweater wanting to see if the beautiful gown would fit me. It was slightly over the top for a first date, but my aunt did say formal and this was as formal as it got.

With great care, I pulled the delicate, long fitted sleeve lace gown over my head and let the rich fabric cascade all the way to the floor. I was draped in French lace; brilliantly sculpting in all the right places. "Oh my lord," I uttered in unrestrained enthusiasm. I simply couldn't get enough of how beautiful it was. After a few acrobatic moves, I finally had the zipper halfway up my back. It felt perfect just the right size giving me a ridiculously flattering hourglass figure. Happier now than I had been in a very long time, I gave a little girly twirl, enjoying the way the gown made me feel.

In mid-twirl I stopped dead at the sight of the shoe-rack – stacked with stylish heels. I just stood there wondering if any of them would match this gorgeous dress. Wouldn't you know it, right there in the middle of the second row was the set that matched perfectly.

"Come here my beauties," I muttered, taking the high fashion pumps off the rack wanting to see if they fit. I tried them on slowly, sliding my foot in. My heart was pounding loud in my ears. My mother's shoes actually fit; not a hint of discomfort.

Unbelievable, I thought doing my best to hold back the tears of happiness. I was the same size as my mother, a revelation I'd never before considered. Touched by how surreal my life had become, I took the gown off carefully, putting it back on the hanger and placed the shoes in front of her dress. I didn't want to start crying again. I fought back the scaling sadness which was threateningly surfacing – ready to ruin my evening. Tonight was my night and I was not about to let sentimental objects get the best of me.

Shaking off the negativity, I traced my hand over the rest of the clothes; my father's jacket's, perfectly pressed shirts; they all hung there in faultless order. I opened the first two drawers of the island, in the middle of the walk-in. My father's cufflinks arranged in an army fashion – perfectly spaced one from the other.

Moments later, I pushed the drawer closed not wanting to feel his absence. I had enough tears for one day.

"Hi, can I come in?" I asked, knocking as I pushed Emily's door open.

She was sitting at her desk scribbling something. She took her eyes off her notepad just enough to look in my direction. "What's up Caitlin?" she asked, as if she didn't already know.

"I need your expertise once again Em, if you have the time? I have a date with Justin at nine and I don't know what to do with this," I said, pulling on my hair.

"Ah, a date with Mr Perfect himself."

"Well, will you help me?"

"Of course, I'd love to help. But first go and take a nice long bath so you can relax and enjoy a few minutes alone."

"A bath? Is that really necessary?" I asked, loathing sitting idle in the water for too long. "How about a quick shower?"

"A bath, and that's an order," she finally said before exiting my room.

I headed to my bathroom only to find the tub filled with a cloud of bubbles, garnished with rose petals. *Emily*, I thought. *She must have foreseen everything.*

I soaked in the tub, actually enjoying myself, wondering what Justin had planned for tonight. I closed my eyes recalling his kisses and embrace. I must have drifted off because Emily's voice cut through my serenity.

"Are you still in there?" she called out.

"I thought you wanted me to relax and enjoy some time alone," I yelled back laughing playing with the bubbles.

"I do, but you don't want to be late, do you?"

"I'm coming," I said reluctantly, getting out of the warm water and wrapping myself with a towel.

"Come to my room when you've dried off."

"I'll be there in a sec.," I said, fiddling with my undergarments.

It was half an hour into my makeover and still no sign of finishing. Emily decided to curl my hair and then changed her mind and picked it all up in an elegant knot.

"Can you use this?" I said, handing her my mother's butterfly hairpin.

She took the ornate hairpin from my hands and fastened it through my hair. "It's perfect. Wait, is this not the one mom gave you on your tenth birthday?"

"Eighth," I corrected her. "Yeah, it is. My mom gave it to your mom, who gave it to me."

"Really? You were only eight?"

Emily put the finishing touches on my hair.

"You used to sleep with it – put it under your pillow each and every night."

"I still do," I smiled. "It keeps her close."

Emily turned to the makeup bag, visibly feeling uncomfortable talking about my mother.

"Where's Kyle, I want to thank him for earlier?"

"He's at Justin's."

"What's he doing there?"

"Helping him, get ready, of course. You didn't think Justin would be able to get through this, being nervous as he is."

"That's silly Em, what does he have to be nervous about?"

"He's finally taking out the one girl he's wanted his whole life. What's not to be nervous about?"

I smiled. "Do you really think his anxious about tonight?"

"I know he is."

"Kyle must be driving him crazy. He's probably joking around about everything."

"I don't think he is, Caitlin. He knows how important this is to Justin. Kyle was the one left to pick up the pieces when you left five years ago."

I looked at her through the reflexion in the mirror.

"Was it really that bad, Em?"

"You of all people should know the answer to that. Anyway, that's all in the past. Now enough about that, we have work to do. I'll be damned if Justin's mouth doesn't drop to the floor at the sight of you tonight."

"You can only do so much."

"Caitlin, when are you going to realize that you are beautiful, even without all this?"

"Em, please! I could have a third eye and you'd still say I'm beautiful."

"I wouldn't go as far as to say that," she laughed.

Having finished my hair and makeup, I got up to go to my parent's room to retrieve the dress and shoes.

"I'll see you downstairs," Emily said, putting all the makeup back in her bag. "The guys are here."

I turned and stared wide eyed. My heart bounced against my chest. "I'll be right down, I promise."

She squeezed my hand. "You need to calm down and don't rush. It'll do him good to wait."

"I'll see what I can do," I said, turning to give her a kiss. "Thanks again."

"Go get dressed," she answered pushing me out the door.

I draped the material over my head and put on my mother's shoes. Not wanting to make Justin wait any longer then he had to I quickly headed to the door, but as I was about to exist my parents' bedroom the corner of my eye caught my reflection in the mirror.

Shocked from the remarkable likeness I had to my mother, I momentarily froze on the spot but refused to allow the revelation to bring me down. Too excited about my date I pushed the sadness deep, deep down and closed the door and my past behind me.

As I came down the stairs Justin's back was turned, engrossed in conversation with Kyle. My aunt, however, noticeably pleased with my transformation, clutched her chest and tenderly slid her arm around my uncle.

Emily beamed a smile of accomplishment while Kyle caught a glimpse of me from the corner of his eye and displayed the brightest and widest smile I had ever seen.

My insides in knots, I stood stunned as Justin turned in my direction. There in front of me was the personification of godliness. He was dressed in a designer dark suit, looking heavenly. I took another deep breath and continued down the stairs.

He didn't say a word – just stared. "Caitlin," he said, his voice trailing off.

"Now that's the response I was waiting for," Emily squealed, looking at Justin's lost expression.

Aunt Leslie wanting to minimize the tension took me by the hand and said, "I have something for you." She held up an intricately designed coat made from woven gold string. It was beautiful. "This should complete the ensemble," she added, helping me put it on.

It was supple and silky-smooth. *Was this my mother's as well?* I wondered

"Yes, it was sweetie," she said giving me a hug. "You enjoy tonight, have fun," she whispered in my ear.

"Now you kids get going and have her back by midnight," Uncle Abbot said, looking at both of us. Justin looked at him questionably, "Okay, okay just get her home at a reasonable hour."

I gave my uncle a kiss for his understanding and let Justin escort me outside.

I looked behind me and saw my family waving at me happy and proud. *My family*, I thought. I was once again part of a family.

Many moments later, talking for the first time since we left the house, Justin asked, "Would you like to listen to some music?"

He was driving unusually slowly, in no hurry to get to our destination. Not waiting for my response, he pushed in a CD and in seconds, the car was infused by an angelic melody, sweeping me away at the sound of each note. It was not the first time I had heard of this piece – I was pretty sure of that.

"This song is you, Caitlin," he said, turning to me and smiling. "You are each note, each piano key."

I closed my eyes taking it in, completely lost in the melody. "Justin, I've heard this before, but I don't remember where or when. It's beautiful."

"You're father wrote this piece a year after you were born. He gave it to me as a birthday present when I was four years old."

"My father...? I can't believe my father wrote something so beautiful, and why in the world would he give it to you?"

Justin smiled. "I was so disappointed to get a CD. I was used to more extravagant gifts from your parents."

I leaned my head back savouring the melody. "I remember my father playing the piano. I know I was small, but I clearly remember sitting on the floor watching his feet move while he played his melodies. The whole house would fill with his tunes."

"He was an accomplished pianist among other things, Caitlin."

I was looking at him suspiciously. "But why would he give you this CD? Don't get me wrong, it's superb, but it's a rather unusual birthday present for a four-year-old."

"I know, right? He told me he wrote it for you."

"For me?"

Justin nodded.

"Winston even made sure I learned how to play it on the piano. He said that each note represented your every mood, your smile, your tears and everything sweet about his little Caitlin; his sweet Caitlin."

Justin took my hand and brought it to his mouth and gently kissed it. The warmth of his lips caused my soul to soar even higher.

"Why didn't you tell me about this before? You've kept this all those years? I can't believe he wrote this." I shifted my gaze back to Justin. "You should've told me years ago Justin."

"I couldn't. It was my secret, besides you never stuck around long enough for me to talk to you. You always scurried away at the mere sight of me."

"I didn't! You're the one who kept your distance. Every time I'd come anywhere near you, you'd change direction and bolt."

We both started laughing at the revelation that we were both acting equally stupid, without even knowing it.

"You should know that I've been listening to this melody each and every night for the last ten or so years. It was a way to be close to you. Your father must've known that when he gave it to me."

I looked at him questionably. "Every night?"

Justin nodded. "You were his world, Caitlin. Don't ever doubt that. He would've given up everything for you."

I stared out the window seeing nothing, feeling even less. My reflection against the darkness was witness to my deep pain, but I wasn't going to let it take over.

"Justin, where are we going exactly?" I asked, refusing to be saddened by the memory of my father.

"Be patient, we're almost there."

As soon as he turned up the driveway I realized that we were at his grandparent's house. *What could we possibly want here?* Nobody had lived in this house since they passed away – years ago.

"Caitlin, do you remember the last time you were here?" he asked, pulling up the driveway, turning off the engine.

"It's been so long. I must've been eleven or so." I said, recalling those wonderful days. "It was at your grandparent's sixtieth wedding anniversary if I'm not mistaken."

The memory was deeply engraved to mind. It was the last time I saw all the members of the three bloodlines together under one roof.

"Justin, I felt really bad for you that night."

"Why is that?" he asked grinning.

"Your grandfather, being tired of dancing with me, passed me on to you. I could tell how uncomfortable it made you feel dancing with me."

"It was our first dance," Justin said recalling the event. "The first time I ever held your hand. I wouldn't call what I felt that day discomfort. I just didn't know what to do with the feelings I had for you. Let's just say that the bond we share was a bit overwhelming for a fourteen-year-old boy."

Kissing my hand one last time he got out of the car leaving me with the memories of that evening so long ago. That night I had stayed up hugging my dress, smelling his cologne on the soft material, not being able to get enough of him. I was not aware back then that he had felt the same way.

Justin came round and held the passenger door open, offering his hand to help me out. It was so chivalrous, so perfect, so Justin.

"What are we doing here?"

"Be patient!" he said, unlocking the door leading me inside.

The splendour of the old manor was still breath-taking. Everything was as I once remembered. He helped me out of my coat and set it on the banister, and then escorted me down the corridor.

We stopped in front of the double doors that led to the assembly hall; the place where the Bradfords would hold their annual anniversary ball.

Justin turned to face me. "Did I tell you how amazingly

beautiful you look tonight Caitlin?" he asked, leaning in and kissing me on the lips.

"What are we doing here?"

"We're here to finish something that we started long ago," he said, pushing open the double doors.

In that instant my heart had stopped at the sight of the large flower arrangements that adorned the walls. The grand crystal chandelier which hung from the fresco decorated ceiling was dimmed to create an unearthly feel. I couldn't believe the humbling beauty of it all. There in the middle of the hall a table set for two awaited us. It was like walking into a dream.

I was still so stunned, so moved, that all I could manage was, "You did all this?" I asked, staring at him in disbelief. "When – how?"

"You only get one shot at a first date, Caitlin." Justin took my hand and led me to the table.

"This can't be real, it's," words had failed me. "How did you do all this?"

"This is how I imagined that night at the anniversary ball. This is how it ought to have been. After dancing with you I promised myself that when we'd grow up I'd bring you back here and do it right."

I started to smile as my eyes filled with tears of joy. He held me close and gently brushed them away with his fingers. I reached up and kissed him with all the love I had to give. His hold tightened around my waist lifting me inches off the floor and twirling me around.

My father's melody filled the grand hall. I turned to see where the music was coming from. And there, in the farthest corner of the hall a white baby grand was instrumentally being played.

"May I have this dance," Justin asked, offering his hand.

"Be warned," I said smiling. "The last time I danced was that night."

He offered his hand again. I placed mine on top of his allowing him to slip his free hand around my back holding me lightly, leading the dance.

"You see, you're dancing."

"Yeah, I guess. I just can't believe all this is real," I muttered. "I...." His urgent kiss, intoxicating as it was, erased every last thought I had in mind. Justin took a small step back and reached in his jacket pocket. "I have something for you," he said pulling out a velvet box. "I've been keeping it for some time."

It was one of those antique jewellery boxes with a lush royal blue velvet encasing.

"Are you serious?" I asked, hardly daring to hope he was. "You've done so much already, Justin. All this is more than enough."

Laughing, he said, "It's not what you think, so you can breathe."

Crimson with embarrassment at jumping to idiotic conclusions, I looked at him confused. "You didn't have to get me anything."

"I didn't, don't worry."

He opened the box to reveal a beautiful heart shaped diamond solitaire pendant. Its luster was not at all extenuated by the deep red velvet it laid on. "It was my grandmother's, Caitlin. She wanted you to have it."

"Your grandmother?" I looked at the beautiful pendant and then met his eyes. "I don't understand. What do you mean 'she wanted me to have it'?"

"A year before she passed on she had a vision of you wearing it. It brought great joy to her to have foreseen us together, so she asked me to give it to you on your next birthday."

Justin took the pendant out of its box. "May I?" he asked.

"She foresaw all this?"

He came round behind me and fastened it around my neck. "Perfect," he whispered, straightening out the pendant; placing it right in the curve of my neck.

"Justin this is too much. I mean, it's beautiful but...." I was speechless for the second time.

He took my hand and raised it circling me around in a slow twirl.

"You are everything I've ever dreamt of Caitlin. More than I could ever have hoped for."

Justin tenderly let his hand touch my back bringing me close to him. Being there, snuggled in his arms, was all I needed in my life. I was sure this dream would have to come to an end at some point, but for now I was content cuddled in his embrace.

The hours had passed and our dinner was delectable; not that I was paying much attention to what I was eating. My mind was distracted by Justin's fingers stroking my left hand. I felt comfortable, not forced to enjoy myself.

Apart from the formality of the occasion and the opulence of my surroundings the atmosphere was relaxed and tremendously enjoyable. We talked for hours, catching up on lost time. Justin brought up his studies – recommending a list of titles for me to read, knowing all too well I'd enjoy each and every book. With every word he articulated, his effect on me was hypnotic, lost in his every syllable and sound. My boarding school experiences were pale in comparison to his university exploits. Being a gentleman, however, he sat across from me listening to my accounts with rapt attention, smiling and taking pleasure in my otherwise pathetic life. He even seemed intrigued with my Head mistress, Ms Leedey and her worldliness. Justin was amazed at how such an experienced and educated person would chose to work in an all girls' school in Stone Hurst, of all places; not exactly the center for culture and scholars.

"Remind me to thank her for taking such good care of you," he said, finishing off his wine.

I kept looking around because I just couldn't get enough of how mind-boggling everything was. I tried to commit everything to memory not wanting to forget any small detail. I was, for the most part of the evening, expecting to wake up from this heavenly dream knowing that all of what I was experiencing was too good to be true.

The waiters having cleaned off our table, scrambled to the kitchen leaving us alone to enjoy the melodies exuded by the piano keys. Enjoying every second I spent with Justin, I tried to brush aside the escalating sensitivity in my right wrist. It was my own doing. I should have kept it from getting wet earlier. Soaking in the tub must have irritated the scar. Now, the friction from the gauze was only adding to the discomfort. Disregarding my wrist I said, "I just can't come to terms with how beautiful it is. I'll never forget this night, Justin. Thank you."

I was about to reach across the table to seal my gratitude with a kiss when the abrupt commotion from the kitchen startled me. The lights suddenly went out, leaving me and Justin in complete darkness. He didn't say a word, just held my hand tightly and pulled me to my feet next to him.

"It's half past twelve," Justin whispered in my ear. "Happy birthday, Caitlin!"

He reached down in complete darkness and kissed me passionately on the mouth. I surrendered myself to his captivating lips.

Unexpectedly, the double doors opened, only to reveal the glow of flickering candles. I could barely make out the faces in the dark. I strained my eyes and realized that Kyle and Emily were the ones holding the birthday cake; candles and all.

Everyone was there. Aunt Leslie, uncle Abbot, Tyler the whole lot. "Surprise!" they all screamed in unison.

I was left standing, gaping in utter surprise. They all stood there singing the traditional birthday song, smiling and approaching Justin and I. In no time at all, the waiters had set up a table on the side wall for Kyle and Emily to set down the cake. They continued to carry in chairs and more tables to accommodate the numerous guests. The help moved so synchronized, like a well-oiled machine. In seconds they had set up a whole array of delicacies for all to eat. Expensive china and crystal glasses adorned each and every table.

"How in the world did you pull this off?" I asked Justin.

He pecked me on the cheek not wanting to exhibit more affection in front of Uncle Abbot. "Are you surprised?"

"Surprised? Surprised doesn't begin to explain what I feel. I can't believe you did this!" I said finding it hard to breath. "They're all here!"

"You did say you preferred a family affair, so here we are." Kyle's voice carried through the hubbub of all the voices. "You must have forgotten how big our family is, little sis."

All three bloodlines: the Falcone, the Bradford and the Cathcart; all under one roof again. Even though not all were blood relatives they couldn't be any more a tight knit family. For many generations growing up together and experiencing each other's happiness and sorrows had fused them together as one.

"Blow out the candles," Tyler yelled, from the back of the group.

Justin took my hand, holding it tight, and led me to the two tier cake. It was lovely – decorated with pink roses and ivy embellished with ribbon and beads. The candles ornamented the top layer with their flickering.

"It's unbelievable – all of this. I don't know how to thank all of you," I said, turning to face my guests.

"Blow out the candles, already!" Emily said impatiently.

Her tone triggered a round of laughter, adding to the merriment of the already happy affair.

"Make a wish," Justin whispered in my ear – kissing me lightly.

I looked around to all their faces and closed my eyes not knowing what to wish for. I already had everything I had ever wanted in that one room; a family again. Tightening my grip on Justin's hand, I blew out the candles, praying that I was indeed finally home. A roar of applause tore the silence.

One by one the older members of the families kissed me and wished me a happy birthday. My cousins, my childhood playmates – people I have known my whole life – my extended family were all there sharing this with me. There was nothing more I wanted from my life. I finally believed, truly believed, that whatever the reason for the secrecy behind my past, it had to be warranted.

Marc approached, holding Emily's hand. She winked at me mischievously. "Happy birthday, beautiful," Marc said, kissing me on both cheeks. "Justin, proud of you man, this is all amazing."

"Thanks," Justin answered hugging his best friend, "I see you finally stepped up to the plate," he added looking at Emily.

Marc planting a sweet kiss on Emily's cheek, and said smiling, "You know how it is Justin, no use fighting destiny."

Emily was blissful by Marc's display of affection – not caring what people thought.

"Happy birthday, Caitlin. Didn't figure we'd do this did you?" asked Emily enthusiastically.

"I wasn't sure what you were planning. But this – this goes beyond anything my simple mind could fathom. Thanks Em, it's the best birthday ever."

"Don't be thanking me just yet. You've got a whole day of celebrating waiting for you in the morning."

My eyes popped open as I said, "What did you do Emily? There's more?"

"Let's just say that tonight is Justin's surprise, the upcoming day's events are going to be all mine."

"Oh great," was all I could say.

Claudius and Sabina Falcone were motioning to Marc. They obviously wanted to see what the new couple was up to.

"You'll see, it'll be fun," she said, walking away with Marc in hand to talk to his parents.

Justin stood there shaking his head. "Unbelievable isn't she? I swear Caitlin, your cousin could effortlessly rule a country – rule the world for that matter. I couldn't have done any of this without her input."

I was about to comment on his remark when Tyler came up to me checking me up and down making me feel a bit uncomfortable in the process.

"You look ravishing," he said, in a deep alluring voice full of underlined meaning. "Justin – don't I get to kiss the birthday girl?"

Justin's posture became tense in response to the way Tyler spoke.

Ignoring Justin's shift in mood, Tyler took me in his arms

giving me a tight hug – holding on longer than the occasion called for. I didn't want to pull away, fearing it would seem rude.

"This sure is killing him!" Tyler whispered in my ear, smiling cunningly at the effect his embrace was having on Justin. I quickly became agitated by his forwardness. He was intentionally provoking Justin.

"Damn it Tyler! Get off!" I sneered wanting to push him off. As my anger escalated so did a mass wave of energy flooding my veins, intensifying at the tips of my fingers and then the unexpected happened. My trifling attempt to discretely push Tyler off went askew by unintentionally throwing him a couple of feet back, landing him on the floor with a loud thud.

The room froze.

Everyone was staring at me.

I hated when people stared.

Tyler's expression was problematic. I immediately went to help him up apologising for my involuntary action.

Aurelia and Marcellus came to their son's side looking concerned.

"Caitlin – are you okay?" They asked, disregarding their son's predicament.

"Is she okay? I'm the one hurt here," said Tyler, irritated by his parents' indifference.

"The only thing hurt is your ego," said Marcellus, turning to his son. "Now get up!"

"You deserved it," said Justin, furiously raising his voice.

"Enough! Both of you! Nobody meant any harm." Marcellus' very severe tone cut through the tension.

"I didn't mean to hurt you Tyler, please forgive me. It just happened. I don't even know how." I needed him to understand that I would never want to hurt him in any way.

Tyler turned his attention from Justin and looked at me. His contemptuous expression completely erased and his features once again softened.

Composed he lifted his hand to my cheek. "You keep sweeping me off my feet, Caitlin," he said smiling "Next time, how about a little warning if you don't mind."

Justin reached out his hand and helped Tyler to his feet. "Next time it'll be me knocking you on your ass, Falcone," he said, sounding intimidating.

Tyler was not one to back off, but being there among family he knew it was not the appropriate place to stand his ground. Devilishly he gave Justin a foreboding smile not saying a word.

"I'm really sorry Tyler. I swear I didn't do it on purpose."

"I sure hope not," he said smiling. Having dusted himself off, he leaned in and pecked me on the cheek. "Happy Birthday, Caity," he added and walked away.

Aurelia put her arm around my shoulders. "Come, let the testosterone settle," she said, as she led me to the corridor.

I could tell Justin was still angry at Tyler, but he did his best to keep his composure not wanting to ruin my perfect evening. Once outside the assembly hall Aurelia took me across the hall to the sitting room. She sat me down in one of the armchairs closest to the door.

"Has your wrist been bothering you today?" she asked, taking hold of my scarred hand.

"It has, actually." I allowed her to undo the bandage. "It's been stinging for the past hour or so."

"Can I take a look?"

"Of course," I said, allowing her to remove the bandage.

I flinched back surprised that the scar had already healed. Shannon came in and sat right next to me, looking at the scar on my wrist, "Don't cover it again," Shannon said, "it will chafe otherwise."

"I took a bath this afternoon. I shouldn't have soaked in the water so long. It probably incited the stinging."

"It wasn't the water, Caitlin. Your scar was healing itself at a rather fast pace," she said, sounding rather alarmed.

"That's a good thing, isn't it?" I asked puzzled at the way her voice sounded.

"Your mark is a living part of who you are. It was just responding to your needs."

"My needs – what does that mean?" I turned to look at Aurelia. "What Shannon means, Caity, is that your body felt somehow threatened by Tyler and reacted accordingly."

"I had no control over what I did to Tyler. I don't even know how I did it."

"Slowly you will grow into your powers, but for now you must control your temper. It would seem that your gift is triggered by your emotions. If you were the slightest bit angrier you could have seriously harmed him."

"I'm so sorry, Aurelia. I didn't mean to hurt Tyler. You must know that I would never do anything to harm him."

"You're precious," she said, with her defined Italian accent. "No need for apologies. Justin was right, Tyler deserved it. No gentleman places a young lady in such a compromising position, even if that gentleman happens to be my intolerable son."

"He didn't mean anything by it. Tyler was just being Tyler," I said, defending my best friend's ridiculous actions.

Shannon stood up and headed for the door "Caitlin, the animosity between Justin and Tyler is only superficial. They both respect each other deeply. Tyler is young and tries to rouse my son, tries to get some reaction out of him."

Laughing quietly, Aurelia stood up as well.

"You have grown into a beautiful young woman, Caitlin. It's only natural to have men fighting over you. It's amazing what high levels of testosterone can make young man do. My son was shamefully stupid to needle Justin, knowing full well that Justin needn't lift a finger to hurt him. But boys will be boys."

"Enough about the male ego, let's return to your wonderful party," Shannon said opening the door. "We're all here to help you through this transition, Caitlin. There is nothing to worry about."

Justin was right outside pacing the corridor. Shannon moved towards her son exchanging words in complete silence. Her face was softer full of love and admiration.

"Thank you," he told her and kissed her on the cheek.

"Come Aurelia, our men are waiting," she said, taking Aurelia's arm and walked back to the grand hall.

I turned and thrust myself into his arms, giving him no time to react. I slipped my arms behind his neck and kissed his marvellous lips.

He groaned under his breath from pure excitement. I backed up just enough to catch my breath.

"Justin, this night couldn't have been any more perfect. Sorry if I ruined it."

"Are you kidding me? Seeing Tyler hit the floor was exhilarating." He chuckled. "Feel free to do that any time and as often as possible."

"Be nice. I could've hurt him."

"Yeah, too bad you didn't."

"You know you don't mean that. I wouldn't be able to live with myself if I hurt anyone."

"I'm sorry, but if I catch him looking at you like that again or even touching you in any way I'll…"

I kissed his mouth in mid-sentence not allowing him to finish his threat. He was jealous and I adored him for it.

"C'mon killer, let's get back to my brilliant party." I said, amused by his frankness.

FIFTEEN

UNEXPECTED

OURS AND MANY glasses of wine later, the party was far from over. Justin, being the perfect host, circled the room making sure everyone was enjoying themselves. Wine glass in hand, I leaned against the far wall observing each and every one, lifting my glass now and then, thanking people for their heartfelt wishes.

For many minutes I stood there alone, allowing my mind to wonder off; thinking about what my reason for being back was. *Could it possibly be that they simply missed me?* I shook my head knowing the answer to that. *Yeah, right – fat chance it being that simple.*

There was much hidden behind all these smiles, maybe not in the younger members of our community, but surely the Ellri knew exactly what was going on. I shrugged the destructive thoughts from my head – refusing to ruin such a beautiful evening.

"Aren't you enjoying yourself?" asked my uncle; leaning as I was with his back against the wall.

"Are you kidding me? This is the best birthday ever."

"Yes, yes it is. It's a wonderful party." He took a sip and crossed his arms across his chest. "I'm truly sorry, Caitlin," he said. "I just wish that the past five years didn't have to happen the way they did. I wish I could've been there for you. I'm...," As he spoke he touched his upper lip gingerly, finding it hard to hold back the tears.

I went very still. I wanted to say that it was truly okay, and that the past belonged in the past, but I couldn't say the words even in my mind. They hung on the air like a spear waiting to pierce my heart. I couldn't lie, not to him. Instead, I hugged my uncle and held him tight.

"You're the reason I haven't blown a fuse yet, aren't you?" I accused, knowing all too well that it was his powers that have kept me as calm as humanly possible in my state of mind from the moment I stepped in Oaks.

He loosened his embrace. "Arguments never lead to answers, sweetie. You have every right to feel whatever you are feeling, but blowing up on everybody would only bring you more grief and you know it. It would have temporarily soothed your nerves, but then what?"

I looked into his deep set eyes knowing that he was speaking the truth.

"You see, you agree sweetie. But you should know that I didn't have to work hard to keep everything in line. You don't have a mean bone in you, Caitlin. You know how to forgive, and that's the biggest gift of all."

"I'm pathetic, that's what I am."

"Why in the world would you say something like that?"

"I can't stay mad longer than a minute, even though at times I want to kill somebody, the feeling simply fades after a few seconds. I hate being wired this way. It's annoying."

"Abbot," said Aunt Leslie, causing both of us to turn and look. "This is our song sweetheart, come dance with me."

My uncle smiled at her and quickly kissed me on the head. He took a great big gulp of the remaining contents of his glass and said, "Happy Birthday, sweetie." He caressed my cheek and walked away.

I could only stare at his back as he led my aunt to the dance floor. They glided in a seamless wave of movement to the music. Seeing him dance brought me back to days long gone, days when he would lift me onto his feet and guide me on the dance floor; twirling me around in smooth flowing steps, making me feel like I was flying.

I scanned the room and saw that everybody seemed to be enjoying themselves. Taking the opportunity of finally being alone, I quietly slipped outside undetected; being around so many people was not exactly my strong suit. Coat in hand, I exited the house through one of the side rooms. The sky was much lighter with dawn approaching and everything was so peaceful. Brewing with satisfaction and glee, I pulled my coat tightly around my body, keeping the cold, crisp air from affecting my mood. This night was beyond anything I had expected. A week before, I was submerged in myself not seeing any way out; stuck in the cold confinement of my dorm room and today, I was dressed in my mother's elegant gown enjoying the best first date of my existence.

How strange life is, I wondered taking another deep breath of fresh, morning air.

"You need to stop sneaking out, little sis," Kyle said, standing next to me, looking up at the break of day with both hands deep in his pocket, trying to stay warm. "It's beautiful, isn't it, Caitlin? The best part of the day and we usually sleep right through it. It's amazing what we all miss when we have our eyes closed."

"Is that supposed to mean something?" I asked, turning to face him. He was rather too insightful, for my taste. "How much did you have to drink, Kyle?" I asked, nudging him in the ribs.

"Not a drop. I'm just enjoying my evening or better yet, my morning." He inhaled deeply and tilted his head back, facing the sky.

Only after a brief moment of utter silence, I spoke, "I wanted to thank you for that incident in my room. If it hadn't been for you, I'd have probably taken a knife to my wrist."

"Nonsense Caitlin," he said, circling his head to face me, "you would never harm yourself or others. You showed great control. Before our ascension we were all a little insane. You simply need to learn your limits."

"How can you say that, Kyle? You saw what I almost did to Justin and Emily. And how about what I did just a few hours ago to Tyler? I have no control of whatever this is."

He stood there quietly for a few seconds. "Come with me. Let me show you something."

He took me by the hand and led me across the lawn to a marble bench under an Oak tree.

"Your gift is amazing," he said, picking up a pine cone from the ground. "Very few can transcend all natural barriers, but what you should always have in mind is that you need to have control and extreme caution."

He placed the pine cone in my open hand. "Now, what I would like you to do is to think about what you would like the cone in your hand to do."

I looked at him like he was stupid or something. "Kyle, you know I can't do anything like that. I'm not telekinetic."

"I know. You are much, much more. Now, stop talking and

pass me the cone," he snapped, "Without moving your hand; using only your mind"

I looked down at the pine cone puzzled and then turned my gaze towards Kyle.

"Pass it to me," he insisted. "Let your mind create an image of what you want it to do, and do it."

"Fine, but there's absolutely no way I'm...." At that precise moment, livid at how persistent he was, I suddenly felt rather odd.

"Picture it," he said. "I know you feel the shift. Pass me the freaking pine cone!"

A tactual sensation as from many tiny prickles; a soft tingling like being stroked with a feather, crept up in my veins. It was subtle at first, inhibited even, but the moment I closed my eyes to concentrate on the image of the pine cone in Kyle's hand, the sensation climaxed, causing my eyes to snap open. It was then that I witnessed the impossible; the pine cone was in Kyle's grip.

"Did I do that?" I asked, at a loss.

"Yep," he said, sounding rather proud. "Do it again, Caitlin, but this time keep your eyes open.

He placed the cone back in my hand.

"Here goes nothing."

I instantly felt the pine cone respond to my thoughts. This time I was more aware of the object in my hands than the actual sensation running up and down my arm.

It inexplicably lifted off my palm, suspended weightlessly in the air, dangling for a mere few seconds before falling into Kyle's open hand.

"You see, Caitlin, it's not nuclear science. It's your God given ability. Just think of your mind as the control panel and your gift your tool. You can wield anything to happen. That's the amazing thing about you; there's absolutely no limit to what you can accomplish. If you start believing in your abilities the flood gates will open and your power will surface."

Flabbergasted by my ability to move an object, I was not in any shape to talk.

Kyle continued to look at me adoringly – happy that his experiment paid off. "You need to keep practicing. You'll be amazed at how fast you'll be able to move things. Start small and work your way to bigger objects." His brow furrowed in thought. "Come to think of it, Caitlin, just picture any old object in your mind and you should be able to control it, no matter the weight or size."

For a moment I was too stunned to speak. He tapped my nose with his finger. "Are you with me?"

I nodded smiling. "Yeah, just give me a minute. It's a bit much to take in."

I dropped my gaze to my scar, wondering how much my life had changed in a mere week.

"Kyle," I said with affection, "my whole life I believed I was different, and now I'm actually one of you. I'm gifted like everyone here."

"I wouldn't go as far as saying like everyone here," he said cracking a smile. "You're way more powerful than most of them combined." He nodded, trying to make me realize how true his words were. "Yes, you are, Caitlin. That's why it's very important, sis, that you don't lose control of your emotions. It triggers a sequence of events in your body and mind. You are its primary concern and anything or anyone that seems to be a threat to its wellbeing will be dealt stealthily menacing repercussions. Poor Tyler got a mere taste of it today."

"I had absolutely no control of that."

"I know. That's what I'm saying. Your gift responded to Tyler as if he were a threat to you. It can't interpret your true feelings, not yet anyway. Happy, sad, mad, tired, it doesn't matter; your gift meshes all of your emotions into one, that of threat. It swiftly responds to protect you."

I looked down at my scarred wrist again, thinking of what a danger I was to everyone around.

"Don't worry about anyone but you," he said, listening to my thoughts. "With time you'll be able to control every bit of your power, until then; you need to be calm."

A serene silence hung over us for many long moments. "Kyle? You can do the same thing, can't you? I saw how you stopped Justin in his tracks."

"It's nothing like what you can do. My gift is limited to protecting others and hearing thoughts. You could say it's like a shield where nothing can penetrate it." He threw the pine cone across the lawn, in one quick motion. "Yesterday, I wasn't shielding you, Caitlin. It was Justin that was in dire need of my gift. Your bond must be evolving, altering alongside your powers because day by day you and Justin seem to be projecting your feelings to one another."

"Tell me about it," I said pushing back a strand of loose hair. "Every time he gets angry, I get sick."

Kyle smiled. "It's no walk in the park for Justin either, I can tell you that. Your rollercoaster of emotions are every bit his own from now on. He's simply more aware of why these changes are happening, more in control of his own gift."

"He's quite powerful isn't he?"

"Yes, he is. Justin's powers matured way before any of ours even surfaced. If Justin wanted to, he could've easily broken out of my hold yesterday. He is much stronger than I am."

I started to smile with pride. "He can move things with his mind as well. I saw him do it," I said, recalling how he forced open the locked wrought iron gate.

"Justin has ascended two years ago. His powers are ripe and quite lethal. He has a remarkable ability to read and manipulate the mind, but he's telekinetic abilities only surfaced, days before you came to town."

"I didn't know that?"

"The Ellri, believe that it's because of you that he can now do all those things."

"Me? What do I have to do with Justin's gift?"

"The bond is redistributing your gifts, giving Justin an advantage."

I exhaled rather heavily. "Why can't I read minds the way he does. Why is our bond only to his advantage?"

Kyle shrugged his shoulders. "It's too early to tell. Your gifts are too raw to know what they are capable of. Justin's more than able to cope with change. He's actually enjoying it – the raw power of it all."

"He hasn't said anything to me about all this."

"Caitlin, this is Justin you're talking about. When has he ever boasted about anything?"

"True," I agreed, knowing how reserved Justin always was; not volunteering anything more than necessary. "Marc can manipulate people's thoughts, can't he?" I asked, wanted to wane from the subject of Justin.

"Marc can only make people do his bidding as can Justin, but it stops there. Having only one specific gift gives him the upper hand; allows him free reign over anyone's mind."

Their powers were perverse. I was happy to move a pine cone and they were capable of inexplicable feats.

"So, tell me Kyle, what's the difference between hearing thoughts and reading them?" I asked, wanting to learn as much as possible.

"Well, I can only hear what you are thinking the moment you are thinking it. Basically, I can anticipate what you're going to do or say seconds before you do it. But my gift has evolved these past few years allowing me to see what other's see, the moment they see it. It's like peeking through a keyhole. I can see everything through their eyes as if they were my own."

"Amazing!" I exclaimed. "It truly is, Kyle."

"I'm not capable of digging in anyone's mind to read long term intentions or plans of action. I'm only an observer. Unlike Justin, who can pick away at anyone's brain, manipulating it as he sees fit. He is the strongest of his kind, you know?" Kyle grinned, knowing how happy it made me feel to hear how special Justin was. "Though, he doesn't much care for his gift."

"Why is that?"

"It doesn't have any power over you or the Ellri. Your gift blocks him and everyone else from your mind, preventing him from controlling your thoughts. He can only read them."

"You make it sound as if that's not bad enough. You know how hard it is to have your boyfriend know each and every thought?"

He chuckled. "Actually, I do. But we're all able to block each other out. Readers like Marc and Justin can break through any block with ease, but they don't, not unless it's absolutely necessary."

I looked at him thinking of what he had said. "Wait, what do you mean my gift blocks him out? Do you mean he tried to manipulate my mind and failed?"

"That night, five years ago, when you left, he exhausted

himself trying to make you see how he really felt, but it was in vain. He had absolutely no power over you even back then, so you see, Caitlin, you were always gifted, just didn't know it. Nobody knew exactly how or when your powers would surface."

My gaze fell to the ground with images of that awful night re-emerging in my mind. "It's a shame that no one has the power to erase the past," I said, shifting my gaze back to him

"Actually, Marc can – not the actual past, but memories of it, but I'd advise you against it, trust me, I know." He shook his head smiling at some past memory.

Kyle quickly stopped, the second he saw my saddened expression.

"Oh, c'mon sis, I didn't bring all this up to make you miserable. It's your birthday and we need to return to your guests, some of them are getting ready to leave."

He stood up and offered his arm for support.

"My lady," he said, bowing in front of me. "May I have the pleasure of escorting you inside?"

His boyish charm had erased every last drop of sadness. I took a deep breath and stood.

"By all means," I said, curtsying; resting my arm on his – giggling at how juvenile we both were.

The main hall was streaming with guests saying their goodbyes. It was a long night for everyone, but they all seemed to enjoy it.

"There you are," said Justin coming to my side. "You have a knack for disappearing on me."

"I was outside enjoying the air and the company."

I could tell Kyle was smiling at my comment. He winked at me and walked off without saying a word.

"It's nice to see you enjoying the evening," Justin said,

intertwining his fingers with mine, pulling me closer against his toned body.

I kissed him softly on the mouth, thanking him for everything. I would have continued with the kissing if it weren't for uncle Abbot's deliberate cough, drawing my attention away from Justin.

"Caitlin, we need to go home. It's five in the morning, child. You need your rest."

"I want to stay with Justin," I said, pleadingly. "Have you forgotten I'm an adult now? I don't need a curfew."

"I don't care what you are, young lady. You're coming home with us, it's late."

Before I could respond defiantly to his order, Justin squeezed my hand ever so lightly turning me to face him. "He's right, Caitlin, it's late and you should go home. But if your uncle doesn't mind, I'd like to drive you back ending our date properly."

Justin was particularly masterful at knowing exactly what to say to get his way.

"You're right young man," said Uncle Abbot. "You should be the one bringing her home. Just make sure you're not late."

"Yes sir, thank you," Justin replied – pleased with my uncle's response.

Every last guest had gone home, leaving the help clean up in the kitchen. Justin and I were alone again. He reached for my hand and twirled me around once again.

"I love you," he said, heaving me closer and kissing me on the lips.

"We don't have to end our date here," I heard myself say, offering all of me with each passionate brush of his lips on mine. I was an addict trying to indulge my need for him.

"What kind of gentlemen would I be if I were to take advantage of you on our first date?" He smiled kissing me again. "I told you, I want to do this right?"

"That's sweet Justin, but not really necessary."

He released his hold and fixed his eyes on me. "You know how much I love you, Caitlin. But I promised your uncle to get you straight home. And that's exactly what I'm going to do – no matter how sweet your pout is."

"Fine, if you feel that strongly about it, I'll comply – for now," I said, disenchanted, wanting the day with Justin never to end.

"Good girl. Now get your things and let's get you to bed."

Once up the driveway, Justin accompanied me to the entrance and kissed me good night. "Sleep tight," he said, snuggling me in his strong arms.

"I would, if you were there next to me." I added, sounding disappointed that he would have to leave.

"Don't tempt me, Caitlin. See you in a few hours. You're in for a treat later on today. Emily has thought of everything."

"Is that supposed to make me feel better?"

"You need to start allowing people to do things for you. Whatever she has planned she's done it out of love. You might as well enjoy it."

I knew he was right – he was always right.

I watched in silence as Justin drove away.

Uncle Abbot was at the foot of the stairs clearly waiting up for me. I gave him a quick kiss on the cheek.

"This was the best night, ever," I said, and wished him good night.

SIXTEEN

LIFE IN A BOX

Y NEED FOR ONLY a few hours of sleep meant that I, once again, had woken before anybody else. This ridiculous attribute was most effective in concealing my true nature to procrastinate. It came in quite handy growing up – allowing me the time to catch up on things I needed to have done.

Unlike most of my classmates, who raced to finish homework assignments, I had plenty of time. I would simply wake up, unforced, feeling completely invigorated with just four hours of sleep. Arousing that early on a school day had given me a plethora of time to do whatever I neglected to do the previous night.

Everyone's still sound asleep, I thought.

Turning in at six in the morning was not exactly a frequent habit for the Cathcart family. I looked at my alarm clock on the side table "Ten thirty in the morning," I muttered, doing the math in my head. "Only three hours sleep. Good going, Caitlin."

I was in bed by six, but my relentless mind kept rerunning my magical night, keeping me wide awake, thinking and missing Justin till about seven that morning, when my body finally gave in.

Now, perched on the side of my bed I took the liberty to look around making a mental note to empty out the contents of the box in the far corner.

I grudgingly pushed myself to my feet. "No time like the present," I muttered.

Pulling the cardboard box from its hiding place, I yanked it open and realized that whoever packed my stuff surely took their time not wanting to break or destroy anything, because every little item was meticulously packed.

"My MP3 player," I squealed in delight, sounding more excited than I should have over the miniscule technological miracle. It was my faithful companion at Stone Hurst – last year's birthday present from Ms. Leedey. Quickly, I put on the earphones and turned on the player. Music was a nice distraction, and a great way to start the day.

Picking through the box I noticed a sealed envelope peeking through under some books. 'CAITLIN' it read, in huge bold letters across the flap. This too, was from my former Head Mistress – that, I was certain of.

The envelope bore her unmistakable penmanship – a crisp, single sweep with a ballpoint pen – accentuating the capital letter.

Even more excited now, I speedily ripped the envelope open, unable to contain my enthusiasm about the contents.

Ms. Leedey was my mentor – the only person I could turn to in those awful days away. Her patience and care were what pulled me through those hard, dark times.

The letter read:

My Dearest Caitlin,

Hope your life is full of love and experiences which will travel you to new worlds and awaken your inner abilities and passions. Have the happiest of birthdays and a full and productive life. It was an honour spending time with a formidable companion.

I came across St. Theresa's Prayer and it reminded me of you, my sweet girl.

'May today there be peace within.
May you trust that you are exactly where you are meant to be.
May you not forget the infinite possibilities that are born of faith in yourself and others.
May you use the gifts that you have received, and pass on the love that has been given to you.
May you be content with yourself just the way you are.
Let this knowledge settle into your bones,
and allow your soul the freedom to sing, dance, praise and love.
It is there for each and every one of us.'

She closed with:

Happy Birthday, Caitlin,

With Love,

Ava Leedey

I was sincerely touched by her kind words. She seemed to know me better than I knew myself. Her letter had captured the essence of what I was going through, and if at all possible, I loved her even more than before. After going over the letter one more time, I stuffed it back in the envelope and tucked it under my pillow – sure to read it again later.

Turning to tackle the remainder of the contents, I noticed another box sitting on the dresser by my door. It was embellished with an elaborate satin bow. Somebody was obviously not asleep because that box was not there when I turned in earlier that morning. They must have brought it in before I awoke.

Carrying the bow bearing box to the bed, I vigilantly untied the black satin ribbon, and wrapped it around my neck in excitement. The box itself was quite big; embossed with the designer label. Carefully, I pulled the cover off, eager to see the contents. I realized that Emily had done some shopping on my account. A small note lay on top of the impeccably folded clothes saying:

Happy Birthday Caitlin! Hope everything is to your liking
Luv ya, Em.

I took each article of clothing out of the box, taking extra care not to wrinkle anything. She was dead on about the style; a contemporary line of casual and somewhat dressy apparel. Nothing fancy – the kind she knew I'd enjoy; expensive, nonetheless. Excited, I quickly slipped out of my flannel jammies and tried on the grapefruit hued, track suit. It was incredibly soft and fitting, providing the ultimate combination of comfort and high-end style. With my new clothes on, I continued to straightening out my room, putting everything in its rightful place.

Not long after, I made my way downstairs only to hear Emily talking to Aunt Leslie in the kitchen.

"Good morning," I said, with a bright smile, twirling on the spot to show Emily that I appreciated what she got me. "I loved your gift – every last piece." Emily hugged me and wished me a happy birthday – eyeing her purchase. "It's perfect! I knew this would look good on you. I bought one for myself in a darker color," she said, sounding pleased.

"You look real nice Caitlin," Aunt Leslie said, kissing me on the forehead. "It's a subtle change from what you usually wear. Good pickings, Emily, and a very happy birthday to you, sweetie."

Did she say a subtle change? Aunt Leslie was trying to be polite. My clothes were monotonous and lacked color. Jeans and a few sweaters was the full range of my personal wardrobe.

I looked at my lovely cousin questioningly. "What do you have planned for today, Em?"

"You'll just have to wait and see. What's your hurry anyway?" she asked, aware of how uncomfortable surprises made me.

"Come and eat breakfast, lunch – whatever it's called at one in the afternoon."

"What time did you guys get up? I didn't hear any of you this morning."

Aunt Leslie handed me a glass of juice. "We've been up for a couple of hours. Emily needed some last minute things, so she dragged me out to the stores earlier."

"You both must be exhausted. Em, whatever you're planning could've waited till you were both well rested. I don't want you to feel drained on my account."

"What are you talking about? We went shopping for heaven's sake! How can that be a bad thing?"

Aunt Leslie had prepared toast and scrambled eggs. She served us breakfast and turned to clean off the counter. "Last night was a blast," she said, placing dirty dishes in the sink. "Haven't danced like that in quite a while. Poor Abbot had a hard time getting to sleep from the soreness in his legs," she continued to say smiling. "That Justin sure knows how to impress a young lady, doesn't he? Swept you off your feet I presume?"

I felt my cheeks redden. "I didn't expect it to be so – so perfect," I admitted.

"Justin was frantic about the details," Emily offered. "He wanted everything to be just right, particularly the music and the pianist. I wanted to kill him at some point for making my life a living hell, but I knew he meant well."

"I can't thank you enough, Em. Aunt Leslie is right, it was a wonderful evening."

Kyle walked in looking disheveled and sleepy. "Good morning girls," he said, kissing his mom on the cheek, pouring himself a cup of freshly brewed coffee. Lazily, he circled his head in my direction. "I'm going to kill Justin," he said between yawns.

"Sit down," my aunt ordered, handing him a fresh bagel and cream cheese. "Why in the world would you say a thing like that? The boy went out of his way to entertain everyone – no small feat if you ask me."

Kyle took a bite of his breakfast and looked over to his mom. "Do you know how difficult he has made it for all of us?"

I looked at him puzzled "Difficult – how?"

"Caitlin, how am I going to compete with last night? Sandy is probably expecting me to come up with something as remarkably romantic."

We all laughed.

"It's not funny," he said, taking a sip of coffee. "What happened to taking your date out for dinner and then a movie? I mean, he might be my best friend and all, but his grandiose gesture to impress you has made my life impossible."

"Oh, shut up, Kyle," Emily said, tossing a cinnamon bun at

him, hoping to hit him on the head. His reflexes were way to fast, catching the bun in mid-air.

"Real mature, Em," he said, returning the bun to its place.

She pulled a face and continued to speak. "Justin is crazy about Caitlin. Last night has been eighteen years in the making. Cut the guy some slack. Just because you're a pig, doesn't mean all men are."

"Sure you say that now, but wait till Marc takes you out for a special occasion and it's something plain and simple. How will you feel?"

Emily smiled impishly thinking of her Marc. "There is nothing simple or plain about anything Marc does," she said beaming.

Kyle rolled his eyes at her, mumbling some nonsense under his breath.

"Both of you need to grow up. You're both being ridiculously immature," my aunt said, putting down the cleaning cloth she was using to wipe down the counter. "And for your information Kyle, last night was perfect – anyway you look at it. If you can't satisfy your girlfriend's needs, don't go blaming Justin for your own shortcomings."

Emily's grin widened even more with content.

I felt bad that he felt the way he did so I turned to him and said, "I'm sure Sandy doesn't care were you take her as long as you're there, nothing else matters."

"Sure, little sis, you say that now, after a flawless night. The guy even wrote you a song. What's that about?"

Kyle was clearly under a misapprehension. "Justin didn't write that melody, my father did."

Aunt Leslie suddenly went stiff, frozen in place by my words. Kyle and Emily looked at me perplexed not knowing what to say.

"Your father?" Kyle asked, dumbfounded. "How can that be?"

I scanned their faces wondering why they were more shocked than I was when I first found out.

"Yeah, well he did write it," I said, shrugging my shoulders. "He wrote it a year after I was born and gave it to Justin as a birthday gift. I had heard it before, but up until yesterday I didn't know it was written for me."

"It figures that Winston would have written such a beautiful song," Aunt Leslie said trying to conceal her discomfort by turning to her chores – avoiding eye contact.

It was in that moment that the sudden need to learn about my parents inundated my thoughts. As I was about to speak, my aunt quickly intervened saying, "Tyler's coming soon to help you with school work."

"It's my birthday today. I thought we were celebrating?"

"Don't worry. You'll have plenty of time for festivities. See what you've missed this week in school and then – well, you'll see." I looked around the room soliciting help from my cousins – it was futile. They both shook their heads refusing to help me out of my horrendous jam.

Only a short time later, Tyler came over, but seemed exhausted. He had as much interest in school work as I did. "Do we have to do this today?" he asked, grudgingly opening his biology textbook. "It's your birthday. Couldn't you get out of it somehow?"

"Don't you think I tried? My aunt insists I get this over with now. Before the festivities begin."

"Oh, yeah, I completely forgot about that."

"Tyler, you're my best friend, right?"

"Last I checked, why?"

"Best friends don't keep secrets from each other, do they?" I asked, trying to elicit information about Emily's plans.

"Best friends don't throw each other across the room either," he answered, poking me in the side, making me laugh.

"That's not fair, Tyler. I've apologized a thousand times for last night." I pouted, trying to act all cutesy.

"Your charms won't work on me, Caitlin," he said, reaching to tickle me. "You owe me dearly for what you did. Now you must pay."

Giggling at his sinister laugh, I attempted to stand up to get away, but he was much faster than me and caught my leg causing me to fall back down.

"You must die," he said, amusingly, pulling me by the leg towards him. Theatrically, he raised his hands in the air preparing to tickle me to death, "Say mercy," he kept repeating

"Never," I yelled, through the uncontrollable laughter.

Tyler pinned me to the floor and continued to tickle me. "Ask for mercy if you want to live."

"Okay, okay. Mercy, mercy," I finally yelled between happy tears.

"Am I interrupting?" Justin's tone was razor-sharp. He didn't seem to be amused by our, otherwise, intimate position.

"You are actually," Tyler answered, without budging.

"Tyler, c'mon. Get off," I said, trying to keep my cool so a repeat of last night would not occur. He sat back, leaning with his back against my bed, looking satisfied for annoying Justin once again.

Mechanically, I brushed myself off and moved towards Justin – beaming with happiness. "This is a nice surprise," I said, nestling in his embrace.

"I came up to wish you a happy birthday," he said, tightening his hold around me, and kissed me tenderly on the lips, "Happy Birthday, Caitlin."

I could tell he was purposely taking his time with the kiss – irritating Tyler in the process. I didn't mind one bit; having his lips on mine was all I cared about.

Tyler sat there, on the floor, shaking his head in discontent. He instantly started collecting his books off the floor attempting to look casual. "Caitlin, I should go."

"No, I don't want you to leave. Why would I want you to leave? We have tons of things to do." It was Justin who in seconds released his hold and turned for the door. "Tyler you don't have to go on my account," he said, "I've got errands to run for Emily."

"She's got you running around too? What's she up to?"

Justin kissed me on the forehead. "It's a covert operation – on a need to know basis."

"I'm on a need to know basis," I said, sounding like a spoiled little brat.

"It's going to be fun, Caitlin. Just you wait and see. I have to get going."

"When will I see you again?"

"As soon as I'm finished," he replied, visibly pressed for time. He gave me a quick kiss and was off.

I turned to look at Tyler who didn't look at all happy with our display of affection.

"So, what's that all about? Are you in love with him now?"

"Do you really need to ask? Isn't it obvious?"

He looked away momentarily. "I guess, but if it's the bond that is making you feel this way than it's not really love," he said, trying to rationalize my feelings for Justin.

"What Justin and I have goes beyond any bond." I needed Tyler to understand what I was feeling. "I'm not whole without him. Even now that he is away on mere errands I feel a bitter void in the depths of my soul, as if part of me has died. Only his closeness can extinguish the overpowering grief I feel in his absence."

Tyler stared at me, finding it hard to take it all in. "I didn't realize your bond was so strong." He looked disappointed for some reason. "I remember how much pain you were in when we were younger, but I had no idea...."

I crossed the room and grabbed his school bag from his hands. "Let's get to work, shall we?"

"I know you love him, but that doesn't mean I have to like it," he added, sitting back down on the floor. "But I'm happy for both of you." Tyler pecked me on the cheek. "I really am."

He scratched his head anxiously looking around to avoid eye contact. Evidently he wasn't as okay as he'd had hoped. "Now, enough with the melodrama and let's get back to biology."

With books sprawled on the floor we got down to work covering all the basics. A few hours had passed and Justin still hadn't returned. I was getting anxious about seeing him again. Tyler had suggested we get something to eat so I prepared some sandwiches and continued to hit the books.

The house was alarmingly quiet. I was sure that everyone was at the thing Emily was preparing.

Tyler unexpectedly jumped to his feet, collecting his belongings, "I can't take anymore reading. I'm going home. Besides, it's almost time for your surprise."

"You're really not going to tell me what to expect, are you?"

He shook his head, "I'm afraid I can't. Just have fun with it. Let Em and the others do this for you. We all had to go through it."

"Go through what?"

Tyler simply stared at me for a second. "Nothing! I'm not

saying another word, Caitlin. You're going to get me into trouble. You've never felt Emily's wrath, and stop looking at me like a wounded puppy, it's not going to work."

"Fine! I'll just have to wait and see," I exclaimed, knowing that I was placing him in a difficult position.

Descending the stairs we realized we were not alone anymore. Nine of the Ellri women were gathered in the foyer talking amongst themselves.

"Hi, ladies," Tyler said, approaching his mother. "Is it that time already?"

Aurelia fumbled her son's hair, "It would seem so. Did you two get anything done or were you playing around up there."

Tyler took a few steps back to distance himself from his mother's attention. "What are we two years old? Caitlin had a whole week to catch up on. We're exhausted."

"Go home and get ready," she told him. "Your father dropped Natalie and Michelle at a friend's house. They'll stay the night. And Tyler, don't be late."

"I won't! Gee mom – think you had enough caffeine for the day?" Aurelia stared him down, and with her Italian temperament, lightly smacking him on the arm, "Go home before I put you over my knee, smarty."

Everyone started laughing.

"I'm going, I'm going!" he said, rubbing his arm – feigning being in pain, "See you soon, Caitlin." Swiftly he pecked Aurelia on the cheek and darted off before she had any time to react.

Once Tyler left – the women all turned their attention to me.

"Did you cover all your missed lessons?" Aunt Leslie asked, leading me to the den.

Midterms
Illustrated For Lines That Bind · Circle of Turst

"Yeah, for the most part."

I looked over my shoulder and noticed that the rest of the Ellri were following us inside. "Caitlin, here have a seat," she said. "There's something we need to talk to you about."

I stiffened at the thought that I was finally going to get my answers. I would have liked Justin to be there, but this would have to do for the time being. Sabina Falcone, Marc's mother, was the first to speak. She sat perfectly upright on the edge of her seat restless – eager to start. "Caitlin, your eighteenth birthday signifies an important stage in your life. Among the gifted it is a time of liminality and transition," she said, sounding rehearsed as though she had on numerous occasions repeated the same words.

I must have looked baffled. I was not exactly expecting for the Ellri to be talking about my birthday. Being prepared for a much deeper, more serious conversation, I was frightfully disappointed that once again I would have to live with not knowing who I was.

"Liminality? What are we discussing exactly?" I asked trying to sound involved in the discussion – not knowing what the word meant.

"For the non-gifted it is the Rites of passage – rituals that have been passed down from generation to generation, differing from culture to culture." Sabina continued to say. "For us of course, it is much more. It defines our metaphysical state of being on the threshold between two existential planes of awareness."

Existential what? Was she even speaking English?

She must have picked up on my lost expression. I clearly didn't understand what she was talking about.

"In short, Caitlin...," she finally clarified, "it's a sacred ceremony to initiate you among the gifted."

Shannon, aware of my confusion, reached for my hand. "The initiation itself is different for everyone. It's nothing to worry about, sweetie. It involves what we call a 'leap' in your psychic and emotional growth. That's what we are celebrating tonight – your rebirth. All the Ellri along with direct members of the three bloodlines will have an active role."

"Why is this the first time I hear of this ritual?" I asked, with a hollow tone.

Shannon's expression changed slightly – saddened in a way. "The first stage of this introduction to adulthood usually takes place within the first lunar cycle of your thirteenth birthday. You were away at the time so you couldn't have known about the ritual."

"What will I have to do?" I asked, "Jump through fire or something?"

"It's not that technical, Caitlin. It's more or less a festive occasion that involves some symbolic steps. You shouldn't feel a thing physically, if that's what you're asking. The transition that you are already experiencing in your powers is the actual stage of Liminality."

"When is this all going to happen?"

Uncle Abbot's sister-in-law, Marlene Cathcart, stood up and moved towards me, shifting her weight onto her cane. She was the eldest of all the members, and by far the coolest to be around. Never caring about etiquette or holding back her tongue, Marlene would shock those around her with her provocatively candid opinions, causing us to burst at the seam with laughter on many occasions.

"Tonight silly, why do you think Emily has gone to so much trouble?" she said, cupping my chin. "Don't look so worried, Caity dear, we haven't lost one yet." Her chuckle filled the charged atmosphere.

Marlene spoke so casually of the ritual that I allowed myself to be convinced that there was nothing to worry about. From the corner of my eye, however, I caught a glimpse of tight-wound Lucille Bradford moving towards the door. Being Justin's favorite Aunt, I couldn't help but foster a deep respect for her. Firm and disciplined, she usually had little patience for Marlene's childish behavior, but with the passing of time the two had become inseparable – completing each other in many ways.

"These rituals have been celebrated for thousands of years among our kind, Caitlin," Lucille said, turning to face me, aware of my eyes on her. "It follows a standard pattern of symbolic death, the gaining of new wisdom and the rebirth to a new self. Justinian will guide you tonight. It's only fitting that you both share this together, considering your bond." She was the only person in Oaks that insisted on calling Justin by his full name – it made her sound rather cold and distant which in reality she wasn't. "Come now ladies, we have several things need attending to before the ceremony," she urged, holding the door open, motioning for everyone to exit.

They all filed out one by one leaving me alone with Aunt Leslie. "You've got about an hour to get dressed and come back downstairs. We will all be waiting for you," she said, patting me on the hand. "It will be exhilarating, you'll see."

"Is this truly necessary?"

"Of course it is. It is a confirmation from us all to you – a commitment of love and teaching. This ritual acknowledges that your transition into adulthood binds all of us as equals. Besides, its loads of fun and a great excuse to throw a party," she said smiling, pushing back my loose strands of hair. "Now go upstairs and get ready," she added, sounding impatient with my unwillingness to participate in a long standing tradition.

SEVENTEEN

LEAP OF FAITH

NLY A FEW YARDS from my bedroom, I stopped and stood motionless. The all too familiar faint, tingly feeling in my blood suddenly became stronger. I picked up my pace and burst into my room only to stop myself at the mere sight of him sitting on my bed, gazing at me, smiling.

His splendor erased all uncertainties from my mind. Completely absorbed in his appearance, I threw myself on him, causing him to fall back on the bed, kissing him enthusiastically.

With his hand on my back, he slowly turned us to the side smiling at my enthusiasm. "If I knew you were going to react like this I'd have returned much sooner," he said, playing with my hair.

"Why didn't you? You of all people should know how I feel when you're not here."

"I wanted to give you guys some time to finish your school work. It wouldn't have been fair to Tyler if I stayed and hovered over you."

"That's ridiculous!"

"The poor guy has had a thing for you for so many years."

I shoved him playfully to the side. "He's my only friend in school, Justin. It's not like that. It's not what you think."

"I can read his thoughts, Caitlin. It's exactly like that. It took all my concentration not to kill him when I saw your compromising position earlier this morning."

"Oh come on!" I exclaimed, feeling the reddening in my cheeks. "We were just playing. It meant nothing to either of us."

Justin kissed me once again – his lips softer than ever, "To you, maybe. Tyler's mind was otherwise occupied."

I outlined his face with my finger, tracing an invisible line around his lips, smiling at his inability to accept something so innocent. "Why didn't you ever tell me about these rituals? A heads-up would've been helpful."

His eyebrow arched up, visibly aware at my feeble attempt to subtly change the subject. "We all had to go through it. It's an amazing event," he said, pulling himself to a sitting position. "Up until I personally went through it myself, I didn't know anything about all this, either."

I scooted over and sat next to him. "So, should I be nervous, scared?"

"There's nothing to worry about. It sounds much more mysterious than it actually is. I'll be right next to you throughout the whole coronation."

Pausing only long enough to exhale, I turned to Justin and said, "Promise – promise it won't hurt."

He chuckled. "I promise – cross my heart."

Clad in a white, long sleeve woven tunic on top of white trousers; looking quite dashing, Kyle poked his head in the door. "Are you guys still up here?" he asked. As he strolled in, he lifted the garment bag that he was holding. "Caitlin, you need to wear this and come downstairs. Everyone is waiting." He addressed Justin in the same hastily manner. "C'mon man, you're needed down there."

Letting go of my hand Justin took the garment bag from Kyle, "You go, I'll be right down."

"Don't be late, everybody's here," Kyle insisted. "You wouldn't want to make Marlene wait any longer than necessary."

"Okay, fine, now go, I'll be right down."

As soon as Kyle closed the door behind him, Justin unzipped the garment bag to reveal a lovely floor length, strapless white column dress. "Is that what I'm wearing?" I asked feeling the exquisitely soft texture of the material.

"Do you like it?"

"How can I not? It's – it's beautiful."

"Everything we do tonight, Caitlin is symbolic like the color of your gown. It's white because everything is present in white. It occurs only when the whole spectrum of light is seen together," he explained, smoothing out the material. "It symbolizes that nothing is hidden, secret or undifferentiated. We believe that it evokes purification of thoughts, actions and hopefully fresh beginnings." My eyes widened reveling in the excitement – he made it sound so mystical and alluring. "Now get dressed and come downstairs. You heard Kyle – don't want to keep the Ellri waiting."

Emily poked her head in the door, smiling radiantly. "Does a certain someone need help getting dressed?" Like Kyle, she was also dressed in a white loose fitting tunic. Hers however, was floor length. She looked like a mythical nymph with her hair cascading down her back.

"I'm glad you're here Em," I said, swaying the lush material back and forth. "Isn't this gorgeous?"

She nodded and lifted the gown against my body. "It's perfect!"

Justin approached and took my face in his hands. "I'll be downstairs, don't be long and don't give Em any grief." He leaned in and whispered, "I love you," in my ear, causing my heart to skip a beat – giving me a hug and a tender kiss before heading for the door.

The dress draped down my form with a soft pleated look. I was happily surprised at how the strapless neckline flattered my figure.

"Brilliant," I said, swirling around feeling pretty.

"Justin picked out the dress this afternoon," Emily said, fixing the hem. "He even dragged Marc and Kyle along."

"You can't be serious!"

"I'm dead serious – now stop moving, will you?"

Emily continued tweaking each and every little detail, brushing my long hair behind my ears. She didn't really do much to it; simply pulled my long bangs on either side and fastened them in the back letting the rest cascade lose.

"I've got to hand it to him, he's got impeccable taste," she admitted, putting the last touches. "All done, let me look," she said, stepping back to get a better view of the overall effect. "Perfect!" She unfastened by birthday pendant and placed it carefully on my dresser. "You won't be needing that, and don't worry about shoes. You won't need them either," she said, lifting her tunic to display her own bare feet. "Let's get going, we're already late."

I had, at first, been terribly happy and excited. When I realized that nobody was downstairs, my first reaction was of disappointment. "Where is everyone," I asked.

"Follow me, you'll soon see."

We headed down the corridor and to the back entrance. My breath suddenly caught in my chest the second I saw Justin dressed similarly to Kyle – all in white.

Emily hugged me tight and kissed me on the cheek. "I can't wait to see your reaction in a few minutes," she said, opening the back door, ever so slightly, barely fitting through the opening – clearly not wanting me to see what was hidden behind the door.

Justin took me in his arms and gazed into my eyes. "You're breath-taking," he said, kissing me. "I should warn you, Emily's gone a bit overboard with the preparations. The ritual isn't an elaborate occasion, but who would dare cross your cousin."

There was no explaining why I giggled, but I suddenly felt giddy, too happy for words. Justin pulled two long white sashes from the coat hanger on the far corner.

"Try to enjoy yourself tonight. It's a once in a life time experience."

My inquisitive gaze met his eyes. "Are those for me?" I asked, pointing to the white material he held in his hands.

"Put your hands behind your back."

I raised an eyebrow of apprehension, but did as he asked.

He tied my hands with the delicate material. "By binding your wrists it signifies the burdens that constrain you in life," he explained the symbolism of his actions really close to my ear arousing the all too familiar feelings that only Justin could awaken.

He continued to tie the second sash covering my eyes and continued to explain, "Blindfolding denotes death and balance," he said softly.

I could sense him looking at me. "Is there something wrong?" I asked, feeling helpless.

"No, nothing's wrong," he admitted. "I'm just admiring how

calm you are. When I was in your place I was literally shaking, didn't know what to expect."

"As long as you're here, I'll be fine," I assured him.

His lips were soft against mine. Not being able to see had heightened my ability to sense his closeness. "Are you ready?" he asked, taking my arm, breathing heavier than usual.

"I guess I am. Unless you want to continue kissing me," I said, smiling at the way he made me feel.

He squeezed my hand even harder, "Having you tied up the way you are," he paused momentarily and within seconds I felt his breath against my ear, "kissing is the last thing on my mind," he admitted deceitfully amused, causing my cheeks to turn crimson from emotion.

"Here we go," Justin said, leading me through the back door. The cool air of the unusually warm November evening, sent shivers down my spine. Bound and blindfolded I was entirely dependent on Justin.

"Marlene being the eldest of the women will be performing the ceremony," he instructed.

Justin took great care to guide me down the steps stopping in mid-stride – letting go of my arm. I sensed that he was not next to me anymore, but I could feel, all too clearly, that he was still quite close.

So much for promises, I thought.

Standing there, feeling awkward, not knowing what was happening around me, I felt a wave of warm air sweep over me and the faint smell of wood burning in the distance.

"You look like an angle, Caitlin."

Unsure of where to look, I used Marlene's voice as a navigational tool to guide my head in the right direction. In spite of feeling awkward, I thanked her and smiled gratefully.

"Follow me," she said, taking my arm – guiding me. The warmth from the fire was more evident with every step. I was standing on something hard – a step of some sort.

"We are all gathered here, in a circle of equals to attest to the rebirth of Caitlin Eileen," Marlene said, emphasizing my middle name in a very serious tone, addressing all those who stood before me. There was no way of knowing how many people were actually there.

To hear the sound of my full name spoken from her lips for the very first time triggered a spiral of dark emotions which inundated my mind. I was suddenly aware of my true feelings – the ones that had been muted from the moment I arrived in Oaks.

It was a voice inside my head that reminded me of all the secrets they withheld – the insufferable nights of fighting off the insatiable thirst to end it all.

Now, standing before me were the people that had hid the truth from me and none were willing to shed light on my past. Surprisingly, my body reacted to my inner thoughts instantaneously, sparking a light quiver down my arm to my scarred wrist. My first thought was that of escape – not wanting to be bound anymore.

The more my thoughts delved deeper, the more intense the pressure against my wrist became. Within seconds the deafening quiet was piercing to my ears. Feeling exposed to the menacing sensation, I stood there with my wet eyes hidden behind the white material; clearly sensing all their eyes on me, but none responded to my agony – left to bear the brute force of my affliction on my own.

I shut my eyes tighter, trying to alleviate the pain – concentrating hard to diminish the rage I felt from their betrayal. Effortlessly, I slipped into my personal solace as I did many times before, looking for a way to extinguish the onslaught of rampaging emotion. This time, however, there was no darkness to contend with.

I was astoundingly able to see through the blindfold, as though someone had lifted it from my eyes, but no one had. It was the vaguest and most uncertain of feelings, but I was very aware of the band of material still tied around my head, the tight knot was taut against my skin, but it surely didn't obscure my vision in any way.

I was just able to distinguish their faces, like peeking through a blurry window. Watching them, I had almost failed to notice that I was standing on something higher than the rest, a raised platform in the middle of three circles.

Marlene was by my side, holding an intricately designed scepter in her left hand.

Seventeen Ellri stood arm's length apart, wearing white robes, illuminated by the moonlight. They formed the inner circle – a much smaller and more intimate circle than the other two that encompassed them. Behind them, a few feet away, the second, larger circle was formed.

Familiar faces stood next to each other holding lit candles, all dressed in white; Tyler and Emily among them, standing among the younger members of the three bloodlines – those who had passed into the first stage of ascension. The largest of the three circles was a ring of fire, created by burning small mounds of logs spaced perfectly apart. It was mystifying.

Wanting to circle my head, to spot Justin among the rest, I quickly felt constrained by my physical body, limiting my ability to look around. I panicked for a fraction of a second, wondering where Justin was. Without recourse, my scarred wrist ignited, responding stealthily to my jumbled emotions. At that instant, the stinging escalated to unwavering proportions, more potent than ever before.

The periods of worry and pain quickly came to a halt as I realized that my hands were not bound; I was free of all restraints in my solace.

Instinctually, I took a step forward wanting to move around. Without warning, I literally stepped out of my body, feeling lighter and tremendously calm – in complete control of all my senses.

I knew I was moving, but I felt absolutely no resistance whatsoever. It was more like a glide than anything else. My physical body remained motionless in the middle of the circle – bound and blindfolded.

The ability to act without externally imposed restraints was invigorating, intoxicating even. My new found ability was, to say the least, mind-blowing, immersing every single emotion into the depths of my inner-self. I felt free, truly free from everything that had weighed me down over the years; my mind a clean slate. At that instant, a startling idea occurred to me, an idea that seemed at the moment, to be new. *Justin*, I thought. *Where's Justin?* The second the thought occurred to me, I felt an acute burn in my wrist and then within milliseconds, I found myself staring right at him; inches from his perfect features. I circled my head in amazement, astonished at how it was even possible to have covered such a distance in a blink of an eye.

Standing on the first step near the entrance along with Marc, Kyle and a few others who had already ascended, Justin's gaze was transfixed to where my physical body stood, oblivious to the fact that I was actually only inches away. I leaned in, able to hear the crisp beat of his heart; his breath was warm against my face. Not knowing if he would be able to sense me, I leaned in even closer and touched my lips to his. His eyebrows furrowed, unsure of what he felt. "Caitlin?" he whispered, putting his hand to his mouth.

"Justin?" I said his name questionably, not knowing if he could hear me. He continued to look straight ahead at where by body stood, smiling contently. At that moment I was sure that even if he couldn't hear me – he felt my presence, all the same.

"Stop playing around, Caitlin. You need to go back," he said, impatiently.

Everybody turned and looked in his direction, unaware of what he was talking about.

Marlene, however, was obviously not amused by my little stunt. Stepping to the very edge of the platform, she raised her hands high above her head and for several minutes stood perfectly still. Only her lips moved, silently, and the reflected flames of the surrounding fires leaped and flickered in her eyes.

Sure enough, the instant she put her hands down she reached Justin and I in a gale forced stride - visibly irritated – enraged even. She stopped about a yard away and just as mad struck the scepter on the ground causing the earth to shake. At once everybody bowed their heads – keeping their eyes tightly closed. Marlene closed her eyes as well – frozen on the spot.

"*Caitlin,*" she yelled, projecting her voice in the wind. I could actually feel her breath on my face, but she was nowhere near me. *What kind of power is this?* I wondered in amazement.

"You need to return my child. This elation you feel right now is very addictive. You don't want your body to suffer. The realm you've entered is not a place to be toying with. It's dangerous for someone so young and inexperienced."

Not wanting this feeling to disappear, I shifted my gaze back to Justin's face and caressed his cheek. He instinctively placed his hand on mine. "Go," he urged, immediately.

I shook my head enjoying the feeling of being free. I was helplessly inebriated by my phenomenal ability.

"Go," he repeated.

"Fine," I said insolently, muttering different choice words under my breath, thinking that nobody could hear.

"Watch your tone, young lady," Marlene said, reprimanding me.

"Okay, okay, I'm going already, geez."

I grudgingly glided back to where my physical body stood, all tied up. I faced myself – not knowing exactly how to return to my physical bind.

"Walk into it," I heard Marlene say. "The rest will happen naturally."

I did as I was told and in seconds felt the limits of my torso – trapped in the uncertainty and the burning.

Opening my eyes I felt the material up against my lashes once again.

"I'm back," I said, under my breath, missing the freedom that accompanied my unearthly state.

At that moment, I felt somebody freeing my hands and untying the sash from around my eyes. Needing a few minutes to adjust to the lights I circled my head to look around me.

"Don't you ever do that again without a guide, do you hear me young lady," Marlene said, louder than ever – in an earsplitting tone. She was deliberately projecting her voice in my head – intent on getting her message across, making sure that it was loud and clear. I squinted from the piercing pain and tried desperately to focus on her face – not being sure why she was so upset.

"It was the only way to extinguish the pain," I said softly.

"No matter what the reason, you do not dally with your powers without proper guidance," she added, lifting the scepter higher with each word. *"Any longer outside and you would have put yourself in mortal danger. Don't you dare do something as asinine as that again, do you understand?"*

Her tone was so intense that it triggered a full blown migraine, "I'm sorry, I really am," I whispered, rubbing my temples to ease the pressure. I mechanically looked around pretty embarrassed of being scolded. Just then, I noticed that nobody was aware of our conversation, apart from Aunt Leslie who bore into my eyes.

Brushing aside the topic completely, Marlene turned her back to me and walked in a complete circle around where I stood, tracing a line in the grass with her scepter – encompassing me in it. In unison all the Ellri started reciting something while Marlene retraced the same circle another two times. Whatever they were mumbling was not in any language I knew. To be honest, I was a bit exhausted to even try to understand what they were saying. Headache aside, I felt completely drained from using my gift. It was much easier this time to slip in and out of my solace – effortless compared to the past, but leaving my body was exhausting. The Ellri were right, with practice it will become second nature to me.

Still surfing on the high of being able to do something as cool as leaving my body, I turned my head to take a quick peek at Justin, remembering the kiss. He winked at me smiling from the distance – motioning for me to turn around.

"Caitlin," Marlene said, drawing my attention, "by removing the bind and blindfold you are reborn into our family as an honorary member. Do you promise to keep our secrets within these circles?"

I nodded yes.

Without any warning, she authoritatively struck the staff once again on the ground triggering yet another tremor. I fought to keep my balance as the ground underneath faltered and a deep crater-like indentation formed about a yard in circumference – exactly within the spot she traced on the ground. I stood motionless, fearing the worst. The only thing separating me and the crater was the solid ground just under my feet. For some unexplained reason it remained leveled – untouched.

Temporarily incapable of putting thought to words, I stood there quietly, fighting back the fear that crept it's way to the surface.

"Do you promise?" Marlene repeated, raising her voice slightly.

"Yes – yes of course," I answered astounded.

She struck the scepter one more time, "Do you trust us?" she asked, triggering a sequence of astonishing events.

I gasped in disbelief – was this even happing? I mean – was I really seeing this?

The second Marlene struck the ground a spine chilling resonance emanated from the earth beneath my feet and in no time at all, hair-thin cracks thunderously extended from where I stood to the line traced in the ground. In an instant the earth started collapsing, crumbling to pieces, causing a deep and endless pit with every rumble. I stood there in utter shock, on top of a vertical shaft in the middle of this gaping hole, fearing that this too would, at any moment, give way. I instinctively looked around for an escape – hoping that somebody, anybody would come to my rescue. Unfortunately for me, all their heads were bowed down – lost to some kind of magical incantation.

"If there is to be trust you need to take the leap," Marlene said, pointing to the bottomless pit that surrounded me.

"You can't be serious," I pronounced, trying to keep deathly still.

"Take the leap of faith, Caitlin," she said, stretching out her hand from across the four-foot gap that encircled me. "Trust us!"

It was not a question of trust, but one of fear. I looked down into the bottomless pit pretty sure that I would not be able to make the jump across. How were they expecting me to leap across when I barely had enough ground to stand on? Any wrong move on my part and I'd be a goner.

"This is your test, Caitlin. Come, take the leap," she repeated, offering her hand again from across the opening.

"Hell with it!" I said, summoning up the courage. If Marlene believed in me who was I to question someone so gifted? I took a deep breath and hiked up my dress off the ground. "Here goes nothing," I whispered and took the leap across without even considering the dire consequences of missing my target.

I felt surprisingly feather-like over the wide opening. I simply glided across with ease. As soon as my feet touched the ground I gave a sigh of relief – thanking the lord that I lived through this whole crazy test.

"Good job," Marlene exclaimed, smiling wider than I've ever seen her. "With this action you have entered the Circle of Trust, congrats Caity."

Without a second to spare she struck the ground again making me turn in the direction of the vast opening in the ground. Faster than a blink of the eye the ground returned to its original form as if someone pressed the rewind button on a video. The gap disappeared completely – replaced by grass laden earth. Like nothing had ever happened.

The Ellri were more powerful than I once thought.

"Anything that you hear or see from this point on is kept among the members. You will not share your knowledge or speak about what you learn with anyone outside these circles," she said, pointing to the people creating the links.

At that moment I understood why no one had ever mentioned my past – they were all bound to secrecy. *How was I supposed to know that any of this existed?*

Shannon approached holding a small plate with something on it. I was not sure what it was. "Do you promise to rise above the bitterness and vileness of life?" she asked, looking lovingly into my eyes.

"I guess," I said, unsure of what she wanted from me.

"You need to be sure, Caitlin. Do you promise?"

"Yes, yes, I do." I finally said.

"Open your mouth then," she said, picking up a morsel from the plate and placed it in my mouth. It was bitter and inedible – I wanted to vomit from the sheer pungency of the taste. "Let this be the last time you taste bitterness in your life," she added, kissing me on the cheek and took a step back.

Aurelia took her spot in front of me and said, "Do you promise to rise above the tears and the sorrow life hands you?

"I do," I repeated. The bitter taste still lingered in my mouth.

"Open wide, Caitlin," she said. The saltiness of the morsel was nondescript. It melted quickly on my tongue, but impossible to swallow. "Let this be the last time you taste tears in your life, child." She too, kissed me and moved to stand next to Shannon.

Lucille was the last to approach me.

"Caitlin, do you promise to enjoy the sweetness life has to offer with all your heart and soul?"

I looked at her and smiled. "Most definitely," I answered, blissfully thinking of Justin.

"Open your mouth, child," she said, placing something incredibly sugary on my tongue. It tasted sweet like honey, in a way. "From this day forward may your last memory be of sweetness and love," she said, kissing me on the cheek.

As soon as all three women returned to their places in the inner circle Marlene said in a loud voice, "Does anyone here tonight have any objection to Caitlin's place in our circle?"

A long silence later, she took me by the hand and walked me around the inner circle stopping in front of my uncle.

"Do you accept her place among us, Abbot?" she asked.

"I do," he answered smiling.

"Do you Leslie?"

"With all my heart – I do," she said, visibly touched.

Marlene took me around to each and every Ellri asking them one by one if they accepted my place in their circle. I was delighted to hear them all agreeing. We returned to the middle – this time she was the one who stood on the raised platform.

"Does the bloodline of Cathcart agree to Caitlin's entrance?"

"We do," they all said, in unison and blew out their candles.

"Does the bloodline of Bradford agree to Caitlin's entrance?"

"We do," I heard them say in one loud voice and then blew out their candles.

"And does the bloodline of Falcone agree to Caitlin's entrance?"

"We do," they all said harmoniously blowing out their candles as well.

"Heck, yeah," Tyler screamed, inciting a roar of laughter among the outer circle.

Marlene clearly amused by my friend's outburst turned to me and showed me my place in the circle.

"Join your family, child," she said.

As soon as I stood next to Emily and Tyler, the whole lot started clapping and cheering. "Welcome – congratulations."

Moments later, Marlene came up to me again and took my hand and led me to where Justin and the rest of the truly ascended were standing – the ones who were a step away from becoming Ellri themselves. "Will all of you accept Caitlin as your equal – allow her in your circle when the time comes?"

"We will," they all said.

Marc being the oldest picked up a wreath made of interlaced stems and was about to put it on my head anointing my new life and my rebirth, when Tyler broke from the circle and headed our way.

"Not so fast Marc, you're not putting that dead thing on her head," he exclaimed sounding annoyed. "Give it to me."

He grabbed the wreath from his cousin's hand without waiting for his response. Justin didn't look a bit amused.

Everybody gathered around us to see what he was up to. Tyler simply took hold of the wreath and in seconds the stems and twigs came to life. Leaves and flowers popping up everywhere. I anticipated his action, seeing his power first hand a week ago when he offered me a rose, but everybody else looked truly shocked.

"Here you go Marc," he finally said, handing him the flower laden wreath, "now it's appropriate for Caitlin," he said, winking at me.

Dumbfounded at Tyler's unusual ability, Marc finally placed the wreath on my head.

"On behalf of our family we await your ascendance to the higher order, to stand next to us – as one of us," he said.

"Here, Here," they all shouted in unison.

Once again there was a burst of applause – everybody cheered and yelled.

"Let the party begin," I heard Emily yell from the back of the crowd.

In seconds music filled the air. The younger members scrambled to set up tables and feed the fires. The women went to the kitchen and carried out numerous munchies for all to enjoy.

The buzz of excitement transformed the solemn ritual to a full-blown party. Each and every last member hugged and kissed me, formally welcoming me to their tight-knit family.

I happily felt Justin's hand slip around my waist, kissing me on the shoulder. "You were remarkable," he said, turning me to face him – holding me much closer.

"It was intense," I admitted, swallowing back the vile. "Do you mind if I go inside. I need to get this horrible taste out of my mouth."

"I'll come with you," he said, leading me indoors.

"Whatever your mom gave me, it's making me sick."

"It's nothing to worry about," he said. "It was a bitter almond paste. Nothing extreme, but it does leave an awful aftertaste."

The music from outside permeated the whole house. "Emily sure knows how to throw a party."

"She organized all this," he said, escorting me upstairs. "The ceremony usually takes place only with the Ellri present, and no one else. It's quite tame and dull, nothing like tonight. She wanted to do it traditionally with all three circles. The Ellri were excited with her proposal, they hadn't carried out a traditional ritual in decades. She must love you a lot because she's never gone to this much trouble for anybody before."

"I love her too," I said, walking quietly beside him down the hall. "That was something. How did they know I'd jump?"

"They didn't," Justin answered holding my door open.

"So you mean I could've fallen in?"

"Well, sort of."

"What's that supposed to mean? Has anyone not jumped – not taken the Leap of Faith?"

Justin nodded. "Sure – many. Not everyone is resilient as you are, Caitlin. If someone doesn't choose to jump it means that their mind is simply not ready for the truth – not ready to face their true calling or accept who they really are."

"What happens to them?"

"Nothing happens to them. The memory of the whole ordeal is simply erased from their mind. They have absolutely no recollection of the event, and believe it to be a real weird dream or something along those lines."

"Only if I knew that beforehand," I said smiling.

Justin's grin reached from ear to ear and said, "You know you would've still jumped."

I smiled even wider, "I know! It was awesome!"

Initiation

Illustrated for Lines That Bind - Circle Of Trust

EIGHTEEN

REBORN

RUSHING MY TEETH, I gurgled an immense amount of water to finally rid myself of the bitter taste. Justin was sprawled across my bed, playing with the wreath I had taken off earlier. "He's got quite a gift," he said, lost in thought.

"Amazing isn't it?" I responded turning off the bathroom light. "Last Saturday he brought a whole rose bush back to life in seconds."

"He's still young. His power will only grow with time." He sat up, setting aside the wreath. "You know, Caitlin, if he is able to bring things to life he'll also be able to take life." Justin said, stealthily pulling me into his lap. I squealed in sheer delight, and kissed him on the lips. "From what I know, he doesn't actually bring things to life, Justin. He can only improve something that is already alive."

"Do you think he can also heal things?"

"Not as far as I know, but won't that be amazing to have the healing touch? Just imagine the possibilities and the good he can do. Tyler can save so many lives."

"It doesn't work that way. There is a balance to a power like healing."

"Balance? What kind of balance?" I asked, interested in my best friend's gift.

"Healing is a difficult and frustrating power to have. You must learn to display great self-control. Once they heal someone they have to transfer the ailment to another living organism – condemning one to save another."

"That's horrible," I exclaimed. "How can they choose between who to save and who to condemn?"

"That's the whole point, they shouldn't have to choose. Healers rarely use their powers in fear of the repercussions. Only when the choice is clearly defined do they act."

"I doubt if Tyler is going to evolve into a healer, but if he does he has the ability to keep that balance." I said, in admiration for my friend's good nature. "Justin, he's amazing!"

"Caitlin, are you okay? You look a bit tired," he asked, changing the subject not liking the way I talked about Tyler.

I wrapped my arms around his neck. "I'm fine. Now what was that you said about tying me up, earlier?"

His laughter lifted my spirits.

"Do you really think that I would make any moves on you, with eighteen Ellri downstairs? Not to mention one of them being your overprotective uncle. Have you forgotten that they can all read our mind?"

I giggled. "Well, I hate to tell you this but if they're reading my mind, we're in serious trouble," I laughed. "It's going to happen sooner or later Justin."

He raised his eyebrow, smirking at my comment. "Don't you think I want this? It's killing me to have you this close especially when you look like this," he explained affectionately, kissing me. "And as if that's not enough for one man, I have to fight off the damn bond that keeps reminding me how much I want you every second of my day."

I trailed kisses up and down his neck paying no notice to his complaints – loving him with all my heart and soul. His breathing deepened taking joy in our caress – groaning under each touch of my lips on his bare skin.

"You're going to be the end of me," he said, kissing me on the mouth.

It was then, that a sudden knock on the door caused me to quickly jump to my feet. My childish response incited Justin's laughter.

"Come in," I said, to our visitor making a smug face at Justin for teasing me.

"Hi, mom" he said.

Shannon stood in the doorway smiling at both of us "We'd like it if you both came downstairs for a few minutes."

"Of course, is there something wrong?" I asked, not being able to read her expression.

"Nothing to fret over, but all the same, we'd like to talk to you both. It's not a problem is it?"

Justin was amused by something and couldn't stop smirking.

"I'll see you both downstairs," she said, and walked out the door closing it behind her.

I smacked him on the arm.

"What's that for?" he complained.

"Why didn't you warn me that she was right outside our door?"

"I didn't know."

"Yeah, right!" I said, sitting next to him. "What's that all about, anyway? I thought the initiation was all done. Do you think they're going to talk to me about my family?"

"Your past is the furthest from their mind. It's your future their mostly worried about."

"I thought none of the gifted can see the future?"

"They can't, but the thing the Ellri are contemplating – let's just say you don't need any special power to know it's imminent."

"Justin, tell me. What is this all about?"

"I can't be the one to tell you. Let them explain it to you," he said chuckling. "Let's go downstairs and get this over with, shall we?"

The minute we reached the foot of the stairs the men were standing on the right hand side near the den and the women on the left – near the study. Justin did all he could to stop himself from laughing.

"Come on son," William said, taking Justin by the shoulder – leading him towards the den.

"Caitlin, this way," Shannon said, guiding me towards the study.

All the female Ellri were there except for Aunt Leslie.

"What we need to talk to you about Caitlin is your relationship with Justin," Shannon started to say the second I sat down. She looked rather uncomfortable with the topic at hand.

"What about our relationship?"

"We realize that you are both adults and it's not our place to meddle, but considering your powers we feel it's our duty to intervene."

I looked at them confused, "What about my powers? And what do they have to do with me and Justin?" I asked, looking around at their faces, relatively frustrated.

Aurelia took my hand and started stroking it not knowing how to start. Marlene, clearly fed up with the way the others sidestepped the topic, stood up looking at all of them. "For heaven's sake ladies, she's not ten. She's a young woman. Give her some credit," she finally said, approaching me.

Lucille didn't find Marlene's outburst at all funny. She shook her head in disapproval and started to say, "Caitlin dear, we're all here to talk to you about intimacy."

"Sex Caitlin – sex is what we need to talk to you about," Marlene cut in, annoyed at her friend's blatant attempt to avoid the bigger topic.

"You're kidding – right?" I asked mortified by the prospect of these women talking to me about the birds and the bees. "I can save us all a lot of time and embarrassment. I've already had the 'sex' talk with Ms. Leedey back in Stone Hurst."

"It's not exactly that simple, Caitlin," Shannon said, from across the room. "You see with your powers being so unstable and so in tune with your emotions we fear that – well – what I'm trying to say is that…,"

Marlene shook her head in utter annoyance "What she's trying to say, Caity, is that until the day you ascend, you must keep your teenage hormones under control and your legs crossed." The other Ellri were completely taken aback by Marlene's rawness. "Abstinence is imperative if you don't want to kill yourself or Justin."

No wonder Justin was laughing.

Mental note to self: Kill Justin for throwing me to the wolves.

"Why would my being with Justin, in that way, be so detrimental? I mean we were born to be together. What's wrong with that?" I asked, trying to reason with them.

"We're not telling you to stay away from him. It's just that you need to have complete control of your power before you go down that path," Sabina said, sitting next to me. "You remember how your body reacted to his touch last week? You don't want a repeat of something like that because next time your power won't be that forgiving."

What I was experiencing at that moment was, by far, the weirdest situation in my life. I couldn't believe I was in a room with eight of the most influential women in my life talking about my sex life or lack thereof.

"Justin and I are always together. I haven't hurt him since nor do I ever plan to in the future."

"That's good to know," said Shannon not too happy with my lack of understanding "Unfortunately, Caitlin, your power reacts without your knowledge. At this point, you can't really sit there believing that you're not a possible threat to yourself and Justin if your emotions get the best of you."

Marlene stepped in once again. "We're afraid that you won't be able to control your gift in the thralls of passion." She winked. "You wouldn't want your first time to be your last, now do you?"

By this point, my cheeks were scarlet and my brain ceased to operate due to the sheer inadequacy I felt with the whole conversation.

"Oh – oh – I see your point," I said, accepting whatever they had to say. "We'll behave, I promise."

I knew I really couldn't promise anything at that point, but I was totally embarrassed of the whole conversation, wanting to merely crawl under a rock and die. I stood up taking it upon myself to cut the awkward meeting short and headed towards the door. "Um, thanks for the warning," I said and headed out the door.

Justin was standing in the foyer smiling. Of course he didn't have to sit and listen to that nonsense – he knew way beforehand what they had in mind. Annoyed at his unruffled composure, I momentarily glared at him and walked right passed him, heading straight for the back of the house to lose myself in the party.

"Caitlin, this is your party," Emily called me over, swaying to the music. "Don't look so glum."

I made my way through the crowd and gave Em a great big hug. "I didn't get to thank you for everything, it's all amazing," I said, trying to sound sincere through my aggravation.

"What happened? Why aren't you enjoying yourself?"

"Em, if you knew what I've just been through, you'd fall down laughing."

"No, they didn't," she chuckled, clearly reading my thoughts. "They mean well. Don't be so upset. They're looking out for both of you, for all of us for that matter."

"I know they are, but still, it doesn't make it any less horrific. You should've heard Marlene – 'sex Caitlin, were here to talk about sex'," I said, failing to successfully mimic Marlene's voice.

Emily burst out laughing unable to control herself. "I should've been there to see Lucille's face on hearing Marlene vocalize the word 'sex'," she said, almost in tears.

Her laugh was contagious. We were both cracking up – hysterically laughing when Marc came to Emily's side. "Let me in on the joke," he said, visibly amused by our mood.

We were in no shape to speak. We couldn't structure a word through the laughter let alone a whole sentence. Marc apparently was too much of a gentleman to read our thoughts – he simply stood there enjoying our merriment.

"The Ellri had the 'sex' talk with Caitlin," she said, ultimately getting control of her laughter.

I looked at both of them as I wiped away my tears. "It was mostly a precautionary seminar," I admitted nervously.

"Well, you should take some precautions before the act," Marc said, obviously not understanding the underlining meaning.

Emily faced him and planted a kiss on his mouth. "They didn't talk to her about being careful. They told her to abstain until she ascends."

"You must be joking! Poor Justin," Marc said, sympathizing with his best friend. "It's going to be torture for him."

"Nothing, I can't handle." I heard Justin say seconds before he slipped his arms around me from behind – pulling me against his chest. "We survived five years of agonizing separation, a few more weeks won't kill us."

Emily and I burst out laughing again not being able to contain it.

"Come on Em, let's get you something to drink," Marc said, cleverly distancing themselves. They crossed the makeshift dance floor and mingled with the others.

With great force, Justin turned me in his arms and simply gazed at me. "Are you still mad at me?"

I nodded.

He leaned his forehead against mine – his breath lingered on my lips, "I'm not afraid of dying, Caitlin. The only thing I fear is losing you." he said, his voice now softer and sensual. "You have saturated my every last thought from the moment you were born. Don't think for once that I don't want this – that I don't want to be with you."

His sweet confession inflamed my desire to be with him all the more. "I want you, too," I confessed, not wanting anything else but to quench my yearning for him.

I took his face in my hands and started brushing my lips to his – not wanting anything more out of life. My heart was racing, beating harder than ever. His hold around my waist tightened all the more bringing me up against his warm body. Justin's strong hold aroused feelings in me that I never knew existed.

"Tonight," he said lifting me inches off the ground surrendering to his longing, "I'm all yours."

I couldn't get enough of him – my blood reacted to his touch, burning through my veins like lava. I suddenly felt aware of my wrist stinging like it did before.

Tormented with the likelihood of hurting him, I forcefully pulled myself back and put some space between us. His need was visibly embossed in his expression.

"We can't – I can't. I won't risk…," I tried to speak but was being cut off in mid-sentence by his kisses.

"I know," he admitted, backing off an inch or two. "They wouldn't have intervened if it wasn't life threatening in any way."

My thoughts submerged in deep misery. *He was twenty-one years old. Why in the world would he want to wait? Nobody was sure how long my ascension would take. He's dated other women before. He might want to move on.*

"Look at me, Caitlin," he said, knowing all too well what I was thinking. "Get those ludicrous thoughts out of your mind. You've always been the only one I wanted."

"You don't need to wait, Justin, it's not fair. We don't know how long this will take," I said, hurt and disappointed by my dilemma.

"You can date other women if you want." I swallowed hard, wanting nothing more than to take the words back. He let out a chuckle, delighted by my juvenile sacrifice. "That's real generous of you, but if you don't mind I'd rather wait for you, forever."

"This is serious, Justin," I urged, attempting to wipe the smile from his face. "What if this takes years? What if I never get complete control of my powers? What then?"

"Till death do us part, Caitlin," he declared, causing me to buckle at the knees. He swiftly held me up – pleased at my response.

"You make it sound as if we're married," I said, getting my bearings.

Justin laughed – knowing all too well that the gifted didn't believe in the westernized idea of marital union – for us it was much more. Recognizing a true partner and consecrating the relationship was one way for the gifted to lock into the natural cycle of life. It was a simple oath taken by the couple as a commitment to formalize a relationship – over several lifetimes. It was not something to be taken lightly. Both their life and gifts became one. Each partner would hold the hands of the other – right hand to right hand, left hand to left – their wrists crossed. The golden ribbon of unity would then be wound around the wrist over the top and around the other, to create the symbol of infinity. Once the oath is taken the couple's powers merge to become one – their souls intertwined, binding them for eternity. That's the reason why with every generation the gifted became even stronger.

"Caitlin, whether you like it or not you're stuck with me," he said, smiling. "Now, would you like to dance?"

I nodded, banishing any ill thought from my mind. "There's nothing I'd like more," I answered, attempting to sound as mature as possible.

The night was beautiful, kept warm by the blazing fires. The younger members danced the night away basking in every moment. Some of the Ellri had retired early – allowing us the freedom to enjoy our night without them hovering over us.

Joyous hours later, we sat on the steps in complete silence. Kyle and Sandy sat on our right while Marc and Emily sat on our left.

"This was a great night, Emily," Marc said, admiring her work.

"Thanks, love," she responded, placing her head on his shoulders only to have it kissed tenderly.

"I have a great idea guys," said Kyle, jumping to his feet to get a better view of all our faces. "Why don't the six of us go somewhere together? Winter break starts in a few weeks. Caitlin I'm sure dad's not going to have a problem with you coming along now that he's certain that you and Justin – can't – won't – ," He started laughing at our expense.

"Cut it out Kyle, it's not funny," Sandy said, at her boyfriend's childish behavior.

"That's a great idea," Marc responded, looking around to see if we all agreed. "We should go somewhere, somewhere warm."

I didn't know how to respond. I needed to get so many things straightened out – vacationing with friends and family was not exactly on my To-Do list.

Justin tightened his grip on my hand. "Sounds like a plan," he said, to his best friends. "Now, who's going to approach the Ellri with the idea of having five of the most powerful gifted vacationing among the rest of the world?"

"Oh c'mon! Marc went to Italy, they didn't have a problem with that and besides we're all living on campus on a daily basis." Kyle was intent on getting Justin to see his point of you.

Marc raised his arm to object, "Actually, Kyle, I was among Ellri when I was there. I didn't really have the opportunity to prance around town. And don't forget that the only reason we are allowed to attend either one of the Universities is because they are close to town and like it or not we are in sync with the Ellri. They know how we feel way before we do."

Kyle turned to me, beseeching my support, "Caitlin, tell them how easy it is to live among normal people."

"We are normal, Kyle," I said, offended by his presumption that everybody outside Oaks was better. "Being restricted inside the walls of residents, I wouldn't go as far as calling it living." I didn't sugar coat it – needing him to understand that I wasn't away on vacation, but exiled. "I didn't have any powers then, so I don't know how it feels to be tempted to use them."

Kyle was determined not to drop the topic. "Justin, what are you saying exactly? You of all people have complete control of your gift; we all do for that matter." He turned and stared at me. "Caitlin is strong, she can control her volatility."

"Thanks for the vote of confidence," I said, knowing all too well that no one else felt the same.

"Fine, if you can talk the Ellri into letting us go, we're all in. But don't be disappointed if they refuse."

"You'll see. It's going to be great." Kyle said, beaming with anticipation. "Where do you think we should go?"

We all shrugged our shoulders not at all sure about the Ellri's reaction to our upcoming request. It was going to be a hard sell, and Kyle above all knew what he was up against.

The evening was flawless. My outer body experience had left me tired and weary, looking forward to a good night's rest. The six of us along with Tyler were left to clean up. It didn't take as long as we thought.

The fires died out slowly allowing us to feel the crisp November air. Kyle took Sandy and Tyler home. Marc had to pry himself off of Emily not wanting to let her go for the night. Leaving unwillingly, Emily said her good night and went to bed leaving me and Justin standing outside in the yard.

"Let's get you to bed," he said, pushing me up the steps.

"Aren't you leaving?" I asked confused, by how comfortable he felt coming upstairs at these small hours – only yards away from where uncle Abbot slept.

"I'm staying the night," he said smiling. His casual tone took me by surprise. "Not with you, Caitlin. Kyle needs me for something and he said it couldn't wait till morning."

"Oh," I muttered.

"Stop pouting, I'll stay till you fall asleep," he said opening the door to my room.

I got ready for bed, turning off the light in my bathroom. I turned to find Justin sprawled on one side of the bed. "Cute nightshirt," he said with a sweet smile plastered on his face.

"My aunt must've put my usual nightwear for the laundry." I pulled down on my white kaftan-style cotton shirt to cover as much as possible. The side splits were not helping out in any way. He pulled back the covers on my side of the bed motioning me to get in. Walking toward the bed I was aware of his beautiful Caspian-blue eyes scanning me up and down. "Don't do that, you're making me feel uncomfortable," I said, tucking myself in.

"I can't help it. You look hot!"

"Stop teasing me. You know I don't." I turned my back to him in defiance. "It's not funny."

"You have absolutely no idea what you do to me, Caitlin," he said in a deep seductive voice.

"It's the bond that makes you feel this strongly about me."

"Like hell it is," he groaned, "Now go to sleep before I change my mind and test the limits of your power."

The Past
Illustrated For Lines That Bind - Circle of Turst

NINETEEN

THE PAST

SCHOOL DID NOT SEEM as tedious with winter break approaching – excluding, of course, the exams which were scheduled to be taken prior to our two-week winter break. With the first school term slowly coming to an end, the days rolled on without a hitch. Even Megan was cordial towards me, keeping her distance with an occasional 'Hi'.

Surprisingly enough, school kept my mind well occupied. Tyler drove me to school on a daily basis while Justin picked me up after, coming round only in the evenings. He knew I needed to study, even offered to tutor me, but having him so close made it impossible for both of us to concentrate.

My powers were growing day by day. Once I was sitting comfortably on my bed with notebooks spread all around me, and couldn't find the will to get up and go to my desk for my Biology text book. Stacked there neatly, one on top of the other – my books, a constant reminder of how much more I had to read. Needing my biology text book, I looked at my desk wielding the book to come. Effortlessly, in milliseconds, it swooped over into my stretched out hand. The speed with which I could move objects was astounding. The second I thought of something, it was already in my procession as if time and space had no meaning.

With each day it got easier. I was able to focus faster and move more than one object at a time. I was proud of my accomplishment, but kept it a secret all the same.

The sudden knock on my door startled me. Impulsively, I placed my Biology book on my nightstand, wanting to hide the evidence of how aimlessly I was using my gift.

"Are you finished studying?" Justin asked, walking in casually – kissing me lightly on the lips.

I pointed to the pile of books behind him. "I'm never going to finish."

"Caitlin, you're overdoing it. You've read everything twice – give it a rest!"

"Easy for you to say – Harvard man. Now that you've graduated you don't need to open a text book – ever."

Justin was determined to get my head out of the books. "It's Saturday night, and I'm taking you out tonight, so get dressed and meet me downstairs."

"Where are we going?" I jumped up excitedly, needing an escape from my books.

"We've decided to take you to the coast for dinner."

"We?" I asked, pushing my notes to the side.

Justin dragged me off the bed impatiently. "Kyle, Marc and I are taking you girls out. Hurry up, get dressed, Emily and Sandy are already ready. Just throw on a pair of jeans and let's go – it's casual, nothing fancy."

"Casual? I can do casual."

"Good. See you downstairs then," he said, giving me a quick kiss and closing the door behind him.

I quickly tucked my jeans into my boots, collected my hair in a ponytail and finished with a comfy tight fitting cardigan – the one Emily got me for my birthday. It took me less than five minutes to pull myself together.

"Where is everyone," I asked, seeing only Justin by the entrance.

"We'll meet them there. Are you ready?"

"I guess? Am I at least dressed for the occasion," I asked, knowing I had a knack for under-dressing. I wanted to make sure.

"You're perfect in every way," he declared, pulling me close and kissing me lightly.

The thing I loved about being in the car with Justin was his ability to hold a conversation while driving at toxic speeds.

I looked out the side window – seeing my own reflection in the dark. "Justin, when do you think the Ellri will talk to me about my parents? It's been almost a month and not a word."

"I don't know. They must have a lot to deal with otherwise they wouldn't be meeting as often as they have."

I turned my back to the window and looked at his perfect features. "I have a strong feeling that I'm the reason for all these gatherings."

He shifted his gaze towards me momentarily – looking at me questionably "Why would you think that?"

"I've been having these nightmares since I came back here," I finally admitted, wanting him to know everything.

Before I even had the chance to describe my dreams, Justin's mood darkened. "Nightmares?" He sounded annoyed. "Why haven't you said anything?"

"I don't know. I thought that they might have been triggered by all the stress, but each time they seem to get stronger as if they're trying to tell me something."

"We have to tell the Ellri."

He unexpectedly made a dangerous U-turn in the middle of the two lanes.

"Now? We have to tell them now? They're dreams, Justin. We can wait to tell them as soon as we get back, tomorrow even."

"You don't get it, do you? For the gifted, nightmares are much more than bad dreams. Someone is reaching out to you, trying to break through your subconscious."

I looked at him noticeably confused. "Why in the world would anyone want to do that?"

"We're going to find out right now."

"Do we have to do this now? Won't the guys be waiting for us?"

"You should have told the Ellri as soon as you saw the first dream," his voice was severe and anxious.

"I didn't know it was that important! Do we really need to do this now?"

Justin shook his head annoyed at my lack of understanding. "This is really important; you have to believe me. Have you had any dreams in the past, while at Stone Hurst?" he asked impatiently, visibly upset by my omission.

"No, I was too busy fighting off bouts of debilitating pain."

He rolled his eyes seeing how irritated I was with the way he reacted.

"You're over reacting. Let's just turn back and meet up with the others."

"You don't know how serious this is. Someone is digging in your mind gathering information while you're asleep, keeping track of your actions." He looked at me out of the corner of his eye. "Whoever is doing this is extremely powerful. He is able to bypass your natural shield. I can't even do that."

"Now you're beginning to scare me. Why would anyone want to keep track of me? I mean, they must have better things to do."

"That's what we're going to find out," he said, and didn't talk again until we got back to Oaks.

He drove to Tyler's house knowing that the Ellri were meeting there. His knock on the door was menacing – pounding with all his might.

"What's your problem?" Tyler asked on opening the door, visibly annoyed by Justin's urgency. "Didn't anyone teach you manners?"

"Where are they?" he barked, sounding edgy.

"Down the corridor, last door to your right. What's going on, Caitlin?" Tyler asked, shaken by Justin's expression

"I'm not sure," I answered, evidently as ignorant about the situation as he was.

Impatient and determined to talk to the Ellri, Justin didn't seem to care for Tyler's questions. "Caitlin, you can talk to your little friend later, this is important."

I looked at Tyler and shrugged my shoulders, not knowing what to say about Justin's state of mind.

"See you in a bit," I said, following Justin down the hall.

We were a few feet away from the double doors when Justin waved them open – revealing the Ellri inside. They were sitting casually; some around the fireplace, others at the tables that were set up with food and drink. They didn't look surprised to see us.

"What brings you here, son?" asked William.

"Caitlin's been seeing nightmares for some time now," he blurted out loosing no time at all.

They all froze, looking at each other deciding who was going to talk first. Uncle Abbot stood up and took me by the arm. "Sit here child. Now tell us when did these dreams start?"

I racked my brain to think of the first time my sinister visitors came to me. "It was my first night back in Oaks, but that one I don't remember. There were others. The worst was the one I had the night I hurt Justin." I turned and looked at him. "That day we went to my parent's house."

Justin's face froze. "My vision," he said, turning pale at his thoughts. "Someone was guiding me as well. I thought it was one of you," he looked around to their faces reading their thoughts.

"Just a second, son. What are you saying?" asked William, clearly concerned.

Justin sat down next to me and put his face in his hands finding it hard to speak. "The night before I took Caitlin to the Korbs' place I had a vivid image of taking her there. I believed it was all of you guiding me; to show her," his voice was distorted from the pain and remorse. "If it wasn't any of you, than who could possibly have the power to reach me?"

William stood in front of his son and placed his hand on top of his head. "Don't worry. You did what you thought was right. This is not your doing."

I took Justin's hand and squeezed it tight. I wanted him to know that he was in no way to blame for anything. He picked my hand up to his mouth and kissed it lovingly.

I turned my attention back to the Ellri. "My dream has been getting all the more intense," I said, not waiting to be asked.

"What do you see," asked Uncle Abbot.

"Well it's always dark and I can feel being followed by two faceless figures. When I first saw them I was scared to death, but then one night when the dream recurred I stopped running and turned to face them only to have them vanish. From that night on I stopped running."

The room went completely silent.

Justin turned and stared in amazement.

"What is it? Why are you all looking at me like that? Did I do something wrong?"

Justin asked in shock, "You're telling us that you have absolute control of what you do in your dream?"

"Yes, each and every time. At first I was not even sure if they were dreams. They felt too real – the smells the textures everything was acute and occurring in fact, not dreamlike. It was like I was transported to a new world." I shook my head to erase the haze. "That's a good thing, isn't it?"

They stared at me, startled, attentive and, it was easy to tell, very much impressed. Aunt Leslie moved her chair and set it down right in front of me. "Caitlin, your ability to control your thoughts is –," She shook her head amazed. "It's amazing for someone so young. Do these faceless creatures ever try talking to you?"

"No, never. Not that I give them the chance. I feel very threatened by both of them as though they're there to kill me," I admitted, shuddering at my own thoughts.

Marlene and her partner Nathan stood up simultaneously like being pulled up by invisible strings. "It's time, she knew," I heard Nathan say. "If she is able to fight off Shadows, she is quite capable of handling the truth."

I looked at the Great Ellri and said, "Shadows? What Shadows?"

Nathan didn't respond but simply gestured to the rest, "Come, it's time."

All the Ellri nodded their heads in agreement. Aunt Leslie and uncle Abbot were the only ones who seemed to disagree. Not that they had any say in the matter. Once Nathan spoke, it clearly meant that the decision was final – he was the oldest and most powerful, an Ellri of the Higher Order.

They all stood up and effortlessly wielded the furniture out of the way leaving Justin and me in the middle of the room.

"Don't be scared," Justin said, responding to my thoughts.

I hadn't wanted to think it – hadn't allowed myself to entertain even the slightest hope that I would ever find out the truth about my past, because I simply was terrified of what knowing will entail. I was surprisingly not ready to face my past. All those years, all those questions were finally going to be answered and I, for some reason, was not ready.

Feeling desperate at the very idea of having come to this crossroad, my heart started beating erratically, leading to uncontrollable breathing. My anxiety seemed to take over my senses.

"Caitlin, calm down, you needn't worry," Nathan said rather keen on my every thought. "We're all here for you. You are part of our family and nothing will ever change that. It's time you learned the truth,"

"The truth," I repeated, nodding my head.

"Keep your emotions under control," Marlene instructed. "The things you are about to see might trigger your powers. You must contain them otherwise we are all in harm's way, especially now that they are so potent. Do you understand?"

They were obviously all aware of my enhanced abilities. I should have known better it was impossible to keep a secret from them. Now, trying to cover my unease, I widened my smile as I struggled for my next words, "What do you mean by 'things I'm going to see'?"

Disregarding my question, they formed two circles around us. Marlene, Nathan, Aunt Leslie, Uncle Abbot, Shannon, William, Lucille and her partner Richard all formed the inner circle – the strongest and oldest of the bunch. The outer circle was formed by the younger Ellri who stood shoulder to shoulder, palm to palm holding hands. At that moment the members of the outer circle concurrently tilted their heads back, closing their eyes to the ceiling, verbalizing words and sounds unintelligible to me. Without a word, seconds later, they simultaneously stretched their joined arms in front of them and placed them on the shoulders of the members of the oldest bunch of the inner circle who followed suit. They, too, held each other's hands and turned their heads to the ceiling, closing their eyes mumbling some ancient verses.

Justin stood up in front of me looking calm and unexpectedly collective. "Don't lose control of your emotions. If you feel, in any way, that your power is taking over just call out to me and everything will stop. You need to trust me," he said, leaning over to kiss me. His lips were soft and sweet. I knew he was a lot more worried than he let on. "Are you ready?" he asked, lifting his hands and placing them on either side of my temples.

"I guess?" I answered not sure what I was in for. I quickly cleared my throat and braced myself.

Justin stood inches away from me turning his head upwards like the others. He took a deep breath and closed his eyes shot. In no time, everyone from the inner circle lifted their joined arms as if to touch him, but only my uncle and aunt did by resting their hands on his shoulders.

Terror rose within me in answer to my scar's menacing response to their touch – burning through my skin, slipping me into my solace involuntarily. The darkness of my abyss quickly disappeared, revealing endless fields of tall grass.

I was outside somehow – somewhere foreign to me.

"Where am I? How the heck did I get here?"

I pushed myself forward needing to look around. The sun was radiant. I could feel it's warmth on my skin. This was not the solace I knew. All my senses were astute, able to feel the grass between my fingers, and smell the earth under my feet.

The stinging in my arm suddenly propelled me forward, gliding me smoothly through the field, barely touching the ground.

In seconds, I traversed a course that would have otherwise taken at least half an hour to trek. I stopped moving as soon as I reached the foot of a hill.

Perched on the hilltop, nestled between the numerous olive trees and endless vineyards, a large structure stood out. Renaissance in architecture, the century old château was, to say the least, breath-taking. I walked on, unaware of what I was to see.

Suddenly, I saw a familiar face.

My father was standing a few yards away, looking much younger than any of the pictures I had of him. My heart started pounding rhythmically against my chest at the sight of him. Though he was not alone, I couldn't peel my eyes off of him. I took a deep breath remembering Justin's words – I had to stay calm. Keep my emotions under control.

I took a minute, and then called out to him, but got no answer. He was not aware of my presence. It was then, that I realized, that I was observing the past, somehow.

"Don't you presume to know what's good for me," I heard my father yell at the other man standing in front of him. He was visibly angry at this person. "If you continue to fight me on this, you will lose me as a son," he added furiously.

"She's not right for you, Winston. Never was and never will be. I'll never allow the unity to take place."

"You have no right father. She's my life and no one will come between us."

"Grandpa?" I whispered, knowing that he couldn't hear me. It was the first time I had ever seen my grandfather; nobody ever spoke of him – not a word for eighteen years and now he was standing a few feet away. I wanted to touch him, to reach out and hug them both, but I fought my natural urges and took a step back. Both men were volatile – neither backing off.

"Be reasonable, Winston," my grandfather continued to say, lowering his voice. "She's not gifted like the rest of us. She does not belong with our kind. Your powers will diminish if you unite with her."

"So be it father. I have never cared to be one of your experiments. You don't see us as human," my father snarled at my grandfather. "You collect us like trophies, breeding us to take pleasure in our power."

"Don't you dare speak to me in that tone! Whether you like it or not, I am still your father and your Ellri. If it were not for people like me, people who care about the survival of our kind, we would not be standing here breathing."

Just then a woman emerged from the back of the house, dressed in a long tunic looking suspiciously familiar. She suddenly stopped and looked around quizzically. "Clancy," she said after a few seconds, "leave him be. He has made up his mind, chosen his partner. We have no right to intervene."

"I'm not going to allow this, Eileen," he said, much angrier now turning his attention back to my father. "Carolyn might be the first born of the McDevitts', but she has no gifts. If you decide to defy my wishes, I will strip you of your name," he warned, turning on his heel and walked away swearing under his breath.

I didn't know what I was feeling at that moment. My attention was on my grandmother's face. I took notice of the many similarities between us. Though our overall features differed our eyes bore the same shape, but not color. Hers a light honey brown, while mine an emerald green, but we had the same long chestnut colored hair and apparently I had her name. I guess my father had named me after her, I thought. He must have loved her dearly.

Rather serious and alarmed, my grandmother turned to my father and took his hands into hers. "Do as I say Winston, no questions asked. You must take Carolyn to the families in Oaks and never look back."

He looked at her confused. "I will do no such thing, mother. How can you ask this of me?"

"Winston please, your father and brothers will never allow this union to happen and she will suffer at their hands."

"Mother, how do you know all this?" he asked clearly baffled by her ability to know the future.

"No questions. Just do as I say," she urged him. "The Korbs must not know of your whereabouts."

"That's not possible and you know it, mother. No one can conceal our whereabouts, not from father."

"You leave that to me. The McDevitts and I have an understanding. They will help in blocking you off – together we can keep you safe. No one will be the wiser of where you are as long as I have breath left in me."

"You contacted the McDevitts?"

"Winston, there's no time to explain. You must leave tonight; otherwise your stand against your father will be in vain." She stretched out her right arm to tenderly caress his cheek. "You must hurry before your brother's suspect anything."

Something on her right wrist had caught my attention. I breathed deep in astonishment – she bore the same exact scar as I did. Impulsively, I moved only inches away to get a better view. Instantaneously, I felt a sharp, piercing pain at the center of my scar. Quickly, I cupped my scarred wrist with my free hand to smother the awful pain. I looked up only to see my grandmother in the same state of mind as I was, holding onto her wrist, looking straight at me.

"Caitlin?" she whispered, closing her eyes.

I reached out my right hand and held onto hers, not knowing if she could feel my touch. She smiled slightly turning back to my father.

My father was clearly puzzled over her expression – not knowing why she was smiling in the midst of all the chaos

"The families in Oaks will assist you in your transition," she told him, sounding more certain then before.

I didn't know how it was possible, but I felt that my presence had eased her uncertainty. My father, on the other hand, was visibly upset. "Mother, how can I just get up and leave? Carolyn needs her family as much as I need mine. Why is father dead set on keeping us apart? Her gifts might not have surfaced, but she is one of us."

"Of course she is, Winston. No one questions that. Your father simply has his own idea of what is right for our kind. He is a Purest, believing that couples should share the same powers so that with each generation that single power is enhanced. He's dead set against mixed couples thinking that the gift lessens in potency for the next generation."

My father must have known all that. She was purposely

explaining things on my behalf – wanting me to understand the reason behind my grandfather's actions.

Somehow she knew I was there, she felt me. She caressed his cheek once again. "Carolyn's latent powers will grow soon enough, but until that happens, you need to leave. It's dangerous here for her. They cannot control you Winston, but someone like Carolyn is susceptible to their gifts, manipulating her anyway they see fit."

"I won't let them touch her," he said furiously. "I'll destroy them all before they lay a finger on her."

I could feel tears running down my face, but when I lifted my hand to wipe them away – my eyes were completely dry. My father was in sheer anguish over his family's intentions. I wish I could have done something to help, but I knew I was there to simply observe.

"Winston, you must leave now. The wheels are already set in motion and you must follow each step carefully. Our balance depends on it."

My father kissed her on the cheek and embraced her – holding on for some time. "I love you mother," he declared and walked off leaving her stand there.

My grandmother turned and stared right at me as though she could see me.

I stiffened – not knowing how to react.

"For you to be here," her voice faltered at the end, "everything went according to plan."

She paused for a couple of minutes again, and then said, "My sweet little girl, I'd give anything to hold you in my arms." Her voice trembled with emotion, but just as quickly tensed up again. "You need to go now, Caitlin, and thank the Ellri on my behalf."

The second she finished speaking, I suddenly slipped into

complete darkness again. I wanted to stay there with her – where both of my parents were still alive.

"Caitlin! Caitlin! Snap out of it," I heard Justin's voice urging me out of my solace. As soon as I opened my eyes, the Ellri broke formation and each took a seat, looking far more exhausted than I was.

"Are you okay, Caity?" Marlene was the first to speak.

I wiped my tears away, looking around to all their faces. "I was with my father and grandparents. It all seemed so real," I said, trying hard to put into words what I had just experienced.

"It was real, child," Nathan said, stroking my hair to comfort me. "Your ability to transcend gave us the opportunity to guide you where your answers were."

"Can I go back? I have so many questions I want to ask her."

Nathan, looking the least exhausted. He smiled at me and said, "Your grandmother couldn't hear you, but being so powerful she was able to sense your presence."

"She wanted me to thank all of you for helping my father," I said, conveying the message.

Aunt Leslie approached me and helped me to my feet. My legs were weak, causing me to fall back in the seat.

"Slowly Caitlin, you need your rest," she said, turning her attention to Justin. "Take her home. We'll be right behind you."

I wanted to know everything – I didn't care how tired I felt. "No, I'm not going anywhere. There are so many questions I want answered."

Justin came to my side and helped me up, supporting most of my weight. "You need your rest, you'll get your answers soon enough."

The ride home was unusually quiet. Justin let me rest not saying a word.

"My grandmother had the same exact mark on her wrist as I do," I muttered, through the exhaustion. Justin didn't speak. His gaze was focused straight ahead, driving much slower than usual. "Justin? Are you feeling okay?"

"I'm a bit tired as well. It took a lot out of all of us."

Once at the house he helped me upstairs and into bed – pulling off my boots.

"Here," he said, handing me my nightshirt. "Change into something more comfortable and rest up."

Justin turned his back to me, fiddling with things on my vanity to give me some privacy. I shrugged out of my clothes and into my shirt.

"All done," I said, tucking myself under the covers – wanting him close to me again.

He went around the other side of the bed. Before he could even sit down, I lifted the covers for him to get in. Justin's gaze was questionable, not sure if he should. He finally gave into my pleading expression and slid his body next to mine, resting his hands on my waist, pulling me up against him. I kissed him on the mouth, lingering hungrily for his response. His wandering right hand trailed up and down my back pushing my shirt along with it. Inch by tantalizing inch, unintentionally, exposing my skin under the covers. His light touch on my bare back was maddening. I wanted him more than ever and I knew he felt the same.

Justin quickly responded to my thoughts, pinning me under him, searching my face, reading my expression. His kisses were full of yearning and hunger, but even thought my wrist was on fire I didn't want him to stop. His hand caressed my outer thigh, burning every inch it touched, and then the all too familiar tinkling sensation in my fingers was back.

Without warning, I felt a rush of energy course through my veins and before I could even warn Justin my gift responded menacingly, thrusting him across the room, crashing him against the wall with spine chilling force. He was thrown back as if hit by a bolt of lightning. I scrambled quickly to his side, hoping I didn't do much damage.

His laugh was welcoming. "Serves me right," he said, shaking it off. "You give a whole new meaning to why abstinence is preferable," he said, smiling at my traumatized expression. "I'm fine, don't worry," he chuckled. "Sorry Caitlin, I just got carried away."

"I'm the one who's sorry. I didn't mean to...," I bit my lip. "The Ellri are so right. My gift can't interpret my emotions."

"If you value my sanity, Caitlin, don't be so willing next time," he said, exhaling heavily into the pillow.

"I'm so sorry. I should've known better then to put you in this position. I wasn't thinking. I have absolutely no control."

"It's not your fault. We're both fighting this against our will. We'll be together soon enough," Justin said, rationalizing the impossible. "I can't seem to control myself when I'm that close to you and the feel of your skin on mine...," he shook his head again, trying to banish the feeling. "Well, let me just say that next time you're going to have to use more force to pry me off because I won't be able to stop myself."

"You'll be willing to lose your life to be with me?"

"Trust me – my sacrifice will be well worth the prize."

"You're never going to touch me again, are you?" I pouted, knowing full well that he would never put me in such a position.

"Not tonight I'm not. I wasn't the only one in imminent danger, just now. My own gift responds just as quickly in protecting me. We're both lucky I have complete control, otherwise we could've easily killed each other."

"Oh great!" I exclaimed, sitting up. "So we're destined to kill each other, is that it?"

He chuckled. "Only if you continue to look as sexy as you do tonight."

I picked up the pillow and threw it at him. "I'm serious!"

"So am I," he said, laughing. "I can't keep my hands off of you. My own feelings aside, the bond is growing, drawing us together. Can't you feel the pull?"

"Of course I feel it." I put my face in my hands. "The Ellri were right, Justin. I'm going to end up killing both of us."

He brought my head round to face him. "And what a sweet death it will be."

I shoved him away playfully. "It's not funny. We'll never be together." I whined, pleadingly. "You'll probably never touch me again."

"I'm not falling for that one, Caitlin."

"Not even a kiss?"

Justin shook his head. "Go to sleep."

TWENTY

DARKNESS DESCENDS

ROM THE TERRIBLE *pounding in my ears to the feeling that my heart was going to shatter from the sheer adrenaline rush, I stood there alone in an isolated world of large ancient woodlands, enveloped in eerie darkness with only the moon to shed light on areas where the dense canopy of bare branches allowed room for a smidgen of light.*

My ears caught nothing but the sound of the erratic change in my breathing. Wandering around uneasily I stopped the moment a slight breeze caught in my hair as with it came a trail of opaque whispers filling the decaying surroundings.

There, in those unnerving seconds, I felt a soft touch on my shoulder and as I nervously turned to see what it was my footing got caught up in one of the many protruding roots, and landed me on the cold moist soil. So terrified by the extraordinary turn of events that I scurried to brighter specks of ground, hoping that whatever was out there would remain in the darkness.

Then came whispers, which continued incessantly, changing in pitch and frequency that served to veil words of any form. There was not a breath of wind to stir the air. I inhaled and listened. There was that flat, oppressive air one senses before a storm, the smothering silence, the terrifying sound that comes only before the most horrid realization that you are not alone. I quickly turned to a sudden movement caught by the corner of my eye.

Two silhouettes emerged from deep inside the darkness, standing only yards away against the poorly lit backdrop. My heart raced, fearing the worst, but just as quick my mind came into focus. This, I was sure, was yet another dream.

The forms took one step closer and then another, testing me, seeing if I would back off. Suddenly, I felt the full force of my power in my fingers. I was not about to budge. This was my mind and they needed to get out.

"What do you want?" I heard myself ask. "Who are you?

Neither answered

I took one step forward determined to prove to them that I was not a bit scared, but this time they took one too.

"What do you want from me?" I suddenly bellowed. "Tears? Hysterics? Is that what you're looking for? Well that's not going to happen. Not today." I took one more step forward. "Now get the hell out of my head!"

The Shadows instantly vanished once again.

It had to be a dream. No other logical explanation.

I took a deep breath and opened my eyes – my head was on fire.

It was the same feeling I'd felt my first night in Oaks, at the pub where everybody was trying to read my thoughts – not as intense though. I was more in control.

"Did you have another dream?" Justin asked, from the far corner of the room.

"This is ridiculous. Why are you sleeping in the armchair? Come to bed."

"I'm fine where I am. Besides this is the place your uncle assigned me for the night. 'Take it or leave it' is how your uncle put it." Justin's imitation of Uncle Abbot's voice was spot on. I felt rather disoriented. I was not completely sure if the culprit was my dream or my visit to the past.

"What time is it?"

"About four in the morning."

I patted the empty space next to me, enticing him to come. "At least stretch out on top of the covers. I'll behave, I promise," I claimed, smiling at him, not wanting him to spend another night in that armchair.

Justin grabbed the quilt that covered him and moved towards the bed. "Fine, but there will be no kissing and no touching of any kind. Do we have an understanding?" He said, positively childishly.

"I promise," I said, laughing whimsically "No kissing, no touching – I get it."

He stretched out next to me with both hands crossed over his chest, fixing his gaze to the ceiling.

I turned my back to him complying with our deal. Justin turned to his side and buried his head in my hair, taking in long deep breaths, kissing me on the head and then wrapped his arms around me.

"Deal breaker" I accused him.

"Temptress," he retorted, kissing me again.

I giggled.

"The headache will soon fade away. Your dream is what brought it on. You shouldn't talk to them you know. It just gives them more power over you."

Justin was doing it again – reading me like an open book.

"I'd love to be able to read your thoughts as easily as you read mine."

"It's not as much fun as visiting the past, Caitlin, now is it? Reading and hearing thoughts are considered basic gifts. With time you might possess either one. There is no rule to how our gifts evolve."

"My grandmother Eileen could see the future, couldn't she?" I asked, turning to face him "She had warned my father and urged him to come here to Oaks."

"She couldn't see the future, nobody can. Eileen had visions of possibilities as did my grandmother. No one possess the ability to see something that hasn't happened yet. With every decision each person on this planet makes, the future changes like a chain reaction. We are all tied together in the web of life. Our every action has an effect on seven billion people. We're not aware that it's happening, but it does."

I looked at him baffled his explanation was hard to believe. "How is that possible?" I asked.

"Well, let's see. How can I explain this," he contemplated his next words. "Okay, imagine a lake with a smooth as silk surface. Now, if our decision was a pebble and we dropped it in this lake it will cause an outward movement of small ripples. Each ripple signifies the repercussions of that one decision." I nodded in understanding. "So, the bigger the decision the greater the repercussions, get it?" he asked, looking satisfied with the lesson.

"Sure, the bigger the pebble the larger the ripple," I said, laughing at how serious he looked at me. "I get it – I got it."

"Go to sleep, smarty." Fairly tired, I snuggled in his embrace and drifted off to sleep.

It was hours later when the roar of Kyle and Emily's arguing dragged me out of yet another bizarre and slightly scary dream where one of the Shadows actually stretched out a hand wanting me to take it. Thankfully, I was abruptly drawn awake by my brilliant cousins.

"That's just stupid," Emily screamed barging in. "Caitlin, can you please tell your fat headed cousin that we'd rather go somewhere hot for winter break. He thinks skiing would be much better."

I stretched to fully wake up. Justin was nowhere to be seen.

"He's in the bathroom," she answered my thoughts.

Kyle perched himself on my bed. "Caity, skiing is much more fun compared to sunbathing all day. You must see that."

"I'm sorry, but what are you arguing about and how did I get involved in the decision making?"

"I didn't get a chance to tell her yet," Justin said, emerging from the bathroom wiping his face off with a towel.

Emily seemed furious.

"Can somebody please tell me what we are arguing about this morning?" I asked puzzled.

"Last night the guys planned a picnic on the beach, bonfire and all." Emily said smiling at the memory.

I was visibly infuriated at Justin. "You let me miss something as wonderful as that?" I glared at him.

"We had more pressing problems to address, Caitlin, and more still."

"I know, but a bonfire, on the beach? How amazing was that Emily?" I turned to her knowing that only a girl would understand my anger.

"It was perfect – full moon and all. They even surprised us with the news."

"What news?"

"The Ellri agreed to let us go anywhere we want for two whole weeks," Kyle spat out triumphantly.

Justin didn't seem so excited. His expression suddenly darkened. "I'm not sure if Caitlin and I are coming," he finally said, staring at me intently.

"Why in the world not?" asked Kyle "If the Ellri allow it, there is no reason for you not to go. Isn't that right Caity?"

"Yes, that's exactly right," I answered, not breaking eye contact with Justin, intentionally provoking him. He didn't want to go for some reason.

"It's settled then, we're all going" Kyle said, content with my answer. "Now, about the place?"

Emily shoved Kyle over and sat herself down. "Sun or snow, Caitlin?"

I didn't want to be the one to decide our destination. The whole ripple effect got to me. "Kyle," I turned my full attention to him, "it's really a simple decision on your part. Would you prefer to have Sandy in a ski-suit or a bikini for two whole weeks?"

It took him all of two seconds to reach his final decision. "Sun it is," he said, jumping off the bed.

Emily squealed in excitement clapping her hands. "Thank you, Thank you," she screamed kissing me on the cheeks several times.

Justin stood there, across from us not saying a word.

"Can you guys leave us alone for a second? I need to talk to Justin."

Emily and Kyle both nodded, heading for the door, closing it behind them.

"What's wrong with you? Why don't you want us to go?" I asked, pushing myself out of bed. My nightshirt was pulled way to high, unladylike, revealing more than it should. I quickly straightened it out and stood up.

Justin's expression remained stone cold. "Do you really want to go on vacation with all this stuff going on?"

I walked up to him and kissed him lightly on the lips. "I've been locked up in an all girls' boarding school for five, long, tedious years missing you every second of the day. What makes you think I wouldn't want to go away with you? Unless it's something else you're not telling me?"

"I want you to get to the bottom of all this. I hate that you question your own existence, hate that you see nightmares. I hate everything these secrets are doing to you. Going anywhere with you is my dream, but I want you to be able to enjoy it, and not worry about anything else."

I folded my hands around his waist leaning my head against his chest. "We have a several days ahead of us. I'm sure the Ellri are going to shed light on everything by then. They wouldn't have agreed to any of this if they thought something bad might happen, would they?"

"No, I guess not. Okay then we'll go. Now get dressed, I want to take you to your parent's house to see why your faceless friends wanted you there in the first place. You're up to it, aren't you?"

"Yeah, sure. No problem," I said trying to sound convincing.

Before leaving for my parent's place we sat for breakfast with Uncle Abbot and Aunt Leslie – Kyle and Emily were still upstairs planning our vacation – arguing about the location.

"The Ellri need to see both of you later on today, so don't plan on going anywhere," Aunt Leslie said, handing Justin a cup of coffee.

Thanking her, he placed it down on the table, and said, "We're going to drive out to the Korbs' Estate, so Caitlin can see her house. We didn't have a chance to see the inside last time."

Aunt Leslie was cleaning up. I could tell she was slightly uncomfortable with our going out there again.

Folding his newspaper, Uncle Abbot directed his attention to me and said, "There's nothing at the house that will cause you any stress. It would actually be nice for you to look around and get a feel of your parents taste. They were so refined."

Aunt Leslie sat down across from me and extended her arm taking my hand into hers.

"Sorry if this whole ordeal has caused you pain. No child should be raised without knowing their past. Tonight you will get your answers and hopefully see that we did what we had to do to protect my beloved sister and you."

Her apology was heartfelt. I always knew deep down that she would not do anything to hurt me deliberately. I was not able to see that at thirteen, but now after seeing my father and grandparents, I was sure they had all the reasons in the world to send me away.

"Aunt Leslie, Uncle Abbot," I said, reaching for him with my free hand. "I could never ask for better parents than the two of you. You have showered me with so much love and attention." My uncle looked at me through teary eyes. "I admit that night five years ago was harsh, but now I'm sure you had your reasons. I never stopped loving either of you. I need you both to know that. I love both of you very, very much."

Uncle Abbot he lifted my hand and kissed it. "We don't deserve you, Caitlin. You were truly a gift to us."

My heart felt like breaking at the sound of his tearful voice. I got to my feet and gave him a great big hug. "I love you both."

"We love you too, child," he said, tightening his embrace. Aunt Leslie also hugged both of us with tear filled eyes.

"Can I get in on the hug?" Kyle said walking in, wrapping his arms around us – squeezing a bit more than necessary. "Justin, was breakfast that good?" he asked, wondering why all the hugging.

We all started laughing at his remark. His comic timing was always just right. "The best breakfast I ever had," Justin said, smiling at me.

We all took our seats once again finishing our breakfast. Emily came waltzing in smacking Kyle on the back of the head. "Damn it Em, knock it off already," he complained.

"What were you guys arguing about this morning," Uncle Abbot asked, picking up his newspaper once again.

Emily poured herself a cup of coffee.

"We can't decide where to go for our vacation," she said, sitting across from Kyle.

Aunt Leslie walked over to the fridge.

"None of you need to worry about arrangements. We got every little detail covered," she pointed out, smiling at our surprised expressions.

"What do you mean, mom?" Emily questioned, fairly taken by surprise.

"We agreed to let you go, but we decide the where," she muttered "Don't worry you won't be disappointed."

"So where are we going?" Kyle asked impatiently.

"You'll have to wait and see. We need to finalize the plans. The only thing you guys need to do is get your bags packed."

Kyle and Emily were lost for words – not sure if they should be happy or sad by the turn of events.

Deep In The Forest

Illustrated for Lines That Bind - Circle Of Trust

TWENTY-ONE

REVELATION

UBTLE IMAGES of my father, and what I had seen of the past continued to dawdle in the back of my mind allowing for a hint of sorrow to crawl its way back into my heart. It was like a knot in my gut that I couldn't seem to untie, getting tighter and tighter as the days wore on.

Justin's whole attitude had undergone a subtle change that day. I couldn't put my finger on it, but a change did occur, a change which he would never fess up to. I didn't question him on it, didn't even bring it up; instead, I remained staring out the side window as he accelerated down the winding road to my parents' home. Once there, Justin was about to wave the burly cast iron gates open, when I beat him to the punch.

"What was that?" he asked, not accustomed to being taken by surprise.

I giggled at his expression. It was not every day that I could catch him off guard. He was always two steps ahead of everybody. "It would seem," I said boasting, "that you're not the only one in this car with powers."

His gaze was filled with suspicion. "That was quite fast. I felt you blocking me."

"I didn't mean to. I just wanted to show off a little." I admitted, innocently. "I've been practicing for weeks and I finally got the hang of it."

"You have, have you?" He said smiling wickedly, putting the car in motion.

The magnificent classical elevation of the house was hidden from view until we broke from the trees. As we approached up the long driveway, the first thing I noticed was the once spacious landscaped gardens on either side now overgrown, in much need of care.

"It must've been beautiful," I whispered, making a mental note of how years of neglect had slowly disfigured the once sculptured landscape.

Even in the disarray of overgrowth and fallen limbs, the area couldn't hide its original splendor. It was surely in impeccable order back then, with its perfectly pruned bushes outlining the far walkway, neatly cut lawns sprawling across the endless grounds, even the grand marble fountain free of all the slimy residue and years of debris; nothing like what it was now, abandoned and left to the elements.

I let my gaze scan the length of the tall pines and aristocratic opulence of the oak trees which cast long shadows over the house and garden, intensifying the mysteriousness of the place.

"So what can you do exactly?" Justin finally asked.

I circled my head to the sound of his voice. "Anything."

"Anything? That's interesting."

"It's really easy. I think about what I want and it's in my hands in no time at all."

"I've got to see this," he said, putting the car in park.

We both got out and climbed the double elliptical stone stairways ascending to the main entrance door, under a Baroque covered porch. I could feel the warmth of the cream colored, hand-wrought, natural stone columns.

Once at the door, Justin looked at me skeptically. "Open it, Caitlin," he said, testing me.

I deliberately turned my back to the locked door and stared directly into his eyes to show him that I could do it with my eyes closed. "Open," I said in a soft, but firm voice, giving him a peck on the lips to prove how effortless it was. In no time, at all, the door unlocked to my command.

Justin proudly kissed me back, happy to see that I was getting the hang of my power.

On entering the house we found ourselves in the middle of an impressive, highly decorative double height sky-lit Foyer. Large family portraits, covered with dust rags, hung on the far walls and twin curving stairways led to the second floor. Stone and plaster details abound; the classical theme permeated the structure. Beautiful wood floors contrasted with the marble and stone. The breath-taking crown moldings and vaulted ceilings captured the eye.

Justin and I decided to go through the framed doorway and into the formal living room. It was an extremely elegant room, once lit by the sparkling chandelier that hung overhead – now, its luster lost to the dust and cob webs.

"You're not forcing it are you?" he asked, surveying our surroundings. "It's all so natural for you, isn't it?"

"I guess it is," I said smiling contently.

"For me it's a force I have to push to wield things. It's like breaking through a natural boundary."

I didn't speak. I simply walked round the room, letting my hand linger behind, tracing over every object, leaving dust tracks in my wake. It was in immaculate condition, considering nobody had lived there for so many years.

The sight of all the furniture being covered with white sheets to protect it from the dust created an eerie atmosphere. The first thing that struck me was the smell of damp and mustiness which, not surprisingly, pervaded the whole house.

Justin drew the rich velvet curtains. Instantly, a cloud of dust lifted off the material. He opened one of the double French doors to let in some fresh air and light.

"How many things can you move simultaneously?" I asked, exploring the room.

He turned his attention to me. "I can move about two objects, but with great effort. How about you?"

"As many as I want. I picture what I want and it happens." I walked to the other side of the long room. "You want to see what I mean?"

"Yeah, go ahead – only if you feel up to it."

"What would you like me to do?" I ventured, wanting to prove that I was finally getting things under control.

"I don't know. Pick up a chair or something."

"I'll do one better than that."

In a split second I had all the covered furniture in the room suspended in mid-air. Justin's bewildered expression was testament to how powerful I've become.

"You don't feel anything? A pressure or any sort of pain?"

"It just happens. I can control each and every piece separately, look," I said, smiling at his astounded face, returning each piece, one by one to its original spot without the slightest sound.

"I can honestly say, Caitlin, you are a wonder. What's the

biggest object you can move?'

"I don't know. I've never thought of it in that way. I don't think about the weight or the size of the object. I just concentrate on what I want it to do. Maybe you should do the same. Why place limits to your gift? You are way stronger than me. By thinking that something is too big for you to handle you're inadvertently blocking your own potential. Just wield it because you want it. Don't let its size or weight limit you."

I could tell he was seriously contemplating my suggestions. He was bobbing his head up and down in agreement. "Yeah, I see what you mean, it makes sense."

Wanting to prove my theory, I pointed to the coffee table in the middle of the room.

"Justin, don't think about what it is just move it," I instructed.

Smiling broadly, amused that the pupil suddenly became the teacher, he swiftly motioned the table to lift with his right hand. In seconds the inanimate object lifted off the floor floating in air.

"Now this," I ordered, directing his gaze to the couch. "Don't think of it in size or shape, just lift it."

Unlike me, Justin used his hand to wield the object. With another quick flick of his hand he did as I said and both objects were a few feet off the floor. I stepped to the heavy armchair.

"Try one more. Simply picture all three suspended," I advised.

Closing his eyes – Justin did as he was told. Instantly all three pieces were weightless in the air defying the laws of gravity.

"How do you feel?"

I could tell he was bowled over – not expecting anything like it. "It's amazing," he exclaimed. "I felt absolutely nothing. How did you figure it out?"

Deciding that he deserved some kind of prize for his feat I reached in and kissed him resolutely on the lips. "At my birthday party," I answered, taking a few steps back to control my sudden excitement. "Kyle showed me how to move a pine cone and told me that I should concentrate only on the action I want done and not on the object itself."

"That Kyle is something, isn't he?" Justin said, returning the objects back to the floor.

I was surprised at how fast he grasped the technique. "It took me a few weeks to learn how to do what you just did in seconds."

Justin frowned at my discontent expression. "I'm more in tune with my powers," he said, trying to make me feel better about my weeks of practice. "I've had them much longer than you. We all learn new things about ourselves on a daily basis. This method will help me evolve even more," he added, pulling me into his embrace and kissing the tip of my nose admiringly. "Now, enough playing around, let's get down to the real reason we're here." He quickly released his hold. "Where would you like to start?"

Uncle Abbot was right, there was nothing left in the forlorn house, apart from the priceless antique furniture. The two story library with spiral stair had nothing but bookcases that stood bare, draped in ghostly white.

I unveiled several portraits – my ancestors stared down at me from the walls, sending shivers down my spine. My grand-parents' portraits from my mother's side – Grandpa Cecil and grandma Cordilia were similar to the ones hung in Aunt Leslie's great hall. I was, however, surprised to see the portraits of my grand-parents from my father's side in plain view, hung in the master study.

"Why would my father display a portrait of grandfather

Clancy? There was bad blood between them. I saw it first-hand."

"Your father loved him, Caitlin," Justin muttered, looking at the portrait, responding to my bewildered expression. "He might not have agreed with Clancy's choices or ideals, but that doesn't mean he loved him any less. It must have been very difficult for both your mother and father to leave their families behind," he continued to explain – putting his arms around me, and pulling me back towards him. "The ties we share with our family are like no other. We are weaved together emotionally, making the distance between us unbearable. That's why we all live in such a close proximity. Your parents suffered being away from their loved ones."

Needing to face him, I repositioned myself in his embrace. His gaze unintentionally scattered my thoughts. Picking up on my light-headedness, Justin leaned in and kissed me lightly, smiling at my love struck response.

"They had absolutely no choice, but to leave," I sighed, regaining my composure. "They were going to hurt my mother. He had no choice but to drop everything and live in exile." I added, at the brief flash of memory.

Hearing my own words I suddenly realized that my parent's banishment was a picture image of my own life. My eyes quickly widened at the revelation.

"Was that the reason I was sent away?"

He held me tighter.

"I don't know, Caitlin. We're going to find out later on today."

I racked my brain trying to recall every detail of those last few days, the days before I had been sent away, anything that could help me piece together the puzzle.

"Please," he breathed, leaning towards me, "don't do this to yourself," he said, keeping his tone light – coaxing my face up.

"We'll get to the bottom of this, I promise."

My head was spinning faster at all the possibilities.

"Was I in any danger back then, Justin? Do you think I'm in any danger now?"

His soft expression hardened.

"Who'd want to hurt me, and why?" I asked, trembling at the thought.

Justin's voice was almost inaudible, his expression slightly fearful. "Don't jump to any conclusions. Whatever it is, I promise I won't let anything happen to you."

The next few minutes seemed to stretch for hours. Nestled in his arms, I was overcome with the fear of knowing it was the only promise he would not be able to keep.

Whatever the outcome, I would never put him in a position to risk his life – not even to save mine. He was everything to me and I was willing to lay it all on the line.

Desperate for his touch, I encircled my arms around his neck, pushing myself up to kiss him. Justin quickly responded by lifting me slightly off the floor, holding me tight against his toned chest.

"I love you," he said, his voice deep with meaning. "I won't allow anything to happen to you."

I looked into his brilliant deep blue eyes – like pools of midnight sky inviting me in.

"You have to promise me," I said, lost in his gaze, "that whatever happens, whatever this is, you're never going to risk your life. Not for me, not for anyone."

"Nothing is going to happen," he tried reassuring me. "And for the last time, Caitlin, you are my life." He brushed his lips against mine. "Who would I be without you?"

Satiated with excitement, I shuddered almost painfully. I

locked my mouth with his feverishly.

The love I felt for him was unquenchable. "I love you," I confessed, rapt in his touch.

The stinging sensation on my wrist returned. The faint sweet smell of his skin was intoxicatingly alluring, pulling me into its trap. Not wanting to torture him any more than necessary, I took a step back kissing him gently on the mouth. "Why did you do that for?" he growled, reaching for me – wanting me.

Teasingly, I smacked his extended hand. "Keep your hands to yourself," I told him, reminding him of last night's deal. "No kissing, no touching, remember? Your rules!"

Justin flashed me one of his devilish smiles, reaching for me. "Rules are meant to be broken," he said, pulling me back into his hold with brute force.

"Not if breaking them, means killing you," I pronounced decisively, pulling out of his vice. "Now behave or else," I threatened, trying not to laugh at his pleading gaze.

He took a step closer, slipping his hand behind my neck, pulling me closer. "I'd die a thousand deaths if it meant having all of you," he said breathlessly, narrowing the space I put between us, leaning in, inches from my lips.

I let out a groan of protest as he quickly stepped back, leaving me wanting more. "But seeing that you're so intent on preserving my life, I promise to behave, for now, at least."

"Good," I finally exhaled in a state of mental numbness, trying to reclaim my balance, trying to bring order to my flailing concentration. His words and sensual actions had stupefied me – left me stand there with a blank expression.

Justin's boyish grin widened. "Let's go check out the second floor, shall we?" I nodded, staring at the only man who could make me weak in the knees. "We have to make it quick. The Ellri are expecting us," he said, taking my hand.

The upstairs was a network of halls leading to the numerous rooms. The walls were discolored in places where paintings once hung. One by one we surveyed the rooms to see if by any chance we would find anything of interest. Most were vacant – not a hint of life.

"Have you decided what you're going to do with the property?" Justin asked, leading me down the hall to the next room. "This is all yours now, Caitlin. You can sell it if it makes you feel uneasy."

Looking around in amazement at the grandeur of my surroundings it was hard to believe that all this belonged to me.

"I haven't thought about it. I mean, I still can't believe my parents lived here. Look at this place!" We continued to survey other rooms. "I don't want to part with it, but that doesn't mean, of course, that I'm ready to live here."

Justin squeezed my hand reassuringly. "I didn't mean to imply that you had to make a decision any time soon. This building isn't going anywhere."

"I know. I just can't see myself selling it. I wouldn't want to see my parent's home in somebody else's hands. If my father wanted to sell it he would've when he was alive, wouldn't he?"

Stopping abruptly, Justin held both of my hands – his eyes wide with intrigue. "Justin, what is it? What's wrong?"

"I can't believe I haven't thought of this before!"

"Thought of what?"

"Caitlin, they left it for you," he started to say, deep in thought, "wanting you to have something that meant a lot to both of them. They told me themselves."

"What do you mean, 'they told you'?"

"Carolyn knew of our bond way before anybody else did. On

your first birthday, she sat you on my lap." He pushed back his hair, shaking his head in disbelief. "I can't believe I forgot all about that."

"What are you saying?"

"I was barely four years old at the time, but she insisted that I hold you, Caitlin. She made me promise to protect you and love you. I agreed thinking nothing of it; you were such a cute little brat, after all."

I looked at him confused. "What does that have to do with anything, apart from the fact that you are absolutely adorable right now?"

His concentration was elsewhere. I could have been a giraffe and he would not have noticed. "Do you know what this means?" he asked me.

I shook my head.

"Caitlin, this proves that your mom was quite gifted." I continued to look at him questionably. "She knew the future, knew that we were going to be together."

"How is that possible? The intensity of our bond didn't start until many years later, after her death. I must've been seven or eight when I first felt the burn. I was sick for two whole days."

"That sounds about right," Justin estimated in his head. "I must've been ten or so when I first experienced it. At times, it was unbearable being away from you. Your parents probably knew exactly what it was, even before the burn had surfaced."

Justin smiled at yet another thought.

"What is it? What's on your mind?"

"I can't believe I didn't catch on to it."

"Justin, you're losing me again."

"Caitlin, your father kept bringing me over the house using piano lessons as an excuse. He had figured out that the closer I was to you, the better we'd feel. He was right. I did feel at peace with you close. When you were about three they had brought us here, to this house."

I looked at him with skepticism. "Are you sure? I don't remember this place. It's my first time here."

"You were only three, Caitlin. I remember it so vividly, it was the first time I'd ever stepped foot in here. They took us around the house showing us all the rooms."

His gaze suddenly dropped to the floor – weighing something in his mind.

"What is it?" I asked, concerned by his altered state of mind.

He circled his head and faced me. His blue eyes looked troubled – darker somehow.

"They knew – knew they wouldn't be around for long," he said, overwhelmed at his own thoughts. "That's why they had brought us here that day. Your parents wanted to make sure I knew about this building. They hadn't said it in so many words, but it was there in their actions."

My heart caught in my mouth. "Are you saying that they had foreseen everything? Even their death?"

He closed his eyes, visibly preoccupied by other thoughts. "Yes, I think they did."

Tears fought to break free, but I refused to give into those feelings. "Justin, what did they tell you, exactly?"

Visibly struggling to find the right words, Justin swallowed hard not knowing what it all meant. "We were in the lounge downstairs, talking about trivial matters," he said, after a long pause. "I enjoyed their company because they treated me like an adult. Your mother was so weak, Caitlin, so fragile. She had insisted on coming along. Your father was dead set against it, but he didn't have the heart to refuse her request."

"But why was she so sick?"

Justin shrugged his shoulders. "I'm not sure. Nobody ever talked about it."

"Figures," I muttered, inhaling deeply to smother the sadness. I noticed from the corner of my eye that Justin was reluctant to continue. "I'm fine," I said, reassuringly, "go on."

"Are you sure? You don't look fine."

"Go on!"

"That day, your mother had explained that the older I got, the stronger my feelings would be for you, and that you would feel our special connection just as deeply. It wasn't as intense as it is now, but the feeling was there, Caitlin, from the moment you were born." Justin's stern features quickly softened. "That day, I realized that it was you who caused me so much pain." He smiled. "To be honest, I didn't much care for you after that. You were the root of all evil, as far as I was concerned."

I chuckled at his admission. "I knew you hated me all along."

"Hate?"

Justin caressed my cheek. "I wouldn't go as far as to call it hate. It was just hard, at that age, to decipher what it was that I felt for you." He leaned his forehead against mine. "Over the years you grew on me."

"Like fungus, you mean?"

He laughed out loud, lifting my spirit high. "No. Not fungus, Caitlin." Justin pecked me on the lips and continued saying, "Your father mentioned that they weren't going to be around forever and that they needed me to remind you of how much they loved you and that all this was done for you. Your mother died a few months later and your father not long after."

Tears sprang to my eyes once again. This time nothing I did could hold them back.

"I wish I had your memories of them, Justin. Mine are so vague. I only have a faint memory of my mother's voice and fragrance. My father is a melody, a hum of sorts."

With a feather like motion, he wiped my eyes dry. "They loved you and they certainly knew how much I'd love you. They were looking out for you, Caitlin. That much I'm sure of." He cuddled me, knowing I needed comforting.

"Why did they have to die so young?"

"Look at me," Justin said, guiding my chin up to face him. "They are not dead. They live through you, Caitlin. You are the continuation of both of them. You carry in you both their powers and love. You must see that."

Justin was once again the adult and I the child – his words had somehow hit home.

"I know," I whimpered. "I just hope I had more time to get to know them."

Several minutes had passed when Justin slightly released his hold and gazed knowingly into my eyes. "Let's go to the lounge," he instructed unnerved. "I just remembered something your mother had shown me. It didn't mean anything back then, but now I'm sure she intentionally pointed it out."

Puzzled at his rapid change in mood, I followed him downstairs.

Back in the lounge, Justin let go of my hand and headed to the far corner of the room – scanning the area for something. He wrinkled his brow in an apparent effort to recollect what it was that my mother had shown him – more than fifteen years ago. His smile widened to a grin. "Here it is," he exclaimed.

Justin pulled out one of the hand carved drawers of the china cabinet, shaking it lightly – smiling with satisfaction.

He carried it proudly to the coffee table, smiling contently at his find. It was completely empty.

"Carolyn showed me this that day, making damn sure I'd be impressed enough that I'd never forget it. It was completely empty back then, but I bet there is something here for you now."

"It's an empty drawer, Justin," I stated the obvious, confused by his enthusiasm.

"Not everything is what it seems, Caitlin," he said, utterly absorbed in the task of pushing down on the base of the drawer.

With a loud click the bottom unlatched, opening like a drawbridge – revealing a secret compartment full of letters.

"I knew it," he exclaimed delightedly. "They had foreseen everything. Why else would she have shown this to a six-year-old? It certainly wasn't to impress me," Justin muttered, sounding as if he were talking to himself now. "She knew, all too well, that most of our hand crafted furniture had some kind of secret compartment. This was certainly nothing special compared to some of my parent's intricately designed ones."

Stunned, unable to move, I stared down at the faded pink ribbon which neatly held the letters in a compact pile.

I tentatively took them out of their hiding place and sifted through them. They all bore the same penmanship – no return address on any but a name: *Eileen Korbs*.

They were all from my grandmother, addressed to my parents.

"This one is addressed to you, Caitlin," said Justin, surveying the contents of the drawer.

"For me? How is that possible?"

I stared at him in disbelief, my mind was a whirl, not sure of what it all meant. I hesitantly reached out my hand to take it.

"You don't have to do this now," he said, aware of my anxiety.

"It's only a letter, right? How bad can it be?" I added, with a shaky voice trying to get up the nerve to open the envelope.

I pulled the correspondence out, timidly unfolding the paper. My heart started to thump rhythmically.

"It's a poem," I winced, expecting something more.

Justin looked at me, not knowing how to react.

"It's one of my favorite poems, 'Sympathy' by Emily Bronte."

"There should be no despair for you
While nightly stars are burning;
While evening pours its silent dew
And sunshine gilds the morning.
There should be no despair – though tears
May flow down like a river:
Are not the best beloved of years
Around your heart for ever?
They weep, you weep, it must be so;
Winds sigh as you are sighing,
And winter sheds its grief in snow
Where Autumn's leaves are lying:
Yet, these revive, and from their fate
Your fate cannot be parted:
Then, journey on, if not elate
Still, NEVER broken-hearted!"

She closed off the letter with a simple:

I love you, Caitlin Eileen.

Your devoted Grandmother,
Eileen Korbs

"I don't know that one. Go ahead, read it," he said, pushing the drawer to the side, giving me his undivided attention.

I positioned myself in his lap and redistributed my weight to sit comfortably – needing him close, not knowing how my grandmother knew that I loved this poem.

"Maybe it was simply her favorite as well," Justin said, answering my thoughts.

"When I first came across Bronte's collection in our school library at Stone Hurst, it was as if it called out to me – relating my every emotion."

Justin traced his hand up and down my back trying to sooth my hesitation. I took a deep breath and recited the words.

Justin caressed my face with his hand and kissed me lightly on the lips. "It's beautiful."

I nodded my head in agreement, unable to speak. I never had the chance to meet my grandmother apart from my bizarre visit to the past. Nevertheless, I knew in the depths of my soul that I loved her dearly.

At that moment, I stood up, giving him a quick kiss, a startling idea occurred to me, an idea that seemed, at the moment an inspiration. "I think I know what it all means." I said in a breathy tone. "I know why she had written this for me." I paused momentarily in front of him, but then started pacing back and forth. "Why did my parents include this letter with the rest?" I stopped and looked at him, clutching the envelope against my chest. "It's the only explanation. Why else would they go to so much trouble to bring us here all those years ago? They wanted to make sure you knew of this hiding place."

I could feel Justin in my head, searching my thoughts. "Do you really think that's the reason?" he asked way before I even got the chance to formulate my theory.

I bobbed my head in affirmation. "I wrote this poem in my diary a few years ago. One of those nights I had difficulty sleeping. She must've sensed my agony of being away or might've even seen me in one of her visions. Either way, it means she was keeping track of me. She was thinking of me."

"It would explain the letter. She wanted you to know that you were really never alone. She was there looking out for you."

"Why was my grandmother keeping tabs on me for all those years, Justin? Why didn't she simply come and visit? Why didn't anyone come? What were they so afraid of?"

Anticipating my desire to learn the truth he got to his feet and collected the drawer.

"Before we head to the Ellri," he said, picking something out of the secret hiding place, "there's one last thing that belongs to you."

He handed me a very distinguished and attractive Victorian silver locket elegantly detailed with etched leaves surrounded by a heart and dart border. The underside was skillfully engraved with the initials - E.K. - in the center.

The collar was long and rare with links which were beautifully pierced through with floral ornamentation. I traced my fingers over the embossed letters. "Eileen Korbs," I sighed "This was my grandmothers."

Justin returned the empty drawer to its rightful place.

"It must've been," I pronounced.

Without wasting any time he came and stood next to me and

took the locket from my trembling hands. With ease , Justin pried open the firmly shut snap and we both smiled at the sight of the picture of me as a baby, in my mother's arms, but the left frame was empty.

"That's odd," I said, turning to look at Justin. "Why would she have a picture of my mother and not one of her own son?"

"I don't know," he said closing the snap. "But, what I do know is that she wanted you to have this. I'm sure she needed you to know that you were very dear to her."

Justin hung the pendant around my neck. "This locket was very important to your grandmother, I'm sure of it. You are very lucky to have so many people who love you."

I tucked the long chain under my sweater, away from prying eyes. "Why wouldn't she have a picture of my father?" I repeated. "It's odd, isn't it?"

"I hate to rush, but we need to get going if you want to get all your answers from the Ellri."

"Of course," I said, taking a deep painful breath as I collected the small stack of letters. "Let's get out of here."

The Estate

Illustrated for Lines That Bind - Circle Of Trust

TWENTY-TWO

THE TRUTH

HE MID-DECEMBER sun, which filtered faintly between soft masses of cloud, was surprisingly warm. I closed my eyes and leaned back in the comfortably padded car seat, luxuriating in the peaceful ride back home. I stopped playing with my pendent, stopped thinking of my parents and allowed my mind to drift into nothingness.

"If you're not up to it, this can wait," Justin told me, aware of my feelings.

"No, I want to do this, for both of us. Learning the truth will help me move forward. It will allow me to leave the past behind, where it belongs."

"Whatever you hear today; however, dark it might be, I want you to remember that I love you and nothing in this world can change that."

"I love you too," I said smiling faintly, and shifted my gaze out the window once again until the lights from the house came into view as we entered the long driveway.

"Everything will be okay, you'll see," Justin reassured me.

The things that bothered me: my relationship with Justin and the rest of my family, my deep rooted unhappiness at missing out on having my parents around, were trivial things in the whole fabric of what truly went on around the world. My family took care of the details. I only had to worry about living my life.

It's a pity, I thought as I looked up at the sky, *that I'm so damn bad at it.*

The weather was turning quickly for the worse. The sun dipped beneath the horizon and the puffy clouds began to darken. The breeze was whipping up so that the branches of the trees had started to sway.

"Let's get inside before it starts raining," Justin said, turning off the engine. Hand in hand we walked up to the door. "This should be fun," he added smiling, knowing something I didn't.

The second the door opened, I knew exactly what he was referring to. The house was a hubbub of activity. I was surprised to see the Ellri so up key. I had thought that we'd find them meditating or something – not that they ever did, but surely not this.

"Oh good, you're both here. Come, have something to eat before we begin," Shannon said, a bit more cheerful than usual.

She took our coats and skipped merrily away.

"Have they been drinking?" I asked, not sure why they were acting so peculiar.

"No – maybe – I'm not sure. They're just happy that this is going to be over with. They're trying real hard to create a casual atmosphere for you; maybe, too hard, by the looks of it."

"They look drunk."

He chuckled. "Trust me, there're not. It hasn't been easy for them to keep all these secrets."

"So why did they then?"

He shrugged his shoulders. "That's what we're here to find out. If you want to get your answers you need to keep an open mind about everything you hear. Keep your emotions under control, no matter what they tell you."

I kissed him on the cheek. "Gee, Justin, you're more worried than I am. Relax, will you?"

He pulled a face. "Funny girl! Just keep your cool, and don't forget that every last one of them had an active part in raising you. It was really hard for them to keep all this bottled up for so many years."

"Okay, I get it! I'll behave!"

I decided that if they were willing to go to all that trouble to make my evening less painful, I would at least play along.

"C'mon, then," I said cheerfully to Justin, "Let's get a bite to eat."

He grinned broadly, eyes shimmering in skepticism. I sensed that he was not buying into my new found positive attitude. Being the perfect gentlemen, though, he played the role faultlessly. "Wait for me in the kitchen," he told me, taking the letters from my hands, and scuttled up the stairs, two steps at a time, and headed towards my room.

After a few minutes he joined me in the kitchen and chewed down on a few scrumptious morsels that Aunt Leslie threw together, listening to some anecdotes William had prepared for our entertainment. Boisterous laughter inundated the air each time Justin's father finished with a story. Justin, however, found his father's talent in story telling childish and out of character – rolling his eyes at each and every punch line.

The few hours that followed were, for me, a time of change, and a time when hours of worry and sorrow alternated with periods of great happiness.

"Have a glass of wine, Caity," Marlene offered. Justin's brow furrowed in suspicion. "It will sooth your nerves and relax your frame of mind," she added.

"If I didn't know any better, Marlene, I'd think you were trying to get me drunk," I told her, taking the glass, not losing the opportunity to accept alcohol form an adult.

She handed Justin a full glass as well, winking at him and exhibiting a conspirator's smile. "Caitlin, it's not me you should be worried about getting you drunk." Her husky laughter filled the air, knowing I'd get the insinuation.

"Ha, ha, very funny Marlene," Justin said sarcastically.

Her smile widened to a grin. "Drink up dear boy," Marlene continued to taunt him. "So much repressed sexual-tension can't be good for any young man."

I strained to catch the words, but my ears seemed filled with cotton balls, and my eyes didn't believe the scene that was unfolding in front of me. I almost choked on my lunch, stunned but not because of Marlene's comment, but because Justin was nodding his head in agreement. His reserved manner quickly evaporated as he lifted the glass to his mouth emptying the contents in one swift gulp.

"Good boy," she consoled him, patting him on the back.

My cheeks were, if nothing else, an embarrassing ruby red. Swooping in on the conversation, Lucille was not at all amused.

"Don't patronize my nephew," she said, looking angrily at her best friend. "Just call them as I see them," responded Marlene, leaving the room, laughing even louder.

"She's incorrigible," Lucille exclaimed rather loudly, making sure that Marlene could hear her down the hall.

"You shouldn't pay any attention to that old bag. The years

seem to have faltered her common sense."

"Sticks and stones, Lucille – sticks and Stones," Marlene yelled, from yards away, booming excitedly.

"You take her way too seriously, Aunt Lucille," said Justin, defending Marlene. His voice loomed and faded to take another sip. "She only says things in good fun, never hurt anyone to laugh."

Her expression was quite severe, but his words managed, nonetheless, to penetrate the icy cold exterior. "Yes, I see your point," she conceded, kissing him on the head, leaving us to finish our meal. "Laughter is always a good thing," she added on her way out.

I looked at Justin disappointedly, nudging him with my elbow. "You agreed with Marlene," I accused him. "Shame on you, and here I thought you were a gentleman."

Justin was already on his second glass of wine, grinning at me mischievously. "As if I could hide anything from a High Ellri. She can read both of us like an open book, Caitlin," he said pausing. "My innate ability to keep myself from ravishing you is amusing to her."

I blushed even more, were that even possible. "You must be kidding!"

"Wish I were, but I'm not. They all find our predicament amusing."

"Oh, that's just great!" I exclaimed, taking a great big gulp of my wine.

A few hours into our merrymaking, Nathan called us into Uncle Abbot's study. "We'd better get started," he said. "Caitlin, it's time you knew the truth."

I went very still. The fear of the unknown came in torrents, but it couldn't outweigh the seeded curiosity that grew stronger and stronger, becoming less easy to ignore.

Standing up had become a greater challenge than I thought. I pulled myself together enough to talk. "Great wine," I proclaimed giggling, turning to Justin.

"Oh, great! That's all we needed," I heard him say, putting his arms around me to lead me to the study. "Marlene, are you satisfied?" asked Justin, really appalled at her for intentionally making me tipsy

"I'm fine," I said, slurring my words. "Let's just sit down and get this over with."

Uncle Abbot showed me to one of the leather chairs, shaking his head in disapproval of my intoxicated state. I lifted my hand and childishly patted him on the cheek. "I'm fine Uncle Abbot, don't worry. I'm not, at all, drunk."

He motioned for me to sit down. "Behave," he ordered, turning to the rest of the guests.

It took a few minutes for the room to finally settle down.

Marlene sat on my right, holding my hand. "Are you okay, Caity?"

"Great, no thanks to you," I smiled, preparing to stand. "We should get more wine."

She quickly pulled me back in the seat. "Later Caity," she said, waiting for me to calm down.

It was not until several moments later when everyone had quieted down, that Marlene began to speak. "Well, I guess the best way to go about this is to dive right in," she said, squeezing my hand. "You've already seen the reason why your parents had to come here twenty or so years ago."

I nodded, giving her my undivided attention – well, almost.

Giddy as I was, I tried concentrating hard, wanting her to get to the core of the reason why I was sent away.

"Your grandmother Eileen along with your grandparents Cordilia and Cecil McDevitt blocked their escape to Oaks. Nobody knew that your parents moved here, apart from us, of course. Your father was given precise instructions to use the Cathcart name in order to secure their anonymity," she started to explain. "This was a little over five years before you were born."

"Okay wait – just stop for a sec," I said. In the heavy silence that followed, I clearly felt the first stirrings of rational thought. "How would changing their surname keep them safe, keep them undetected?"

Marlene looked over to her life-partner for help. Nathan hesitated a few seconds, sorting out his thoughts, fumbling with his sleeve. "You see Caitlin," he began to explain, "over thousands of years each generation of Ellri has developed ties with our immediate family which allow us to home in on any living blood relative. It's a safe-guard to assist each other in a time of dire need. We simply concentrate, think of that person and we can read their thoughts and vision their actions."

My eyes unintentionally widened thinking about my grandmother's letter. *That's how she knew about the poem,* I thought. The connection she had with me permitted her to see and feel me. Instantly, I turned my gaze to Justin needing to let him in on my discovery, but quickly realized that he, too, came to the very same conclusion. It was in the way he looked at me.

Aunt Leslie stood up, too anxious to remain seated. "Your grandparents were quite remarkable, both in character and especially in power," she boasted. "Eileen Korbs and my mother Cordilia both possessed the power to block thoughts. They could erase any tie a family member might have to an Ellri, making it impossible for anyone to sense the one they shielded. However, what they couldn't do is erase your parents off the map completely, because your grandfather Clancy's unparalleled ability to read minds could have easily located them through the thoughts of others, using anyone who verbalized the name Korbs as a homing device."

My aunt walked the length of the room and rested on the edge of the desk, continuing with her explanation.

"Abbot just happened to have a cousin named Winston somewhere in Europe. We took the window of opportunity and introduced your father to the town folk as a blood relative; no one was the wiser. The secret was strictly kept among us."

Surprisingly calm, thanks to the glass of wine; I scanned the room looking at all their faces.

"If you were the only ones who knew about their real identity then how did Justin figure it out?"

"Caitlin," Justin said, drawing my attention to him, "I only found out the truth only a few days ago when I had the vision. When your parents had taken us to the house I was unaware of their true identity. I, along with the rest of the town folk, believed him to be a Cathcart."

"But still," I said unconvinced, "Wouldn't the names Winston and Carolyn have alerted my grandfather? How many people could there possibly be with the same name?"

Nathan looked quite pleased with my perceptiveness, in spite of my half-drunken state, and said, "Our ability allows us to seek only our own blood relatives. Carolyn, your mother, was undetectable as far as Clancy was concerned. He couldn't locate her, unless she willed it. Besides, both your parents bore first names that went back generations. There are several people with the same name scattered around Europe. Oaks, was the last place your grandfather would have looked."

"Then why? Why all the secrecy? You could've easily told me

everything once my parents passed away. There was no need to keep me in the dark, was there?"

Lucille was uneasy, wringing her hands nervously. "We didn't anticipate one significant factor in our equation," she regretfully informed me, "You Caitlin. We didn't anticipate you," she added.

I slid a glance full of uncertainty at Lucille. "Me? Why was I the hitch to your plans?"

"Your parents were together for several years, and never once talked about having children."

"So, what does that mean? Are you saying that I was an unplanned pregnancy? That my parents didn't want children?"

"No – no, Caitlin. You're running ahead of yourself. I'm saying no such thing. Your emergence to our world was clouded by both jubilation and fear."

"Fear?" I looked at her bewildered.

"Yes child, fear. You see, your mom was the first born of the McDevitt bloodline as was Winston for the Korbs. Both families being the oldest secured you the highest level of their gifts. They were the purest of their generation. Carolyn might not have displayed her power, but it was there all the same."

I absently stood up. I didn't know why or where to head, but I stood up anyway. "But that still doesn't explain my part in all this," I heard myself say. "Why was I the problem?"

There was a long, painful silence. No one seemed willing to speak. Even the air around them seemed to be charged with high emotion. Immersed in dark and mazy thoughts, I didn't for some time notice their eyes on me, following me around the room. Somehow, a cold pit had opened in my stomach. I turned to find Justin standing against the far wall, but the look in his eyes was calm and resigned, and when he opened his arms and I stepped into them, only the rapid beating of his heart hinted at his anxiety. His strong hands secured me in his embrace and for a moment my fears had vanished.

"Caity," smiled Marlene, reading my reaction to Justin's touch, "It is quite rare for two firstborns, like your parents, to unite under the Oath of Unity. Even rarer is the power that is passed down to their offspring. It ties the child to both bloodlines."

"I'm aware of that, Marlene. But even so, it doesn't...,"

She motioned for me to stop. "A few months before you were born your grandfather Clancy must have sensed you. It was your blood ties to the Korbs that summoned him, enabling him to locate your father. Winston probably feared that they would come for them – for you, especially."

"What would they want with me?" I gasped.

"Your powers, silly?" she said, sounding amused by my ignorance "The Korbs have a long standing tradition of breeding only the finest powers. Yours would have been the rarest of all."

I tightened my grip on Justin's hold, unsure if I wanted to hear the rest. It was Shannon who stood up and addressed us in a soft, calming tone. "A few months before you were born we were told that your grandfather Clancy had decided to send your uncles, Caradon and Brett, to Oaks to persuade your father to return home. Your mother was too weak to fight them off and your father was no match for both brothers. So they moved in with Abbot and Leslie, so that we could all be closer to them, ready to defend them in any way necessary."

"My two faceless shadows," I exclaimed, louder than I intended. The interruption stopped her cold. Stunned, she turned to my uncle. His face was white and set. "Uncle Abbot? Is that who keeps visiting me in my dreams – my uncles?"

My remark caused a commotion amongst the Ellri. They

didn't need to talk, but I could tell by their expression it was not going to mount to anything good.

"We're getting ahead of ourselves," said Marlene, trying to calm the room. "But then again," she paused and looked at me, "you never know with the Korbs. They never came for your father. They never came to Oaks eighteen years ago."

"Why is that?"

"Well, at first they thought it would be easy, being that Winston was one of them. You see the Korbs know that we have little to no respect for their ideals. They truly thought we'd simply hand him over – wipe our hands of the whole ordeal. The brothers didn't consider one thing. They didn't factor in the deep friendship we all had with your parents. Korbs or no Korbs, your father was family."

I turned away and retreated into Justin's embrace, holding back my tears by will alone.

"Caitlin, they knew better than to go against all eighteen of us," Marlene added. "Unfortunately, that hasn't stopped them. They've been trying ever since to gather all their Ellri for support."

I sniffed back the torrents of emotion and turned my gaze to her. "Support in doing what?"

"Support in getting their hands on you."

"Me?"

She nodded. "Dating back thousands of years has left the Korbs with a legacy of fifty extremely powerful Ellri. Combined, we are no match for them, sweetie. We would have had to summon the other Ellri – our families from Europe to fend them off."

My eyes widened in sheer terror as I fully understood the import of what she meant. "Eighteen of you, against fifty of them?" My breath caught in my throat as I took the words in.

Marlene smiled warmly and said, "Don't look so worried, Caity. It hasn't been easy for your uncles to gather up enough people to press the issue; not all of their Ellri share the same ideals. They haven't stopped trying to reach you, nonetheless."

Her words soothed my trembling nerves. "Are you sure they've been trying?" I finally asked. "I mean, my nightmares only started after my return to Oaks. I was perfectly fine at Stone Hurst. I didn't feel threatened in any way."

Before she had the chance to answer, we all turned our attention to the commotion in the back of the room. Nathan's need to remain standing seemed to go against his physical capabilities. William quickly got to his feet, offering the High Ellri his seat.

"Where have the years gone?" Nathan asked, patting William on the shoulder.

"To that mass you call a belly," Marlene laughed cynically, at her own words. "How do you expect your flimsy legs to support all that weight, love?"

Nathan waved her away dismissively. "Not now Marlene," he complained. "I'm old, that's all."

"You're not old when your off drinking with your buddies, are you?" she said, looking to all his collaborators.

The men in the room quickly turned their gaze away, looking at anything but her.

"Men!" she exclaimed, shaking her head.

Nathan chuckled. "Boys will be boys, love."

His boyish smile broke her stern expression. "I guess your right dear. Boys will be boys," she said, surprising us all. It wasn't like Marlene to let the ball drop – to lose in any argument – to allow someone to have the last word. "But…," she quickly added, causing us all to hold back our laughter. Nathan's brow lifted in anticipation awaiting her witty retort.

"But darling, that saying is like milk," she told him. "It has an expiration date, and we all know what happens to milk when it's well past its prime."

Nathan's face beamed in delight. "Point taken, love," he said. "Oh, that reminds me...,"

"What is it now?" she said, clearly annoyed.

"Love, we need to go to the market later." Marlene looked at him questionably. "We're out of milk, remember?"

Nathan incited a round of laughter. Marlene joined in as well. "You old fart," she said, pecking him on the cheek.

Enjoying the pleasant break into our, otherwise, serious conversation, I closed my eyes and let my head fall back against Justin's chest.

"Everything will be fine," he whispered, kissing me on the ear.

Loud, roared the dreadful thunder, as the rain deluged the entire area, causing me to jump out of my skin.

"Caitlin, relax," he said, tightening his hold.

The sound of wind against the shingles was a non-stop ominous rumbling. I inhaled deeply, holding my breath to calm my nerves. The room was suddenly quiet again.

"Now, where were we," Marlene said, in a serious tone.

I took a few steps forward and leaned against the antique desk. "I was fine at Stone Hurst," I started to say. "My nightmares began here in Oaks."

"Caitlin, you need to understand that as long as your grandmother Eileen was alive they had no power over you. She made sure to block them out of your thoughts," Marlene started to say. "However, Eileen knew that when she'd pass away, Caradon and Brett were sure to reach you. Her gift gave her glimpses into your future. She was the one who arranged your stay at Stone Hurst, not us."

"My grandmother sent me away?" I shook my head as if to set right the muddle that Marlene's words made of my understanding. "So you guys didn't want me to leave?"

"Of course we didn't, Caitlin," Aunt Leslie told me, teary eyed. "We had no choice. It was the last thing I wanted to do, but it was for your own good. You must understand that it was done to keep you safe."

"How did sending me away help exactly?" I asked, unable to understand their logic.

"It was the only way to get them off your tracks," said Nathan, after a quick sip of water. "To the Korbs you are like a beacon. They can sense you wherever you are. Eileen arranged for your departure with strict instructions. She knew that your uncles wouldn't miss the chance to come to Oaks after her death. It's why we had to make you disappear while she was still alive. Keeping you in the dark about the events surrounding your departure is what has kept you safe for the past five years. The less you knew, the less they knew."

Utterly baffled by the turn of events, I turned to Justin for clarity, but he looked as confused as I was – running his fingers frustratingly through his hair. "Wait just a second," he said, looking towards his mom. "I get the part Eileen played in the whole scheme, but she passed away a year after Caitlin left Oaks. How is it possible that Caitlin was safe at Stone Hurst? Who was powerful enough to block her location from the Korbs for the last four years?"

Shannon paused, waiting for me to realize the great significance of what she was about to say. "What you both don't understand is the unprecedented dilemma we were forced to undertake. We had no sooner realized that your bond existed that we had to tear you apart." Shannon cupped our faces lovingly. "It was agonizing for us to separate you, knowing the pain that you both would have to endure, but your safety, Caitlin, came first," she added.

"Mom," Justin said, pulling her gaze to him. "That still doesn't explain how she was safe at Stone Hurst? Eileen wasn't able to block her whereabouts for the past four years."

Shannon's face went blank. She didn't want to be the one to relate this part of the story; that much was clear. Expressionless, she took a few steps back allowing my aunt to speak.

"Eileen had thought of everything," Aunt Leslie started to explain. "She had arranged for one of the Higher McDevitt Ellri, my aunt – your great-aunt, Caitlin, to move to Stone Hurst and assist you in your time of need. Eileen knew that the Korbs would have never suspected a McDevitt to help. The two bloodlines, the Korbs and the McDevitts have been on a war path for a span of 1000 years."

"That's impossible," I cried. "For the last five years I was all alone. There was no one there, none of our kind anyway."

My aunt took my hand. "You weren't alone, sweetie. Ava was there. She was the one blocking your location for all those years. She couldn't make her identity known. It would've incited a barrage of questions on your part."

My mouth went completely dry. "Ms. Leedey?" I exclaimed, finding it hard to swallow. "You're all telling me that the Head Mistress at Stone Hurst was my great-aunt? An Ellri?"

"An Ellri of the Highest Order," Aunt Leslie corrected.

I was totally floored – It did explain, however, Ms. Leedey's need to be around me. I always thought it was because she had no children of her own, but never, in my wildest imagination, did it ever occur to me that she might have been there to protect me – not in that sense of the word.

"Ava McDevitt-Leedey is your great-aunt from your mother's side of the family, Caitlin, your grandfather Cecil's youngest sister. After her husband, Christopher Leedey passed away she decided to travel around the world to look for other gifted people outside the bloodlines, to guide and help them find their way. My father, your grandfather Cecil had asked for her help, knowing that her ability to shield people was far greater than any other. Kyle has taken after her, acquired her great gift," Aunt Leslie said, boasting about Kyle's ability. "Ava was excited to help. She doesn't care much about the Purist ideals that some Korbs uphold."

"Really?" I was still in shock "Ms. Leedey?" I shook my head unable to get my mind round it all. "Wait," my brain finally found clarity, "If I was safe at Stone Hurst why did you summon me back to Oaks?"

"For two entirely different reasons," William said, in a deep husky voice. "For one, your bond to Justin was getting much stronger with the years. It was becoming unbearable, as you both well know. If the distance between you continued to exist it would have eventually killed both of you," he said, looking away from Justin, unable to picture his son in harm's way. "The second reason was that all these years your uncles believed that you were like your mother; with no gifts. The minute you started using your powers to reach the place you call your 'solace', they were able to sense you, but not locate you. The stronger your powers, the easier it would be for any blood relative to find you. So, with that in mind, we decided that it was best you return home where we could be with you in case they decided to show up."

"What do they want me for?" I asked frightened, staring at William, not sure of how I would be of any use to them.

"To put it simply, Caitlin, we find ourselves in a custody battle."

"Custody?" I looked around to all their faces. "I'm eighteen. What right do they have over me?"

"Your age is insignificant to our kind, and you know it."

"Still..."

"They're claiming their right; you being a Korbs. Your parents, on the other hand, have designated Abbot and Leslie as your only sole guardians. As you can imagine the Korbs weren't very happy with that decision. The Council of Nobe has recently gotten involved with the issue, seeing how pressing the problem is for all of us. It has been deliberating for the past fifteen years, trying to find the delicate thread of balance. They don't want to incite animosity between the bloodlines."

"Why is the Nobe finding it hard to decide? Why don't they simply ask me? I'm an adult. I'm capable of making my own choices. Why not put an end to this, by simply asking me who I want to be with?"

"Caitlin, the Council of Nobe knows what you want. The point here is what's best for us all, for our future. If the Korbs disagree with their ultimate decision, the gifted would have to choose a side. It can mean the end of us all. A war between the bloodlines is not something to be taken lightly. If we have to defend our beliefs we will do so, without hesitation."

The Ellri all nodded in agreement at William's declaration.

The chilling facts were like a slap across the face – my blood froze at his revelation. I was finally driven so close to the edge, I thought I might go over it. I was the cause of all this. My eyes were huge, wide with panic, dazed and horrified. I had placed everyone I loved in danger. Knowing that they would give up everything defending me only heightened my desire to turn myself over to the Korbs, willingly.

Just then, I realized they were all aware of my dark thoughts – Justin above all. He simply pulled me back into his embrace and kissed me on the head. "Don't worry about anything. We won't let things go that far," he promised.

A wave of unadulterated fear washed over me as Justin's consoling words rang hollow. With trembling hands and tear filled eyes, I quickly, straightened up breaking free from Justin's embrace, realizing that they were all so willing to sacrifice themselves for me. I knew I couldn't let this happen.

Figuring out a way to stop any of this from unfolding was my prime concern, now. I was determined not to let anyone get hurt on my account. But first, I needed facts – information to see how I would handle things. So, I wiped my tears away refusing to let fear take over.

"Why am I so important to them?" I asked, needing to clearly understand the root of their actions. "There must be something more. Why would they be risking so much, trying so hard?"

"We're not sure," Uncle Abbot answered. "They must know something we do not, something only immediate family members know. Your parents surely knew what this secret was; otherwise they wouldn't have taken such great steps to protect you. Eileen was aware of everything as well, but never said a word to any of us."

"So – what – what do I do?" I paused, struggling to get the words out.

"We, not you," Uncle Abbot corrected me "we have to wait for The Nobe to deliberate. To see what their final decision will be."

"How long will that take?"

"A minute – an hour – a life time."

"Gee, Uncle Abbot, thanks for narrowing it down."

He smiled. "Nobody can be sure. All we can do is wait and see. From what we can tell, it will take quite some time."

"But you can't say that for sure, can you?"

He solemnly shook his head no.

Marlene stood up and faced me. "I bet you're glad I gave you that wine, aren't you?" she said laughing, trying to uplift our mood. "Nobody will be bothering you anytime soon. Your relatives on the other side of the Atlantic know better than to act before the Council's decision."

Detecting no false hope in her words, I shrank against Justin's hard body once again allowing him to encircle his arms around me – his secure hold eased my anxiety.

"I want to thank all of you," I sighed, looking at each and every one of them "What you have done for me, for my parents was...."

"Nonsense," interrupted Aunt Leslie. "You needn't thank us. That's what families are for. To be there for one another in times of happiness and in times of need. Now, enough about the past, you need to give yourself some time to register everything. We bombarded you with quite a lot today."

I hugged and kissed each Ellri as they exited the study. I wanted them to know that I was grateful to them for standing by my parents in such trying times.

My mind was reeling from all the information I had only moments before learned. As I took the words in, I could feel a surge of fear and doubt beginning to push its way through the barrier of shock. My whole body was starting to shake. When I tried to stand up, my legs were like jelly and I sank back down again.

Immersed in silence, Uncle Abbot's study was veiled in spine-chilling stillness apart from Justin's pacing, so agitated he couldn't seem to make himself stop.

"Justin, what is it," I cried.

"I'm not going to let anyone hurt you, ever again," Justin told me a while later, with his back turned to me; his voice was rough with emotion. "I don't care how gifted they are, Caitlin."

Now I was staring in cold disbelief.

His eyes closed as he sank back in one of the large leather armchairs. For many minutes Justin sat, deep in thought.

I finally stood up, and tried to sound reassuring. "You heard what Marlene said, there's nothing to worry about. The Nobe will decide what's best."

Justin remained still and quiet.

Though the worst seemed to have passed now, I was still shuddering and shivering as a new wave of panic found its way to the surface. I had no answers. All I knew was that something was happening to me.

I felt my knees buckle – my limbs felt gravely numb. A pain like a hot pincer seared my marked wrist – surely ignited by my mixed emotions.

Scared that I might fall, Justin swiftly attempted to reach for me. "Stay away!" I screamed – he was dangerously close. "Give me a minute to collect myself. I don't want to hurt you." I fumbled for the sofa. "Please, stay away. I can't control this force just yet."

"Look at your wrist, Caitlin," he gasped in surprise; frozen in place.

I shook my head in vigorous denial, not wanting to believe what I was seeing. My once insignificant, barely visible scar was now raw and throbbing from the sheer pressure. Unable to hold back the pain, with a blood chilling scream I cried out in pure agony and clapped my other hand to my scarred wrist. In one blinding instant I was thrown back against the sofa by a forceful electric current which darted up my left arm and straight to my forehead. I went to my knees, crying out from the pain in my ears.

"Caitlin!" Justin's voice rang in the air like a bell. "Let go of your wrist!"

Suddenly, thousands of images slammed into me as they boomed and echoed in my head, like a movie reel in fast forwarded motion fleeting across my mind's eye. Quickly, I let go of my wrist and the flashes vanished only to be replaced by an agonizing headache.

Sick and shaking, I huddled in the corner of the sofa as a vortex of thoughts and images and emotions raged through my mind. The uncomfortable feeling of something ominous heading my way was growing steadily stronger. I had a momentary image stick in my mind of a shadow stalking through the woods, the scent of pine so strong it almost tickled my nose. I blinked the sensation aside at the sound of the door opening.

"Caitlin, are you okay?"

I felt my uncle's worry-filled voice try to infiltrate my brain. I kept my eyes tightly shut, feeling nauseous and unable to speak.

My mangled thoughts spun into a gray swirl of confusion as a random image of a man burst with startling clarity into my mind. He was in black, his features concealed against the night.

"Caitlin," my uncle insisted. "Caitlin, concentrate!"

I drew a sharp breath and noticed that the room was once again filled with some of the Ellri – most had already gone home.

I caught the troubled look in my uncle's eyes. "Caitlin, are you okay?" he asked again.

I nodded

"Justin, what happened," asked my aunt, turning her attention to him, knowing I was in no shape to answer.

Justin was crouched over, holding his head in pain. "Look at her wrist," he gasped, shaking his head to relieve the tension.

They all looked down at my hand – nobody risked coming more than a few feet closer.

"Amazing," said Nathan, in awe at the site of my throbbing scar. "Whatever you do Caitlin, don't touch it. You're not ready to face that part of your gift just yet."

"To late," I said, through clenched teeth.

"Well then, I'm sure you won't be trying that anytime soon," laughed Marlene, amused at my predicament.

Everyone in the room gave her a cross look.

She waved them away. "Don't worry, Caity, your headache will subside momentarily."

I looked up at her puzzled. "What the hell was that? What did I see? It was so fast – so powerful?"

"You unintentionally triggered your visions," Marlene explained. "Your gift felt the need to show you everything we revealed to you earlier. It takes quite a long time to get a grip of that particular power. But don't worry Caity, soon enough you'll be able to separate the past, the present and those images of the future. But it does take time to master."

"You're kidding me, right?"

She shook her head. "As I told you before, sweetie, you are the offspring of two very powerful individuals. You're coming into your inheritance."

"What does that mean?"

"You're gifts, sweetie, that's your legacy. Both of your grandmothers possessed the same power, but it takes great skill and patience to master such a gift. You must exhibit ironclad control to sort everything out. For now you need to get control of your other...," She pointed to my wrist, "more deadly gift, before you delve into controlling the visions."

William put his arm around Justin's shoulders to comfort his son. "You'll both be fine son, don't worry," he assured him. "Her gift is slowly augmenting, meeting her needs. No telling what she'll be able to do," he explained, looking concerned at Justin's taut expression. "For some reason your bond connects you in more ways than one; allowing you a taste of what she feels."

Hating myself for putting him in harm's way I attempted an apology. "Sorry about that. Are you okay?"

"Am I okay?" he smiled at my concern. "I only felt a hint of what you must've experienced. I'm perfectly fine. It's you I'm worried about."

"It's all been too much," I choked, as tears streamed down my face. "The stress..."

"It's all right," said my uncle. "Just sit for a moment."

I sat back and closed my eyes, taking deep steady breaths, feeling the throbbing gradually fading away.

Opening my eyes, shortly after, I found myself staring at masklike faces. It was impossible to read the thoughts and feelings that lay behind them.

"Much better," I said, trying to get some kind of response. "It'd be nice if someone could give me an idea of what to expect in the future."

"Unfortunately, nobody can help you with that," Aunt Leslie answered, taking my hand. "We are complex beings. Inheriting our ancestor's powers doesn't allow us to know which of their gifts will surface. For some, it's quite clear from birth, for others, like Justin for example, still experience changes in their power even though they have ascended. Only time will tell how far your powers will evolve."

Uncle Abbot helped me to my feet and turned to Justin. "Take her upstairs," he muttered, "she definitely needs her rest."

The rains waned and the soft brightness of the evening sky shone briefly through my window. I pulled my pillow over my head smothering the light from my eyes – kicking off my shoes in the process.

"Relax," Justin said, plucking the pillow from my tight grip.

Newly formed clouds again brought rain and darkness.

After carefully arranging a number of beautiful embroidered pillows, Justin stretched out his built frame in a manner that could hardly have provided great comfort. "That was something else, wasn't it?" he said, turning his attention to me.

Slowly opening my eyes I felt light-headed with relief at the sight of his beautiful smile. "I'm still a bit dizzy," I confessed, pushing myself to a sitting position. "The wine wasn't such a good idea, after all."

"It's your gift that's spurring your wooziness. You need to sleep. Lay back down," he ordered, pulling back the covers "Where're your pj's?" he asked.

"Only if you stay," I scoffed, pointing to the first drawer of the eighteenth century dressing chest.

"Fine," Justin mouthed, making it sound like he wanted nothing less. He handed me a cotton jersey T-shirt and matching jersey trousers and turned to face the wall. "But only till you fall asleep, I don't want to break any more house rules. Abbot has been more than understanding about allowing me up here."

"This whole arrangement is ludicrous. We're both adults for heaven's sake!"

I was doing two things at once, complaining and wrestling

with my night wear. I wrestled with the bottoms – rolling side to side to pull them up.

"All done," I finally said, tucking myself back into bed.

Justin slowly turned around, "You've been an adult for only a couple of weeks, Caitlin. If you ask me Abbot's been quite lenient. Emily is older than you and yet Marc isn't allowed anywhere near the upstairs of the house. I come and go as I please."

"Yeah, I didn't think of that. Guess you're right. They all realize that I need you here because of the bond..." my voice tattered off, I didn't want it to sound the way it did. I wanted to take each syllable back.

There was an instant flicker in his eye. His eyebrow lifted ever so slightly, responding to my miss worded statement. "What are you saying, Caitlin?" He perched himself on the bed, "The only reason you want me around is because our closeness diminishes the burn in your veins?"

My eyes grew wide in disbelief. "What in the world are you talking about? How can you even think that?" I said curtly, pulling myself back in a sitting position – sounding rather hurt at his assumption. "Justin what I ...."

With apparent spontaneity, Justin moved closer cutting me off by his rather unexpected kiss. I surrendered entirely to his attack wanting nothing more than the taste of his lips on my mouth. Gently pushing me back on the pillow he inched away gazing into my eyes.

"Now get some sleep, you've been through enough today."

"I didn't mean it to sound," I tried explaining, "I love you," I said, needing him to know that there was nothing in this world more important. He was my core – the reason for being.

Sadly, the three little words didn't come close to describing the unfathomable feelings I felt for this man.

"I surely hope so," he smirked, satisfied by my admission. "Now go to sleep." As he tucked me in more snug than necessary he leaned in and whispered, "You're mine to keep, Caitlin," and then kissed me on the forehead.

Happy to have him in my life and on my side, I hugged Justin tightly knowing that I was finally where I belonged and even if the days to come hid something far darker than any of us could ever fathom, I was certain that I would not be alone in unraveling the lines that bind me to these inexplicable events.

But for now, looking at Justin's brilliant smile, my tomorrows seemed much, much brighter.

"A person often meets his destiny on the road he took to avoid it."
— Jean de La Fontaine

LINES THAT BIND

PART TWO

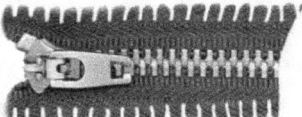 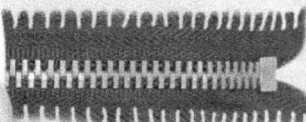

ANNA LAZARIDIS

WITHIN *the* WHISPERS

When do you cross the line between seeking the truth and getting lost in the lies?

www.linesthatbind.com